From Robin Jones Gunn

THE CHRISTY MILLER SERIES

1 • *Summer Promise*
2 • *A Whisper and a Wish*
3 • *Yours Forever*
4 • *Surprise Endings*
5 • *Island Dreamer*
6 • *A Heart Full of Hope*

7 • *True Friends*
8 • *Starry Night*
9 • *Seventeen Wishes*
10 • *A Time to Cherish*
11 • *Sweet Dreams*
12 • *A Promise Is Forever*

From the Secret Place in My Heart: Christy Miller's Diary
Departures (with Wendy Lee Nentwig)

CHRISTY & TODD: THE COLLEGE YEARS

Until Tomorrow

As You Wish

THE SIERRA JENSEN SERIES

1 • *Only You, Sierra*
2 • *In Your Dreams*
3 • *Don't You Wish*
4 • *Close Your Eyes*
5 • *Without A Doubt*
6 • *With This Ring*

7 • *Open Your Heart*
8 • *Time Will Tell*
9 • *Now Picture This*
10 • *Hold On Tight*
11 • *Closer Than Ever*
12 • *Take My Hand*

THE GLENBROOKE SERIES

1 • *Secrets*
2 • *Whispers*
3 • *Echoes*
4 • *Sunsets*

5 • *Clouds*
6 • *Waterfalls*
7 • *Woodlands*

Mothering by Heart

ROBIN
JONES
GUNN

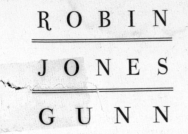

Until
Tomorrow

CHRISTY AND TODD · THE COLLEGE YEARS

BETHANY HOUSE PUBLISHERS
MINNEAPOLIS, MINNESOTA 55438

Until Tomorrow
Copyright © 2000
Robin Jones Gunn

Cover illustration and design by Lookout Design Group, Inc.

Published by Bethany House Publishers
A Ministry of Bethany Fellowship International
11400 Hampshire Avenue South
Minneapolis, Minnesota 55438
www.bethanyhouse.com

Printed in the United States of America by
Bethany Press International, Minneapolis, Minnesota 55438

Library of Congress Cataloging-in-Publication Data

Gunn, Robin Jones, 1955–
    Until tomorrow / by Robin Jones Gunn.
        p. cm. — (Christy and Todd ; 1)
    ISBN 0-7642-2272-4
    1. Americans—Switzerland—Fiction. 2. College students—
Fiction. 3. Switzerland—Fiction. I. Title.
    PS3557.U4866 U58 2000
    813'.54—dc21   00-008271

ROBIN JONES GUNN loves to tell stories. Evidence of this appeared early when her first-grade teacher wrote in Robin's report card, "Robin has not yet grasped her basic math skills, but she has kept the entire class captivated at rug time with her entertaining stories."

When Robin's first series of books for toddlers was published in 1984, she never dreamed she'd go on to write novels. However, one project led to another and *Until Tomorrow* is Robin's forty-ninth published book. Other series include THE CHRISTY MILLER SERIES, THE SIERRA JENSEN SERIES, and THE GLENBROOKE SERIES. Combined sales of her books are over two million, with worldwide distribution. Many of the titles have been translated into other languages.

Robin and her husband, Ross, have been involved in youth work for over twenty-five years. They have lived in many places, including California and Hawaii. Currently they live near Portland, Oregon, with their teenage son and daughter and their golden retriever, Hula.

Visit Robin's Web site at www.RobinGunn.com

For Luanne, who said in the spring of our twenty-first year, "Why don't we go to Europe this summer!" And so we did. (I still have the wild flowers we picked in Adelboden, Lulu.)

For Laurie, who shared her rationed cotton balls and 1006 lotion that sweltering night in the Paris youth hostel.

For Carol, who led us laughing all the way on our journey to find the statue of the *Little Mermaid* in Copenhagen.

For Laraine, who kept us searching until we found the best gelato in all of Florence. (Remember, Lola? You said the Amaretto at Vivolli's was "exquiz.")

And for Chuck, who told me to close my eyes right before we entered the Blue Grotto. Thanks for paying for the pizza that night at the train station in Roma. I think I still owe you.

"Old friends are as close as a memory when the heart is always young."

Robin Jones Gunn

The morning light had not yet tinted the June sky with the promise of a new day as Christy Miller hurried down the cobblestone street of Basel, Switzerland. With long-legged strides, she turned the corner and realized that her heart was racing toward the train station faster than her legs.

This time I'm not going to cry when I see him.

Christy remembered how weak and awkward her endless stream of tears had made her feel last Christmas when she had gone home to California. Todd had just stood there as if he didn't know what to do with her.

I'm a stronger person than I was at Christmas. I won't cry.

At the end of the street she turned left. Only six more blocks to the station.

And I won't let Katie talk me into anything I don't want to do, either. If Katie, Todd, and I are going to get along while we travel around Europe for the next three weeks, then everything needs to be a group decision.

Christy grasped her long, nutmeg brown hair to check how wet it was after her hasty, early-morning shower. She reminded herself that in a month she would celebrate her twentieth birthday. Certainly at twenty she should be facing life as a strong, independent woman, right?

It's time I take a stand for myself. Katie will not rule my choices. I won't let her.

Decision making had never been Christy's strength, which was why she felt determined to make a fresh start with her closest friends. She would show them how much she had changed and how strong she had become during her school year in Switzerland.

The fragrant aroma of freshly baked bread floated her way from her favorite bakery, or *Konditorei*, at the end of the street. Every Saturday morning Christy would make a trek to this special pastry shop. It had become her way of treating herself for making it through another difficult week of classes and volunteer work at the orphanage.

A much better "treat" will be arriving on the 6:15 train from the Zürich airport, she thought with a smile. *The first thing Todd and Katie and I will do is come back here to my Konditorei, and I'll treat them to some Swiss pastries.*

Christy tilted back her head and drew in a deep breath of the delicious aroma. She stood still a moment, quickly folding her hair into a loose braid and fastening it with a clip she had stuck in her jeans pocket. The sky had just begun to lighten with soft shades of lavender and gray. Glad-hearted songbirds twittered in the trees.

Christy hurried the final stretch to the station with light steps. Smiling at the two large stone lion statues that guarded the entrance to the Basel *Bahnhof*, Christy entered and checked the schedule. Todd and Katie's train was to arrive in seven minutes on track four. She rushed to the platform so she could be there the moment they stepped off the train.

Christy was surprised at how noisy and crowded the station was compared to the quiet streets she had just walked. She arrived on the platform facing track number four only moments before the train pulled in. Carefully positioning herself in the middle so she could see Katie and Todd no matter which part of the train they exited from, Christy waited for her two best friends.

Throngs of early-morning businessmen and business-women exited the train. Christy thought she heard a familiar squeal over the roar of rushing footsteps. She looked right and left, expecting at any moment to catch a glimpse of Katie's swishy red hair. But Christy didn't see her in the crowd.

Turning her head to check the other end of the train, Christy felt everything around her slip into slow motion. She didn't know if she was experiencing a dip in the adrenaline she had felt pumping through her veins on her walk to the station or if the crush of people rushing past her made her feel dizzy. One thing she was sure of—the screaming silver-blue eyes she had spotted could only belong to one person.

"Todd!" Her lips formed the name she had held in her heart for half a decade. Pushing her way through the crowd, Christy rushed to her favorite blond-haired surfer boy.

Todd quickly unclasped his backpack and grabbed Christy's arm, pulling her close. In an instant his arms were around her, his eyes locked on hers, and his lips were only inches away.

"Kilikina," he murmured right before his lips met hers.

Christy melted whenever Todd called her by her Hawaiian name. Absolutely melted. Add to that the sweetness of his kiss, and she couldn't take it all in. Uninvited tears coursed down her cheeks.

Todd pulled away from their reunion kiss, his expression hesitant.

"Hi," Christy said, quickly wiping her damp cheeks.

"Hi," Todd returned. His smile widened, showing his dimples. His solid jawline was rough with stubble, and she smelled chocolate on his breath.

Christy playfully brushed the back of her fingers along his jaw. "Hard day's night?"

Todd ran his thumb under her left eye, catching the last tear. He seemed to be studying her, trying to read what she held behind her clear, distinct blue-green eyes. His eyebrows raised as he said, "You all right?"

Christy nodded and smiled warmly. "I told myself I wasn't going to cry."

"And I told myself I wasn't going to kiss you," he said with a teasing grin.

His eyes were locked on hers. Christy felt as if Todd could see right through her, all the way to the secret place deep in her heart.

A settled peace came over her in the noisy station. The peace seemed to cover the two of them like an invisible canopy. They stood completely still, holding hands, basking in each other's presence. Christy wondered if she would spend the rest of her life gazing into those silver-blue eyes that now seemed to be searching her soul.

"Sorry, Todd, to interrupt," a male voice with an Italian accent said, breaking in between Todd and Christy, "but I am parked for only a short time."

Christy pulled herself away from Todd and was stunned to see Antonio, an Italian friend of theirs who had been an exchange student in California.

"Christiana," Antonio said, reaching for her shoulders and planting a kiss on each cheek. "So good to see you. You are surprised?"

Christy felt off-balance. "What . . . how. . . ?" Before she could form her question, she heard a squeal that could only come from Katie. Christy's ever-exuberant best friend pushed her way past Antonio and threw her arms around Christy. As Katie did, the frame of her backpack hit Christy's forehead.

"Ouch!"

"Ouch? You haven't seen me in months, and all you can say is ouch?"

"Ouch and hi!" Christy said, giving Katie another, less aggressive hug. "You look great."

"So do you," Katie said.

"Did you know Antonio was coming?" Christy asked.

Katie's green eyes flashed. "Yes. We just figured it all out two days ago."

Christy turned to Todd. His grin grew wide. "Tonio set it up for us to go camping in Italy with him."

"Camping?" Christy echoed.

"We can talk as we go," Antonio said, taking Katie's pack and carrying it for her. "My car . . ." He indicated the door he wanted them to move toward.

Todd strapped his backpack on his broad shoulders and grabbed Christy's hand, pulling her with him out of the station. Katie latched on to Antonio's arm as if she never meant to give it back, and the two of them led the way out of the station at a fast clip.

"So we're going camping?" Christy asked.

"Yep. Tonio has the equipment. It's all set up."

"What about Scandinavia?"

"What about Scandinavia?" Todd asked.

"I thought we were going there first."

Todd stopped walking. "Did you tell me that? Because I didn't think we had a plan yet. That's why I set this up with Antonio. If you told me and I didn't catch that email, I apologize."

"No, you're right." She knew she didn't want to be the one to start an argument. Not here. Not now. "We don't have a plan yet. This is fine."

Christy was having a hard time thinking straight. She thought Todd had mentioned starting their journey in Norway and working their way down to Italy. But now she wasn't sure. Maybe Katie had suggested that itinerary.

Tonio led them to his small white minivan illegally parked across from the Bahnhof. He opened the side door, and Christy noticed a large dent on the front bumper.

Tugging a gray canvas bag out of the open area in the center of the van, Antonio said, "Give me some help. This must go on the roof."

The four of them moved all of Antonio's camping gear out of the van and onto the roof, securing it with ropes under a tarp.

"How did you two plan all this?" Christy asked Todd, trying to sound calm.

"Through email." Todd shoved his and Katie's travel packs into the van's belly and climbed in. A bench seat ran the back width of the van, and along the van's sides were built-in cupboards. The van's center was empty except for their packs.

Katie gave Christy another excited hug before climbing into the backseat next to Todd. "Are we going to have the adventure of our lives or what?"

Christy nodded numbly. She settled into the front seat and fastened her seat belt, but not a moment too soon. With only a quick glance over his shoulder, Antonio hit the gas pedal and pulled out into the traffic with a roar. Christy clutched the edge of her seat and sat as still as she could as Antonio yelled at the other drivers in Italian and darted his way down the street.

From the back of the minivan, Katie laughed hysterically because, as the car lurched, she had crashed into Todd.

"Tonio," Katie cried out, "we're not in Italy yet! Do us a favor and let us live long enough to get there."

Tonio glanced at Katie in the rearview mirror with a grin. He slowed down and put on his turn signal for the first time. He was pulling onto the main highway that led out of town, the opposite direction from Christy's dorm.

"We need to go the other way, Antonio," Christy said. "The university is that way."

"No, I have been to Basel before. This is the road we take back to Italy."

"No!" Christy practically yelled as panic took over. "We can't go to Italy now!"

"Why not?"

"I don't have any of my things!"

Antonio said something in Italian that sounded like an apology, jerked the car onto a side street, and then stopped. He looked at Christy with a friendly expression and said simply, "Which way?"

With Antonio at the wheel, they reached Christy's dorm in a few minutes. During the drive, she calmed down and tried to think straight.

"We'll wait here," Antonio said, stopping the car in another illegal parking place.

"I'm not exactly ready," Christy said, looking at Todd and Katie for support. "I didn't know anything about this. I mean, I'm mostly packed, but it will take me a few minutes to finish getting all my things together."

"I want to see your room," Katie said, crawling out of the back of the van. "Come on, you guys, let's all go in."

"They're really strict about parking around here," Christy told Antonio.

"We'll wait here," Todd suggested. "In case we have to drive around the block a few times."

"And we'll hurry," Katie called over her shoulder as she followed Christy into the brick building.

Christy scurried to her room and opened the door.

"Wow! This room is a lot smaller than I thought it would be," Katie said, looking around. "Wait until this September when we're at Rancho Corona University. The rooms are

twice this size and for just two people, not three. It's way better than here."

"Hey, it's great here, too," Christy said defensively.

Katie looked startled. She quickly reached over and gave
Christy's arm a squeeze. "Oh, I'm sure it is. Don't get upset. I
was just saying how it's only going to get better in the fall
when we're all together at the same school. Don't you agree?"

Christy nodded slowly. Nothing was going the way she
had imagined it would. They were supposed to be sitting in
the bakery right now, calmly discussing their plans over coffee and pastry. Instead, they were bolting out of town in Antonio's rocket-mobile.

"So," Katie said, clapping her hands together, "what do
you need to pack? I can help."

"That bag is ready to go," Christy said, pointing to the
backpack in the corner. "I need to grab a few more things for
my day pack, though."

Katie suddenly threw her arms around Christy in a
breathless hug. "Can you believe we're standing here, in your
dorm room, casually talking as if we do this every day?
Christy, we're in Switzerland!"

"Yes, we are, aren't we?"

Katie pulled back and put her hands on her hips. "Okay,
what's with you? What's wrong?"

"I'm just trying to think of what I need." Christy reached
for her day pack and began to fill it with items from the desk.

"You would tell me if you were upset about anything,
wouldn't you?"

"Of course."

Katie picked up one of the travel books from the desk and
said, "You're not planning to take any of these, are you?"

"A few of them. At least one."

"They're too big," Katie said. "We don't need tour books.
We're on an adventure! Why would you want to haul them

all over the place and look like tourists?"

Christy ignored Katie's comment. She grabbed the book on top of the stack and stuffed it into her pack. "I'm ready. Let's go."

Katie carried Christy's pack out for her and commented on how much lighter it was than hers.

"I hope I'm not traveling too light. I can't think of what else I need." Christy pursed her lips together, trying hard to come up with anything she might have forgotten.

The guys were waiting in the van with the engine running. Todd had moved up to the front seat.

Christy climbed into the back of the van and said, "I was thinking maybe we could stop at the Konditorei before we leave. It's the best bakery in Basel, and it's only a few blocks away. It would give us a chance to talk through our plans."

"I'm not hungry at all," Katie said, clambering into the van. "Are you guys?"

Todd shrugged.

"Then we will hit the street," Antonio decided.

Katie laughed and playfully tagged him on the shoulder. "You mean hit the road, Tonio."

"Yes, hit the road. Here we go."

The van lurched forward as Christy grabbed for her seat belt and fastened it tightly. She stared out the window as Tonio roared past the bakery and headed toward A-2, which would take them south to Italy. For weeks she had dreamed about going to her special Konditorei with Todd. When they were in London together a year and a half ago, the two of them had walked hand in hand down the streets until they found a small bakery. They sat in a booth in the back corner of the tea shop and opened their hearts to each other. During that conversation, they decided they weren't ready to commit to a more serious relationship.

But that was a year and a half ago.

In her dreams and in her waking hours of sitting alone in the Basel Konditorei, Christy had imagined the conversation she and Todd would share over tea and scones. Now she drew in a deep breath and exhaled slowly. She felt ready to move on and to define their relationship more solidly than ever before.

What if Todd isn't ready to move on? What if I'm ready to make a stronger commitment and he's not? At least I think I am. At the moment, Christy was so frazzled she didn't know if she should trust any of her thoughts or feelings. The only thing she was sure of was that her seat belt was buckled as tightly as it would go, and they were on their way to Italy.

2 Katie wiggled into a comfortable nest she had made with their packs in the middle of the van. She jabbered a mile a minute about how incredible all this was.

Christy smiled at Katie and nodded every now and then. But her gaze kept going to the back of Todd's head. All her thoughts were about what was going on inside that head, under the short, sun-kissed blond hair. Or more important, what was going on inside his heart?

How do you really feel about me, Todd? Are you in love with me? Really in love?

Christy realized again, with sadness, that their chance to bend their heads close together in quiet conversation at her favorite thinking spot had been snatched from her. They were part of the group now. The gang. And if Todd was true to form, he would be a team player the rest of the trip. That meant he would give equal attention to everyone. He was like a mellow golden retriever—always loyal, ready to go along with the others on a moment's notice, and generally content with life no matter what the circumstances.

Christy knew she didn't want to become the hyper schnauzer of the group, *yip-yip*ping the whole time.

"Hey, Tonio," Katie said, "where exactly are we going?"

"*Italia. Mi Italia,*" Tonio said dramatically. "I am taking you to my favorite camping ground. You will love it. At night, hundreds of baboons come from the forest and eat everything they find in the camp. This is why you must close up your tent."

"You must mean raccoons," Katie said. "I doubt any baboons are in Italy."

"Ah yes," Antonio said, looking at Katie in the rearview mirror. "Raccoons. Once again you are right. Where would I be without your helpful lessons in English?"

"Admit it, Tonio. You've missed me."

"I've missed you, Katie," Tonio stated loudly.

"Go ahead, tell me you can't live without me," Katie continued.

"I can't live without you."

This was typical banter for Tonio and Katie. They used to tease each other back in California all the time. And a tinge of romance had existed between the two of them. At least Katie had thought so—or was Antonio just being a romantic Italian? Christy wished she and Todd could express themselves boldly like Antonio and Katie—only not as a joke, but sincerely.

Will I ever hear Todd say, "I can't live without you"?

"He's crazy about me," Katie said, turning her attention back to Christy and smiling broadly. "Hey!" She leaned closer to Christy. "If Tonio and I decide to get married this week, you will be my maid of honor, won't you?"

"Of course." Christy's voice came out small and thin. These topics weren't laughing matters for her. The day she would ask Katie to be her maid of honor, Christy knew she would be asking seriously.

Katie laughed. "This all feels like a dream, doesn't it? I don't care if it is a dream. If it is, don't wake me. I've never been happier in my life. Deliriously happy!"

For the next few hours, as they roared down the highway

through Switzerland and into Italy, Antonio and Todd kept a tight conversation going between themselves. Christy couldn't hear what they were saying since the windows were open and the van was noisy. Katie scooted her nest closer to Christy and filled her in on all the details of what had been going on with their friends back home.

As Christy listened to Katie, she found herself settling in. Their journey might not have started off the way Christy had thought it would, but they were on their way. She was determined to be a team player and not give in to moody contemplation.

They stopped only once for gas, or "petrol," as Antonio called it, before arriving at the campground. Their spot had a large open space for tents under a circle of tall trees. Christy had no idea where they were, but she was surprised that the terrain was so similar to what she had become used to in the hills around her school. It seemed odd to think of Italy as having the Alps, too.

The fresh air invigorated the four travelers as they unloaded the van and set up their two tents. Katie playfully drew a line in the dirt with her heel and said, "Girls on this side, boys on that side."

"Only one problem, Katie," Christy said. "The kitchen is on the boys' side."

Katie carefully walked around the end of her dirt line and said, "This is the path to the kitchen. All starving campers may pass this way." She went over to the wooden box Antonio had brought and opened it up. "Okay, I see some mugs in here, a coffeepot, and a frying pan. Where are you hiding the food?"

"Over there," Antonio said with a nod of his head as he hammered the last tent stake into the ground.

"I don't see anything but trees," Katie said.

"Beyond the trees is the refrigerator," Tonio said. "Come.

I'll show you." He put his arm around Katie's shoulder and led her down a narrow trail through the woods.

"Listen to that," Todd said. He had been stringing up a hammock between two trees when he stopped and looked up, listening closely.

Christy knew what he was referring to. She closed her eyes and listened to the sound of the wind rushing through the treetops. All kinds of memories came riding in on that breeze. Her strongest memory was of the wind in the palm trees at a certain train station in Spain. That's where Todd had placed a gold ID bracelet on Christy's wrist a year and a half ago. The word "Forever" was engraved on the bracelet. Christy ran her finger over the bracelet now, her eyes still closed, her face toward the sky. A smile graced her lips as she said, "They're clapping, Todd."

"Bravo," Todd said in a voice that sounded faint.

Christy opened her eyes and saw that Todd had climbed into the hammock and now swayed contentedly with his hands folded behind his head.

"Hey, you got it strung up," Christy said, walking over to the hammock. "Good for you."

"Did you have any doubts about my ability?"

"Not you, nature boy. I believe you could be the world's premier expert in hammocks." Christy grabbed the side and pulled the hammock toward her. She let go and the hammock swung wide, making a creaking sound where the ropes looped around the tree. Suddenly a rope snapped and down came the hammock, dumping Todd on the ground with a thud.

Christy felt like bursting out laughing, but she held back and quickly checked to make sure Todd was all right. He looked startled but not hurt.

"I'm so sorry!" Christy giggled. "Are you okay?"

Before Todd could answer, Katie came tromping through

the woods with Tonio right behind her. "There's no food over there. Tonio's 'refrigerator' happens to be a lake! We're supposed to catch our own dinner."

"Cool," Todd said, getting up and dusting off his backside. "Did you bring poles?"

"Poles, hooks, everything," Tonio said.

"What are we supposed to eat in the meantime?" Katie asked.

"Jerky," Todd suggested.

"What did you call me?" Katie spun around to face Todd.

Christy felt like laughing again, but Katie's red face told her she had better bite her tongue.

"I didn't call you anything. I was just saying I brought some beef jerky. It's in my pack in the van. Help yourself."

Todd and Tonio were bent over the box of camping gear, twisting together a collapsible fishing pole. Todd rummaged through a plastic box of lures and hooks.

"What you need is an afternoon cappuccino," Antonio said to Katie as she paced in front of them like a cougar.

"I didn't happen to see any coffee shops on the way in," Katie said sarcastically.

"I have coffee right here," Antonio said, lifting a small box from the middle of the camping supplies.

"Do you have any food in there?" Katie asked.

"No, only coffee. Hey, Christy, you start a fire, will you? Todd and I will get some fish."

The guys took off, and Christy gathered kindling.

"I don't want coffee," Katie said with a slight whine in her voice. "Do you?"

"No. I'm hungry, though. If they don't catch some fish right away, let's break into Todd's jerky supply."

"What happened to the hammock?" Katie asked, examining the end of the hammock rope.

"I pushed Todd a little too hard and it broke."

"It didn't break. The rope is fine. The knot must have come out. I doubt that Todd knows as much about knots as I do. This rope needs a Katie special knot."

Katie went to work on the hammock as Christy dropped twigs onto her stack of kindling and returned to the surrounding woods for more. She managed to haul a good-sized log over to the fire pit and then opened the wooden chest to see what she could use for a grill over the top. Everything she needed was in the chest. She hummed as she set up their camp kitchen. All she would have to do was light a match when the guys returned.

"You know what this reminds me of, Katie?"

"What?" Katie had settled herself into the hammock and answered Christy without opening her eyes.

"Remember that time I cooked Christmas breakfast on the beach for Todd, and the sea gulls came and ate the bacon and eggs?"

Katie didn't answer.

Christy went over to the hammock. It was wide enough for two people. The ropes and knots looked strong enough. Golden rays from the afternoon sun slipped through the trees, and Katie had turned to catch their full warmth on her face. Christy pushed Katie's legs over gently and said, "Make room. I'm coming aboard."

"I couldn't move if I wanted to," Katie said, her eyes still closed and her hands folded across her middle.

Christy tried to hold the hammock steady as she climbed in with her head at the opposite end from Katie's. "This is pretty comfortable."

"Just don't kick me in the face, and everything will be fine," Katie said, her voice fading.

That was the last thing Christy remembered hearing until the sound of Todd's voice called to her from a few feet away. "Anybody hungry?"

Christy forced her heavy eyelids open. The brightness of the afternoon had faded. In the early evening shadows she made out Todd's form standing there, holding up a fish about a foot long. She could smell smoke from the fire pit and turned to see Antonio starting the fire.

Christy patted her friend's legs. "Katie, they're back. Wake up."

Christy noticed how stiff she was. Stiff and cold. She carefully tumbled from the hammock and shuffled to the fire, where she warmed her hands over the low yellow flames.

"Some campgrounds in Europe won't let you make an open fire," Antonio said. "But here it is allowed. This fire is just the right size, Christy. *Grazie.*"

"No problem."

"How long did we sleep?" Katie asked, joining the four of them with a yawn.

"A couple of hours at least." Christy yawned, as well. "I'm glad you guys caught something. Was it hard?"

"Just took a little time," Todd said, cleaning his fish with a pocketknife.

What also took a little time was cooking the fish. The stars had all come out to watch them before they had finished eating. As they gathered their plates, Antonio started some coffee in his charred camp coffeepot.

Christy smiled. It officially felt like summer now.

Every summer since she was fourteen Christy had gathered with her friends around a campfire on the beach in southern California. There, under these same stars, they sang to the Lord, roasted marshmallows, and opened their hearts to each other.

Being here, beneath the cloudless heavens with her closest friends, made Christy feel something she hadn't felt in a long time. She had several friends at the university that she would go out with. They would sit around talking and drinking coffee on Saturday nights. But it wasn't the same as being with Todd, Katie, and Antonio. What Christy had with these friends was deeper, sweeter, and different from what she experienced in other friendships. At this moment, she felt as if she could close her eyes, take one step toward the star-filled heavens, and be swallowed up in eternity.

"Come here," Todd said, inviting Christy to scoot closer.

She leaned her head on Todd's shoulder and felt herself warming all over. She remembered a phrase she had heard long ago, something about how *"God is in His heaven and all is right with the world."* That's how she felt. All was right between her and Todd. Just right. And God was near.

Christy hummed softly. Todd picked up the tune, and the four of them began to sing. The woods around them resonated with the sound of their praises for the One whose breath rustled in the treetops and whose whispers hummed low through the Earth on which they were seated.

As the night around them grew darker, Christy began to shiver. Todd put his arm around her and drew her close. Together they sang softly and poked the embers of their dying fire with long sticks.

"I'm going to get my jacket," Christy said, finally pulling away from Todd. "Anyone want anything from the van?" Then she remembered. Her jacket was still hanging on the back of her door in the dorm room.

"Oh no," Christy said. "Did anyone, by any chance, bring an extra jacket?"

"You didn't bring a jacket? What kind of an expert happy camper are you?" Katie said with a snap in her voice.

The comment rubbed Christy the wrong way, and suddenly the special tone of the evening evaporated. "I packed in a hurry, if you remember. I didn't exactly have a lot of time to plan out what I needed for camping."

"Sorry," Katie said, but Christy didn't think Katie sounded apologetic.

"Hey, I have a sweater," Antonio said, going to the van. He grabbed a hand-knit wool sweater that had been wadded up on the floor.

"You don't need it?" Christy asked as Tonio tossed it to her. She took one whiff of the sweater and regretted asking for it. It smelled as if it had lined the bottom of a birdcage, then been used to wrap up fish, and finally to wipe off the bottom of a farmer's boots.

"And here is your blanket," Antonio said, tossing another smelly, woolen object at her.

"No sleeping bags?" Christy asked. As soon as she said it, she regretted it. She couldn't stand it when she sounded like a spoiled American who couldn't cope with Europeans' simpler approach to life.

Katie echoed Christy's surprise at their rationed one-blanket-per-camper. "Are you serious? This is all we get? No air mattresses? What about pillows?"

"Use a sweater," Todd suggested.

Christy knew she wasn't going to rest her face on Antonio's fish-gut sweater.

Todd rose to his feet, and what remained of the closeness of their evening together immediately dissipated. Stretching and yawning, he made his way to the guys' tent. "I'll take one of those blankets, if you have another, Tonio. Good night, Christy. Night, Katie."

"Good night," they echoed in unison.

Christy crawled into their tent and tried to make the best of the smelly sweater and wool blanket. She stretched out the sweater underneath her to use as padding. She then tucked the wool blanket all around her and used a pair of clean shorts and a folded-up T-shirt as her pillow. It didn't work. She was too cold to fall asleep.

Katie managed to doze right off. That irritated Christy since she had wanted to ask Katie how she felt about Antonio and if more than teasing was going on between them. Now Christy would have to wait until tomorrow.

From the boys' tent across the line in the dirt came the steady sound of Antonio's snoring. At least Christy thought it was Antonio's.

What if it's Todd's? What would it be like to be married to a guy who snored like that? I'd never get any sleep.

Christy heard a twig snap right outside their tent. She froze. *Robbers? Are they coming into our camp to take our gear? What if they hot-wire the van and leave us here? Should I scream?*

Another twig snapped. Christy grabbed Katie's arm and shook her. "Wake up, Katie! Did you hear that?"

"What?"

"Listen," Christy whispered.

"That's just the guys' snoring. Go back to sleep, will you?"

"No, it's not snoring. Something's out there. Listen."

Katie turned on her flashlight, and Christy immediately grabbed it and turned it off. "Don't turn it on!"

"Come on, Christy, cut it out!" Katie reached over in the darkness and felt around until she found the flashlight in Christy's hand. "The idea is to scare them away."

Katie unzipped the tent and poked her head outside, shining the light around. Suddenly she pulled back and caught her breath. "Christy, you aren't going to believe this."

"What is it?" Christy's heart raced.

3   "You have to see this. Come here." Katie leaned to the side. Christy joined her and peered into the darkness. The flashlight caught on something by the fire pit that shone back at them like a dozen tiny, round reflectors.

"Tonio's baboons," Katie said.

"Man, Tonio wasn't kidding. Look at all those raccoons. What are they eating?"

"Fish guts."

"Gross."

"I wonder if Tonio left them out on purpose?" Katie twirled her small light around. The eight or nine scrawny raccoons continued to devour their treat, unmoved by Katie's attempt to scare them away. "That is one gang of mean-looking raccoons."

"Maybe you shouldn't get them all nervous with your light," Christy suggested.

Katie laughed. "Why? You afraid they're going to turn on us after the fish guts and come pouncing over here, clawing their way into our tent?"

"I'd feel better if they went away. Can we zip the tent back up? It's freezing."

Katie pulled herself back in the tent and zipped it up. "Do me a favor and don't wake me again unless it's something over six feet tall." She burrowed back under her blanket and added, "With dark hair and brown eyes and lots of money."

Christy had to smile. No matter how upset Katie got, she never lost her sense of humor. "So is that your latest criteria for the man of your dreams? Tonio could almost fill that, you know. Except for the height."

"And the money," Katie added.

"What? You don't think his family has money?"

"Call me crazy, but I'm thinking only really poor people go camping without sleeping bags. Or food."

"I guess that makes us really poor people, doesn't it?" Christy curled up into as tight a ball as she could on top of the wool sweater and tucked the blanket all around her in hopes that the cocoon method would make her feel warmer. "So how are things going between you and Tonio?"

"Fine."

Christy waited for more details. When Katie didn't offer any, Christy prodded. "Do you think you guys might have some feelings for each other like you had last summer?"

"It's all just a game, Christy," Katie said in a low voice. "You know that. I'm nothing special to him. It's no big deal."

"But how does that make you feel?"

"It's my life, Chris. I'm everybody's buddy and nobody's honey." Katie adjusted her position and added, "I don't want to talk about guys right now. I'm really, really tired. Can we get some sleep?"

"Sure," Christy said, wishing she felt warm enough to sleep. She tried rubbing her legs together and pulling the blanket over her head.

Katie's rhythmic breathing soon indicated she had fallen asleep. Christy lay awake for hours, shivering. None of her thoughts could be trusted, but she allowed all of them to parade before her. Thoughts of Todd. Thoughts of what would come next for them in their relationship. Thoughts of getting married. Thoughts of what precise words she would use when they finally had their heart-to-heart talk.

When dawn came, Christy felt exhausted. She wanted to drop off into a deep, dreamless sleep. But the others were up with the birds, coaxing Christy to join them for some of Antonio's specialty coffee.

She gave in, thinking the coffee would at least wake her up. Crawling out of the tent with the blanket around her shoulders, Christy couldn't believe how grungy she felt. Her face and teeth felt sticky, her hair was a tangled mess, and she knew she now carried with her the disagreeable odor of the knit sweater she had slept on all night.

Todd, however, looked fresh and friendly. He bent down and reached for the coffeepot on the grill. "Hey, how's it going?" he asked, holding out a coffee mug to Christy.

She replied with a groan before sipping the strong coffee, trying hard not to make a face. Tonio's special morning brew had to be the thickest, strongest coffee she had ever tasted. If she had a spoon, she could have eaten it like hot pudding. He had added lots of sugar, which made it seem even more like a dessert than a beverage.

"This should wake me up," she said, noticing that Todd's hair was wet. So was Antonio's. "You guys didn't tell us they had showers here. Which way?"

Antonio's face lit up with a mischievous grin. "Right through there." He pointed to the trail through the trees. "Same place where we get our food."

"Very funny," Katie said. The morning sunlight poured through the trees like golden syrup, spilling all over Katie, who sat on a log, sipping her coffee.

"How cold is the water?" Christy asked.

Todd and Antonio looked at each other. "It's refreshing," Todd said.

Christy knew all about Todd's idea of "refreshing" water. "Would it be okay if I use this pot to heat some water?" Christy bent down to pick up a well-used cooking pot and noticed part of a fish head in the dirt. "Did you guys leave the fish guts out on purpose for the raccoons last night? Those were mean-looking critters."

"I heard you and Katie talking to them in the middle of the night," Todd said.

"We were not talking to them," Katie stated. "We were talking about them. There's a big difference."

Christy took another sip of coffee and deduced that if Todd was awake, listening to them talk about the intruders, that meant Antonio was the one doing all the snoring. Somehow that little bit of information brought great comfort to her.

"What's on the schedule for today?" Christy asked. What she really wanted to ask was "When do we pack up and get out of here?"

"Antonio and I were just leaving to get breakfast," Todd said. "Do you two want to come with us?"

"Sure. Are you driving into town?" Christy thought the idea of breakfast at a quaint roadside café sounded wonderful, but she was far too grubby to go as she was. She hoped they wouldn't mind waiting for her while she cleaned up.

Tonio laughed.

"They're going back to the refrigerator for breakfast," Katie said. "Doesn't some fresh fish sound good to you right about now?"

"Oh. In that case, I think I'll stay here and warm up by the fire. I was freezing all night."

"Doesn't look like you got much sleep," Antonio said.

"I didn't."

Katie decided to go with the guys, and as soon as they left, Christy slipped into the tent to snatch Katie's blanket. She headed for the hammock, which was bathed in a stream of sunlight. Within minutes she was wrapped up in the scratchy wool and rocking herself into a deep sleep.

When the others returned with the fish, Christy could hear them discussing whether they should wake her. She was too groggy to respond. Even when the scent of fried fish floated her way, Christy kept snoozing.

She didn't wake until hours later when the sound of a rattling metal pot roused her from her stupor. Through bleary eyes Christy saw a mangy cat prowling for treats among their cooking gear.

"Get out of there," Christy shouted. She untwisted herself from the blankets and tumbled out of the hammock. The day around her had turned warm, and even though the sun had shifted and the hammock was in the shade, she had been sweating inside her tightly wrapped nest.

"Katie? Todd? Antonio?"

No answer.

Christy noticed a piece of a cardboard box propped up in front of her tent. It looked as if her friends had left a note written with the end of a burned twig. All it said was "Went hiking."

"That's great, you guys," Christy muttered. "Leave me all alone in the wilderness with a gang of wild animals on the prowl for fish guts."

Christy's feelings of abandonment lasted only a few moments. She was determined to get cleaned up. Unzipping the tent, she was assaulted by the horrible smell of the pungent wool sweater. She pulled out the sweater and hung it over a low tree branch to air it out. Then she returned to the tent, changed into her bathing suit, and collected everything she needed for a refreshing wash. She headed down the trail to the "refrigerator."

To her surprise, the lake was close. The trees were so thick that they blocked the view from the campsite. She noticed two boats on the shimmering blue water. One was an old, wooden rowboat manned by two boys who appeared to be fishing. The other was an aluminum fishing boat with a small outboard motor, making all kinds of noise as it skimmed across the water. To the right of Christy stood a small bridge.

Tightening her towel around her waist, she strode over to the bridge and discovered a narrow stream that fed into the lake. Two children floated on an inner tube as the stream carried them on a leisurely journey to the lake. *"Ciao!"* one of them called to her. She waved back and smiled.

Christy walked along the stream's shore until she came to a sun-baked gravel cove where the shallow water felt warm to her touch. With careful steps and a deep breath, she waded in and lowered herself into the water. The cool, refreshing sensation shocked her and delighted her at the same moment. Turning on her back, she floated with her face to the sun.

I feel like such a nature child! This is exactly what Todd said it was, refreshing.

Christy undid her long braid and reached for her soap and shampoo. Luxuriating in the shallow water, she hummed as she lathered up. A small brown bird perched on a low branch a few feet away and cocked its head at Christy as if trying to figure out what she was doing. With slow movements, Christy leaned back and dipped her hair into the water to rinse it. The current from the middle of the stream pulled her tresses away from her head.

I feel like I'm in that old oil painting in the university library. The one with all the women swathed in sheer ivory fabric as they bathe at some primeval cove with fat cupids fluttering around the waterfall.

Christy didn't see a single flying cupid as she emerged from the stream and dried off. But the exhilarating sensation of being refreshed fluttered about her as she made her way back to camp.

The others still weren't back yet, so after she changed, she took extra time brushing her hair and letting it air dry in the glorious sunshine. From a campsite not far away came the sound of children's laughing. It made her think of the children at the orphanage where she worked in Basel.

For a long while Christy rocked herself gently in the hammock and did something she hadn't had the luxury of this past school year. She thought about her life, her future, her hopes, and her dreams. She evaluated her school experience in Basel and thought about how much the work at the orphanage drained her emotionally.

What am I doing wrong, God? I want to serve you, and I thought I was by helping at the orphanage. But it has worn me out. Is that the way it's supposed to be?

The only answer to her questions was the sound of the wind in the branches above her.

And what about Todd? What's next for the two of us? Does he still want to live on some remote island and serve you by being a Bible translator to an unreached tribe? Am I the only one who's thinking about us getting married someday?

She knew God was listening to her heart. It had never been difficult for Christy to believe that God heard and saw and knew. Gazing up into the pale blue sky that was now streaked with feathery, thin white clouds, Christy whispered, "But really, Lord, could you see me living on a tropical island? I mean, bathing in the stream is about as close to roughing it as I've ever come. You wouldn't really have that in mind for the rest of my life, would you?"

Christy tried to convince herself that river bathing wasn't that terrible. It was actually sort of exotic. She pictured herself sleeping every night in a hammock like the one she swayed in now. She thought about eating fish every day. Fish and mangoes. Todd liked mangoes.

Cooking outside is fun. I do love seeing the stars at night. But I can't stand the way everything gets dirty so fast. Dirty and smelly. And being hungry, like I am right now.

Christy found the remainder of Todd's beef jerky in the van and ate it. She glanced around their remote campsite and began to feel less exhilarated about her solo afternoon. The surrounding woods, with their curious birds and slumbering, nocturnal wild raccoons, no longer felt enchanting. For months she had been on a rigid schedule and constantly around other people at school and at the orphanage. Many times she had wished for an afternoon exactly like this one, in which she could be all alone to think and daydream. But now she was ready for her friends to return. It was too quiet.

To busy herself, Christy collected lots of wood and cleaned up the campsite. She lit a fire and hiked down to the stream, where she filled the large pot with water and hauled it back to camp.

Maybe I could learn to be an organic, wilderness-type woman after all. This isn't so bad.

After heating the water, she washed the frying pan, their four coffee mugs, and four forks. Every time she heard the slightest noise, she looked around, expecting to see her friends returning from their hike. When the late afternoon shadows stretched across the campsite, Christy started to feel irritated as well as frightened.

Why did they leave me alone like this for so long? We should have a few rules on this trip, such as never leave anyone alone for an entire day.

Just then she heard footsteps coming through the woods, and she got ready to deliver the lecture of her life to her so-called friends for putting her through this agony. However, the footsteps didn't belong to Todd, Antonio, or Katie. They belonged to a man wearing a plaid cap and a thick knit sweater like the one Christy had left on the branch to air out. He carried a string of medium-sized fish and greeted Christy in Italian.

"Ciao," she replied without much expression. She hoped if she acted as if she meant to be here all alone and as if she knew what she was doing, the man would keep on walking past her campsite.

But he entered. And he spoke to her again in Italian.

Christy thought fast. During her time at school, she had learned the best response was to answer in German.

"*Ich verstehe nicht*," she said, which meant, "I don't understand."

The man moved closer to where Christy sat by the fire pit and spoke to her again, with longer sentences and more hand gestures.

"Ich verstehe nicht," Christy said quickly.

Undaunted, the man continued to speak. He removed two of the fish from his line, then pulled at his sweater and laid the fish in the clean frying pan.

"I don't understand you," Christy said.

With more hand gestures, the man removed another fish, laid it in the pan, and patted his chest. He looked at her as if waiting for an answer.

"*Danke*" was all Christy could think to say, assuming, hopefully, that he was just being a kind person and sharing his daily catch with her since it was obvious she had no dinner cooking in her pot. Then, because she remembered how to say thank you in Italian, she added, "Grazie."

"*Prego*," the man said with a nod of his head. He said something else, patted the sweater again, and was on his way.

Christy sat frozen. Only her eyes moved from the man's

retreating back to the fish in the pan. The distinct odor of fish guts hovered over her. It was more than fish guts, though. It was the strong scent of fish guts mixed with lining from the bottom of a bird cage and the bottom of a farmer's boot.

Oh no! Christy jumped up and dashed around to the back of the tent by the trail's opening. She looked around where she had hung Tonio's smelly sweater. It was gone.

Before Christy could run after the fisherman and demand that he return Antonio's stinky sweater, Todd's voice called to her from the woods, "Hey, Christy! You awake yet?"

She ran down the trail, met him halfway, and flew into his arms. But her hug lasted less than two seconds. With a frustrated push against his chest, she said, "Where were you guys? You left me here alone! Some guy came and traded me fish for Antonio's sweater, and I didn't know what was going on!"

Todd seemed to be looking at her hair, which hung straight down over her shoulders and was tousled wildly from her running about. "You smell good," he said.

"Did you hear anything I said?"

"Yes. He left you with three fish. Have you started to clean them yet?"

Christy looked at Todd incredulously. "No."

"Come on, I'll help you. Tonio and Katie are going to be here in a few minutes."

"Where were you guys?"

Todd grinned. "We got turned around on our hike."

"You were lost?"

"A little."

"How can you be a little lost, Todd? Either you're lost or you're not."

Todd slipped his arm around Christy's shoulder. He seemed amused by her raving comments and acted as if nothing were wrong.

Christy became acutely aware of how good she smelled in contrast to how Todd smelled. And when the other two arrived and gathered around the fire pit while Todd cleaned the fish, Christy realized how pointless and rather agonizing it was to be the only clean, sweet-smelling person in a group.

She apologetically told Antonio what had happened with the fish and the sweater.

He laughed. "You should have held out for five fish, minimum. My grandmother made that sweater. Next time, hold up your fingers like this and say, 'Cinque.' "

"Your grandmother made it? Antonio, I feel so bad."

"No, don't. It was an old sweater. She makes me one every Christmas."

"It's actually a God-thing, Christy," Katie said. "Can you imagine how long it would take us to catch some fish for dinner? This is perfect. We get back, and dinner is waiting. Well, almost waiting. Provided, at least."

Katie continued to talk, bubbling over with stories of their beautiful hike, how she was certain they must have walked at least thirty miles, and that she would never agree to go anywhere with those two again.

"Believe me, Christy, you made the right choice to stay here and sleep all day. I'm exhausted. And starving. This living off the bounty of the land takes time, doesn't it? Is there any beef jerky left?"

"No, I ate it."

"How long before the fish is ready?" Katie asked.

"Not long," Tonio said, fanning the fire and feeding it more of the twigs Christy had collected.

"You know, you guys, we could just find something to eat along the way," Christy suggested. "The raccoons would be happy if we left the fish for them."

"Along the way where?" Katie asked.

"Along the way to wherever we're going to stay tonight."

Christy's three friends stopped what they were doing and looked at her. She scanned their expressions and said, "Or were you guys thinking we would stay here another night?"

"Of course," Antonio said decidedly. "I don't have to be to work until Saturday. We will stay here four more nights."

When neither Katie nor Todd balked at the possibility of spending the rest of the week here, Christy kept her mouth shut, more from shock than anything else. She remained quiet the whole time they ate their fish. Todd let her borrow his navy blue hooded sweat shirt. She sat huddled next to him by the fire with the hood up, hiding her face from him and only halfheartedly joining in the singing with the others. She couldn't imagine spending five more days of their three-week vacation here with the masked midnight prowlers dining on fish guts while she tossed and turned on the hard ground, shivering like crazy.

Christy went to bed wearing Todd's sweat shirt pulled over her head, which at least helped to keep some of her body heat in. But without the smelly knit sweater, the hard ground poked her and chilled her more miserably than the night before.

Christy listened to Katie's steady breathing. Then a band of scavenging cats got into a fight with the raccoons over their midnight helping of fish guts. Christy cried tiny, silent tears. This wasn't the vacation she had dreamed of with her friends. How could she say anything to them, when obviously she was the only one who thought continuing to camp was a bad idea?

Christy shifted uncomfortably on the tent's floor and

rubbed her stockinged feet together. *I'm not much of a nature woman after all, am I?*

A wind picked up, and the canvas tent's sides began to billow. With the wind came a sudden downpour of rain. A leak in the tent's corner next to Christy's head caused the rain to come flying in with the wild wind. Within a few minutes, the sweat shirt's hood was soaked.

"That does it!" Christy shouted, jumping up and vigorously unzipping the tent.

"What's going on?" Katie mumbled. "Can't you just ignore the raccoons tonight?"

"Katie, it's pouring rain! I'm soaked. I'm sleeping in the van."

Running through the downpour, Christy yanked open the side door of the minivan and climbed in. She pulled the door shut and settled herself onto the back bench seat. *Why didn't I think of this last night? It's much warmer in here.*

The rain pelted the van's roof, but Christy was safe, dry, and almost warm. She pulled her scratchy blanket up to her chin and thought she might actually get some sleep now.

Just then the van's door slid open. "Make room, I'm coming in! Our tent is flooding." Katie sprang inside, accidentally smashing Christy's index finger against the seat's underside metal frame.

"Ouch!" Christy yelled.

"What happened?"

Before Christy could answer, the van's side door opened again, and Todd hopped in. "Guess you two had the same idea."

Antonio stood right behind him in the pouring rain and shouted, "Hey, come on! Make some room!"

"You guys are all wet," Katie said.

Todd held a flashlight and turned it toward Christy. Tears streamed down her cheeks as she pressed her lips together and held her smashed finger tightly.

"You okay?" he asked.

Christy shook her head but couldn't speak. Todd motioned with a chin-up gesture and said, "Did you hurt your hand?"

She nodded, and he reached for her hand, shining the flashlight on it. Antonio moved in, and all four of them peered at Christy's finger. It throbbed like crazy, but there was nothing to see. It wasn't swollen, cut, or black-and-blue. It just hurt like everything. The way her three friends looked up at her made Christy feel again like a failed nature woman.

"It'll be all right," Christy said quietly, pulling her hand out of the light.

"Well, then, since we are all together," Antonio said, "what should we do?"

Christy leaned back on the bench seat and tried hard to keep from crying over her throbbing finger. Todd made himself comfortable on the van's floor, leaning against her legs. At that moment she didn't want anyone to touch her or to press against her. Not even Todd. The tight quarters were beginning to smell like wet wool socks and mildewed boots. She knew if she popped open one of the windows, the wind would bring in the rain.

"We could tell detective stories," Katie said. "Or play chess. Have you ever played chess in teams? Guys against the girls. What do you think, Christy?"

Christy didn't feel like playing any kind of game. She didn't view this as the impromptu slumber party everyone else seemed to think it was.

"I have another flashlight somewhere," Antonio said, fumbling through the cupboards.

Todd turned around and said to Christy, "Listen to the sound of that rain. Isn't it amazing? What does it remind you of?"

When Christy didn't answer, Todd added, "I'll give you a hint. Think of an open jeep and a sudden downpour."

Antonio turned on a large flashlight, illuminating the enclosed area. Todd appeared surprised when he saw the expression on Christy's face in the light. "What? Did I say something wrong?"

"No," Christy said, trying to change her aggravated expression.

"Then, what's wrong?" Todd looped his arm across her knees and looked at her with concern.

"It's nothing."

"Oh, come on, Christy, it's obviously something," Katie said. "We all know you too well for you to try to hide whatever it is. Just tell us."

Christy hesitated. She hated the way she felt right now. Holding her still-screaming finger, she spouted, "I'm not particularly enjoying this downpour the way you guys are, and to be honest with you . . . I don't know if I can do this."

"Do what?" Katie prodded.

"This!"

"Camping?" Antonio ventured.

"Yes, camping and all this. I mean, you guys love the adventure of roughing it, but this is the first time in my life I've ever been tent camping, and I hate to be the big baby of this group, but this is hard! I'm cold, wet, and hungry, but you guys all think this is great and want to live this way for the rest of the week. Or for the rest of your lives, for all I know!"

They all stared at her.

"I'm sorry, but this isn't what I had in mind when we said we were going to travel around Europe."

Looking at Todd again, she decided she had better keep going while she was at full speed. "You guys, we only have three weeks to see everything in Europe. Three weeks! And if you want to spend the first week sitting here in the rain, eating fish, I guess that's okay, but I have to tell you, it's not as easy for me as it is for you."

Christy felt hot tears coming to her eyes. She forced them to back off. "I'm sorry I'm being like this, but I feel as if the three of you would have a much better time without me. I mean, you took off and went hiking without me. You could have just done this whole Italy camping thing without me, and I could have caught up with you on your way to Norway or something."

"Is that what you want?" Katie asked. "You want to go to Norway?"

"I don't care about Norway. I thought *you* wanted to go to Norway." Christy raised her voice. "Weren't you the one who sent the email about seeing a fjord and the country your great-grandmother came from?"

"Sure, I want to get to Norway eventually," Katie said. "No rush."

"But that's what you don't understand. You don't just say, 'Oh, let's go to Norway today' and arrive in time for lunch. You have to find out when the trains are scheduled. Some trains require reservations. And what if we want to stop and see something else along the way? We need to have a plan. Why can't we have a plan?"

"We can," Todd said. "We can make a plan."

"Three weeks isn't as long as you guys think," Christy said, calming down.

"So what's your plan?" Katie asked. "Give us a plan."

"I don't have a plan."

"Neither do we," Katie said defensively. "That's why we were just letting things happen as they came along. This camping trip with Antonio is a once-in-a-lifetime opportunity."

"No." Antonio held up his hand and shook his head. "Christy is right. The once-in-a-lifetime opportunity is more than this camp, this lake, these trees. You must see the Sistine Chapel and the Eiffel Tower. Europe has much to offer you. More than what you are seeing here. Five days is too long in one place when there is so much to see. We will go in the morning, okay?"

"Antonio," Christy said quickly, "I didn't mean we had to leave right away. I was just trying to say we need a plan. That's all. We need to work together as a team."

All four of them were quiet for a moment. The sound of the pounding rain on the van's roof made Christy realize how loud her voice had been as she had tried to make her point.

"Where would you like to go next?" Todd asked Christy.

"I don't really care."

"Oh, come on, Christy," Katie said. "You can't give us a big pep talk like that and not have something in mind."

"Well, okay. If it were up to me, I'd like to see other parts of Italy," she said cautiously.

"So would I," Todd said.

"It's settled." Antonio clapped his hands. "As soon as the rain stops, we take down our tents, and you go see more of Italy. Mi Italia. You will love it all."

The others seemed to agree with Antonio, which made Christy feel better.

However, the rain didn't stop when the morning came. In a miserable group effort, the four tired and hungry campers took down their soaked tents in the rain, tied them to the van's roof, and lugged the wooden box of camping gear to the back of the van, where they tied it to the bumper. Christy was certain she was soaked all the way to her skin. None of them had anything waterproof to use as a cover-up. Not even a plastic bag. They took turns changing clothes in the van and chugged their way across the muddy gravel road that led to the highway.

"Let's stop at the first place we come to that has food,"

Katie pleaded. "I don't care what kind of food it is."

Antonio drove faster when he reached the paved highway. "At my house, my mama will be happy to feed all of us. You will love her."

"No doubt, Tonio," Katie said, "but how far is it to your Mama Mia's Pizzeria?"

"That is very good, Katie. Mama Mia's Pizzeria. That is funny. It is not a long drive. We will be there within the hour."

Christy felt the hour was awfully long as they drove past green, rolling hills and huge fields of sunflowers. The rain had settled into a fine mist with a few sun breaks once they left the foothills. She stared out of a corner of a side window, watching the sun pierce through the clouds and send golden spears of light down on the grape fields. The light turned the leaves a vibrant lime green. Somehow, she found comfort in the beauty of the pastoral scene, which helped because she was still feeling twinges of guilt over being so upset and making everyone pack up and leave because of her.

She glanced at her smashed finger and noticed it had turned a deep shade of purple. Her spirit felt bruised to a deep purple, as well.

Todd slept stretched out on the backseat, and Katie slept on the floor. Christy envied their ability to sleep anywhere in any position. She couldn't sleep, no matter how hard she tried. She noticed that Todd's arm hung over the side and rested on Katie's shoulder since she had backed herself up against the bench. They, of course, didn't mean to be touching in such a cozy manner, but they were. Christy didn't like seeing Todd and her best friend casually flopped over each other that way. She kept glancing back at them.

When Antonio pulled off the main road and headed into town, Christy asked, "Is this it? Is this where you live?"

"Not far," he answered. "This is Cremona."

"It looks so old," Christy said, gazing at a tall tower that rose above the rooftops.

Antonio pointed to the tower. "That is the Torrazzo. The 'big tower.' Built in the thirteenth century."

"It's beautiful," Christy remarked.

"My family is related to the Amatis of Cremona." He made the statement with great pride, as if it should mean something. When Christy didn't respond, he added, "You *Americanos*. You do not know Amati, do you?"

"No, sorry," Christy said.

"Perhaps you know the apprentice of Amati—Stradivari. He is the one I am named after. Antonio Stradivari."

"Is he the one who invented violins?" Christy asked. "Stradivarius violins?"

"*Si!* You have heard of him. But it was my relative, Andrea Amati, who created the violin. Stradivari only perfected it. This is the town where they both lived. Stradivari made violins here more than three hundred years ago. They still make violins in Cremona. Musicians from all over the world come here to buy them."

For the first time, Christy began to feel excited about being in Italy. This was the kind of intriguing blend of history with the present that she had hoped they would discover and explore.

"You see that street there?" Antonio continued. "I work down there at a restaurant near the cathedral. I tell all the tourists that Antonio Stradivari made by hand 1,200 instruments, and I am named for him. No one believes me."

"They don't believe you about the 1,200 instruments or that you're named for him?"

"Both. They think I am making it all up."

"Well, I believe you, Tonio. And I think it's amazing." She stretched to catch a final glimpse of the cathedral.

With a few more turns on the narrow road, they came to

a wide bridge and crossed a large river before Antonio headed down a poorly maintained road. It led them to a modest whitewashed farmhouse with a red tile roof. The place reminded Christy of the Wisconsin farmlands where she grew up.

Antonio honked the minivan's horn. Katie and Todd stirred from their slumber, and Christy smiled at the woman coming out the side door of the humble house, who was waving and blowing kisses to them.

With a round of warm introductions to Antonio's "mama," the filthy, starving campers were welcomed into the small kitchen. Mouth-watering aromas met them as they entered. Tonio and his mother spoke to each other in rapid Italian as she kept motioning for Christy, Todd, and Katie to sit at the table.

Christy liked the woman at once. And she liked the kitchen. The chairs they pulled from under the table had woven straw seats, and the wood was painted a royal blue. On the wall in front of Christy was an ornate wooden plate rack painted the same blue. It held bright white, yellow, and blue pottery dishes with a matching water pitcher.

Antonio continued to speak with his mother in Italian while she scurried around the kitchen gathering ingredients and talking at the same time Tonio was.

Christy felt like laughing. So much commotion for this obviously beloved son and his three weary friends.

"She says you can take a bath if you want while she makes some pasta." Antonio looked at Christy. "You want me to bring your bag in?"

"Sure. I'd love to take a bath. Are you sure she doesn't mind?" Christy could tell his mother didn't mind. If anything, she probably didn't appreciate these filthy people in her nice, clean kitchen.

"I'll go first, okay?" Christy said, glancing at Todd and

Katie. She knew if she looked anything like the two of them, a bath would be a vast improvement.

Tonio showed Christy to the small bathroom with a tile floor and a strange-looking tub. It was short and deep and had a hose sort of fixture attached, which Christy figured must be the shower. It took her a few minutes to figure out how to work everything, but once she did, the warm water pouring over her head felt like a dream. She scrubbed up quickly and dressed in one of her last two clean outfits.

Katie was waiting as soon as Christy exited the bathroom. "Todd and I just washed some clothes, and guess where you do it. Outside in a big tub with one of those old-fashioned washboards. Then you hang it on a line strung between two trees. Is this bizarre or what?"

Christy noticed that Katie was all wet.

"Oh, we had a water fight. Todd and me. I won. You should see him. He barely needs a bath anymore."

Christy left cheery Katie to her bath and went out back to scrub up her clothes. Todd was in the sun, drying off. He and Antonio sat in straight-backed chairs, talking like two old men. Antonio leaned back and commented on how warm and clear it was here compared to the hills where they had camped. Todd acted as if he was completely at home, adding his own comments about the weather.

When Katie's around, he has water fights. When I come out, he barely notices me and sits there, talking about the weather. I feel like the big, bad meanie. We left the campgrounds because of me. It's probably nice and sunny there now, too, and we could be washing our clothes in the stream. Have I ruined everything?

Within an hour and a half, they were all cleaned up and seated around the kitchen table, eating a banquet of delicious food. Todd raved about the pasta. Katie kept taking more of the sausage, and Christy especially liked the ravioli. Antonio relayed messages to his mama about how much everyone was enjoying the food. She smiled and motioned for them to eat more, more, more!

Christy was sure she didn't have room for another bite, and yet loads of food was left over. "Would you please ask your mom if we can help clean up?"

Antonio asked. His mother motioned with hand gestures that they should shoo and leave her alone in her kitchen.

"We can at least do the dishes," Katie suggested.

That was agreed to, and the four of them set up an assembly line to wash and dry the blue-and-yellow ceramic plates as well as all the pots and pans. It didn't take much time with all of them crowding around the sink and laughing. Christy had a feeling Antonio's mom was glad to have them leave her small kitchen in peace.

They all set to work unloading and cleaning up the camping gear with the assistance of one water hose and one rough scrub brush. It took all afternoon to clean everything, dry it in the warm afternoon breeze, and repack. Christy noticed that Todd and Katie were working almost side by side. After they finished, Todd challenged Katie to a game of chess, and they sat under the shade trees, heads bent close in serious contemplation of the board.

"Can I help your mom get dinner ready?" Christy finally asked Tonio after she got tired of watching Todd and Katie.

"No. She is not so comfortable with someone else in her kitchen."

A few minutes later Antonio's father came in from working the fields. It was nearly sunset. Christy thought Antonio's father seemed stern, or maybe he was tired. He was shorter than Antonio and more muscular. He welcomed them to his table warmly and had Antonio ask them questions while they ate. One of the questions he directed to Christy was "Where did you get your beautiful eyes? From your father or your mother?"

"I don't know. Maybe from both of them," Christy said, feeling her cheeks warm.

"My father says they are the most beautiful eyes he has ever seen." Antonio smiled. "And he is right."

Christy lowered her head and concentrated on her pasta. She felt as if everyone was watching her. Tilting her head and glancing up at Antonio's father shyly, she said, *"Molte grazie, signore."*

"Ahh!" Antonio's father exclaimed with surprise at the way she thanked him so politely in Italian. He rattled off more quick words and playfully swatted Antonio on the arm, pointing at Christy and swatting him again.

"What did he say?" Christy asked cautiously.

Tonio looked embarrassed. He answered his father in Italian, and suddenly Tonio's parents both turned to Todd with surprised expressions.

Todd gave Tonio a half grin and said, "What did you say? What am I missing here?"

Looking at his plate, Antonio used his hands along with his English as he interpreted for his American friends. "My father asked why I have not proposed to Christy already. I told him she was your girlfriend."

Christy looked at Todd. *This is it, Todd. Go ahead. Tell them you're crazy about me. Tell them you can't live without me. Let me hear you say it.*

Todd hesitated. Christy knew Todd was open-ended about much of life, and several times he had let her know she was free to come and go from their relationship as she pleased. And she had done that. And so had Todd. But was he ready now to publicly close at least one of those open ends? All he had to do was declare that Christy was his girlfriend.

As everyone looked at Todd, Christy pressed her lips together and waited.

With a trademark chin-up gesture Todd said, "Please tell

your father I'm flattered by his question."

What is that supposed to mean?

At first Antonio's father looked surprised at Todd's vague response. Then a smile grew, and he nodded his head. With a deep chuckle, he shook his finger at Todd and merrily rattled off a string of Italian words.

Christy wasn't sure she wanted to hear the interpretation from Antonio.

"My father says you have learned early in life the secret, which is to always keep a woman guessing."

Oh yeah, that's Todd's specialty. Always keep a woman guessing. And where does that put our relationship? Obviously not as far along as I thought it was.

Something inside Christy squeezed shut. The hurt in her heart pounded on that invisible shut door. It was an old, familiar hurt.

Don't do this, Christy. Don't sink into this depression. He's not rejecting you. He's just being his usual, noncommittal self. You and Todd have been through five years of a very special kind of friendship. A forever friendship. For now, that should be enough for you.

But deep inside, Christy wanted so much more.

5 Christy woke the next morning to the sound of a car horn in front of Antonio's farmhouse. She slipped out of bed while Katie slept and padded across the rug to the halfway open window. Pulling back the white lace curtains, she peered out at the taxi that had pulled into the driveway.

A tall, slender Italian about Antonio's age was paying the driver. The passenger wore dark, straight jeans and a white dress shirt with the sleeves rolled up. Christy stared at the handsome, dark-haired stranger.

"Ciao!" he called out as he turned and apparently spotted Christy at the window. Then he waved with one hand, lifted his suitcase with the other, and headed toward her. She quickly pulled back, letting the curtains shade her from his view.

"Katie!" Christy whispered, hopping over to the bed and shaking her sleeping friend. "Katie, wake up."

"What?" Katie sounded grouchy, as she usually did first thing in the morning.

"Katie, you have to see this guy. I think your order for tall, dark, and handsome just arrived!"

"What are you talking about?"

"Come here. Get up." Christy pulled on Katie's arm.

"Quick, before he comes in the house."

Katie groaned, "Why can't you ever leave me alone when I'm sleeping?"

A voice behind Christy made her jump and turn away from Katie. "Ciao." The visitor was standing at their bedroom window. Since there was no screen, he simply had raised the window the rest of the way and pushed back the curtains with his hand.

Katie screamed, but he laughed and spoke to them in Italian.

Christy self-consciously wrapped her arms around her baggy nightshirt and quickly reverted to her emergency response, "Ich verstehe nicht."

The visitor spoke to her in German.

Katie grabbed Christy's arm and said, "Who is this guy, and what in the world is he saying?"

He laughed again and said in English, "I know who you are now. You are Antonio's American friends, aren't you? I have heard about you. Are you Christiana?"

Christy nodded.

"And you are Katie. Ciao, Katie."

"Yeah, hi," she said, pulling the bed sheets up to her neck.

A knock on their bedroom door interrupted the awkward introductions, and Antonio entered, speaking Italian with their visitor and using lots of hand gestures.

"You have met my cousin Marcos?" Antonio asked Katie and Christy.

"Sort of," Katie said.

"He's on his way to Rome. You want to go with him?"

Ten minutes later Christy was seated in the kitchen, sipping strong coffee and eating round rolls that were soft inside and crusty on the outside. Around her swirled a lively conversation, partly in English and partly in Italian. Spontaneous plans for the next part of the journey came together effortlessly.

Marcos had arrived by way of an early-morning train that enabled him to stop in for a quick visit with his relatives. Since he was on his way to Rome, the three "Americanos" could join him. Marcos would show them the sights after he made a delivery to one of his father's clients.

"We better pack," Katie said when she found out the train to Rome left in an hour. "I still have clothes out on the line."

Christy glanced at good-looking Marcos and found his gaze was fixed on her. She looked away quickly, feeling her cheeks warm with embarrassment. It was the fourth time during breakfast that she had glanced at him, and each time he was gazing at her.

"Care to join me?" Katie said, rising from the kitchen table and tugging on Christy's arm.

"Sure." She rose and carried her dishes to the sink despite Antonio's mother's protests. "Grazie," Christy told her and comfortably received the woman's kiss on her cheek. Christy had gotten used to a lot of cheek kissing during her time in Europe, and she gracefully kissed Antonio's mom back, thanking her again in Italian.

Katie hung back, offering a stiff nod and saying, "Thanks for the chow."

The two of them turned to exit the kitchen, and Christy glanced at Todd. He was looking at her. She quickly swept her gaze past Marcos. Marcos was more than looking at her. He was watching her every move.

As soon as Christy and Katie were out the back door and away from the open kitchen window, Katie grabbed Christy by the elbow and yanked her around the side of the house by the clothesline. "What in the world are you doing?"

Christy couldn't believe how red Katie's face was. "What do you mean? I'm not doing anything."

"Oh yes, you are! You're flirting with Marcos right in front of Todd! What are you thinking? I've never seen you like this, Christy."

"What are you talking about?"

"What am I talking about?" Katie lifted her hands in a gesture of disbelief. "We're all sitting around the table talking, and all you're doing is taking tiny little bites of bread, and after each bite, you look at Marcos."

"I wasn't doing that."

"Trust me, that's exactly what you were doing. And then you would sip your coffee and pretend he wasn't staring at you. Did you even notice Todd sitting there, watching you flirt?"

"Katie, I was not flirting!" Christy lowered her voice and looked right and left to make sure they were still alone. "I don't know what you thought you saw in there or what you're thinking now, but I wasn't doing anything."

Katie shook her head. "Then that had to be the most intense case of subconscious flirting I've ever seen. I mean, I'm the first to admit that the guy is absolutely gorgeous, but come on, I could feel the heat passing between the two of you."

Christy felt baffled by Katie's statements. "I didn't feel any heat."

"You are so naïve."

"I am not."

"Just do me a favor," Katie said, going over to the line and yanking off her stiff, dried clothes. "Don't do it."

"Don't do what?" Christy felt her anger rising.

"Don't pull a Rick Doyle on us. Not now. You're smarter than that." With a swish of her red hair, Katie turned and marched off, her arms full of clothes.

Christy stood frozen in place, her mouth open in disbelief. *What was that all about? She knows Rick was a big-mistake* crush . . . how many years ago? Four? And what's more, Katie made the same mistake herself when she fell for Rick!

Christy aggressively pulled her clothes off the line and marched back into the house through the front door to avoid seeing anyone in the kitchen. She made a beeline for the guest bedroom and closed the door soundly behind her. Katie stood five feet away, jamming her clothes into her travel bag.

"That was completely unfair and mean," Christy growled at Katie. "Why are you mad at me? You wouldn't be acting mean unless you were mad at me."

"I'm not mad," Katie said without stopping her quick packing job. "Can we just forget it? They're going to be ready to go, and I don't want them waiting for us because we're sitting here having a fight."

Christy was so mad now she could hardly think straight. *I can't believe this is happening! Why is Katie being like this?*

Katie zipped up her bag and, without looking at Christy, lugged it to the door. "I'll be out front with the others."

Slumping down on the edge of the bed, Christy stared at the stiff pair of jeans she held in her lap and tried to calm down. She knew Katie well enough to realize pressing her to talk when she wasn't ready would be a mistake.

Why would she say all that? Was I unconsciously flirting? Was Marcos really staring at me like Katie said? Did Todd think I was flirting with Marcos?

Of course Christy had been aware of Marcos's steady gaze at the breakfast table. But that didn't mean she was flirting with him, did it?

I sure don't get stares like that from Todd. Am I feeling sorry for myself because Todd didn't take a stand about our relationship last night? The way Marcos looked at me this morning is the way I've always wanted Todd to look at me.

A knock on the door pulled Christy away from her evaluating. "Yes?"

The door opened, and to her surprise, Marcos stepped into the room with a grin on his face. His deep brown eyes met Christy's. "Do you need some help?"

Christy felt her heart pounding. "No. Thanks. I'm fine. I can get it. I'll be out in a minute."

"It's no problem. I will wait and carry your luggage for you."

Christy pushed her clothes into her bag and nervously tugged at the zipper.

"Here, let me get that for you." Marcos stepped over to her side and reached for the stuck zipper.

Christy pulled away. She felt self-conscious and nervous about this guy, who was acting as if he had free access into her private space. "Thanks," she said, grabbing her day pack and making sure she hadn't left anything on the dresser. "I'll go on out with the others." With that, Christy left Marcos to wrestle her bigger bag out of the house.

She found Todd and Katie loading their luggage into the back of Antonio's clean minivan. Christy said good-bye to Antonio's mom with another kiss on the cheek and then claimed the front passenger seat. She certainly didn't want to be in the back of the bus with Marcos and Katie while Todd sat in the front seat.

As Antonio steered his van down the bumpy road, Christy kept looking straight ahead. *This is all my fault for making such a scene about leaving the campground. If we were still there, we wouldn't be on our way to Rome with a guy who makes me incredibly nervous. Katie wouldn't be mad at me. Todd wouldn't be ignoring me. At least Antonio is still speaking to me.*

"Do you like Rome?" Christy asked Antonio, trying to start a conversation.

"Yes, very much. But I'm not going with you."

"You're not?"

"No," Antonio said, "I do not have money for travel."

Christy realized then that the camping hadn't cost anything. Even the fish were free. "What if we all pitched in and gave you some money?"

Antonio took his eyes off the road and smiled at Christy. "You sound sad because I am not going with you. That's nice, Christiana."

"I am sorry," she said, turning her attention back on the road and hoping Antonio would do the same. She couldn't figure out why Antonio could be sweet and flirty with her yet she never felt uncomfortable. He had been that way with all the girls when he was in California, and they all had loved it and called him the "romantic Italian." It felt different with Marcos.

Why? Because he's exceptionally good-looking? He must know how handsome he is. Does Marcos just expect all women to swoon over him? Or is it me? Am I somehow looking for more attention? What's going on?

Antonio pulled the minivan into an illegal parking place near the train station and left the motor running as he worked to unload their luggage. Christy felt sorry that they didn't get to stay and explore Cremona.

"Christiana," Antonio said, motioning for her to come around to the other side of the van, away from the others. In a low voice he said, "I told this to Todd and Katie while you were in the house. When I came home from California, I told Marcos about the decision I made in America to dedicate my life to Christ. Marcos said he is not ready to make the same choice. I think your going to *Roma* with him is what Katie calls a God-thing. This is the reason we left the camp. You can show Marcos God's love the way you showed me, and I am sure he will decide soon."

Christy felt her stomach tightening. "I wish you were going with us."

Antonio kissed her soundly on both cheeks. "Maybe you

will come see me again before you leave Europe. You are welcome any time."

"Thank you so much, Tonio." Christy felt the tears welling up in her eyes. "Grazie."

"Prego," he said. "I will be praying."

"And I'll pray for you, my friend. Ciao!"

"Arrivederci," Tonio said, handing Christy her luggage. He then hurried over to say good-bye to the others.

Christy suddenly realized how selfless Tonio was being. She knew he had gone to school in California at the expense of a generous uncle. Marcos's father, perhaps? Antonio's family obviously lived very modestly. The camping trip had been Antonio's vacation. A very inexpensive vacation. When Christy had complained and they had left the campground, that meant the end of Antonio's vacation, even though he didn't give any hint of it at the time. Christy wished again that she hadn't complained.

She followed the others into the train station and watched as Marcos arranged for them to pay extra on their Eurorail train passes so they could ride with him in first class. Marcos offered to pay for all of them, but Todd told Marcos they would rather pay. Christy chimed in with Todd and insisted on paying. Marcos held up his hands in surrender, and the three of them each paid for their first-class passes.

"Well," Katie said under her breath to Christy as they hurried to the train track. "He sure gave in when you told him how you wanted things to be."

Christy pressed her lips together and tried not to let herself become angry with Katie all over again. "Can we not do this, Katie?"

"What?"

"Pick at each other. I don't want to fight with you."

Katie looked down. Todd called for them to come on. "Okay," Katie said and took off for the train.

As they boarded, Christy tried to let go of her frustration with Katie and everything else. She felt little bubbles of excitement building up inside her. She loved traveling on the trains in Europe and had been looking forward to this part of the adventure.

Christy made sure she was seated next to Todd on the nicely upholstered train seat. Katie and Marcos sat on a matching seat directly across from them. Their luggage was stowed on shelves over their heads, and the four of them had the small, first-class compartment to themselves.

"How long will it take to get to Rome?" Katie asked.

"About five hours," Marcos said.

"That long?" Katie said.

"We could stop in Florence, if you like. I do not have to meet with my father's client until tomorrow morning."

"I have a tour book," Christy said, reaching for her day pack. "I could read about some of the things to see in Florence, and then we could decide if we want to stop there."

"We don't need a tour book," Katie said. "I'm sure Marcos can tell us what to see."

"I'd like to see the tour book," Todd said.

Christy felt relieved. Todd was on her side. The two of them could sit close and read about all the great sights awaiting them in these fabulous cities. At least that way they would know some of the history behind the things they saw.

With her sweetest smile, Christy handed Todd the tour book and hoped he was in the mood to snuggle with her while they read. That, more than anything else, would convince Katie and Marcos that Christy and Todd really were a close couple and that Christy wasn't flirting with Marcos—subconsciously or any other way.

Todd took the thick, soft-covered book from Christy, thanked her, and placed it between his head and the glass window of their train compartment. "Perfect," he murmured, closing his eyes. "Wake me when we get there."

"So it is up to you," Marcos said, staring at Christy. "Would
you like to go to *Firenze* first? Or directly to *Roma*?"

"What do you think, Katie?" Christy was eager to
get Marcos to stop looking at her.

"Rome, I guess. Doesn't matter."

"There's a lot of art to see in Florence," Christy said. "Like
Michelangelo's statue of David."

"Are you saying you want to stop in Florence so you can
see a statue of a naked guy?" Katie asked.

Marcos laughed.

"Of course not!" Christy snapped. "You're missing my
point, Katie."

"And what was your point?"

"We might be sorry later if we don't stop to see Florence
while we have the chance."

"Fine. I don't care. I think it's all great. The only thing I
really want to see is Venice. That is the place where they have
the gondolas, right?"

"Right," Marcos said. "That is where I live. *Venezia*."

"You live in Venice?" Katie said.

Marcos nodded.

"Do you have water right outside your front door and ride
around in gondolas?" Katie asked.

"Of course. Venezia is built on more than a hundred islands. Nearly everyone has water outside the front door. My
father owns a jewelry store near the Piazza San Marcos. Carlo
Savini Jewelers. If you go to Venezia, you must go to his store.
Carlo Savini. Don't forget."

"That is so cool. Let's definitely go to Venice," Katie said.

"After Rome," Christy suggested.

"Sure. After Rome and whatever that other 'frenzy' city
was."

"Florence," Christy said, using the English pronunciation
of the city.

"Firenze," Marcos corrected her.

"There is one place I'd like to see in Italy," Christy said. "I
don't know where it is. It might be in Venice."

"If it is, I would know it," Marcos said. "What is the
place?"

"The Blue Grotto. Have you ever heard of it?"

"Of course. It is on the Isle of Capri. Not in Venezia."

"Where's Capri?"

"South. The way we are going. You take a hydrofoil over
from *Sorrento* or *Napoli*. It's only a few hours from Roma. It is
best to see it in the morning. By afternoon there are too many
people, and it's not worth the trip."

"That's good to know," Christy said. "Thanks."

"You could go there tonight," Marcos suggested. "Capri
has some of the most expensive hotels in all of Italy, but I
know a place you can stay. You would then take the first
morning tour boat to the *Grotta Azzurra*. Then you go to
Roma, and I can meet you in the afternoon."

"That sounds like a good idea." *Katie can't think I'm flirting
with Marcos if I'm planning how to get away from him.*

"What's the Blue Grotto?" Katie asked. "And why do you
want to go there?"

"It's a cavern I've heard about," Christy explained. "You

take a boat in, and the refracted sunlight makes the water a unique shade of blue."

"I remember hearing about that place," Katie said. "Didn't we know someone who went there and was always talking about it?"

"Rick Doyle," Todd said without opening his eyes or giving any other indication he was awake.

"That's right!" Katie's green eyes sparkled at Christy. She reached over and slapped Christy on the leg. "Rick called you from Italy on your birthday. I remember you telling me. That's why he took you out to an Italian restaurant for your big date—because he was in Italy the day you turned sixteen."

Sometimes Christy wished Katie suffered from memory lapse. Unfortunately, Katie remembered every word Christy had told her so many years ago. And Katie seemed to feel compelled to recount every detail now in front of Todd and Marcos.

"And Rick went to the Blue Grotto that morning, on your birthday. You were in Maui, and he called you there and told you the water was the same color as your eyes. That's where I've heard of the Blue Grotto."

Todd opened one eye and turned his head toward Christy. She looked at him, knowing she had nothing to hide yet still feeling put on the spot.

"Rick was here in Italy when he called you?"

Christy nodded. Then she noticed Marcos was staring at her again.

"I think he is right," Marcos said. "Your eyes are the color of the water in the Grotta Azzurra."

What is it with Italian men and my eyes?

"Well, then," Todd said, adjusting his position and handing the tour book back to Christy, "guess we better go to this famous Blue Grotto and compare the two for ourselves."

Christy couldn't tell if he was upset or teasing her.

"I'm going to find the dining car and get something to drink," Todd said, standing. "Anyone else want anything?"

"I'll come," Christy said. She was glad for the chance to have a few minutes alone with Todd.

"Wait for me," Katie said, joining them.

Christy gritted her teeth. *Can't you tell I want to be alone with him, Katie? We haven't had a chance to talk privately this whole trip.*

Leading the way down the narrow hall, Christy didn't turn around to look at Katie and Todd until they were in the dining car. Rather than a simple snack bar with a few booths, like the snack car where she and Katie had eaten on a train in England, this dining car had cloth-covered tables and uniformed waiters who seated them and brought the food to them. She had been in a dining car like this last summer with her friend Sierra when the two of them had visited the school in Basel.

Christy sat first, and Todd slid in across from her. Katie slid in next to Todd instead of sitting next to Christy. He leaned across the table and said, "So you're the Blue Grotto girl, huh?"

Christy wasn't sure what to say. She reached over and brushed her fingers along Todd's unshaven chin and said, "And are you the mountain man?"

"I thought I'd let it grow. What do you think?" He leaned back and turned his chin to the right and then the left to allow Christy a thorough evaluation.

"I guess it might take a little while," she said cautiously. Todd's hair was so blond it barely showed unless the light hit it just right. Most of the time, she had noticed, it looked like a faint shadow or as if he hadn't washed his face. "Ask me again after it's been growing for a week."

Todd laughed. "I haven't shaved for a month."

Christy laughed with him. "Oops! Sorry."

Todd rubbed his chin with his thumb and forefinger. "I guess growing facial hair isn't one of my talents."

"Try a goatee," Katie suggested, reaching over and touching Todd's chin.

"You think?" he asked.

"Sure," Christy agreed. "Try shaving all of it but this part." She reached across the table and rubbed the soft fuzz across his chin. "It's actually a little darker there."

"Really?" Todd held up the back of a spoon and tried to catch his reflection. Then, without looking up, Todd asked, "Do both of you want to go to Capri?"

"I do," Christy said.

"Sure," Katie agreed. "Does this mean we have a plan?"

"I guess so," Todd said, putting down the spoon and ordering a mineral water from the waiter who now stood before them. Christy ordered the same.

Katie shrugged and said, "Okay. Another one of those."

The waiter looked unclear as to what she was telling him.

"Tre aqua minerale," Todd ordered for them.

Christy was impressed and gave Todd a look of admiration.

"It's so close to Spanish," he said. "When I was in Spain last year I picked up a few key phrases."

"Good," Katie said. "Teach me how to ask, 'Where is the bathroom?' "

"Out that door and to the left," Todd said. "We passed it on the way in."

"That doesn't do me any good," Katie said. "I'm serious. Teach me whatever phrases you know. I get nervous when I can't communicate."

"And I get nervous when you do communicate," Christy said under her breath.

"What was that?" Katie leaned forward, her arms resting on the white tablecloth.

Christy hesitated before deciding honesty was the way to go with her friends. "I've been having a hard time not getting upset at you all day, Katie."

"Why? What did I do?"

"First, this morning you had all those accusations outside Antonio's house after breakfast. I think you'll notice from the way things are going that those assumptions weren't completely accurate."

Katie tilted her head back and forth as if weighing Christy's words. "I still see some potential, but you're right. It doesn't appear to be what I thought it was earlier."

"I can assure you, from my perspective, it is not." Christy glanced at Todd.

"Am I supposed to know what you guys are talking about?" he asked.

"No," Christy said quickly. She went right on to her next point. "And the whole thing about Rick was more than needed to be said, Katie."

"Why? What did I say wrong? Todd didn't mind. Did you, Todd?"

Todd shook his head. "We all go through different stages in life. Some relationships last and others don't. That's reality."

Christy thought his evaluation was a little too down-to-earth, even for Todd. It sounded as if he could be referring to another relationship, a larger one than the brief handful of dates Christy had with Rick.

Maybe he's talking about his relationship with Rick. The two of them shared an apartment in college with some other guys, but now Todd and Rick never see each other.

"Can you let me out, Katie?" Todd asked. "I'll be right back."

"Nope. Not until you say it in Italian."

"I don't know how to say it in Italian," Todd said.

"Then too bad. You're stuck."

As Christy watched, a little-boy grin appeared on Todd's face. It was the same look he and his buddy Doug used to get at the beach when they were about to pick up one of the girls and throw her into the ocean. Todd reached under the table, and Katie immediately gave in

"Stop squeezing my knee," she said with a giggle as she swatted at Todd.

How did Todd know her knee was so sensitive? I didn't know that.

He exited as the train swayed back and forth. "Katie, I mean it about the flirting stuff you said this morning," Christy continued. She didn't feel she had been able to say everything she wanted to earlier, since they had been talking in code in front of Todd. "That really upset me, and I don't want us to communicate like that on this trip."

"Fine," Katie said. "What else do you want to say to me before Todd comes back? Because if you don't have anything else to yell at me about, I have something I think I should mention to you."

"I'm not yelling at you, Katie."

"Okay, is there anything else you want not to yell at me about?"

"No."

The waiter arrived with their bottles of mineral water and the bill on a small tray.

"I've got it," Christy said, pulling some money from her pocket and placing it on the tray. He gave her some change, and she thanked him in Italian.

"I'll pay for something next time," Katie said. "Now, do you want to hear my observation?"

"Yes." Christy meant it. She really did appreciate Katie's insights. She always had. But she didn't always like them when she first heard them.

Katie leaned forward. "Okay. First, I should tell you that

Todd and I got into a big discussion on the plane. We talked about how he and I are more the outdoorsy type. We were talking about camping, and he said he wasn't sure you would want to do much roughing it on this trip. I told him he didn't have to worry, that you could handle anything we threw at you."

"Guess I proved you both wrong, didn't I?"

"Don't worry about it," Katie said. "Todd and I talked about it yesterday while we were washing our clothes and you were in the bathtub."

"You and Todd talked about me again?"

Katie swished the air in front of Christy with her hand as if to brush away any misunderstandings Christy might be formulating. "I told him we should be sensitive to you and try not to do anything that would push you over the edge. He said you were probably still stressed from school and working at the orphanage and everything. We both know it's been a difficult term for you."

"Well, you know what? I don't know if I appreciate your analyzing me whenever I'm not around."

"It was no big deal, Christy. I think you should be glad that Todd feels comfortable enough to talk with me about you."

Christy wasn't sure she agreed with that. She sipped her bubbly water and reluctantly listened as Katie continued.

"Can I just say that I think you have way too many expectations of yourself, of me, and of Todd for this trip? Either that, or you're living too much in the past."

"And what is that supposed to mean?"

"If you think about it, Christy, you could be having some kind of weird flashbacks to our trip to England, but this is nothing like that trip."

"You're right. It isn't." Christy felt certain this trip couldn't be compared in any way to that one. In England they were

with a group on a short-term missions project. At the beginning of the trip, Christy had been dating Todd's best friend,
Doug, because Todd was long gone from her life. Or so she
thought at the time. Christy had ended up seeing that she
and Doug were incompatible but how perfect her friend Tracy
was for him. Christy broke up with Doug during the first
week of the trip, and now, a year and a half later, Doug and
Tracy were married.

"I don't see how the two trips compare at all," Christy
said.

"That's my point exactly," Katie said. "This is a completely
different trip, and all the circumstances are new. You
shouldn't allow yourself subconsciously to make any com-
parisons to the challenging stuff that happened to you on
that trip and think it's all going to happen to you again just
because you're in Europe with your friends."

Christy didn't follow Katie's thinking until she delivered
her last line, which was a zinger. "I mean, it's not like you and
Todd are going to break up on this trip or anything."

The dining car door slid open, and Todd entered with
Marcos behind him. "I went back to get the tour book, and I
talked Marcos into joining us so we could a make a plan for
the next few days."

Marcos slid into the booth next to Christy. Katie scooted
over, and Todd sat next to her.

Christy felt her heart pounding so hard it throbbed in her
ears. Katie's words bounced off the inside of her head with
each pound of her heart. *"It's not like you and Todd are going to
break up on this trip or anything."*

All the odd little pieces began to fit together. Todd had
been happy to see Christy at the train station and had given
her a sweet hello kiss, but since then he had barely touched
her. Except for when they sat close by the campfire.

Todd didn't agree that I was his girlfriend in front of Antonio's father. Why? Has he realized we're an uncomplimentary match? He loves roughing it, and I fall apart when it starts to rain.

Christy remembered how, during the England trip, she had seen clearly that she realized she and Doug weren't a good match. She wondered if Todd had made that same discovery about her.

Is he just waiting for the right time to tell me? Knowing Todd, he wouldn't break up with me for good unless he was convinced God was telling him to. . . . Christy's mind raced through a number of facts. Todd was nearly finished with college. He had only a few more credits to go, and they both were planning to attend Rancho Corona in the fall. A year from now, Todd would be graduated and twenty-four years old. That was old enough by anyone's standards to be married.

But where is it written that he has to marry me? I was the girl-friend of his teen years. He's a man now. Definitely. Facial hair and everything. He can have any woman he wants. Why wouldn't he marry someone more outdoorsy and easygoing like he is? Someone who is fun to be around and a good friend. Someone like . . .

Christy's heart pounded wildly, deafening all her senses as she stared across the table at her red-haired best friend.

Someone like . . . Katie.

7 Christy felt numb all the way to Rome. As the others in the dining car talked and planned, she barely responded. When the group discussed going straight to Naples and skipping Florence, Christy merely nodded in agreement.

Everything inside her felt shaken by the thought that Katie could be a better match for Todd than Christy was, just as Tracy was a better match for Doug than Christy. When the earthquake inside her stopped, all the pieces were in places they didn't belong. She scrambled emotionally to pick up whatever wasn't shattered and to find a safe place to store her feelings in her heart.

Why would Todd have kissed me at the train station in Basel if he's been thinking about our breaking up?

Then she remembered his words after she said she didn't want to cry. *"And I told myself I wouldn't kiss you."* That's what Todd said. *He didn't want to kiss me. He's probably waiting until the end of this trip before he tells me it's over between us.*

In her numbed state, Christy thought of the water fight between Todd and Katie. The way they had bent their heads close together over the chessboard. The way he knew where to squeeze her knee. Was it possible something was going on between them right under her nose, but she hadn't read the signs?

The four of them ate lunch. Christy didn't taste a bite. They returned to their first-class compartment, and she sat like a blob while the rest of them discussed the sights they should see, which included some of the museums and churches Christy had marked in the tour book. It was what Christy had wanted all along; they were making a plan, and they were working together as a team. Yet Christy was with them in body only. She kept watching Todd and Katie for any further signs of special interest in each other.

At the train station in Rome, Marcos directed them to the track for their next train. Katie tugged on his arm and said, "Marcos, I want you to come to Naples with us." She tilted her head and gave him a smile. "It won't be the same without you."

"Okay, why not?" Marcos said. "I'll ride the train with you to Naples, and when you go on to Capri, I will take a train back to Rome."

Christy thought Marcos might change his mind when they found out the first-class section on that train was booked. But he didn't. Instead, the four of them ended up in second class, which was radically different. They stood part of the way until Marcos found two seats in a different compartment.

The seats turned out to be more like twelve inches of open space. At Marcos's insistence, Christy and Katie wedged their way into the space while the guys stood in the walkway. The woman next to Christy held in her lap a large straw basket that smelled of garlic. The basket slumped onto Christy's lap as the woman slept. As the close smell of perspiration and garlic grew in intensity, Christy drew in little breaths with her hand over her nose. No one else in the compartment suggested opening the window. Everyone seemed content. Finally, Christy couldn't take it any longer. She rose and told Katie she needed to get some fresh air.

"I'm right behind you," Katie said.

The guys followed them to an open window in the wobbly train's hallway. Katie was the first to burst out laughing. "Whoa! What were you trying to do, Marcos, cure us of ever wanting to travel on a train again?"

"This is why it is better to pay more for first class," Marcos said.

"How much farther is it?" Todd asked. "I don't mind standing here if you guys don't."

"The conductor may tell us to move, but until he does, we can stay," Marcos said. He checked his watch. "I would say we should be in Napoli in less than an hour. This is a direct train. That means two hours exactly from Roma to Napoli."

Christy stood next to her luggage with her arms folded on top of the open window frame. The rush of warm afternoon air helped to clear her thoughts. Todd was standing right beside her. If he wanted to, he could easily put his arm around her. Or lean his head next to hers and whisper something sweet.

But he didn't. He stood back just slightly so they weren't touching. His attention was on Katie. She was busy plying Marcos for useful Italian phrases, and Todd was repeating them along with her. Marcos seemed to enjoy the role of tutor in their tight quarters. He also seemed to enjoy Katie.

Christy thought back on how Marcos had pretty much ignored Katie that morning. Now Katie had two ardent admirers, and Christy felt heartsick.

Relationships have to be two ways. Todd wouldn't be interested in Katie unless she let him know she was interested in him. And she is, isn't she? Maybe that's why she's being so cute with Marcos now. Maybe she's trying to make Todd realize how wonderful she is.

Christy watched. At that moment, with her tumbled spirit

in agony, she found it easy to imagine anything.

It was one thing for you to go out with Rick after I did, Katie, but at least you waited until after I'd broken up with him.

She ran her thumb across her gold Forever bracelet. When Todd had given it to her on New Year's Eve almost five years ago, he had said it meant that whatever happened in the future, they would be friends forever.

Is this about to become part of the "whatever"? Are we going to finally tell each other we're just friends? A year and a half from now will Katie and Todd be married like Doug and Tracy are?

Christy would never have expected herself to feel so overwhelmed. Katie was right about one thing she had said in the dining car: It had been a difficult school term for Christy. Her notes home had been cheerful, and almost all her diary entries had been positive. But that was because she only wrote when she felt good.

During most of the past ten months she had gone to classes, given all she had emotionally to the needy children at the orphanage, and returned to her dorm room, where she fell asleep while doing classwork.

That's one of the reasons her Saturday morning trek to the Konditorei had become so important to her. It was her way of treating herself for making it through another week without collapsing.

Christy wondered if part of what she had been feeling the past few days was the result of so many stressful months and such a rigid schedule. She didn't remember how to relax and have fun. She didn't know how to be anybody's girlfriend. Maybe Katie was right, that Christy's expectations of herself and her friends were too high. Maybe she had only imagined the invisible canopy of peace when Todd arrived. Maybe this relationship was never meant to be anything more than what it was right now. If that was true, Christy had to know now, not at the end of the trip.

"Todd," Christy heard herself say, touching him lightly on the shoulder. He turned, and she said, "Could I talk to you for a few minutes?"

"Sure." He leaned against the windowsill with his back toward Katie and Marcos.

Christy felt awkward. She hadn't thought this through. "I guess what I meant was, could you and I go to another part of the train to talk for a few minutes?"

"Sure." Todd picked up his pack and slung it over his shoulder. "Hey, Marcos, Katie, we're going to the next train car for a while. Where should we meet in case we get separated when the train stops?"

Marcos gave Todd instructions, saying that they needed to go right to the bus that would take them to the harbor. At the harbor they would purchase their tickets for the hydrofoil, not the boat, to Capri because the hydrofoil was twice as fast. He emphasized to all of them that Naples wasn't the best city for tourists and that they should watch their belongings carefully.

"Got it," Todd said. "When we get off the train we wait for each other."

Marcos added one more bit of instruction. "When you get to Capri, go to the Villa Paradiso. A friend of my father owns it. Be sure to tell him you know the son of Carlo Savini. He will give you a good price."

"Thanks," Todd said. He and Christy made their way through the train with their bulky travel bags. It seemed they wouldn't be able to find any open corners anywhere. They were about to give up and go back to where they had left Katie and Marcos, but then, in the very last train car, they found a corner in the passageway.

Christy dropped her pack and jiggled the window until it opened to let in a welcome rush of air. The train was rolling past a grove of old olive trees. Some of them had gnarled trunks that were at least three feet wide. A small village appeared on the hillside as the train curved to the left. Noting the charming whitewashed houses with their red-tiled roofs in the distance, Christy thought about how they were probably much older and much more humble up close than they looked from a distance. At least that had been true of Antonio's home.

Christy turned her face to the open window and let the rushing air dry the perspiration on her face.

"How are you doing?" Todd asked.

Turning to face him, she said, "Todd, I need to ask you something."

"Sure."

"I know you'll be honest with me." She looked into his strong, steady face and hesitated before going on.

"I'm always honest with you," Todd said. His short, sunbleached blond hair stood straight up as the wind blew over him through the open window.

"I know you are. And I really want to always be honest with you."

"So what's going on?" Todd asked, turning to give her his full attention.

Christy pulled her eyes away from his piercing gaze. She didn't know what to say. It seemed that for years she had been the one to ask the are-we-more-than-just-friends question. She was the one who always wanted to know where their relationship stood and what was expected of her. Todd didn't seem to need to know. While she needed a plan, he seemed content with the adventure of it all.

Christy said the first thing that came to her mind. "Katie said she thinks my expectations are too high for myself and for the two of you. Do you think that, too?"

"Maybe," Todd said.

"What do you mean?"

"I guess I'd have to know what your expectations are, exactly, to know if they are too high or not."

"Okay, forget I asked that. This is what I really want to know. Do you think we've changed?"

Todd paused and then nodded slowly.

"I mean, have we changed a lot? Maybe changed too much? Or maybe we haven't exactly changed but become more of who we really are. And is it possible that the true people we are now aren't the same people we were five years ago? Or the people we will be five years from now."

Todd ran his hand across the stubble along his jawline. "Can you give that to me again?"

Christy looked down at her hands. Her fingernails were all broken off from the camping trip. Her injured index finger had gone from deep purple to black-and-blue. Inside, she felt as rough and bruised as her hands looked.

"Todd, do you want to break up?" She spoke the words in a thin voice without looking at him.

Todd didn't answer. Since he didn't immediately protest and say, "No, of course not," Christy took it to mean only one thing. Her throat tightened. All her hope drained out of the soles of her feet. Slowly raising her head, Christy glanced up at Todd. His face was turned to the open window, and she could see him swallowing several times.

"You know," Todd said after a full minute of only the consistent sound of the railroad tracks thundering in their ears. "I think I'd like to talk about this later, if that's okay with you."

Christy couldn't stop the tears that sprang to her eyes. "Okay," she managed to say.

Several people were coming down the passageway, forcing Todd and Christy to move out of the narrow aisle.

"Maybe we should go back to where Katie and Marcos are," Christy suggested, lifting her bag.

"Okay," Todd said.

Each step Christy took through the train became heavier than the last. Her mind raced through her options. Once they reached Naples, she could take a night train back to Basel and be there by morning. Back to her safe dorm room. Back to her routine and everything that was familiar. She could pour herself into the children at the orphanage. They needed her and wanted her. Why stay with Todd and Katie if they neither wanted her nor needed her?

Her stomach twisted in a huge knot. *All these years for what, God? Was this whole relationship with Todd a big joke on me? A testing of my emotions? Well, I failed, didn't I? I seem to be doing that a lot lately.*

As the train slowed, more passengers and their luggage crowded into the narrow aisles. They soon became so clogged it was impossible to move. That's how Christy felt inside, too. Stuck. Uncomfortably waiting for the inevitable.

When the train came to a stop and the doors opened, the crush of people pushed Christy out onto the platform. She stepped away from the stream of noisy travelers. Todd was right beside her. Neither of them spoke as they watched for Marcos and Katie. The mass of people moved past them, and the two of them waited, still not seeing their friends.

"Do you think they got off before us and went straight out to the bus?" Christy asked.

"We can go see." Todd headed for the exit. His voice sounded flat and low.

Is he hurting over this as much as I am? We have to talk! This is too painful.

Todd found the bus to the harbor, and they looked all around for Katie. The driver indicated that if they wanted to go, they had to board the bus now or wait for the next one.

"I wonder if she got on an earlier bus?" Christy said. "What should we do?"

"She might have thought we went on to the harbor," Todd said. "Let's take this bus."

They rode to the harbor standing on the crowded vehicle, neither of them looking at the other or talking. Christy kept looking out the windows, expecting to see Katie running after the bus, waving and yelling.

But at the harbor there still was no Katie or Marcos.

"Should we go back to the train station?" Christy asked.

"We could end up passing each other on the way," Todd said. "I think we better stay here and wait. She's with Marcos. He'll make sure she's okay. It's possible he sent her on to Capri. She might be on her way to the hotel already. I'm going to get something to eat. Are you hungry?"

Christy couldn't imagine how Todd could be hungry in the midst of all this emotional tension. Her stomach was aching, but she guessed it was from emotions, not lack of food.

They waited in line at a pizzeria while the city's deafening noises roared all around them. From the street came the continual honking of car horns, the squealing of old brakes on city buses, and noisy hordes of people walking along, many of them using their hands as they talked.

Christy kept watching for Katie. When Christy got up to the window, she felt like her stomach was in too many knots to eat. But she was learning on this trip that it was best to take food whenever it was available.

Their pizza slices came wrapped in newspaper, and the extra gooey mozzarella cheese stuck to the cheap paper. They found a corner of cement that was in view of the bus stop yet away from the main flow of pedestrian traffic. Taking off their packs and using them as seats, Todd and Christy quietly ate their pizza and watched for Katie.

"Did you hear Marcos talking about this cheese on the train?" Todd asked.

Christy shook her head. She didn't remember any such

discussion. Her thoughts had been and still were absorbed in what she was feeling.

"Marcos said the food in southern Italy is best, and the cheese here comes from buffalo milk."

"Was he serious?" Christy asked, quite certain she didn't feel hungry now.

Todd nodded and chomped into his second slice. "It's good, isn't it?" He didn't sound enthusiastic when he said it, but as if he was trying to come up with small talk to keep them from having the conversation they really needed to have.

"What should we do if we don't find Katie?" Christy asked, making her own contribution to changing the subject from the obvious one that hung over them.

"I'll go check at the booth over there where we're supposed to buy the tickets for the hydrofoil. Maybe they'll remember seeing a redhead going through the line." Todd stood up. "Will you be okay here?"

"Sure."

Christy didn't feel okay. She didn't want Todd to leave her. Ever. Watching him walk away from her made her ache in a symbolic way. When she had watched Doug walk away after their breakup talk in England, she had felt strangely content. She remembered feeling confident that she had done the right thing. She didn't feel that way at all about letting Todd go.

But then, we haven't exactly had our breakup conversation yet, have we? It's not really over yet.

As Christy watched the mobs of people move past her, she noticed a man in tattered clothes approaching, mumbling something in Italian.

She was not in the mood to deal with beggars and got up, determined to walk away, even though it meant carrying her pack and Todd's, which he had left with her.

"Hey!" Todd called to her as she was hoisting his heavier pack onto her back. "Christy, let's go!" He ran toward her and grabbed her bag. "The last hydrofoil for Capri already left. We missed it. We have to run to catch the boat that's leaving right now. Come on!"

"What about Katie?" Christy yelled at Todd as they dashed to the boat.

8 Todd jogged ahead of her and let out a shrill whistle to keep the gangplank from being pulled away from the large passenger ferry. The uniformed employee looked irritated as Todd waved their tickets at him and ran onto the boat with Christy right behind him.

"That was close," Todd said, entering the enclosed passenger seating area.

Christy, who was right behind him, caught her breath. "Do you think Katie might be on board this boat?"

"She might. I'm guessing we missed her in the crowds, and she caught the hydrofoil. Maybe Marcos went on to the hotel with her."

Christy thought about how Katie, Todd, and Antonio had gotten "a little lost" on their hike a few days earlier, and she felt less than confident that Katie would be waiting for them at the hotel.

"I'll walk around the deck to see if I can find her," Christy said.

"Okay, I'll stay here and watch our stuff. It looks like a seat is back there by the window."

Christy didn't expect Todd to walk around the large ferry

with her, especially since it meant they would have to lug their packs if they both went. But it still made her feel alone when he sat down in the very last row, with their bags taking up the narrow space next to him.

Christy physically ached as she stepped out onto the deck in search of Katie. The longer she and Todd avoided having their big conversation about breaking up, the larger her ache grew.

Katie was nowhere to be found.

Instead of going back inside to tell Todd, Christy found a bench that was blocked from the wind. She sat with her arms wrapped around herself, as much for comfort as for warmth.

The lights of Naples were coming on all along the large bay they had just left. Tall cliffs, studded with villas and ancient monasteries, rose from behind Naples. The demanding form of Mount Vesuvius towered to the south. Even in her numbed state, Christy remembered Marcos talking about Vesuvius and saying they should visit Pompeii, the ancient Roman city that was destroyed by the now-sleeping volcano.

From this distance, Christy thought the volcano looked harmless. The crescent-shaped bay of Naples appeared to be a magical fairyland, twinkling in the fading light of the late spring evening. None of the traffic, drunken beggars, or street confusion could be viewed from this distance.

A clear, intense memory came to Christy. On her sixteenth birthday, Rick had called from somewhere in Italy. Right here in Naples, perhaps? Or from Capri? Christy and her family had gone to a luau, she had opened her presents, and then she and Todd had sat alone on the balcony lanai of her uncle's Hawaiian condo, watching the moon shimmering on the Pacific Ocean. Christy remembered the way Todd had sat beside her that night, holding her hand, rubbing his thumb over the Forever bracelet. He had told her to look out at the island of Molokai.

Instead of thousands of lights, like the ones she was now watching come alive in Naples, two lights from Molokai twinkled at them like stars, right next to each other on the shoreline. Todd had given Christy one of his famous object lessons that night. He said that just by looking at the lights from a distance, you couldn't tell which one you wanted to go to. You had to get closer and closer until you could see clearly what was there. Then you could decide if what you saw was what you really wanted.

An overwhelming sense of grief came over Christy. *All this time Todd has been getting closer and closer to me, and now that he's close enough to see what I'm really like, he knows I'm not what he wants.*

She couldn't sit there another moment with the lights of Naples winking at her, mocking her for being such a dreamer and for believing that she and Todd would go on forever. She rose and made another round of the deck with deliberate, long-legged strides until she came to a portion of the railing where no other people were around.

A taunting voice in her head dared her to rip off her gold bracelet and heave it into the sea. Better for her to do it now than for Todd's fingers to unfasten it later. Numbly unclasping the bracelet's catch, Christy held it in her fist and stared at the dark water.

She knew that the "Forever" on the bracelet meant far more to her than being Todd's friend forever. The "Forever" also represented her commitment to God. When Christy gave her heart to the Lord five years ago, she had told God that her promise wasn't just for the summer, but that it would last. It was a forever promise. A promise that she would trust God always and love Him more than anyone or anything.

Tears fell on Christy's closed fist as the wind whipped her hair, pulling long strands out from her loose braid. She shivered in the strong sea wind.

I've failed again, haven't I, Father? I'm not trusting you with all my heart. I'm not loving you more than anything or anyone. I'm all wrapped up in myself, my feelings, my needs, my wants. I'm sorry. Change my heart. I surrender everything to you, God.

Christy suddenly felt a warm breeze, as if the boat had hit a warm pocket of air. But it didn't come up from the Mediterranean Sea. It felt as if it came from behind her. Christy turned. No one was there. No giant heater pointed in her direction, yet the warm air still poured over her, calming her.

She was about to turn her attention back to the sea and finish her prayer when she noticed Todd. He was seated inside the ferry, next to the window, not more than ten feet away. She hadn't realized when she walked around the deck that she had ended up in his view.

But Todd wasn't looking at her. As she studied him more closely, Christy could see that his eyes were squeezed shut, his chin was tilted heavenward, and his lips were moving rapidly.

He's praying, too.

Christy watched Todd for a few moments, still caught in the soothing pocket of warm air. She opened her hand and peered at the gold ID bracelet that lay in her fist.

I meant it, Lord. My promise to you is forever. I want what you want for my life. If you want Todd and me to be together, I'll be grateful. If you want us to go our separate ways, I'll still be grateful. And I mean that. I trust you, Lord. I love you first, above all else. The future is in your hands, not mine.

The aching in the pit of her stomach seemed to ease up. She found she was breathing more deeply, and she noticed her jaw hurt from clenching her teeth for so long.

Here we are, just two tiny people lost in all our complex emotions, and yet you see us. You care. You're here. I know you're here. I feel you're so close right now, God. It's almost as if I can feel you breathing on me. Keep breathing on me, God.

Just then the boat rolled forward, as if it had gone over a speed bump in the water. Christy lost her balance and started to fall. Then her gold ID bracelet flew out of her open hand.

"No!" Christy screamed, lunging forward. She came down on the deck on both knees, her head down. As the bracelet slid toward the edge of the deck, the wind whipped Christy's hair madly, and for a moment she couldn't see. Pushing her hair away from her eyes, she frantically scanned the deck.

It was too late. Her bracelet was gone.

"Christy!" Todd's voice called to her. She turned and saw him coming toward her, lugging their gear. Todd dropped it all and knelt beside her. "Are you okay?"

Christy couldn't speak. She couldn't cry. She couldn't utter a sound. Todd waited, staring at her.

"I lost it," she finally managed to squeeze out of her tightened throat.

"Lost what?"

Christy pulled herself up from her precarious kneeling position and moved over to a bench seat along the back of the ferry. Several people had been watching her, but she didn't care. Todd didn't seem to care, either, because he pulled their gear over to the bench and sat down next to her, patiently waiting for her explanation.

"This is a very bad way for us to end." Christy's voice was shaking. "No matter what, I should have been more careful. I shouldn't have taken it off. I'm so sorry, Todd."

"What are you sorry for? I don't understand."

Christy turned and looked into Todd's eyes. They looked red, as if he had been crying, too.

"Todd," she began, trying to draw in a deep breath but finding it difficult. "Todd, I don't blame you for wanting to break up with me, but I should have been more careful with—"

"Wait!" Todd grasped her elbow. "What do you mean I

want to break up with you? I don't want to break up with you."

"You don't?"

"No, of course not! I thought you were saying on the train that you wanted to break up with me! That's why I couldn't answer you right then. I didn't see it coming."

"No, Todd! No! I don't want us to break up. I thought—"

"You honestly don't?"

"No! I thought—"

Christy wasn't able to finish her sentence because Todd suddenly reached his arm around her shoulders, pulled her close, and silenced her with a kiss. When he slowly drew his scruffy chin away, Christy could barely breathe.

Todd looked at her. Then he laughed aloud and wrapped both his arms around her in a tight hug. As he let go, his hand smoothed her hair, stopping halfway down her back.

"Todd, you don't understand," Christy said. "I lost our Forever bracelet."

"No, you didn't."

"Yes, I did. It was really dumb. I was all emotional and I took it off, and I was going to throw it in the sea because I thought you wanted our relationship to end. But then I realized that the 'Forever' on the bracelet meant my relationship with the Lord as much as anything, and that part of my life will never end. No matter what. I started to pray, and then I saw you praying, and then the boat tipped and—"

Todd gave the end of her matted hair a little yank.

Christy interrupted her speech with a small "ouch" before finishing with "And I honestly wasn't going to throw the bracelet overboard in the end, but it slid off the deck, and I'm so sorry, Todd."

Todd just grinned at her.

"What? You think I'm a nut case, don't you?"

"No."

"Then why are you smiling?"

"Give me your hand."

Christy held out her right hand. Todd moved his arm that had been around her shoulder. With a wide grin he produced the gold ID bracelet in his hand and clasped it around Christy's wrist.

"Where was it?"

"Caught in your hair."

"You're kidding! I can't believe it."

"Believe it," Todd said. Then, taking both her hands in his, he leaned close. Looking into her eyes he said, "Also believe something else, Christy. Believe that I want our relationship to continue. I want us to grow closer to each other and closer to the Lord."

Christy silently nodded.

"Do you believe that, really?" Todd asked.

"I believe you," Christy said. "And do you believe that I want the same thing?"

"I do now," Todd said, drawing in a deep breath and letting go of Christy's hands. He put his arm across the back of the bench and drew her close to his side. "That's not what I was thinking the past few hours."

"I know," Christy said. "Me either. I've been bombarded with doubts all day long. I started thinking about how I'm not a very good camper, like Katie. And how this could be like the whole thing with Doug and Tracy, and I wondered why you would want to be stuck with wimpy me when someone more perfect for you was out there, like Katie."

"Katie?" Todd said, raising his eyebrows. He looked at Christy as if the thought of being interested in Katie had never entered his mind.

"Katie or someone else. I figured as you got to know me better and saw me so close up, you were realizing I wasn't a good match for you. It's like those lights on Molokai, when you said you have to wait until you get close enough to see them for what they are to know whether you want to go there or not."

Todd gave her a look that showed he was even more confused now. "Molokai?"

"Never mind. It's just that when Antonio's father asked about us at dinner, you didn't really answer him."

"And that's what got all your doubts started?"

"That and at the Basel train station, your saying you hadn't planned to kiss me."

Todd grinned. "Oh, I planned to kiss you, all right. I'd been planning that one for a long time. I thought you knew I was being sarcastic when I said that."

Christy looked at her hands, feeling ashamed for her reactions to everything.

"As for Antonio's house," Todd continued, "I thought that whole conversation might be making Katie feel bad."

"Katie? Why?" Christy looked up at Todd.

"Think about it. You know how she was interested in Antonio last year. And here we were, sitting in front of his parents, and they were telling Tonio he should propose to you. I thought all the attention on you might make Katie feel bad, so I tried to get them off the topic."

Christy leaned back and shook her head. "I didn't even think of that. You are so right, Todd. Man, when my eyes are turned on myself and all my feelings, I sure miss out on what's going on around me."

"Don't be too hard on yourself," Todd said. "You're not supposed to know everyone's thoughts and feelings every moment. Only God can do that. That's why His mercies are new every morning."

Christy smiled.

"As I see it, we all need a little fresh mercy every morning."

They felt the boat slowing as they entered the harbor at

Anacapri. The sun had set while they had motored to the island, and now the world before them looked like Naples had from a distance, a fairyland of lights.

"Everything okay now?" Todd asked, gently smoothing back her hair with his hand.

Christy nodded and gave Todd a tender smile.

They rose and slung their packs over their shoulders. A shimmer of light from the harbor caught on her bracelet, and Christy, in her glowing mood, smiled and winked back at her bracelet.

You amazing little Forever bracelet, you. You have more lives than a cat!

"Do you remember the name of the hotel Marcos told us to go to?" Todd asked as they exited the boat side by side.

"It was Villa something," Christy said.

"We can ask at the harbor. They probably have some sort of information kiosk."

Christy and Todd moved with the rest of the crowd down the gangplank. A long line of taxi drivers stood outside their cars, reaching in to honk the horns and yelling at the new arrivals in several languages.

"Let's take a taxi," Todd suggested. "It'll save time."

They stopped at the first cab in the line only to realize there didn't seem to be any system to the taxi service. Several cabs already were pulling out of the line and taking off with customers.

"Can you take us to the Villa Hotel?" Todd asked once they were in the backseat with their luggage.

"Villa Nova, Villa Rialto, Villa Paradiso?" the driver asked with a thick accent.

"I think it was Paradiso," Christy said.

"Villa Paradiso?" he asked.

"Yes," Christy said. "*Sì.*"

With a roar, their taxi pulled onto the narrow street. The

driver yelled out the window at another cab driver, using aggressive hand gestures with his left hand and turning up the radio with his right hand. He appeared to be steering only with his knee.

Christy reached for Todd's hand, held it tight, and squeezed her eyes shut.

"Come on," Todd teased her, leaning over and whispering in her ear. "Didn't Tonio's driving prepare you for this?"

"If you want to live, don't bother me," Christy muttered. "I'm praying my little heart out for us both at the moment."

When the cab came to a screeching halt in front of a small café, Christy opened her eyes. "This looks like a restaurant. Where's the hotel?"

The driver took the money Todd paid him and, with lots of fast Italian words and pointing, seemed to communicate that the hotel was behind the café.

"Grazie," Christy said, sliding out of the backseat.

She and Todd ventured down a wide alleyway next to the small café. It was well lit and was marked by a tile sign with an arrow that read *Villa Paradiso.*

"Hey, cool!" Todd said when they reached the end of the alley. Before them rose an ornate garden with a large pool in the center. Violin music floated toward them from a white gazebo, where guests were seated at small tables. The guests were wearing evening clothes.

"I think the cab driver brought us to the back entrance," Christy said. "He probably took one look at us and knew we weren't the usual Villa Paradiso clientele. Do you think we should leave?"

"No," Todd said. "This is the only place Katie knows to meet us. Let's go around the block and enter the front of the hotel. Katie might be there already. Then we can find some place we can afford to stay in."

"I sure hope she's there," Christy said as they walked

down the alley past the café. She drew in a wonderful aroma and realized she was very hungry. "What would you think of coming back here to eat after we find Katie?"

"Sure. Smells good, doesn't it?"

"Really good," Christy said.

They strolled uphill past small houses pressed right next to each other along the narrow street. A crazy chorus of night sounds spilled out of the open windows above them. Babies cried, televisions blared, mamas called out for their children to come inside. A cacophony of smells came to them, as well: garlic, hot olive oil, strong wine, and a hint of sweet almond.

Something profoundly clear seemed to be settling inside of Christy. She felt ready to let go of the doubts she had carried for so many years and calmly walk beside Todd, taking each step to whatever came next in their relationship. Along life's road, she decided, she wanted to be a good traveling companion, no matter how long or short the journey would be with Todd. She wanted to make each day, each moment, count.

Todd reached for her hand. He gave it a squeeze and said, "This is what I thought our trip would be like."

Christy smiled. "Me too. You and me, lugging our bulky backpacks up cobblestone streets, holding hands, and just being together."

"This feels right, doesn't it?" he said. "This fits. You. Me. Not trying to figure out tomorrow. Just experiencing the mercies God put into this day."

She suddenly felt it again, the canopy of peace. She and Todd were under that invisible canopy, and she knew she had been the one who had stepped out from under it.

"Let's not do that should-we-break-up stuff again, okay?" Todd said. "I don't think my heart can take it."

Christy gave his hand a squeeze. "Neither can mine."

Todd stopped walking. In the amber glow of the evening

light, he turned to Christy and gazed deep into her eyes. "Promise?"

Christy smiled. "I promise."

They stood on the narrow, uneven street, holding hands and looking at each other as if they were both trying to memorize every detail. A balmy island breeze wrapped them in a private circle of quiet. All doubts flew from Christy's heart. She knew in that moment that she had changed. She was no longer a teenager, caught on an endless emotional roller coaster. She was a woman. And as a woman, somehow she knew that no matter what the future held, she would forever be in love with the man who now stood before her.

CHRISTY AND TODD · THE COLLEGE YEARS

9 Christy and Todd lingered only a few seconds in their private world before two women came around the corner and bustled past them. With their hands firmly clasped together, Todd said to Christy, "Come on, let's keep going."

Christy thought his words reflected their relationship as much as the private moment they had just shared under their invisible canopy. She felt ready to go on. Todd hadn't indicated that he viewed her or their relationship any differently than he had before the breakup question had driven a wedge between them. All she knew was that she was different. She loved Todd. Maybe he felt the same way about her. Maybe he didn't. Maybe he would have the same internal revelation soon—but maybe he never would.

Somehow none of that bothered Christy. It was enough to know that she loved Todd and, more important, that she fully trusted God with what would happen next in their relationship.

As they walked uphill hand in hand, Christy said, "I think I'm beginning to figure out a few things about myself."

"Oh?"

"I think I need to trust God more."

"Don't we all," Todd said.

They turned the corner and found themselves at the front of the large, salmon-pink hotel. The entrance wasn't especially huge or dramatic, but the intricate designs on the building's front made it look old, grand, and very expensive.

Christy scanned the front of the hotel for any sign of Katie. She wasn't there. They entered the lobby and treaded lightly across the rich burgundy- and gold-patterned carpet. Christy hoped Katie was sitting on one of the thick, upholstered chairs or couches, but she wasn't.

"Let's ask at the desk," Christy suggested. "Maybe she left a message."

"Or maybe she got here before us and got kicked out," Todd muttered. "Marcos didn't tell us this was a five-star hotel."

The uniformed desk clerk looked up at Todd and Christy with a smile that noticeably diminished when he took in their backpacks and casual clothes.

"Sorry. We have no vacancy."

How did he know we speak English? Do we look that much like typical Americans?

"That's okay," Todd said. "We don't want a room. We just wanted to check if any messages had been left for us."

The clerk looked at them impatiently. "If you do not have a room, we would not have kept a message for you."

Christy stepped in and tried to explain, giving him her best smile and making sure he noticed her eyes. That feature seemed to have helped her with other Italian men, and she figured it couldn't hurt this time. "We were supposed to meet our friend here. Katie Weldon. By any chance did she leave a message for Christy Miller?"

"No," he said with a flat expression, without even checking. Apparently Christy's eye color wasn't a novelty with this Italian.

"Grazie," Christy said, reverting to her limited Italian.

"Molte grazie." Speaking Italian had scored points with Antonio's father but had no effect on the desk clerk. She smiled her best eye-sparkling smile at him one more time, then turned to leave. She figured they could go back out on the street to decide what to do next.

"One more question," Christy heard Todd say to the clerk. She turned around and noticed that a distinguished gentleman in a black tuxedo had joined the clerk behind the desk. She was afraid that it wouldn't matter what Todd said. By the looks on the two men's faces, Christy guessed she and Todd were about to be thrown out of the hotel.

Todd stood his ground and said, "Do you happen to know a guy named Marcos? We're here only because Marcos told us to come and to tell you that we know him. His father is Carlo Savini."

Both of the gentlemen froze.

Christy had a terrible feeling that she and Todd should start running for their lives.

The man in the tuxedo exclaimed, "Carlo? You know Marcos and Carlo Savini? Why did you not tell me you were friends of Carlo Savini?" He rushed around to the front of the hotel registration desk and kissed Christy on both cheeks. Then he grabbed Todd and kissed him on both cheeks, too. If Christy hadn't been so stunned, she would have burst out laughing at the expression on Todd's face.

"I am the manager of Villa Paradiso, Emilio Mondovo. How do you know Marcos?"

Todd explained the connection through Antonio, and Mr. Mondovo patted Todd on the back enthusiastically. "You are welcome here. You will be my personal guests." He turned to the desk clerk and said, "Put our guests in the Galleria Suite."

"We really didn't plan to stay here," Christy said.

"That's right," Todd agreed. "We thought a friend of ours might be here waiting for us."

The manager rattled off something in Italian and swatted the air in front of Todd's face. "You are my guests," he repeated aggressively in English. "You and your friend you are meeting here. You are all my personal guests. *Per favore.* Please. Stay."

Christy had the feeling this man would be offended if they didn't accept his offer. She also realized that the money she would spend at this hotel for one night would gobble up the entire amount she had budgeted for three weeks' worth of youth hostels. She gave Todd a desperate look, hoping he would know what to say next.

"We would be honored to stay in your hotel, sir," Todd said.

Christy felt like slugging him. *What are you thinking, Todd? We can't afford this place!*

"Giovanni here will check you in and call for assistance for your bags. Please call on me if you have any problems at all. You are my guests." The dramatic Mr. Mondovo stepped away from them to greet another guest who had just exited the elevator.

"Your key, sir," the clerk said. It was the same businesslike tone he had used with them a few minutes earlier when he said he had no vacancies.

"Thanks," Todd said, taking the key. "And for Christy?"

The clerk handed Christy a second key. It didn't have a room number on it. "What room am I in?"

"The Galleria Suite, miss."

"I thought you said Todd is in the Galleria."

"He is."

"Well, I need a separate room."

"That's right," Todd said. "I thought you understood that."

The desk clerk looked at them with a cold glare.

"And if you would be so kind," Christy said, leaning closer

and lowering her voice, "could you give me one of your lower-priced rooms? I don't know how expensive the Galleria Suite is, but I'm on a limited budget."

"The Galleria Suite is the nicest room in the hotel."

Todd immediately put his key back on the counter. "Oh, well, then could you please give me one of your lower-priced rooms, as well? I'm on a tight budget, too."

The clerk appeared put out with Todd and Christy. He pushed the same keys back at them and stated with staccato words, "You are Signore Mondovo's personal guests. The room is *gratis*."

Christy and Todd looked at each other, still not understanding.

"Gratis," the clerk repeated. "No charge. Free. You are Signore's personal guests. Anything you wish in the hotel is yours."

Christy was so stunned her mouth dropped open.

"Cool" was all Todd said.

"Your keys," the clerk repeated, pointing to them. He rang a bell on the counter twice, and a young man in a burgundy uniform with gold braid around the arms immediately appeared and picked up Christy's pack. He offered to take Todd's bag, but Todd said he could take it himself.

The clerk then walked away from the desk as if dismissing Todd and Christy.

Todd picked up both keys and said to Christy, "Let's check it out. Then we can find Mr. Mondovo and explain that we need two rooms. I'm sure Katie will be here by the time we figure all this out."

Christy followed the bellhop to the elevator. He pushed a button, and they rode to the top floor. He then ushered them down a long, carpeted hallway to the door at the very end marked *Galleria Suite*.

Todd unlocked the door. Christy followed him in, and

once again, her mouth dropped open as she took in the huge living room area with a brilliant golden chandelier hanging in the center. Straight ahead was a fireplace with an elaborate golden mantel. To the left were large windows covered with elegant gold brocade drapes. To the right were a huge entertainment center and a round dining room table.

The bellhop walked over to the curtains and opened them, displaying a view of the enchanting lights of the town below. A sliding-glass door opened to a balcony trimmed in salmon-pink wrought iron. He went to the door on the far left, opened it, and motioned for Christy to enter.

As she strolled through the door, she saw a huge bedroom with two large beds, a table, a couch, a television, and an adjoining bathroom with a sunken bathtub. She had never seen anything like this!

She returned to the living room area to find that the bellhop had opened another door on the far right side, past the bar. Todd was examining a separate bedroom as extravagant as the one Christy had just seen.

"Here you go," Todd said, pulling some money from his pocket to tip the bellhop. He refused to take Todd's money. "Enjoy," he said with a smile and then left.

For a full minute and a half, Christy and Todd stood in the opulent living room, staring at each other without saying a word.

Todd spoke first. With an overly calm, chin-up gesture, he said, "Cool."

Christy burst out laughing. "Cool? That's all you can say? Cool? Todd, this is unbelievable!" She did a little free-spirited gypsy dance and said, "Look at this place! Two separate rooms and everything! Katie is going to freak out when she gets here. Did you see the bathtub in my room?"

"And just who says that's your room?"

"Oh, you want to race me for it?"

Without answering, Todd took off sprinting across the room.

"No fair!" Christy squealed, dashing after him.

Todd arrived at the sunken tub first and said, "Cool!"

"You can't have it. This is my bathroom and my room. Did you even check out what kind of bathtub you have?"

Todd grinned again and said, "Race you!"

He took off first, but Christy was ready this time, and she almost tied with him.

"I only get a shower," Todd said, catching his breath.

"Look at this thing," Christy said, opening the double doors. The shower offered eight separate shower heads coming out of the tile at different heights.

"It looks like a compact car wash," Todd said. He reached in and turned the knob. They both laughed as the water squirted out in all directions.

"We better go find Katie," Christy said after Todd had turned off the shower and they had returned to the living room. "Do you think she got mixed up and ended up at one of those other 'villa' hotels the cab driver mentioned?"

"Good deduction work, Sherlock. Now tell me how we missed her."

"Did we take the last boat out of Naples?" Christy asked.

"No, we missed the last hydrofoil, but a couple more boats were scheduled for tonight. Or at least one."

Christy didn't feel very confident of Todd's calculations. "What should we do if she doesn't show up?"

"Eat," Todd suggested.

Christy had to laugh. "I should have guessed that would be a priority for you. Then what do we do?"

Todd headed for the door and opened it for Christy. "If Katie doesn't show up, I think we should figure out other arrangements for where we stay. It wouldn't be right for us to be in this suite, just the two of us."

Christy knew Todd was being wise and using good discernment, but she couldn't help feeling a twinge of disappointment. The suite was incredible. Staying there would be a treat. But Christy knew that being alone in such a place could easily awaken dreams that needed to stay asleep in innocent bliss. This would not be the right time to give those dreams a place to unfold.

"You're right," Christy said. "That's what we should do."

They exited the room and headed for the elevator.

"Do you have the room key?" Christy asked.

"Right here," Todd said, patting his pocket. "I hope they have fish at that café. Doesn't fish sound great right now?"

"I take it you didn't get enough while we were camping."

"I can never get enough fresh fish," Todd said as they reached the elevator and pushed the button.

"Or mangoes," Christy added.

Todd gave her a surprised look. "How did you know I like mangoes?"

"I take notes."

"You know," Todd said after they had stepped into the elevator and began going down, "that's what amazes me about you. You know me, Christy. You probably know me better than anyone else. Even better than my mom and dad. You know me, and yet you still want to be around me. That amazes me."

"I feel that way about you, too, Todd. That's what I was trying to say about the lights and Molokai. I keep thinking that the closer you get to me and the more you get to know me, you'll see what I'm really like. When that happens, I'm afraid you won't want to be around me anymore."

"No." Todd shook his head for emphasis. "It's not like that at all. The closer I get to you, the more you amaze me."

"But we're so different."

"Haven't you ever heard of opposites attracting? Besides, I

don't think we're completely different. We're alike in a lot of ways. You're good for me, Christy. And I think I'm good for you."

As the elevator reached the lobby level, Christy did something she had thought of many times before but never had allowed herself to do. She leaned over and kissed Todd tenderly on his stubble-covered cheek.

Just then the elevator door opened, and before them stood Katie. Frazzled, red-in-the-face Katie.

"Oh well!" Katie exclaimed, holding up a hand for dramatic emphasis. "Don't let me interrupt anything between you two. I'll just go back to being lost for a few more hours."

"Katie! What happened?" Christy exclaimed as she and Todd both rushed to hug their friend.

"Don't ask. You won't believe me when I tell you. Have you guys eaten yet? I'm starving."

"We were just on our way to a café we saw earlier," Christy said. "I'm so glad you're here. Are you okay?"

Katie nodded as Todd pulled her pack off her back.

"I'll take this up to our room for you, and then we can go get some food," he said.

Christy led Katie to a couch in the elegant lobby. Katie motioned toward the desk clerk and muttered, "That guy sure isn't going to win any awards for his love for Americanos. Even though I dragged it out of him that you two were registered here, he wasn't real thrilled about letting me join you. Didn't you tell him I was coming?"

"Yes, he knew. Don't worry. It's all fine. Thanks to Marcos and his dad, all three of us are the honored guests of the hotel manager. We get to stay here for free."

"Free?" Katie spouted way too loudly.

Christy nodded, hoping Katie would lower her voice.

"Awesome! What a God-thing! Good ol' Marcos!"

"I know," Christy said. "Good ol' Marcos."

"Hey, I'm sorry I said all those things this morning about

your flirting with him. By the way, what was going on with you and Todd?"

"What do you mean?"

"I saw you two snuggling and kissing in the elevator. That's a little more, shall I say, 'expressive' than you two usually are. What did I miss?"

Christy nodded, feeling shy about divulging any of the details. "We had a couple of good talks. I had misunderstood a few things."

"Oh, like that has never happened with you before," Katie said. "What was it this time?"

In years past Christy had told Katie almost everything. But Christy didn't want to share all the details from her latest roller-coaster ride over Todd. She wanted her exchange with him to be between just the two of them, especially since part of Christy's inaccurate imaginings had involved Todd's being interested in Katie.

"It was nothing, really. I realized I need to stop trying to have everything in life figured out. I need to trust God more and not always be worried about having a plan."

"Yeah, well, I've certainly changed my opinion about having a plan on this trip," Katie said, stretching out her legs. "Plans are our friends. I'm telling you, I am a reformed traveler, Christy. If we hadn't had a plan to meet up here, I don't know where I'd be right now."

"What happened? How did we miss you at the train station?"

Todd arrived in the lobby just then, so Katie waited until the three of them were seated at the café and had ordered before jumping into her crazy story. She described, with great detail, how she had decided to use the rest room on the train right before they pulled into the Naples station. She had leaned her large backpack outside the door of the bathroom stall, and when the train came to a stop, her backpack fell against the door, locking Katie in the stall.

Christy tried not to laugh too hard. "What did you do?"

"I yelled and pounded until poor Marcos had to come into the women's rest room to let me out."

"We thought you got off the train before we did and that you went straight to the first bus and took off," Christy said.

"Hardly! Marcos and I barely jumped off the train before it pulled out of the station. He took me to the bus stop and waited with me for the next bus. Then a huge car accident happened about a block away. It was awful! You could hear the metal as it crunched. Marcos went down there, and when he came back he said no one was hurt. But it took forever to clear the road so the bus could get through. I think I caught the last boat out of Naples. Marcos wrote down the name of the hotel and gave me his home phone number, too. He was really great about watching out for me."

"I'm glad you got here okay," Christy said.

"Well, I hate to admit it, but you were right, Christy. We did need a plan. I'm glad we did, otherwise I don't know what would have happened. Marcos is going to meet us tomorrow in Rome. He wrote down all the information. Like I told you, I'm a reformed traveler. From now on, we stick together, and we always have a plan."

Christy smiled at her friend, but her smile wasn't prompted just by Katie's admission that Christy was right. She was smiling because Todd had reached his arm around the back of her chair and was fingering the end of her hair. She was thinking of how far their relationship had come in this one, very long day.

She was still thinking about it after Katie had fallen asleep in their luxurious bedroom. Katie had gone crazy over the free, first-class accommodations. She treated herself to a bath and crawled into bed still commenting on every gorgeous detail of their room. Sleep found Katie when she was in mid-sentence and took her away someplace very quiet.

Christy lay in the silence, smiling. She tiptoed over to the window for one last glimpse at the sky on this enchanted evening. Curling up in the chair next to the large picture window, Christy tucked her bare feet under her and wished she had a new diary so she could record all her feelings about being a woman and knowing she was in love with Todd. She leaned back and gazed into the heavens.

What an amazing night, Father! All those stars! It looks like you embroidered a thousand twinkling diamonds to the velvet train of midnight's sweeping cape.

She thought of when she was on the boat and God had felt so close that she could feel His breath. *Sweep over me, God. Breathe on me. I always want to feel as close to you as I do right now. And I always want to trust you completely.*

Christy closed her eyes and fell asleep in the chair. She woke sometime later with a stiff neck and cold feet. Padding back to bed, she slept and dreamed deep, luxurious dreams.

The next morning, Katie woke early. Christy could hear her on the phone trying to order eggs and Italian sausage for breakfast. When Katie noticed that Christy had her eyes open, she said, "Do you want the same thing?"

"Sure. Tell them to bring three orders. I'm sure Todd will want to eat, too."

They rose and dressed, still in awe of their glorious surroundings. Todd was the one who answered the knock on the door when room service arrived. He was dressed, packed, and ready to embrace the new day.

Christy ate the huge breakfast too fast and felt her stomach doing flip-flops as they arrived at the Marina Grande and boarded a motorboat that took them to the entrance of the Blue Grotto. They were instructed to transfer two at a time into small, narrow rowboats that would enter the cavern. A guide wearing a blue-and-white-striped shirt manned each boat. The men also wore straw hats with blue ribbons hanging down the back.

Christy could tell this was all daily tourist business for them. But as she stepped into the boat and settled herself in front of Todd, she felt as if she was about to experience a dream come true. For some reason, the Blue Grotto represented the end of the world to Christy. She thought of it as the ultimate I've-been-someplace-rare-and-exotic-and-now-I-measure-my-life-with-a-different-ruler experience. She didn't know exactly why this remote corner of the world had come to represent so much to her, but she was ready to have her horizons expanded. Leaning back against Todd's chest and ducking as the guide paddled their boat through a small opening in the rock, Christy felt tingles on the back of her neck.

After a moment, her eyes adjusted from the brightness of the morning they had just exited to the muted light of the grotto. The guide paddled them to the center, giving them the dimensions in English, German, and Italian. Christy caught that the cavern was almost one hundred feet high and about fifty feet wide. But she didn't care for any more details after that. All she wanted to see was the water, the clear blue-green water that caught its light from refracted sunshine as it poured itself on the ocean and slipped under the rocky overhang.

Christy squinted at the wonder around her. The light really did seem to rise up from underneath them, from the water itself, illuminating this cave that otherwise would have been deathly dark.

"It's like my life," Christy whispered to Todd.

"Like your eyes? Yeah, that's what I've heard."

"No, like my life. It's like the way God's light shines in the dark places of my life, and He makes it come alive."

Todd wrapped his arms around her and put his lips right

beside her ear. "And that's what I see in your eyes. I see His light shining through you."

Christy's heart soared.

Their guide tilted his chin to the roof of the grotto, and in a rich, reverberating voice he sang, *"O Solo Mio."*

They spent less than five minutes inside the Blue Grotto. By 10:30 the three of them were on the modern hydrofoil jetting their way back to Naples, where they would catch a train at noon so they could meet Marcos in Rome at two.

Katie remarked again about how unmonumental the Blue Grotto was in her opinion. "I still can't believe we came all this way just to duck into some little cave and listen to a fat guy in a straw hat sing to us. We should have stayed in Rome with Marcos."

Christy didn't respond. She was still smiling. And still feeling euphoric over her experience in the Grotta Azzurra. Not even Katie's sarcasm could spoil the event.

In every part of her being, Christy felt as if she had connected with God in a deeper way during the past twenty-four hours. She felt as if she had stepped into womanhood with both feet. God held the "tour book plan" for her future, and she was ready and eager for whatever happened next.

What happened next was Rome.

After an uneventful forty-minute ride on the hydrofoil and a smooth train ride from Naples to Rome in first class, Christy, Todd, and Katie made their way through the gigantic, ornate train station in Rome and caught a taxi to the hotel where Marcos told them to meet him. Even though the front of the hotel was unassuming, Christy suspected it offered five-star lodging like the Villa Paradiso.

"Is it just me," Katie asked as they entered the lobby, "or is anyone else beginning to guess that Marcos's family has a little more money than Antonio's?"

"I hope Marcos and his dad are buddies with the manager

of this hotel, or we're going to spend a whole lot of money tonight," Christy said.

"We don't have to stay here," Todd said. "We can find the youth hostel and stay there."

Christy was thinking about how nice it would be to stay in a fancy hotel again. They could stay on cots in a youth hostel anytime. Before they could discuss their options, Marcos came toward them, looking dashing in a dark business suit with his hair combed straight back.

"Boy, do I feel like a bunch of fish guts the 'baboons' dragged in," Katie said under her breath.

"Ciao!" Marcos greeted them, kissing the girls on the cheek and shaking hands with Todd. "You are here! This is good. I have finished my lunch meeting. Your timing is *perfecto*. I have one small problem, though."

"You're embarrassed to be seen in public with us," Katie quipped.

Marcos looked surprised at her comment. "No, of course not. My problem is that I must return to Venezia tonight. I can only show you around Roma for a few hours."

"That's okay," Katie said. "We'll take what we can get. Where do we go first?"

"Would you like to leave your luggage at the hotel?"

"We haven't checked in anywhere yet," Todd said.

"And I can tell you this place is a little over our budget," Katie added.

"Then at least leave your luggage here with mine," Marcos said, motioning to the bellhop.

Christy knew then that no more soaks in sunken bathtubs were in her near future. Their luggage could stay at the hotel for free, but they couldn't.

Back in a taxi they went. Marcos directed the driver, and they darted about like a drunken hornet through unbelievable traffic. Hundreds of noisy motor scooters zipped in and out around the cars as if they were in a race with death through a gauntlet of motor vehicles. The noise was deafening. Christy closed her eyes. She didn't want to see how they were getting across town. All she cared about was arriving in one piece—preferably still breathing. Marcos pointed out fountains and statues, and Christy only opened her eyes long enough to catch a glimpse of each before squeezing her eyes shut again.

The taxi came to an abrupt stop, and they climbed out while Marcos paid. "Follow me." Marcos briskly led them past several small shops and cafés and up a wide set of stairs. At the top they saw a long line of people wrapped around one of the many gray stone buildings in the area.

"This way," Marcos said. He directed them past the long line of tourists at the building's front and took them around to the side. A guard, dressed in a purple-and-gold-striped uniform that was so colorful it looked like a Mardi Gras costume, stood at the side door. The guard recognized Marcos immediately. The two men greeted each other and spoke in rapid Italian.

"Where do you suppose we are?" Christy asked Katie.

"Like I would have any clue," Katie said. "Does any of this resemble pictures in your tour books?"

The guard motioned for them to come closer. He opened the side door with a key and greeted each of them heartily as they walked past him and into the ancient building.

"Welcome to the *Cappella Sistina*," Marcos said. "Come, I will take you to the room with the most famous painting."

"This is the Sistine Chapel?" Katie asked.

"Yes, Cappella Sistina."

They entered a main hallway, where a thick line of tourists shuffled forward. Most of them wore headsets and held brochures as they glanced at the paintings and statues on the walls. Christy noticed the spectacular tapestries that hung from the floor to the ceiling. She fell behind her friends when she stopped to admire a particularly striking wall hanging.

Katie turned and motioned for Christy to catch up. She hurried, and as soon as she reached Todd, she linked her fingers with his. "I can't believe we just got in here the way we did," she whispered to him. "This is the Sistine Chapel."

"I know. Cool."

Marcos stopped walking and motioned for them to look up. Above them on the ceiling was the famous Michelangelo painting of God's outstretched hand giving Adam the spark of life as their fingers touched. Seeing the actual ceiling of the Sistine Chapel didn't amaze Christy the way she thought it would. As a matter of fact, her neck got sore staring up at it while so many other tired, perspiring tourists bumped into her in the crowded area.

Christy heard a tourist with a British accent say to her companion, who apparently was her husband, "It says here Michelangelo started in 1508, and it took him only four years to paint this ten-thousand-square-foot ceiling. How long do you suppose it will take you to finish painting the kitchen?"

"Look, Christy," Todd said, pointing to another section of the large ceiling. "It's the story of the whole Bible."

Katie pulled out her camera and was about to snap a photo when a guard reached over to block her view with his hand. He spoke to her in French and then repeated his demand in English. "No flash photography."

"Sorry," Katie said, slipping her camera back into her day pack.

"Come," Marcos said. "If you want to take pictures I will take you to the top of the *Basilica di San Pietro*. I will show you the seven hills Roma is built on. Come. It is not far."

Christy had read a lot about this gigantic cathedral in Vatican City. Saint Peter's Basilica was one of the largest churches in the world and could hold one hundred thousand people.

They entered through the massive main entrance. Christy felt overwhelmed by the basilica's size and its ornate decor. Marcos took them first to the famous sculpture, the "Pieta." He told them that Michelangelo was only twenty-two years old when he sculpted this statue of Mary holding Christ after the Crucifixion. That bit of information seemed to stick with Todd.

Marcos walked them past the breathtaking altar and past a huge statue of Peter seated, holding the keys to the kingdom. Peter's left foot was positioned forward from his right foot on the five-foot-high, thick base. Marcos told them to stand back and watch.

Soon a short woman with a dark scarf on her head approached the statue. She rose on her tiptoes and kissed Peter's marble foot. That's when Christy noticed that Peter didn't have any toes on his left foot. She looked at Marcos with a surprised expression, indicating that now she knew why he had them stop to watch.

"For centuries people have kissed his foot," Marcos said. "And now it is rubbed smooth."

Katie wanted to see who else came up to kiss Peter's foot, but Marcos persuaded her to go on to the elevator that would take them part of the way to the top of the basilica's dome.

"He was only twenty-two," Todd mentioned again after they got off the stuffy elevator and climbed the endless winding stairs on their way to the top of the dome. "Can you imagine being able to direct all your talent and passion into something like that when you're our age?"

Christy only said, "Amazing, huh?" in response because she was beginning to feel light-headed. They had to tilt to the side as they climbed the rounded dome. The heat rose along with them. Even though the view of Rome was spectacular from the top, and all of them took as many photos as they wanted, Christy felt as if she couldn't appreciate it fully because all she could think about was finding something to drink.

The refreshment she was hoping for came after they took the subway to the Colosseum. Marcos directed them to a *gelato* cart across the street. Christy soon discovered that gelato was the best ice cream she had ever tasted. It came in cups, filled by a metal spatula instead of a scoop. Her two flavors of choice were strawberry and chocolate, which tasted especially good together.

"We will take a quick tour of the Colosseum, and then I will go to the station," Marcos said.

Todd had been studying a small sign near where they were standing. "Hey, check it out. This was a prison. The Mamertine Prison. It says Paul was held prisoner here."

The prison was almost level with the sidewalk and appeared to be a maze of subterranean prison cells.

"Do you suppose Paul wrote his prison letters from this cell?" Todd asked.

Marcos shrugged. "It is possible."

Christy noticed that Todd's eyes had lit up with wonder over what appeared to her to be an insignificant discovery. He looked at her and said, "Can you imagine? Paul could have written his letters to the Philippians while looking out this very window."

Todd and Christy had a special verse from that book of the Bible. He had written Philippians 1:7 on a coconut years ago and mailed it to her from Hawaii. She still had the coconut in a box at home. The verse simply said, "I hold you in my heart."

Christy stood next to Todd and stared at the gray rock structure with the narrow slit for a window. "Do you think Paul was actually sitting in there when he wrote, 'I hold you in my heart'?" Christy asked.

"Possibly," Todd said.

Christy felt the hair stand up on her arms. She shivered at the thought of Paul's writing such beautiful words while in such a dismal place. "That astounds me," she told Todd. "I mean, it isn't as if I had pictured Paul writing all those letters in a hammock while sipping pineapple juice, but here? Right here?"

Todd held her gaze, equally amazed. "I know. It gives new meaning to Paul's New Testament letters, doesn't it? Paul knew what it meant to suffer for what he believed."

Christy couldn't shake the feeling that came over her as she looked into the dilapidated cell window with Todd. The taste of sweet strawberry and chocolate gelato lingered in her mouth, making a sharp contrast to the realization that many who walked these same streets centuries before had been persecuted for their Christian faith. Many had even been martyred.

They moved on to the Colosseum, which was massive, overwhelming, and fascinating. Yet Christy felt as if she couldn't take in any more sights or information. She stared down into the remains of the underground compartments beneath the Colosseum, taking pictures and listening to Marcos describe how the first-century Romans had kept the lions in those cells. She could see the ramps used to bring up the lions to face the gladiators.

"Weren't the lions set loose on the Christians, as well?" Todd asked. "I know I've heard about Christians being fed to the lions while Emperor Nero watched. Was that here?"

"It is possible," Marcos said. "They burned Christians alive on poles to light the garden parties for Nero."

"You're kidding!" Katie exclaimed. "That's awful! I can't believe civilized people would torture and kill other humans over their faith in God. It's barbaric."

"It still happens today," Todd said. He leaned against one of the stone pillars.

"Where?" Katie asked.

"All over the world. We just don't hear much about it. People are martyred all the time for putting their trust in Christ. There may come a point when we'll be challenged to take a stand. If that day comes, I want to know that my relationship with Christ is so solid I'd be willing to die for Him," Todd said.

Christy felt like sitting down. This was all too much for her. She had never seriously considered the possibility that one day she might have to make such a choice. Her eyes swept across the Colosseum's vast ruins.

What she saw with her mind's eye wasn't the Hollywood glamour of a Ben Hur–style chariot race. As deeply as the light of the Blue Grotto had pierced her soul that morning, an image came alive inside her mind under the pounding afternoon sun. She saw the rows and rows of Colosseum seats that now circled her filled with a wild, cheering crowd. Starving lions were about to be let loose. All she had to do was denounce Christ, and she could go free. If she remained steadfast in her commitment to the Lord, the lions would maul her.

Oh, Father God, with all my heart I hope I would be true to you in such a situation!

CHRISTY AND TODD · THE COLLEGE YEARS

11 In the cab on their way back to the hotel, Todd and Marcos discussed what they believed about Christianity. Christy had her eyes closed again to avoid seeing all the near-accidents their driver barely skirted around. She also was glad to avoid the heavy discussion. Her head and heart felt overwhelmed with all that she had seen that day.

"But that's not enough." Christy listened to Katie as she jumped into the discussion with Marcos. "You can't just be a good person and try to live a good life and think God will let you into heaven. Have you ever heard that verse in Romans 10:9? That if you confess with your mouth Jesus is Lord, and believe in your heart that God raised him from the dead, you will be saved."

"Romans?" Marcos questioned.

"Oh yeah, Romans! Hey, cool!" Katie said. "I didn't realize it until this minute. The book of Romans was written to the people that lived in this very city! That is so amazing!"

"This is in the Holy Bible?" Marcos asked.

"Yeah," Katie said. "There's a whole book written just for the Italians."

Christy smiled. The coincidence of Katie's choosing to

quote Romans while they were in Rome was definitely a God-thing.

"No one can get to heaven on their own efforts," Katie continued. "It says that in the book of Romans, too. 'All have sinned and fall short of the glory of God.' And what's that other verse in Romans about the gift of God?"

"Romans 6:23," Todd said. " 'For the wages of sin is death, but the gift of God is eternal life in Christ Jesus our Lord.' "

"See?" Katie said. "We can't earn eternal life. It's a free gift from God. But we have to accept it. We can't earn it."

Christy wondered if Marcos thought Katie was coming on too strong. But Christy also understood how impossible it was to have been confronted with everything they had seen in the last few hours and not be passionate about one's faith.

"Doesn't God love everyone?" Marcos asked.

"Yes," Todd answered.

"Then good people have nothing to worry about. God will let them into His heaven," Marcos concluded.

"It doesn't work that way," Todd said. "You know what it's like? It's like when we went to the Villa Paradiso. On our own, they would never have let us in just because we were good people. But when we mentioned your name and your father's name, we were welcomed with open arms. All the riches of the hotel were ours for free."

Christy opened her eyes, stunned at the perfect example Todd had just given. Surely that made sense to Marcos.

Marcos was sitting in the cab's front seat and had turned around to talk with Todd. "It helps to know the right people in high places," Marcos said with a grin.

"Exactly. It's the same way with eternity," Todd responded. "It's not what we do, it's who we know. We knew you and that opened the door to the Villa Paradiso. Knowing Christ opens the door to the eternal paradise."

"Antonio has tried to convince me of this, as well," Marcos

said. "He told me I must have a relationship with Christ. It is different from how I was taught all my life. I must tell you, though, I see something more in Antonio's life since he has come back from California."

"That 'something' is really 'Someone,' " Katie said.

Just then the taxi stopped in front of the hotel, and the four of them got out. This time Todd insisted on paying for their ride. "It's a free gift from me," Todd said, giving Marcos a friendly, chin-up gesture. "Just accept it, man."

Christy knew Todd's words had a double meaning and wondered if Marcos caught it, as well. They went into the fancy hotel, retrieved their luggage, and walked back out to the street to say their good-byes.

Christy felt sad as she received Marcos's parting kiss on her cheek. With Antonio she could say good-bye more easily, knowing she would see him again in heaven, if not before. With Marcos, this might be the last time she ever saw him, in this life or in eternity.

Christy looked into his handsome face. She remembered how Katie had persuaded Marcos to go to Naples with them, and with a charming grin equal to Katie's, she said, "Marcos, I want you to come to heaven with us. It won't be the same without you. Please surrender your life to Christ."

He looked surprised at her oddly worded farewell. "You have me thinking. Antonio gave me a Holy Bible. Maybe I will read this part for the Italians."

Christy stood on her tiptoes and kissed him lightly on the cheek. "*Buona,*" she said because she was pretty sure that meant "good" in Italian.

Marcos smiled. He stepped into a cab and waved as it lurched into the traffic, heading for the train station.

"And now are you going to tell me that was supposed to be a 'holy kiss,' Miss 'Christiana'?" Katie teased.

"Yes, it was." Christy thought for only a moment how different it was to kiss Marcos's smooth-shaven cheek compared to Todd's prickly face. But the comparison went nowhere else in her imagination. In every way, to Christy the kiss was pure and holy.

Then, because she couldn't resist, she said, "When in Rome, do as the Romans do."

Todd laughed. Katie only shook her head. "Can I just say that I've noticed you've certainly become the little kissing bug since you've moved to Europe?"

"You don't see me complaining," Todd said with a grin still on his face.

"Okay, let's drop the kissing talk," Katie said. "I'm getting depressed being around you two happy hearts. Let's find a place to dump this luggage."

"Where's your tour book, Christy?" Todd asked. "Does it list places to stay?"

Christy reached inside her day pack and said, "Shouldn't we at least go down the block a little? I feel kind of tacky standing in front of a hotel looking for a cheap place to stay."

"Nobody knows that's what we're doing," Katie said. "I feel safer standing here than in the middle of the street with our backpacks announcing to the whole world that we're tourists."

"Here," Christy said, handing the book to Todd. "You look it up. My brain is fried."

Todd suggested a *pensione* he saw listed in the book. He said it was a house that rented out rooms, like an American bed-and-breakfast. The best feature was the low price and the closeness to where they stood at the moment.

Walking six blocks in the early-evening heat, they found the pensione, only to be told no rooms were available. Undaunted, Todd consulted the tour book again as they stood against the side of a shop that sold leather jackets. The shop was closed, its windows barred shut.

"A youth hostel is listed here, but if I'm reading the map correctly, it's on the other side of town. We could take a cab."

Christy felt her teeth clenching at the thought of trusting her life to another Italian cab driver. "Isn't there anything else?" She took the book from Todd when he offered it and scanned the lodgings page. "I had another little book I should have brought because it was only about Italy, and it listed dozens of places to stay in each of the big cities." She tried hard not to place her frustration on Katie, who had said they didn't need tour books because they were on an "adventure."

"We could jump on a train and go to that 'frantic' city," Katie suggested.

Christy gave her a pained expression. "Do you mean Firenze? Florence?"

"Yeah. The frenzy place. I mean, tell me, what is there left to see here?"

"Lots," Christy said.

"Like what?"

Christy took off her backpack with exaggerated motions, as if she knew this would be a long discussion. "There is a lot of art, fountains, statues, and churches."

"That's what Marcos showed us all day. What's to see in Florence?"

"Fountains, statues, and churches," Todd said.

"Fountains and statues and churches, oh my!" Katie quipped, smiling at her joke as she took off her pack. "I don't think we're in Kansas anymore, Toto!"

Christy didn't laugh. She wanted to tell them again that this was why they needed to have a plan. How could they make decisions like this when they were all tired and hungry?

"Let's find a place to eat," Todd suggested. "We need to sit down and discuss all our options."

Fortunately, a pizzeria was only half a block away. The

food was fast and delicious. The only drawback was they had to stand and eat at small, round tables with high legs. They were discovering it was popular in Italy to grab a quick plate of pasta or a slice of pizza and eat it standing up around tables that came up to Christy's elbows. The food helped, but the standing didn't make for a relaxed discussion.

"I think we should go on to Florence," Katie said. "Or Venice, or what about that leaning tower? Where did you say that was?"

"Pisa."

"Oh yeah. The Leaning Tower of Pisa. How could I forget? Where's Pisa?"

"North," Christy said flatly.

"North near Venice?"

"No, north but the opposite direction. It's actually closer to where we went camping."

"We should have gone to see it then."

Christy couldn't control her tongue another minute. With spicy breath from the pizza sauce, she said, "That's why I said we should have a plan. If we just jump on a train and take off for Venice or Florence, we might miss something we really wanted to see."

"So what do you really want to see?" Katie asked.

Christy couldn't come up with a specific answer. She wanted to see everything.

"I'd like to see Pompeii," Todd said.

"Marcos was telling me about that place," Katie said. "How the whole city has been excavated, and you can walk around and see what happened after the volcano erupted and destroyed it. He said the volcanic ash actually preserved some of the people who were running to get away."

Christy had read about Pompeii in her other Italian tour book. It didn't sound appealing to her then, and it sounded even more depressing now. She didn't find herself fascinated with the same things that intrigued Todd and Katie.

"I'd like to go there, too," Katie said. "I know it's south, not far from Naples, because Marcos showed me Mount Vesuvius while we were waiting for a bus."

Christy remembered seeing Mount Vesuvius from the boat deck on their way to Capri. "That means we go back to where we were this morning. That would take two hours or more to get there, and then what? Find a place to stay in Naples or Pompeii?"

"I wouldn't want to stay in Naples," Katie said. "Marcos told me some stuff about that city. It's not the safest place for tourists."

"So we would stay in Pompeii?" Christy flipped through the tour book. It listed a whole page of interesting facts about Pompeii and how to get there, but it didn't list any lodgings.

"We could stay here and take a morning train," Todd suggested.

"But where? The youth hostel?"

They stood in the pizzeria for almost an hour, discussing all the possibilities. Their final decision was a surprise to Christy, and she couldn't figure out quite how they ended up agreeing on it. They would go to Oslo, Norway.

Instead of staying in Rome, they decided to catch a night train north. The logic that emerged from their lengthy discussion was that they would shoot straight up to Norway and spend the rest of their trip working their way down until they ended up back in Basel, Switzerland, by 8:00 Monday morning, June 27. That's when Christy's summer classes began. Todd and Katie's flight back to California left that afternoon from Zürich.

The part of their plan Christy liked the most was that the long train ride would give them plenty of time to talk and plan so that the remaining sixteen days of their journey would be thought out. She hated to admit it, but she was exhausted. Her stamina hadn't exactly been at a high point when they had started this trip, and their fast pace had worn her out. With a bittersweet twist, Christy wished they were still camping so she could curl up in the hammock or bathe in the stream and feel her senses come alive again. If they had stuck with Antonio's plan, this would have been their last night camping.

As they strapped on their packs and walked the sixteen blocks to the train station, Christy decided she was glad they hadn't stayed at the campground after all. She wouldn't have wanted to miss Capri or Rome for anything.

They stopped at a small shop that carried mostly magazines and cigarettes just inside the train station. Katie wanted to buy some candy bars, and Christy was curious to see if they sold any tour books in English.

She didn't find a tour book, but she did find a blank journal with a brown leather cover. Years ago her uncle Bob had given her a diary, and he had told her to write out all her thoughts and feelings on the diary's pages, trusting that it would become a good friend. His words had come true.

The night before Christy left for this adventure with Todd and Katie, she had written on the final page of her diary and had felt a strong sense of loss. For the first time in almost five years she didn't have a special place to record her heart's secrets. That diary had become a close friend.

She paid for the leather-bound journal, having no idea if the price was fair. *It sure would be helpful to have Tonio or Marcos around now.*

Christy studied the change the salesperson had placed in her hand. So many coins. To her surprise, the salesperson muttered something in Italian and placed three more coins in her hand.

Does he think I just figured out he shortchanged me? How funny!

I don't have a clue how much I paid or how much I now hold in my hand.

She continued to hold the coins in her hand without turning away. For fun, Christy glanced up at the man and gave him an expression that said, "Shame on you for trying to cheat me."

This time he didn't mutter anything in Italian. He simply leaned over and handed her three more coins and two paper bills.

Still uncertain as to just how badly she had been treated, Christy decided to get while the going was good. She stuffed the money in her pocket and exited the small shop while trying to keep from bursting out laughing. Todd and Katie were waiting for her out front, and after Christy recounted the story to them, Katie said, "Hey, I think I'll go back in there, hold out my hand, and give him the evil eye. He probably overcharged me for these two candy bars."

"I don't know if it would work after you've already left the store," Todd pointed out.

"Let's go to that shop over there," Katie suggested, indicating another small store inside the train station. "It looks as if they sell food. I think we should pack ourselves a picnic."

"I'm all for that," Todd said. He was the first one in the shop.

As Christy watched, he selected several hard, round rolls; some small, oval-shaped tomatoes; and a triangle of white cheese. Christy was more interested in buying something to drink for the train. She found liter-sized bottles of water and bought three of them.

Katie purchased two more candy bars and stood at the register, examining with a critical eye the change she had been handed. The woman behind the counter appeared irritated at Katie and rattled off something in Italian, motioning for Katie to move so the next customer could pay.

"Guess I'll never know if she ripped me off or not," Katie said as they entered the main terminal. "You just have the right look, Christy."

"Okay, now we're getting organized." Todd walked over to the computerized schedule board and read the departure times. "This is the one we want. Roma to Venezia departing at 20:35 at platform . . ." He glanced at his watch. "Come on! We're going to have to run to catch it!"

Todd took off at a sprint, and Christy fell in line behind him. She glanced over her shoulder to make sure Katie was with them. As they jogged through the crowds, Christy felt her pack dig into her shoulders and hit her repeatedly on her hip. The spicy pizza in her stomach threatened to come up for another visit.

Despite all the discomfort, they made it to the train. And, thanks to Todd's quick thinking, they arrived in time to upgrade to first class at the ticket window. First class was packed. It seemed everyone was leaving Rome on this Friday night. Christy figured second class was even worse. They found two seats at the end of an aisle, which Katie and Christy took while Todd stood, studying the tour book.

The train rumbled out of the station, and Christy closed her eyes and tried to find a comfortable position. They were definitely on an adventure now, and they were also coming up with a plan. It seemed to her that both wishes were being fulfilled. She hoped that meant the next two weeks would be less stressful.

During the five-hour trip to Venice, Christy slept some, walked around some, and visited the rest room with Katie so Katie could demonstrate exactly how she managed to lock herself into the stall in Naples. Christy laughed at her crazy friend and thought how glad she was that they were getting along this well. Much of the earlier tension they both seemed to have struggled with had dissipated. Now Christy felt that the wide gap that had spread between them while she was in Switzerland was closing, and they were getting back to being the close buddies they had been for so many years.

About an hour before they arrived in Venice, Todd and Christy left Katie so they could sit across from each other in the dining car, sipping cappuccino and discussing plans. Todd had done some serious reading during the past few hours, and he now was a huge fan of Christy's travel guide. His eyes glimmered as he told Christy about the sights that lay before them in Scandinavia.

"And this Fredericksborg Castle in Denmark sounds pretty interesting," he said. "I know you like castles. It's only about half an hour from Copenhagen, so when we go through there, I thought that might be a place you would like to stop."

Christy smiled at Todd. "You remembered that I like castles."

"Hey, you remembered that I like mangoes. Maybe we've both been taking notes on each other for a long time without realizing it."

"I'd love to see at least one castle on this trip. More, if we can fit them into the schedule. What about you? What do you want to see? I doubt many mango trees will be along the way."

"There's this museum in Oslo." Todd pointed to a short paragraph in the tour book. "It says they have the original *Kon-Tiki* on display there."

Christy waited for an explanation. "*Kon-Tiki*" sounded Polynesian, which would explain why Todd, who had lived in Hawaii when he was young, would be interested. She just didn't know why a museum in Norway would have something Polynesian.

"It's Thor Heyerdahl's raft. He sailed it from Peru to the Easter Islands to prove that early civilization from South

America could have found its way to the islands of the Pacific."

"Oh," Christy said. "And Thor was Norwegian, I take it."

Todd nodded. "I think Katie is going to want to see this." He pointed to the words *Lille Havfrue* in the tour book.

"What's that?"

"It's a statue of the *Little Mermaid* from the Hans Christian Andersen fairy tale."

"We'll definitely have to see that," Christy agreed. "This is going to be fun."

"It's already been fun." Todd reached across the table and gave a playful little tug on a strand of Christy's hair that hung over her shoulder. "It'll only get better."

With a smile at Todd that reflected all the delightful anticipation she held in her heart, Christy said, "I can't wait until tomorrow."

At 2:00 in the morning, their train pulled into the Venice station. They grabbed their packs and headed through the ornate terminal, trying to find their connecting train north to Salzburg, Austria.

In the middle of the platform, Katie stopped and said, "You guys, we have to talk."

"We can talk on the next train," Christy said. "We have to make that connection to Salzburg."

"No, we need to talk now. I have to be honest with both of you about something."

Christy thought Katie was going to say she had felt left out during the past hour when Todd and Christy had gone to the dining car to sip their cappuccinos. Christy already was preparing her apology for excluding Katie and planning their transition to the next train, which left for Salzburg in forty minutes. If they were among the first on the train, Christy hoped they would be able to find better seats than they had had to settle for on the ride from Rome.

"I want to stay here," Katie said.

"Stay where?" Christy asked, looking around the platform.

"In Venice. The one thing I wanted to see was a gondola.

Marcos lives here. He told me a lot about Venice. Remember? His dad has the jewelry store. I'd like to stay here for a day or two and then go on to Norway."

"Okay," Todd said. "We can do that."

Christy felt reluctant to agree. She wanted to see a gondola, too, but for the past hour, Todd had been telling her about Scandinavia, and now she had visions of castles and mermaids floating in her head.

"I know I should have said something sooner," Katie said. "I kept going back and forth in my mind, trying to decide if I was being a team player by bringing this up. I guess it just hit me when we stepped into the station. This might be the closest I'll ever be to a real gondola. I want to see one. I don't have to ride in one; I just want to see one."

"We'll need to find a place to stay," Todd said, turning and heading for the exit instead of for the track to board the train for Salzburg. "Let's ask at information. It's the middle of the night, so we'll have to take what we can get. Are you guys okay with that? It might be pretty expensive."

"I think it would be worth it for one night," Katie said. "Besides, we haven't had to pay for a single hotel yet. We have money to burn."

"I wouldn't go that far," Christy said.

"Or you know what?" Katie said. "We could call Marcos and see if we could stay with him for free."

"Doesn't that seem a little pushy?" Christy asked. "It's like we're following him. He left Rome on the 6:00 train, and we followed him here on the 8:30 train. That feels odd to me."

"Okay, we don't have to call him," Katie said. "We can find a place for tonight and then stop by his dad's jewelry store tomorrow. I'd like to see Marcos again."

Christy tried to evaluate what was going on. Was Katie's real passion for the elusive gondolas? Or was she attracted to Marcos the way she had been attracted to Antonio last summer? Their train ride to Venice was the first time only the three of them had been traveling, except when they went from Capri to Rome. Christy wondered if Katie had felt the loss of a counterpart when Todd and Christy went to the dining car. Maybe Katie didn't like the idea of being number three when Christy and Todd were a couple, and she was trying to delay the odd numbering by touring around with Marcos a few more days.

Todd took the adjustment to their plans in his easygoing stride. He suggested Katie and Christy wait with the luggage on a long, polished wooden bench in the center of the station while he did some research.

Christy tried to think of a delicate way to ask Katie about Marcos and if she was feeling brushed aside by Christy and Todd. But her mind grew foggier and foggier as she sat with the noises echoing off the high ceiling and reverberating inside her head. The cappuccino's caffeine seemed to wear off in a single, crashing moment, and Christy could barely keep her eyes open, let alone discuss Katie's psyche with her.

Christy was glad to see Todd returning. Once they were settled in a hotel, had slept a bit, and then ate a good breakfast, Christy thought she would feel a lot more optimistic about their sudden change of plans.

"I found a place we can stay," Todd said. "And it was no small task since it's the middle of the night. But they only accept cash. How much do both of you have?"

Katie, Christy, and Todd pooled their money and found that between the three of them they didn't have half the cash needed since the hotel was pretty expensive.

"Why won't they take traveler's checks?" Christy asked.

"Don't know. It's their hotel. They answered the phone. They get to set the rules, I guess."

"Isn't there a place here in the station where we can change our money?" Katie asked.

"I already tried that. They don't open until 6:00 in the morning. If we had a credit card or an ATM card, we could use the machine. Guess none of us thought of that ahead of time."

"So what you're saying is that we have to wait here until 6:00, change some money, get ourselves into Venice by water taxi or whatever, and by around 7:00 we can check into the hotel," Christy summarized.

"You got it," Todd said. "And check-out time is noon."

"I don't want to pay all that just for a place to sleep for five hours," Katie said.

"We could sleep on these benches," Christy suggested.

"Or take a train to Salzburg," Katie said in a low voice. "I'm so sorry, you guys. I messed everything up."

"No, you didn't."

"Yes, I did. We had a plan, and now we've missed the train, and we didn't make arrangements ahead of time for here so we can't do anything. We're stuck."

"I checked a couple of the train schedules," Todd said. "A train leaves at 8:02 for Salzburg. It has only one stop in Villach at noon and has a three-hour layover before it leaves for Salzburg. We would be in Salzburg by 7:00 tomorrow night."

"That's all day on the train," Katie said. "Wasn't the night train we were going to take direct, without any stops?"

Todd nodded. "Yes, but we can't look back. We're here now. What do you guys want to do?"

"What time is it?" Christy wished she had a watch. Her old one had broken months ago, but she never had replaced it.

"It's 3:10."

"No wonder I feel as if I've been run over by a truck," Katie said. "I say let's get out of here."

"And go where?" Christy asked. "Roam the streets of Venice?"

"They don't have streets. They have canals, remember?" Katie said. "No, let's just get on the next train and take it wherever it goes."

"What about seeing a gondola?" Christy asked.

"Right now, I don't care. I made a bad decision when I insisted we stop and get off track after we had set up a schedule and everything. Let's go back to the schedule as much as we can. Only, can't we get to *Sound of Music* land without it taking all day?"

Todd consulted a small pamphlet of train schedules as Katie talked. "Because I'd kind of like to stop and see some of Salzburg. It's the only Austrian city I know anything about."

Christy added, "That's because you've seen *The Sound of Music* a hundred times." She thought of lyrics from one of that movie's songs, "How do you solve a problem like Maria?" and felt ready to sing her own version, "How do you solve a problem like Katie?"

"Looks like a 10:30 train out of Innsbruck gets into Salzburg at 2:30," Todd said. "We could find a place to stay and then look around Salzburg that afternoon."

"Does that mean we sleep here for the next two hours?" Christy asked.

Todd examined the four long benches placed back to back. "You know, I always wondered what a homeless person felt like. Now I'll get to find out."

Christy had never wondered such a thing. *Only you, Todd.*

Todd and Katie had no trouble catching some Z's on the hard benches. Christy, on the other hand, couldn't fall asleep. She felt nervous about people walking by, seeing them asleep, and taking their gear, even though they had fastened their packs all together and anchored them to the benches. The train station wasn't full of people, but enough travelers were coming and going to make Christy nervous.

The more she thought about it, the more frustrated she

became with Katie for the way she had thrown their plan off course. Christy tried to be understanding and forgiving. She reminded herself how everyone had been kind to her when she had melted down in the minivan on the camping trip. They all had agreed to alter their plans to accommodate her. She knew she wasn't being fair to begrudge Katie the same courtesy everyone had shown Christy.

Since she didn't want to get any more upset with Katie, Christy turned her thoughts toward Todd. Her scruffy-faced sweetheart lay curled up on the wooden bench across from hers, with the hood of his navy sweat shirt pulled over his head. Christy was amazed that he could clock out whenever he wanted to, although she knew she shouldn't be surprised. Over the years, Todd had managed to clock out emotionally at times when she was wide awake, so to speak, in her feelings for him. Or at least that's how it had seemed to her.

So what have we decided, Todd? We're not going to have any more should-we-break-up conversations, but where does that put us? Where we've always been? Friends? Close friends? Friends-forever kind of friends for another five years until your internal alarm clock goes off and you wake up to me? I'm here. I'm wide awake. I know I'm in love with you, and I always will be. I'm ready for more. Are you?

Christy closed her eyes and turned over on her side. She tried with all her might to force herself to go to sleep, physically and emotionally. Her efforts didn't meet with success. Instead, her thoughts wandered off to her family. She knew her parents had grown used to her calling home only about once a month and writing a quick note every few weeks. As a matter of fact, she had talked to her mom for about twenty minutes the day before Todd and Katie had arrived, and her mom had told Christy again how she hoped Christy would have a great time on this trip. Maybe Christy should call her parents now. What time was it at home? Her mind was too tired to do the calculations.

And what exactly would she tell them? "Hi. We're sleeping on benches in the Venice train station, and we haven't exactly been eating balanced meals or managing to stay together all the time, but don't worry about anything. The trip is going great so far. The three of us are getting along just peachy."

Christy knew she couldn't call them. Not now. Not when she didn't have a positive report. It wouldn't help to let them know details at this point, she decided. It would be better to call them at the end of the trip, after she was back in her dorm room and life was normal again.

Things will get better in Austria. They have to. Then I can send a postcard home, and nothing in my news will be false or strained.

The train ride to Innsbruck and then on to Salzburg turned out to be comfortable. Their compartment had pull-out beds called *couchettes,* and Christy stretched out and slept deeply for the first four hours. When she woke, Todd said he had breakfast for her. It turned out to be one of his oval tomatoes, some cheese, and a hard roll. Christy ate it gratefully and shared her water with Todd and Katie.

They barely made it to the train that took them to Salzburg. But, once settled in, they found their window seats provided a fantastic view of some of the most spectacular scenery Christy had seen since she had been in Europe. It was much better than the view out of Tonio's van. This was the kind of experience she had hoped to have with Todd, and she scooted closer to him as they gazed out the window so they could comment on the dramatic mountain ranges that seemed to go on forever.

Katie was noticeably quiet by the time they arrived in Salzburg. They found a *Gasthof* that was recommended in the tour book and checked into two rooms. The friendly owner of the Austrian-style bed-and-breakfast told them that *Jause* would be served between 4:00 and 5:00. She explained that was a traditional coffee time. However, they were too hungry to wait and politely excused themselves to go find a full meal.

They left their heavy luggage, exchanged their money, and went off to see the sights. Christy wished they had taken time to shower and change before hitting the streets. She promised herself that a shower would feel even better that night when they returned.

Deciding on a restaurant they could all agree on turned out to be easy. Two blocks from the Gasthof they came to a large, open-air restaurant. It offered plenty of outside tables under umbrellas, allowing them to sit below an austere fortress on the top of a hill and watch the horse-drawn carriages promenade by on the cobblestone streets.

After they had eaten *Schnitzel* and discussed what to do next, Katie said, "We need to find the fountain where all the Von Trapp children danced and sang. I think it had statues of horses in it."

Todd consulted the tour book while Christy savored her cherry strudel dessert. She didn't feel the need to run and see and go and do. Salzburg seemed willing to strut by and show Christy plenty of her charms. A young couple strolled past the outdoor café walking a small, fluffy dog. The woman laughed a light, airy titter at something the man said, and Christy saw him wink at her.

Someday. Someday you and I will stroll side by side, Todd. And someday you'll wink at me like that.

Christy turned her attention to two women at a table next to them. As the women carried on an afternoon chat, she thought about how different the Austrian people were from the Italians. Here the local language around her flowed like a broad river with earthy, rolling sounds. In Italy she had felt as if the entire population was eager to get its point across with whatever amount of drama required. At one point, when they were at the top of Saint Peter's Basilica in already close quarters, Christy remembered thinking that about Marcos's style of communicating. She felt as if he were trying to lick her nose at the top of his voice.

"Hey, this sounds like something Christy would want to see," Todd said, reading an entry from the tour book. "It's a castle called *Schloss Hellbrunn*. We should go there first, in case they close in the evening."

Christy felt warmed inside knowing that Todd had been taking notes again and that he remembered her saying she wanted to go to as many castles as they could find. She let Todd figure out how to get to the Schloss Hellbrunn, and once there, she continued to feel charmed by Salzburg's unique beauty as they toured the castle. The guide told them to pay attention to the outside dining table. It looked as if it was made of cement with individual cement seats. Suddenly jets of water shot straight up from the seats and from the middle of the table, spraying the tour group with a light mist.

After the laughter subsided, their guide said, "Yes, Marcus Sitticus, the host of Schloss Hellbrunn, had a grand sense of humor. He enjoyed surprising his guests this way at summer picnics. To appreciate such innovation, remember, this was all built in the early 1600s."

The tour guide directed them to the garden exit. On both sides a line of spraying water shot into the air and formed an arch for the visitors to run beneath. Todd and Christy went first, holding hands and moving quickly under the refreshing mist. Katie was right behind them, but when she jogged through, the direction of the water changed, and she was doused with a jet of wet stuff that came at her from all sides.

Dripping and laughing, Katie said, "Now I know why the ladies from that era wore those long dresses. It was protection from crazy dinner hosts like this guy. I wonder if his guests ever came back a second time?"

When Christy snuggled under her down comforter at the Gasthof late that night, she thought about how she wanted to come back to Salzburg a second time, if ever the invitation was given.

She wrote that in her new diary the next day on their train ride through Germany. Part of her entry read,

The charm of that happy city will never leave me. When we walked past Mozart's birthplace this morning, I thought of how his music still resonates here in a timeless, majestic way. The tour book said that people lived in Salzburg five hundred years before Christ was born, because of the salt deposits found here. That astounds me. All Katie seemed to be impressed with was the number of fountains we found as we walked around yesterday evening. At every fountain that had a horse statue in it, she made us stop and listen to her sing, "Doe, a deer, a female deer, ray . . ." etc. Poor Katie tried so hard to get Todd and me to stand on the edge of the fountains and sing with her, but we let her do a solo every time.

Their train rolled to a stop at the Munich station in Germany a fast two hours after they left Salzburg. Christy threw her diary into her pack and followed Todd and Katie off the train. It took them a while to figure out which train they wanted to take next. With the help of an attendant at the ticket window, they made reservations on one of the newer direct trains. The attendant told them the train would shoot them to Hamburg in the northern part of Germany at 165 miles per hour. They had to pay an extra amount, but they had become used to that in Italy.

Instead of compartments, the train to Hamburg had comfortable seats similar to first class in an airplane. Each seat came equipped with earphones and a dial so all the passengers could select their own favorite music.

"This is a big change from the Italian trains," Katie said.

"How long are we going to be on this one?"

"I think she said it was six hours to Hamburg." Todd settled into his seat next to Christy and said, "Not bad, huh?"

"We'll have to stop in Hamburg to buy hamburgers," Katie said. Her seat was directly across from Todd's and Christy's. They all stacked their day packs in the empty seat next to Katie.

"Do you suppose Hamburg is where hamburgers were invented?" Christy asked.

"Your handy tour book might help us." Todd unzipped his pack and pulled out the book.

"Didn't some cook invent hamburgers for an earl of something?" Christy said.

"You're thinking of sandwiches," Todd said. "I've heard that before, too. The Earl of Sandwich. His chef invented sandwiches for him. I don't think any Earls of Hamburg existed. Although it says here that Hamburg dates back to the medieval times. But the city was almost destroyed in World War II. That's awful."

"Can I just say," Katie said, leaning forward, "that you have your face in that tour book just a little too much to make me believe we're really on an adventure, Todd."

"It's a great book," he said, looking up. "But it doesn't say anything about hamburgers in Hamburg."

"It might have said something about Hamburg in one of the other books I left back at my dorm," Christy said.

"You had more books?" Todd asked.

"Seven. One of them was just about Italy and another one was about Scandinavia."

"You should have brought them. I'm really getting into finding out some of the history of these places," Todd said.

Christy glanced at Katie and gave her friend a sassy little see-I-told-you-so expression.

"I didn't stop you from bringing your books," Katie flared

at Christy. "All I said was that they would take up a lot of space, and they would. Don't blame me, Christy. You could have brought them if you really wanted to."

Christy hadn't expected such a reaction. "Katie, it's not that big a deal. I think the book I brought is the best one. It's helped us out a lot."

Katie turned away, fiddled with her earphones, and then curled up in her chair with a sweat shirt over the front of her like a blanket. The air conditioning was blowing right on them, and Christy felt chilled, too. She slipped her arm through Todd's and cuddled up close to him to get warm.

"What are you reading about now?"

Before Todd could answer, Katie stood and, pulling off her earphones, said, "Six hours is a long time. I'm going to walk around and see if I can meet some people."

Christy felt the words "Just don't lock yourself in the bathroom this time" burning on the tip of her tongue. But she made herself keep quiet.

Then, as if Katie could smell the smoke from Christy's burning words, she said, "Don't worry. I'll be back before we reach Hamburg."

With that, she brushed past Todd and Christy and took off down the long aisle.

As soon as Katie walked away from Todd and Christy, Christy
thought, *Good. Now Todd and I can snuggle and
talk quietly, just the two of us.* But then another
thought marched into her mind. *Katie looked
really upset. I better go after her and find out what's
wrong.*

"Do you think she's okay?" Todd asked.

Christy continued to struggle. She wanted to hold tighter
to Todd's arm and brush off Katie's mood as normal Katie behavior. With a sigh, Christy said, "I don't know. She's upset
about something."

"I'll go check on her," Todd said.

"No, that's okay. I'll go."

"Actually, Christy, I think I should go. What if she's mad at
you?"

Christy felt her defenses rise. "Mad at me? What for? What
did I do?"

"I don't know," Todd said calmly. "That's what I might be
able to find out."

Christy reluctantly pulled her arm out of Todd's and took
the tour book as he handed it to her. He didn't even look back
but strode down the aisle in the direction Katie had gone.

This is just great! Since when did Todd become everyone's coun-

selor? That used to be Doug's job. Todd should be here, with me.

Christy watched Todd until he passed through the sliding door to the next compartment. She wondered if she should write out her frustrations in her new diary. She didn't feel like writing the way she had from Salzburg to Munich. Instead, she pulled Todd's navy blue sweat shirt from his pack and draped it over her to protect her bare arms from the air conditioning, and to feel close to him. If his real arms couldn't be around her, then she would settle for the arms of his sweat shirt.

With her eyes on the door, Christy waited, watching for Todd and Katie to return. She considered going to find them, but then she would have to carry all their packs.

The earphones came in handy as she waited. The scenery outside the window resembled what they had seen in Austria—green hills, small towns, tunnels, and an occasional small train station. The main difference was that all these things were going by so fast everything was a blur of color. Inside the air-conditioned train that was traveling at such great speed, Christy had a hard time absorbing that they were in Germany now rather than Austria. On the second-class train in Italy, when she had to hang her head out the window to breathe because all she could smell was garlic, she had known she was in Italy.

Selecting classical music on her radio dial, Christy let the sounds of a cello be her companion and comfort. She tried not to make a big deal out of Katie's exit and Todd's going after her.

To distract herself, Christy looked through the tour book. What caught her eye in the section on Germany was a picture of a light blue castle with several pointed turrets rising into the sky. The castle was set on a high place overlooking a brilliant blue lake and vast, rolling green hills. The forest, like a velvet green skirt, hugged the base of the huge castle grounds.

The words *Famous Neuschwanstein Castle* appeared underneath the photo.

Christy pulled out a pen and marked the places she really wanted to see. She had just drawn a circle around a Rhine River castle boat tour when Todd returned and sat next to her.

"How's Katie?" Christy asked.

"Good. She just needed some space."

"Is she mad at me?"

"It wouldn't hurt for the two of you to talk everything through."

"What do you mean by 'everything'?"

"You would have to ask her that."

Christy's irritation built toward Todd as much as toward Katie. He made it sound as if some big, unsettled issue lay between Christy and Katie.

"Should I go talk with her? Where is she?"

"She's sitting by herself in the next car."

"I'll go talk with her." Christy really didn't want to. She wished Katie would come back so the three of them could all talk openly. Slipping past Todd, Christy put his sweat shirt back on the seat and said, "Sure you don't want to come with me?"

"You want me to come?" He sounded surprised.

"Yes. I think it would be better if we could all discuss whatever this is about. We're on this journey together, you know."

"I think you're right," Todd said, looking past Christy. "But you can sit down. Katie's coming back."

Christy returned to her seat. Katie plopped into the seat across from her. "Okay," Katie began. Her face was red. "I just decided I don't want to be alone and have my own space any-more. As soon as Todd left, this really creepy guy sat next to me and asked if he could buy me a beer."

"What did you do?" Christy asked.

"I told him to get lost, but when he didn't move, I came crawling back to you guys. I'm sorry I took off like that."

"It's okay," Christy said.

"No, it's not. I need to tell you something, Christy. I told Todd, but I told him not to tell you because I wanted to."

Christy braced herself.

"I met this guy," Katie said after a long pause. "I met him the last week of school. Great timing, huh? I didn't tell you about him, Christy, because there wasn't much to tell. He plays baseball on the team at Rancho Corona, and I happened to go to the last game. His name is Matt. Number 14. That's all I know. We talked after the game for a while. We hit it off great. The problem is, I've been thinking about him day and night for the last two weeks."

Christy didn't think that was too unusual for Katie. When she got going on a project—any project, including relationships—she jumped in with both feet. That's how she was with Michael, the guy she had dated her senior year of high school.

"Will you see him again?" Christy asked.

"I'm pretty sure he's coming back to Rancho in the fall. But that's not my problem. My problem is that I'm being eaten alive with jealousy. I'm so envious of you and Todd that I can't stand it. I know this is really bad to tell you, but Todd said it was better to get things out in the open than to let them burn holes inside of me."

"I agree," Christy said. "So what should I do to make things more comfortable for you?"

"Nothing. That's just it; you're not doing anything to make me feel this way. If anything, I think both of you are holding back and not being as close to each other as you would like because you don't want me to feel left out."

Christy glanced at Todd. He had a calm, steady expression on his face and was concentrating on Katie. Christy could tell from the way Katie was talking that this was difficult for her to discuss.

"I really, really wish a guy were in my life," Katie said. "I want what you two have. Is that wrong to wish for?"

Just then an older guy who was walking down the aisle stopped and looked over at Katie. He looked as if he hadn't bathed for a month. When he saw Katie he said, "There you are."

Christy could tell from the paralyzed expression on Katie's face that this was the same guy who had offered to buy her a beer in the other train car.

"That seat isn't available," Todd said without moving any of their day packs.

"I don't see anyone sitting there," the guy said. He talked like an American, and from the way he slurred his words, Christy guessed he was either on drugs or drunk. "Unless you paid money for that seat and can prove it, that seat is open." He picked up the first pack and dropped it on the floor by Todd's feet.

Christy's heart pounded. She had never seen Todd confronted like this. Would he stand up and punch the guy in the nose?

"We were just leaving." Todd spoke in a calm, even tone. He picked up Christy's pack and handed it to her, motioning with his head that she should stand up. She stood. Todd handed Katie her pack with the same gesture to stand.

"There you go. The seat is all yours," Todd said to the guy. Then Todd stepped into the aisle with Katie and Christy right behind him. Without a word, he led them to the dining car.

"Is he following us?" Katie muttered over her shoulder to Christy. "I don't want to turn around to find out."

Christy cautiously glanced back. "Nope. He's going to the car behind ours."

"Do you want to go back to our seats, Todd?" Katie asked. "I think he took your hint."

"No, I'm not very good at trying to talk to drunk guys. We might as well eat since we're halfway to the dining car."

It turned out they were a full eight cars from the dining car, and when they arrived, a line of people was waiting to be seated. Christy knew it wasn't unusual for Europeans to eat their main meal at two in the afternoon. That's what they did at the orphanage where she worked in Basel. Since this was Sunday afternoon, people were more likely to linger a long time over their meal.

"We could be here awhile, you guys," Christy warned them.

"It's too far to go through all eight cars again, turn around, and come back here in half an hour," Katie said. "I don't mind waiting, if you don't."

"No, that's fine." Actually, it was pretty squishy. Christy wouldn't have minded being this close to Todd if it hadn't been for the way they had left Katie in midconfession over her struggling as she watched Todd and Christy together. Christy knew this wasn't the time to wrap her arms around Todd and lean on him in an effort to condense space.

They didn't talk. It was too noisy with all the conversations going on around them. The four people in front of them spoke in a deep, loud German dialect and laughed even louder.

By the time the three of them finally were seated, they were eager for a huge meal. The dining car chef on this deluxe supertrain didn't disappoint. They all had roast beef with potatoes, carrots, turnips, a creamy broccoli cheese soup, and dinner rolls. Christy ordered hot tea to drink with her dessert of apple cake, and the tea came in a white ceramic pot with a matching creamer.

"Katie, when we move into the dorms this fall, let's find

some little teapots like this and buy two of them. Then, on long nights, when we need to keep ourselves awake, we can brew up our own little pots of tea and have a midnight tea party."

Katie smiled at Christy's suggestion. The excellent food had done wonders for all of them, and just like the "locals" seated around them, they took their time over dessert.

Katie commented on how dark and rich her coffee was and asked Todd about his cappuccino.

"Not as good as I had in Italy. But not bad."

"Katie," Christy said, holding her teacup in her hands to warm them from the chill of the air conditioning. "Do you want to talk some more about what you were saying before that guy came and interrupted us?"

"I don't know. Sometimes I make too big of a thing out of nothing. We can drop it. It doesn't matter."

"I think it matters because it's been bothering you, and if you stuff it away, it might come back and bother you again before the trip is over. I'd like to talk it through now, if we could."

"It's dumb. I know it is. I get my eyes off the Lord and my perspective goes crazy. I told you guys I was jealous, and I am. But I know that's wrong. I know God says we're not supposed to envy what someone else has. The thing is, I don't know what to do with my feelings. I try to ignore them, but then they overwhelm me."

"Pray," Todd suggested immediately.

Katie sighed and looked down at her half-empty cup of coffee. "Yeah, pray. That's what I should do. I don't know why I don't. I get tired of confessing the same thing over and over. But whenever I do talk it through with God, I always feel better."

"And He always forgives us no matter how many times we come to Him," Todd said. "I think it helps to find out what triggers those weak areas and recognize the warning signs before you get blindsided."

"What do you mean?"

"Well, what triggers the jealousy?"

Katie paused a moment before saying, "I see somebody with something I wish I had, and I start to compare myself. Then I get jealous."

"We all do that," Christy said.

"That doesn't make it right," Katie said.

"I know," Christy agreed.

"One thing that helps me is when I see the cycle beginning. I can almost stop the sin in midair before it hits me," Todd said. "Like the comparing part. I memorized a couple of verses that relate. Whenever I start to compare myself with somebody else, I repeat those verses and get my heart back on track with God."

"Then you better teach me those verses, quick!" Katie said, "Because I have a horrible problem of comparing myself with other people."

"One is real short. It's in Isaiah 45:9. It just says, 'Does the clay say to the potter, "What are you making?" ' The other verses are in the same book, Isaiah, in chapter 64, verses 6 and 8. The first time I read this it put me in my place, if you know what I mean."

"Yes, I think I probably know what you mean," Katie said. "What are the verses?"

" 'All of us have become like one who is unclean, and all our righteous acts are like filthy rags; we all shrivel up like a leaf, and like the wind our sins sweep us away. Yet, O LORD, you are our Father. We are the clay, you are the potter; we are all the work of your hand.' "

"Let me see if I caught the same meaning here that you did," Katie said. "When you start to compare yourself with someone else, you think of those verses and how all of us are basically the same before God. Like the clay."

Christy jumped in and said, "And God is the artist. The craftsman. He's making something out of us, the clay. We're not supposed to say to Him, 'Why did you make me like this?' or 'Why can't you make me like her?' "

Todd nodded. "Exactly. Each person's life is a different work of art. God's design for me is different than what He has planned for you."

"Does that really work for you?" Katie asked.

He nodded again. "I find it hard to be jealous when I realize God is the one in control, not me. If He chooses to bless someone more than me, who am I to tell Him what He's doing isn't fair? Do I ever say it's not fair when someone is going through a tough time? Do I tell God it's not fair because He hasn't given me as many difficulties as the other person?"

"You better write those verses down for me, Todd. This is a huge area in my life. I think I have it figured out, and then it comes back stronger." Katie downed her last sip of coffee. "You guys ready to go back to our seats and see if my guardian hobo is still waiting for me?"

He wasn't there when they returned. Instead of sitting beside Todd, Christy sat down next to Katie. She had a lot of questions for her friend and started by saying, "Thanks for being so open, Katie. I'm glad you let both of us in on what you're feeling."

"I wasn't going to. I was going to try to figure it out myself. But Todd was right when he said it's better when we get everything out in the open."

"Then I want you to explain something to me," Christy said. "I don't quite understand how the guy from Rancho made you feel as if you wanted a boyfriend. I mean, why him? Didn't you feel that way around Antonio or Marcos?"

"No. I can't explain it, Christy, but when I met Matt, I thought he was awesome. The only other guy I've ever felt that way about was Michael." Katie turned to Todd and included him in their conversation. "Do you think love at first sight is a big lie?"

Todd rubbed his hand across his jaw. It looked as if he was trying to hide a smile.

"What's so funny?" Christy asked.

Todd looked at Katie and said, "All I can tell you is that the first time I saw Christy I knew." He glanced at Christy.

"Knew what?" Katie asked.

Todd's voice lowered and became deep and dramatic. "I knew that she was God's gift to me and I would never consider anyone else."

For a moment Christy felt overwhelmed by Todd's romantic words. Words he had never before expressed to her. Then she doubted his words and thought he must be teasing or even mocking her.

"You did not!" Christy said, reaching over and whacking Todd on the leg. "The first time you saw me I had just been tumbled by a huge wave and was spit up on the shore covered with seaweed."

"My little mermaid," Todd said, his grin returning. "God's gift to me from out of the sea."

"That reminds me." Christy turned to Katie, eager to change the subject before Todd had a chance to tease her any more. "Todd found out from the tour book that in Copenhagen they have a statue of the *Little Mermaid*. We definitely will have to go see it."

"Okay," Katie agreed.

"Anyone for a game of chess?" Todd asked.

"Are you interested, Katie?" Christy said. "Because I'd like to go back to reading the tour book."

"Oh, I wouldn't want to keep you from your precious tour book," Katie teased.

Todd unpacked the chessboard and set it up. Christy had

just turned to the Denmark section of the tour book when Katie leaned over and quietly said, "Thanks, Chris."

"For what?"

"If the Big Artist upstairs isn't ready to paint a boyfriend into my life, thanks for letting me share yours."

CHRISTY AND TODD • THE COLLEGE YEARS

Their train rolled into the Oslo station at 10:00 Monday
14 morning. They had been riding trains for more than twenty-four hours. And Christy had decided that Katie's idea of "sharing" Todd no longer felt like a comfortable, friendly arrangement.

The reality was that Katie hadn't shared Todd at all. She hogged him. When they changed trains in Hamburg and rode through the night in a sleeper car, Christy had stretched out on one of the bunks and managed to fall asleep.

She woke up sometime around 6:00 in the morning and found herself alone. Todd and Katie showed up an hour later, laughing and carrying on about what a great time they had had staying up all night drinking coffee and talking. Todd had helped Katie memorize the verses in Isaiah he had told her about. In every way, the two of them seemed to have shared a wonderful time together while Christy slept.

The worst part was that now Christy was the one who found angry bats, poisoned with jealousy, flapping around in her belfry. "Get outa here," Christy muttered to the evil bats.

"What did you say?" Katie asked as they exited the station. "Which way is it out of here?"

"This way." Todd led them into the brilliant light of the

new day. "We should find a place to stay first, then do some exploring. What do you think?"

"Do you have a place picked out, Christy?" Katie asked. "You were the one who studied that tour book."

"I marked a couple of places." Christy pulled out the book. "This one sounded the best to me, but if you guys want to go someplace else, that's fine, too." She was surprised at how calm she felt now. Maybe Todd's theory of stopping a sin in midair really worked. "This place is a guesthouse like the one we stayed at in Salzburg. It says it's near the train station."

"Sounds perfect," Katie said. "Which way?"

Christy read the map and led them to the *pensjonater*, as their hotel was called. A three-story, square building, it was adorned with a gorgeous stained-glass window above the front door. Christy liked the winding staircase that led them to their third-floor rooms. The first thing she did was open the window's shutters, which unlatched in the middle. Both sides opened outward, letting the sunlight stream into their room. Bright red geraniums spilled over the edge of the window's flower box. Christy drew in a deep breath. Clean air filled her lungs and made her feel invigorated and ready to see the sights.

Katie flopped on the poofy bed and said, "The power of a real bed should never be underestimated."

"You're not thinking of going to sleep now, are you? We're in Oslo! Finally! Fjords are waiting to be visited and folk museums to be explored."

"You and your folks can visit all the museums you want. I'll be here. You can come back and tell me all about it."

Christy pulled on her friend's foot. "We're in Norway. This is the home of your ancestors and all that. Aren't you even a little bit excited about exploring? What happened to your 'We're on an adventure' motto?"

"I've traded in that motto for a new one, 'Sleep is sweet.' "

Christy gave up. She knew in a few minutes Katie would sink into slumberland, so Christy quietly unpacked and made herself at home in the quaint room with the painted wooden furniture. The small desk in the corner was white with tiny red and blue flowers painted along the edge. The matching chair had a high back with a woven straw seat. The wooden bedposts were also painted white with red and blue flowers. A small vase of blue glass held a handful of yellow, white, and blue wild flowers.

After pulling out all her dirty clothes from her backpack, Christy decided to go down the hall to the shared bathroom and wash what she could in the sink. With the sunshine and fresh air pouring through the window, her clothes would dry quickly.

On her way to the bathroom, she knocked on the door to Todd's room. She wondered if he had discovered his bed the way Katie had and had also taken on her "sleep is sweet" motto. Christy hoped he was still awake. She felt ready to explore with him for a few hours. They could let the sleeping redhead get her beauty rest.

Todd didn't answer. But the door to the shared bathroom opened, and he emerged, freshly showered and shaven, wearing a crumpled but clean T-shirt and shorts.

"You shaved!" Christy said.

"Too itchy."

"You look good."

"Hope I didn't keep you guys waiting. A shower sounded too wonderful to pass up."

"A nap sounded too wonderful for Katie to pass up. She'll be out for at least a couple of hours. Do you want to go exploring and then come back and get her?"

"Sure. As long as food is included in that exploring." Todd glanced at the mound of clothes Christy held. "Were you going to wash those?"

"Yes, I thought they would dry in the fresh air that's coming through our window."

"That's a good idea. Why don't we plan to leave in about ten or fifteen minutes? I'll take my stuff to the bathroom on the second floor."

Christy decided to wash more than her clothes. In twelve minutes flat she showered, shaved, washed her hair, changed, and washed her clothes and hung them on a collapsible rack in her bedroom's sunshine. She was just finishing her note to Katie when Todd appeared at her open door. He smiled when he saw Katie asleep with her shoes on.

"Do you think she'll be okay?" he whispered.

"I think so. I'm leaving her a note."

As they walked out, quietly closing the door behind them, Todd slipped his arm around Christy's shoulders and pulled her close. He planted a tender kiss on her temple, halfway on her still-wet hair and halfway on her skin.

Christy was surprised and about to ask, "What was that for?" But when she turned and looked into Todd's clear blue eyes, she knew the answer. He was happy. Happy to be with her, happy to be in Norway, happy to be alive. She decided it was a kiss of contentment and would only retain its magical happiness if she didn't ask to have it explained.

Reaching her arm around his waist, Christy leaned close as they tried to walk down the narrow, winding stairs side by side. She giggled when the curve made them bump into the railing. The owner of the pensjonater met them at the bottom of the stairs and smiled.

"Can you tell us a good place to eat?" Todd asked the cheerful woman. She gave them directions to a place nearby that served what she said was the best *koldtbord* on this side of town.

The restaurant offered outdoor seating. That made Christy happy. She was eager to soak up all the pure air and sunshine. The day felt so fresh to her. The koldtbord turned out to be an abundant buffet. Todd went back twice and ate more salmon than Christy could imagine eating in a lifetime. She tried a stew that the waiter later told her was made from lamb and cabbage. She never would have ordered it if she had known what it was, but she found she liked it.

Lunch wasn't cheap, but Christy felt they had gotten their money's worth. She had eaten so much she felt uncomfortable as they walked hand in hand to the bus stop. The waiter had told them this bus would take them to the *Kon-Tiki* Museum, which Todd was so eager to visit.

They sat close on the bus, holding hands and talking about what they would see after the museum. Christy pulled her tour book from her day pack and noticed how worn it was beginning to look. Todd pointed out a couple of places of interest. The one that intrigued him the most was the *Norske Folke Museet* because on the map it appeared that the *Kon-Tiki* Museum was part of it.

"You know," Todd said, "I was going to tell you, Katie and I looked up a bunch of stuff in our Bibles last night when we were talking, and I found out that Paul didn't write the letter to the Philippians from the Mamertine Prison. He was in Rome when he wrote it, but under house arrest. Apparently he could come and go from the house, and people could visit him."

"So he didn't write anything while in that dungeon?"

"Yes, he wrote his second letter to Timothy. Nero was the emperor at the time."

"Didn't Marcos say Nero was the ruler who used Christians as human torches to light his garden parties?"

Todd nodded.

"That overwhelms me," Christy said. "I mean, to be tortured and killed like that because of what you believe."

"I know," Todd said. "I read the whole book of Second

Timothy last night and tried to picture Paul in that dismal cell, within view and earshot of the Colosseum, where other Christians were being fed to the lions. And there he was, in chains, writing stuff like, 'For God did not give us a spirit of timidity, but of power, of love, and of self-discipline.' "

Christy felt like crying.

"At the end of the last chapter," Todd added, "Paul even said, 'But the Lord stood at my side and gave me strength.' And he wrote about how he was delivered out of the mouth of the lion."

"When we were at the Colosseum, the whole idea of persecution really hit me," Christy said. "I stood there and felt as if I could see that arena come alive with spectators watching as the lions were let loose on the Christians."

Todd looked at her intensely. "I felt that way, too."

"I prayed that if I ever was in that situation, I would be able to stand firm in my commitment to the Lord."

A gentle smile came across Todd's lips. "You know what I want? I want to be confident like Paul so that no matter what the circumstances, I'm willing to give my life for Christ. Because the truth is, we all die. And once we've stepped into eternity, all that will matter is if we remained faithful to the Lord through this short life on earth."

Christy felt a tear roll down her cheek. "I agree," she said in a whisper.

"Do you know what, Kilikina?" Todd caught her tear with his finger and then pressed his finger to his chest, directly over his heart. "This is where I save all your tears. Right here, where I hold you in my heart."

The bus pulled up at their stop for the folk museum. Christy pulled herself together, blinking quickly as she followed Todd out onto the street. She felt as if she had been conversing with him in a different realm, another world beyond the stars. Yet here they stood, with both feet on solid earth, and the blue sky spread above them like a sealed dome, locking out that other realm's secrets.

Holding hands and not speaking much, Todd and Christy toured the Norwegian Folk Museum. More than one hundred antique Norwegian buildings were reconstructed and set up like a village under a grove of large trees. A dirt path linked the houses. Some of the houses had sod roofs and faded, stencil-like paintings over the fireplaces and doorframes. One of the houses seemed especially small, and Todd joked about the Vikings actually being a race of short people who wore really tall hats with pointed horns to make them look ferocious.

Christy liked the simple, reconstructed church that originally was built almost eight hundred years ago. "Just a little different from Saint Peter's Basilica in Rome, don't you think?" It intrigued her to see how people through the ages built special places to worship God. The inborn longing to make a meeting place where humans could connect with the eternal God carried on from generation to generation. She was even more amazed to see something this humble stand after eight hundred years.

Todd wasn't overly impressed with the ancient church, but he came alive when they toured the *Kon-Tiki* Museum. They stood side by side, staring at a very small raft constructed of logs that had been intricately roped together.

"Can you believe six men spent one hundred and one days floating on this raft in the Pacific?" Todd studied the raft from every angle. "That's unbelievable. Don't you think that's incredible?"

"Yes," Christy agreed.

"They must have driven each other crazy. There's barely enough room for six people to sit on that raft, let alone sleep and carry supplies. But, man, what an adventure!"

Christy didn't want to admit it to Todd, but she knew if

she were sent to sea on such a small raft with Todd and Katie for one hundred days, she would go crazy. She was challenged enough to be with them twenty-four-seven for just three weeks. This little break alone with Todd was refreshing to her.

They also viewed the *Ra II*, which was the second craft Thor Heyerdahl built. This one he constructed in Egypt out of reeds to test the theory that such a boat could have reached the Americas before Columbus did. For whatever reason, the *Ra II* didn't astound Todd as much as the *Kon-Tiki*.

"You know, I've been thinking about getting a new surfboard," Todd said.

"What happened to old Naranja?" Christy asked. Todd's orange surfboard had been a part of his life long before Christy had entered it. She couldn't imagine him giving up Naranja.

"I'll keep Naranja around, but I've been looking at this really sweet board that was made by a guy I know in San Clemente. If I buy this new board, I'm going to name it *Kon-Tiki*."

Christy smiled as they strolled back to the bus stop. The afternoon seemed to grow only more beautiful under the clear skies. She knew that at this time of year, in this land of the midnight sun, they could expect more than eighteen hours of daylight. The light felt different to her, even at 2:00 in the afternoon, because the sun came at them from a different angle than she had ever experienced. Norway felt like a crisp, clear, completely different world than the one she had spent her life in.

Christy tried to express those thoughts to Todd as they took the bus back to their lodgings. The more she tried to describe it, the more Todd nodded, and the wider his grin became.

"Do you realize how close we are to the Arctic Circle?" he asked.

"How close?"

"We could take a train out of here tomorrow morning at 8:00 and cross the Arctic Circle at 4:00 that afternoon."

"Wouldn't it be all frozen?" Christy hadn't missed her jacket since their camping trip. A visit to the Arctic Circle didn't seem like a good idea unless a person had at least a jacket for the journey.

"It's not the North Pole," Todd said. "The Arctic Circle is basically the line where the Atlantic Ocean stops and the Arctic Ocean begins. A dozen or more Norwegian towns are above the Arctic Circle."

"It sounds like the end of the world."

"I know." Todd's expression lit up. "So how about it, Kilikina, do you want to go to the ends of the Earth with me?"

15

As adventuresome and appealing as Todd's invitation sounded to Christy, they had only one problem with going together to the ends of the Earth: Katie.

"I can't explain it," Katie said during dinner that night in downtown Oslo. Even at 8:00 the city was as bright and warm as it had been at 3:00 that afternoon. "I just don't want to go to the ends of the Earth with you guys."

"We can't go without you," Christy said, remembering her parents' restriction that she and Todd should never travel alone.

Katie looked at Todd and then back at Christy. "It sounds boring to spend all that time on a train just to see some marker in the ground and herds of reindeer. Sorry."

They had been discussing their options for more than an hour, and clearly Katie wasn't about to budge. As much as Christy hated it, she knew what she needed to say. "Todd, why don't you go by yourself? You really wanted to go to Pompeii, and we didn't make it there. I think you should go to the Arctic Circle. Katie and I can take a boat ride around the fjords tomorrow. If you decide to fly back, like you were saying earlier, then maybe you could fly into Copenhagen instead of here. Katie and I would take the train to meet you there."

Todd studied Christy's expression. "Are you sure?"

In truth, Christy liked the idea of traveling north to the ends of the Earth with Todd, but she still was bothered about not having a jacket. And it did sound a little boring. With their limited travel time, she wanted to see Copenhagen more than she wanted to see an Arctic Circle marker and herds of reindeer.

"I'm sure," she said.

"Oh, now I feel like the toad of the week," Katie said.

"Don't," Christy said. "I think this will work out fine. We'll stay here tomorrow night and then take the train down to Copenhagen to meet Todd. You said there were openings on the flight out of Narvik, right?"

"Right. That would work out perfectly," Todd said.

Christy couldn't tell if he was sounding calm because he was disappointed she wasn't going with him or if he was just being his easygoing self.

The next morning, when Christy and Katie walked Todd to the train station and sent him off for what Katie called his "male bonding with the polar bears," Todd appeared much more enthusiastic about his solo journey. Just before he boarded the train, he reviewed the details of where and when they were to meet in Copenhagen.

"We'll be there," Christy said. "Have a great time."

"Say hi to Santa Claus for us," Katie said.

The conductor called out something, which Christy guessed meant "All aboard" in Norwegian. Todd grabbed her, wrapped his arms around her, and kissed her soundly. Then he leaped onto the train and waved good-bye as if he were a soldier going off to war.

"Well!" Katie said. "Good thing I'm along on this excursion to chaperone you two. When did Mr. Casual turn into Captain Passion?"

Christy smiled. Her lips still tingled from Todd's kiss. She remembered when he had kissed her that way once before. They were in Maui, and he was about to jump off a high bridge. Her heart had cried out with fear that he might not surface from the water below. But he had. Now she had confidence he would return from this "leap," as well.

"Do you want to find a little Konditorei and have a morning pastry with me?" Christy asked, changing the subject as they left the train station.

"You're going to put food past those lips while they're still sizzling?" Katie teased. "Man, if I were you, I wouldn't be able to use my lips for a week."

"Katie, come on. It wasn't that wild."

"You should have had the view I did. It was wild. In all the years I've been around you guys, that was about the most intense outward flash of emotion I've seen from Mr. Cool. Or does he kiss you like that all the time, and I just never see it?"

"No, he doesn't kiss me like that all the time. He doesn't kiss me very often, actually."

"That must be hard."

"No, I think it's just right. It would be hard if we were more expressive." They entered a café, and Christy tried to change the subject. "Do you want to sit here, or should we buy something to take with us and go on down to the harbor? I think the next tour boat of the fjords leaves in an hour."

"Let's take it with us," Katie said. "I don't want to miss the boat."

They bought several delicious-looking pastries and decided to take a cab to the harbor. Katie found it humorous that the taxicab they rode in was a Mercedes. "Only a slightly different experience from our taxi rides in Rome, wouldn't you say?"

About two hours into their relaxing boat tour, Katie brought up the subject of Todd again. "How do you guys keep your kisses to a minimum?"

"What?"

"I want to know how you and Todd have stayed so pure and controlled for five years. I think it's hard. It was hard for me when I was going with Michael. I mean, you want to be close; yet the closer you become, the more you want to be even closer. Do you know what I mean?"

Christy nodded. She knew exactly what Katie meant.

"So what's your limit? Where do you guys draw the line?"

Christy had to think a moment. "Light kisses, I guess."

"And you're going to tell me what I witnessed at the train station was a 'light' kiss? I don't think so, honey."

"He doesn't usually kiss me like that," Christy said quickly, although she did remember that his kiss when he arrived at the train station in Basel had pretty much taken her breath away. And then the kiss on the boat to Capri hadn't been light.

"Have you guys ever talked about it?" Katie asked.

"Not exactly. It hasn't been a problem."

"I'm sure it's helped that you haven't been on the same side of the globe for half of your relationship, whether Todd was leaving or you were." Katie leaned back in her seat on the deck of the tour boat. She closed her eyes and took the sun's full force on her face. "I'm going to have so many new freckles by tonight, but doesn't this feel incredible?"

"I love it." Christy looked over at an inlet their boat was about to enter. Dramatic, sharp cliffs shot straight up from the water and towered above them like a great stone ogre with a gnarled face. "Look, we're entering another fjord."

Katie only opened one eye and glanced, unimpressed, at

the magnificent sight. "Yeah, it's gorgeous. Just like the last twenty-five fjords we've visited. You see one fjord, you've seen 'em all."

Christy thought it was funny that there they were, finally in Norway, Katie's destination of choice, and they were on a tour of the one thing she wanted to see, fjords, but she was about to take a nap.

The silent time Christy now had to herself was a precious gift. She basked in the sun's warmth and felt comforted by the boat's peaceful motion as it motored through crystal water. The quietness gave her a chance to reflect on what Katie had said about kissing.

Christy wondered if she should draw up some guidelines and standards for herself. She never had to consider that before because over the years Todd had been so slow and sparing in expressing his feelings for her. She had broken up with Rick before kissing had become a problem. It never had been an issue when she went out with Doug because he had made a personal vow never to kiss a girl until his wedding day, and he had succeeded. A special sense of celebration had filled the air at Doug and Tracy's wedding because of their intense purity.

I'm glad Todd has given me his kisses over the years. Each one has meant something different. If Todd saves my tears in his heart, I save his kisses. And I'm saving thousands of kisses to give back to him if we get married.

Christy allowed herself a few moments to consider the possibility that she and Todd wouldn't get married. She had no regrets about the kisses and tears she had bestowed on him over the years. But she also knew that she didn't want to give him a whole lot more, just in case it would be too hard to stop. The full expression of her dreams of passion was wrapped in innocence, and she wanted that delicate wrapping to stay on those dreams until her wedding night.

Pulling her new diary from her day pack, Christy wrote her thoughts out as quickly as they came to her. Part of what she wrote was,

> *I have so much saved up inside my soul that I'm sure it will take me a lifetime to fully express physically my love to my husband. I want to save all of that until we enter into "holy matrimony." I think that's part of what makes it holy. I think God honors virginity in a special way. When He chose to send His Son to earth, He did it through the body of a virgin. I want my marriage to be holy before God. For the first time I've begun to think that maybe I need a plan instead of just assuming that's how everything will go. At this point in my life, I assume I'll marry Todd. But I don't know that for sure. It's as if I need to save myself from him to save myself for him.*

The concluding thought on the topic came to Christy that night as she and Katie walked through Oslo's streets at 9:30 in what felt like broad daylight. The sky carried only a tinge of tangerine-shaded dusk as they strolled past a row of shops. Dozens of people were out, walking or sitting in open-air cafés, talking as if it were lunchtime.

"I can't believe we waited this late to eat dinner," Katie said. "Although it hasn't exactly felt late. But I am starving."

Christy saw a vendor across the street and said, "Do you want a pretzel or whatever he's selling?"

"No, I don't want to waste hunger like this on a pretzel. I'd rather save it until I can have a real, full, long-anticipated dinner. Are we almost to that restaurant you and Todd liked so much?"

"One more block this way," Christy said. Her mind was spinning with Katie's words. She wanted to remember them and write them in her diary. It made so much sense. She did have a hunger in her life for passion. So did Todd. It was a natural, wonderful gift from God to feel that way about someone you loved.

What was it Katie just said about not wasting such hunger on a pretzel? She wanted to save her hunger for the real, full meal. That's exactly what I want. I don't want to waste my physical longing on some incomplete expression of affection that could never be satisfying. I want to wait for the real, full expression that can only come in marriage.

As they loaded up their plates at the koldtbord, Christy kept formulating her purity plan. Her parents had never talked about this with her, and they had never given her a purity ring, like her friend Sierra had received from her parents. It was up to Christy to make a plan, and Christy liked plans. She always felt more secure when she had a plan.

I'm going to save my really big kisses for Todd and tuck them away, safe and warm, in the secret place in my heart. When we're together and I feel like kissing him, I'll just tell myself to save that kiss. It will be like saving pennies in a piggy bank. One day I'll give that piggy bank to my future husband, whoever he is. And I'm quite sure that piggy bank will be full! Christy smiled.

The huge dinner and the short but good sleep they had that night prepared Christy and Katie for the ten-and-a-half-hour train ride to Copenhagen. They left on the 7:30 morning train, which arrived in Copenhagen at 5:30 that evening. The scenery of endless green forests and of lakes with huge floating lily pads was beautiful and refreshing. Katie and Christy rode comfortably in the modern train. They wondered aloud about Todd and how he was enjoying being on top of the world.

Then, about four hours into their journey, Katie surprised Christy. She asked if she could see Christy's tour book.

"I don't know . . ." Christy said.

"Why not?"

"I'm afraid you're going to throw it out the window or something."

"No, I just want to see it."

For the next several hours, Katie became an even bigger tour book maniac than Todd. She read everything about Denmark aloud to Christy and even made Christy repeat Danish phrases back to her.

"Okay, now, this is how you say, 'Where is the bathroom?' *'Hvor er toilettet?'* Try it, Christy."

"Hvor er toilettet," Christy repeated. "You do know, don't you, that we have no idea where the accent should be, so we could be saying these phrases completely wrong."

"At least we're trying to say them. Now say, *'Tager de kredit-kort?'* "

"What does that mean?"

"Do you take credit cards?"

Christy laughed. "We don't have any credit cards."

"Okay, fine, if you're going to be that picky, try this: *'Er der nogen her der taler engelsk?'* "

Christy felt reasonably certain that Katie had slaughtered the pronunciation of that sentence. "And what was that supposed to mean?"

"That means, 'Does anyone here speak English?' "

Christy burst out laughing.

"What? That's a useful expression."

"But, Katie, if anyone speaks English, couldn't you just ask in English and that person would understand you?"

"Oh." Katie buried her nose in the book and muttered, "Never mind."

"Let's decide where we're going to go after we drop off our luggage. I'm glad Todd had us call the hostel and make reservations before he left. This is the first time we've actually known where we were going to stay before we arrived in a city."

"The *Little Mermaid* statue is a must-see, in my opinion," Katie said. "And this Tivoli Gardens sounds fun. They have rides, free concerts, puppet shows, fireworks, and get this—

they even have ballet performances. Oh, and I definitely would like to go to this one palace or whatever it is that holds the Danish crown jewels. I love that kind of thing. Remember when we saw the British crown jewels at the Tower of London?"

Christy remembered the cold, old tower and that they had climbed lots of stairs. She didn't remember much about the jewels. But she said, "Crown jewels would be fun to see. Where should we go first?"

"Either to see the *Little Mermaid* or Tivoli Gardens."

"Let's check out the mermaid," Christy suggested. "I think Todd will want to see Tivoli Gardens when he gets here, but I don't think the mermaid is at the top of his list."

Christy was feeling pretty confident as the two of them set out from their youth hostel in search of the *Little Mermaid*. She had worried a bit earlier that the two of them traveling together might attract a few drunken hobos like the one Christy had seen in Naples or the guy on the train who had bothered Katie a few days earlier.

But traveling, just the two of them, had been fantastic so far. They were getting along wonderfully. No one had tried to harass them. The youth hostel was easy to find, and they hadn't gotten lost yet.

Katie led them down the clean, darkly paved streets of Copenhagen, reading the tour book aloud as she walked. "It says the statue of the *Little Mermaid*, or the *Lille Havfrue*, as they call it, is at the Langelinie Harbor."

"Katie," Christy said with a finger to her lips. "You don't have to announce where we're going to the whole world."

"They don't care," Katie said, glancing around. "It's obvious we're tourists. Hey, that's the bus we're supposed to take. Come on!"

They dashed to catch the bus, and Katie asked the driver, "You are going to the harbor, right?"

"Yes, the harbor."

"Great."

Christy and Katie took two seats near the front and disembarked when the driver turned and, pointing to the large Tuborg Beer factory, said, "The harbor."

"Thanks," both of them said as they headed toward the water. They were at a huge harbor. Sea gulls swooped down to snatch treats from the large fishing boats. Katie and Christy walked and walked all around, looking for a statue in the water but with no success.

"You'd think they would have a few signs up or something," Katie said. "This is ridiculous."

A huge ferry pulled in while Katie and Christy walked back to where they had started. As they stopped to rest for a moment, the monstrous craft released a long line of cars from its underbelly. Hundreds of people stood on the deck. A group of children all wearing bright yellow T-shirts lined up at the guardrail and called down to Katie and Christy.

"Wave," Katie said. "They're being cute and friendly."

Christy didn't feel very cute or friendly, but she waved. The children got excited and waved and yelled even more enthusiastically. It was as if they had been playing a game, trying to make someone notice them, and Christy and Katie were the first to play along.

A familiar pain brushed across Christy's heart. It was the hurt she felt whenever she worked with the children at the orphanage. *So many children in this world are crying out for love and attention.* She wondered how all the little ones were doing back in Basel.

"I see a bus coming," Katie said. "Let's take it back to town. I've lost all interest in the missing mermaid."

To their surprise, the driver was the same person who had dropped them off a half hour earlier.

"We didn't see any mermaids," Katie told him, taking the

seat right behind him. "I suppose she was diving under the water, and that's why we couldn't see her."

The driver turned the large steering wheel on the bus and smiled at Katie in the rearview mirror. Christy wondered if the poor man had any idea what Katie was rattling on about. He then looked at Christy in the rearview mirror. She felt obligated to try to translate for Katie.

"We were looking for the statue of the *Little Mermaid*," she said slowly.

When he didn't respond, Katie pulled out the tour book and said, in a voice that Christy thought was way too loud, "*Lille Havfrue*. We're looking for the *Lille Havfrue*."

Christy was certain Katie's accent was wrong. But the driver somehow still understood. "Ah, *Lille Havfrue*." He broke into a deep, jolly laugh. "*Lille Havfrue* is not at the harbor."

"So we discovered," Katie said. "Where is she?"

"I will take you," he said, still laughing. Then he added with his delightful accent, "She is not large like your Statue of Liberty."

Christy glanced at Katie.

"Well? How was I supposed to know? It says here she's at the harbor."

The driver stopped by a park and opened the door. "Here," he said. "You will find the *Lille Havfrue* here."

"Thanks." Christy smiled at him as they got off. She couldn't help but feel that as soon as the door of the bus closed, the whole busload of Danish people would burst out laughing at the crazy American girls.

"Well," Katie said, undaunted. "I guess we made his day a little brighter."

"He did seem humored," Christy said. "This place looks totally different from where we just were."

"And look! There's a sign. '*Lille Havfrue* this way.' " They followed the pathway through a garden area.

"It pays to consult the tour book and to learn the local lingo, doesn't it?" Katie asked.

Christy couldn't pass up the opportunity to tease her friend. "Oh, what's this about consulting the tour book? Does that mean we are no longer on a free-spirited adventure?"

"I know, I know. I deserved that. I'm a reformed traveler, though, remember? Don't be too hard on me. I didn't understand the power of the written word."

"It sounds as if you're talking about the Bible."

"Now, there's a good analogy for you," Katie said. "We'll have to tell that one to Todd. The Bible is like our tour book for this journey through life."

"And the part about adventures? How does that fit in?"

"In case you haven't noticed yet, Christy," Katie said, "I think adventure tends to find you and me. We don't have to go looking for it."

Christy smiled at Katie. "We always were a couple of peculiar treasures, weren't we?"

Katie tilted back her head and let loose her carefree laughter. "I haven't heard you use that term in such a long time! You're right, Chris. We are a couple of peculiar treasures. And so is this little Havfrue statue, if she actually exists."

They walked a long distance before seeing the water, which appeared as flat and shallow as a pond. Then, suddenly, there she was. The *Little Mermaid*. A bronzed statue only about two feet high. She had taken on a weathered, green tinge, and she sat gracefully on a flat, reddish-colored boulder, gazing down at the water. Her back was turned toward Katie and Christy.

"Look at that, will you? We come all this way, and she won't even turn around." Katie said.

"She's a lot smaller than I thought she would be," Christy commented.

"Now I know why the bus driver thought we were so

funny," Katie said. "Can you imagine this little statue being situated somewhere in that harbor? She would be run over in an instant by all the cargo ships and ferries."

"So," Christy said flatly, "this is the famous *Little Mermaid statue*."

"Yep, that's her."

They stood for a moment, staring at the statue. Then, turning to look at each other, Christy and Katie burst into the kind of laughter that could only come from two peculiar treasures caught in the midst of an adventure.

16

Christy wrote about their experience in her diary that night. She entitled her entry "In Search of the *Lille Havfrue*." Her last paragraph read,

> I hope I never forget the lesson I learned today. Some of the things I set out to find in life aren't as grand as I thought they would be. When those discoveries turn out to disappoint, may I always be blessed with what I had today: (1) a peculiar treasure of a friend to laugh wholeheartedly with me over the disillusionment and (2) enough money for bus fare to take me on to the next episode of the adventure.

Christy closed her diary, turned off the flashlight she had borrowed from Katie, and fell asleep with a contented smile on her lips.

The next morning both Christy and Katie found only cold water in the shower. They had slept until 7:30, which, in this circle of travelers, apparently was considered sleeping in.

If everything went according to schedule, Todd was to arrive at the youth hostel at 9:00 that morning. Christy and Katie found a bakery down the street that was packed with young international travelers who had stayed at the hostel and were on their way. Backpacks bumped into one another as the travelers stood at the counter to place their orders.

"Do you want to go someplace else?" Christy asked.

"Just tell me what you want, and I'll wait in line for both of us. Why don't you see if any tables are free outside."

Christy tried not to appear obvious that she was watching the diners like a hawk, waiting for one of them to make even the slightest movement indicating that he was ready to leave. Two guys wearing hiking boots and shorts began to stand up, and Christy slid over to their table to grab it. As soon as they walked away, she pulled out one of the three chairs and plopped down.

Almost immediately a tall, slender guy wearing a leather jacket and orange-tinted sunglasses pulled out the chair next to her and sat down. *"Godmorgen,"* he said.

From Katie's drills on the train, Christy knew that was Danish for "good morning." She wished the tour book had listed how to say, "Get lost."

With a simple nod to acknowledge his greeting, Christy turned her head to see where Katie was in the line. The guy said something else, and Christy pulled out her well-used "Ich verstehe nicht."

Unfortunately, he answered her in German, but she didn't understand what he said. She didn't want to say anything in English because then he would know she was an American, and she couldn't fake a British accent well enough to pull that off.

Before Christy could decide what to do, Katie bustled out the door with her hands full. She was about to drop one of the pastries she had balanced on top of Christy's cup of hot tea.

"Hey, grab this quick, Christy," Katie said before she reached their table. Then turning to see the guy in the orange-tinted glasses, she added a friendly, "Hi. Is it okay if we sit at your table with you? It's really crowded here this morning, isn't it? Must be a good place to eat."

Oh great, Katie! I was trying to get him to leave.

Their table host graciously pulled out a chair for Katie and in perfect English said, "So where are you guys from?"

"California," Katie said.

He looked disappointed. "Me too. Fresno."

"Really? That's cool. We're from Escondido," Katie said.

Christy was stunned that this guy had managed to convince her he was a local. She lowered her head, closed her eyes, and said a quick prayer before tearing off a corner of her pastry, which was covered with powdered sugar.

"Your German is pretty convincing," he said to Christy. "I wouldn't have guessed you were an American."

Christy lifted her head. "Thanks." She liked fitting in and not sticking out. After she had been at school in Basel for a few weeks, she had decided she didn't want everyone to know she was from the U.S. She found it easier to slip in and out of everyday life if she wasn't always known as the foreigner.

"How long have you been here?" Katie asked. "I'm Katie, by the way. This is Christy."

Christy didn't feel particularly comfortable letting this stranger know her name, even if he was from the U.S.

"I'm Jade. I've been in Europe since May. This is only my second day in Copenhagen."

"It's our second day, too," Katie said. "Christy has been in Europe since last fall. She's going to school in Switzerland."

"Oh really? Where?"

Christy didn't appreciate Katie telling Jade all the details of Christy's life. She gave him basic information about the university she attended and concentrated all her attention back on her breakfast.

"What have you seen here so far?" Katie asked.

"Seen?" Jade asked.

"Have you been to Tivoli Gardens?"

"No, I'm just hanging out."

"We went to see the *Little Mermaid* statue yesterday," Katie said. "Now, that was an adventure! Not necessarily one I would recommend, but it was an adventure."

Jade gave them a look as if to say he couldn't believe they were running around looking at points of interest. Christy guessed he had a different agenda for his travels.

"You know," he said, "a good dance club is on Nysted. The band was pretty good last night." He looked at Christy. "You want to go with me tonight?"

Christy tried not to sound too shocked. "No, thanks."

"Would you come if I found a date for your friend here?"

Christy shook her head.

"Not very friendly, are you?"

When Christy didn't look up or answer, Jade said, "Yeah, well, maybe I'll see you there." He stood up and gave Christy a light punch on the arm, as if trying to get a reaction out of her. "Take it easy."

They watched him saunter over to some other girls who sat in the shade. They were smoking and offered Jade a cigarette.

"Once again," Katie said, "I, your ever faithful friend, stand by and watch guys drool over you while I mysteriously become invisible."

"Like you were really interested in that guy, Katie." Christy tried to take a sip of her tea, but it was too hot.

"I would have gone to the dance club with him," Katie said.

"Yeah, right," Christy said.

"I think guys like that are intrigued by you because you get all shy around them. And it's not an act. I know that. You start blushing, pull back, and look away. It's all very natural for you. I think they see it as a challenge and try to get you to open up. I, on the other hand, am an open book. And obviously not a bestseller."

"Katie, you're perfect just the way you are. One day a guy will come into your life who will be so stunned that you are *you*. He'll also be glad that you didn't go to dance clubs with guys in leather jackets named after cold green rocks."

Katie smiled. "You better keep reminding me of that, Chris. The longer I wait for my handsome prince, the better those green rock-heads look to me."

Christy shook her head. "You know, it always bothered me in Basel when I would see Americans like that. It's as if they're trying to figure out who they are."

"And we're not?"

"I guess we are. It just seems different to me. Almost like they are wearing a costume. You know, the leather jacket and orange glasses. Then they come all the way to Europe to try out their costume and to see if anybody believes that's who they are."

"You sound like an old lady, Christy."

"I do not."

"I liked his glasses. I was about to ask him if I could try them on. I wanted to see if they clashed with my hair."

Christy decided to play along with Katie rather than make philosophical observations so early in the morning. She casually glanced over her shoulder. "You know, you could still ask him, Katie. He hasn't left yet."

"Maybe if I keep looking over in that direction, Jade will get the hint that I want him to come back over here," Katie said.

"Please don't. My arm still hurts from where he punched me."

"Do you miss Todd at times like this?" Katie asked.

"Yes. Although I'm really glad you and I had a chance to be together for a couple days. It's been fun."

"I know; it has. I kind of wish Todd were going to be away a few more days. I liked being the old Katie with the old Christy for a while. We haven't been *us* for a long time. I've missed that. Being around you brings out the real me."

"Do you feel it's hard to be that way when Todd is around?"

"No. Well, sometimes. But it's not because of anything you've done or haven't done. I think it's just the reality of where we are in our lives. You and Todd are getting closer, and that means there's a little less room in your life for me."

Christy was about to protest when Katie cut her off. "That's not a bad thing. It's good. Isn't this what you've wanted? I know I've put in a prayer or two over the years that you and Todd would reach this point. It's nice to see a few of my prayers answered. Even if they are prayers for my friends and not for me."

"I hadn't thought of it that way, but you're right. Todd and me still being together is a little miracle, isn't it?"

"I think the miracles have only just begun," Katie said. "And I like watching you two as you're getting more serious about each other. I'll probably be even more excited than you on the day he finally proposes to you."

Christy looked into Katie's mischievous green eyes.

"What?" Katie leaned forward and grasped Christy's hand. "What was that look? Has he already proposed, and you've kept it a secret from me? You wouldn't do that, would you?"

"No, of course not, Katie. Todd hasn't proposed. We haven't talked about it at all. I was just looking at you like that because it sounded so strange to hear you say it. I mean, I think about it sometimes, but I don't say it aloud."

"Well, then I'll say it. Todd is going to propose to you, Christy. It's only a matter of time."

Christy felt her heart pounding.

"You look so shocked!" Katie laughed. "Why would that

shock you? I mean, strangers coming up and asking you to go dancing, that should shock you. But why would Todd's proposing shock you?"

"I don't know. It just does."

Katie looked behind Christy, and with a widening grin on her face, she said between clenched teeth, "Don't look now, but he's back."

Christy didn't turn around. She had thought Jade would be happy hanging out with the girls he had found at the other table. "Don't say anything to him," Christy said in a low voice, looking straight at Katie.

Katie's grin was obviously for the guy who now stood behind Christy. Katie gave the guy a chin-up gesture and said, "Go ahead and kiss her. She's been hoping you would."

"Katie!" Before Christy could reprimand her friend further, the shadow of an unshaven, not-so-great-smelling man came over her. Dry, chapped lips suddenly were being pressed against hers.

Christy pulled away, grabbed her cup of hot tea, and shot the steaming liquid into the face of her perpetrator.

Todd screamed.

Springing from her chair, Christy looked at Todd and then at Katie and yelled, "Why didn't you tell me it was Todd?"

Everyone was looking at them. Someone offered Todd a paper napkin. Both his hands were covering his face.

"Todd, I'm so sorry," Christy panted. "Are you okay? Let me see your face." She gently touched his arm, and he pulled away.

"I'm okay," he said slowly.

Christy could see big, red splotches on his forehead. He wiped his eyes with the napkin and lowered himself into the chair next to Christy's with his backpack still on.

"It's okay," Katie announced to the onlookers. "He's all right."

"Does it still burn?" Christy asked, sitting down and trying to get a good look at him. "Should we find a doctor?"

"I think some cold water might help," Todd said.

"The youth hostel is just around the corner." Christy tried to help him up.

Todd pulled his arm away from her, and she remembered more than a year ago, when he had been burned seriously. If she tried to help him do anything, he would get irritated with her. So now she reminded herself that, when he was hurt, she should do what he said, get what he wanted, and then back off.

None of them spoke as they walked quickly to the youth hostel. Todd checked in and headed for the guy's side of the dorm. Christy called out, "We'll be in our room."

Like two naughty children who had been sent to their room, Katie and Christy shuffled off in the opposite direction.

"It was my fault," Katie said firmly. "I can totally see now how you thought I was talking about Jade. You had no way of knowing it was Todd."

"I should have looked before I threw the hot tea on him. I feel so awful."

"You were just reacting," Katie said. "Don't blame yourself. I was the one who set you up. I'm really sorry, Chris."

"That's okay. I know you were just having fun. It was an accident." Christy leaned against the side of one of the wooden bunk beds. "I feel so terrible."

Katie and Christy spent the next hour quietly reading on their beds while other youth hostel guests came and went. One girl came in, collapsed on a lower bunk, and appeared to fall into a deep sleep. Christy was reading from Psalms, which is where she usually went when she needed some comfort.

The God-breathed words of Psalm 61 especially helped. *"Hear my cry, O God; listen to my prayer. From the end of the earth*

I call to you, I call as my heart grows faint; lead me to the rock that is higher than I."

Christy thought of the astounding, soaring-to-the-heavens rock formations they had seen on their boat ride a few days earlier. *God, you are my rock. I rely on you. I may not have traveled to the end of the Earth with Todd, but I feel as if that's where I am right now in my heart.*

The door to their dormitory room opened, and a young woman who worked at the registration desk said, "Is there a Christy in here?"

"Yes?" Christy called out.

"Someone wants to see you in the lobby."

"Thank you." Christy hopped down from her top bunk and asked Katie if she wanted to come with her.

Katie put down the tour book and said, "I think I better go with you. I want to tell him it was my fault."

They walked to the lobby close beside each other. Todd was sitting on the long, wooden bench that ran along the left wall of the lobby entrance. He grinned at them as they approached.

"I'm so sorry, Todd," Katie began. "It was my fault. Christy thought it was Jade, and believe me, she didn't want Jade to kiss her."

Todd raised his eyebrows. Christy could see a big red swollen splotch across his forehead. It looked bad but not awful.

"Jade, huh?" Todd said.

Katie quickly explained who Jade was.

Christy sat down next to Todd. She gave him a sympathetic look. "I'm sorry I reacted like that without seeing who it was."

Todd brushed a long strand of hair from her cheek. "I guess I don't have to worry about you knowing how to take care of yourself. You have quick reactions, Christy. That's good."

"Except it's not good when you get hurt."

"It'll heal. So what have you guys been doing, besides turning down invitations to dance clubs?"

Christy could tell Todd was okay. He wasn't mad, and he wasn't seriously injured. Katie must have come to the same conclusion, too, because she sat down on the other side of Todd and plunged right in with a proposed itinerary of what they should do that day, as well as a long list of all the other sights they should see.

Todd looked at Christy with surprise as Katie continued to spout her knowledge of all the hot tourist spots.

"She's been reading the book," Christy told him.

Todd laughed.

Christy felt good hearing his laugh again. And good being close to him and knowing that everything was okay.

"Before we go anywhere, I want to hear about your adventure," Christy said.

"Right," Katie agreed. "And then we'll tell you about our little adventure with the *Lille Havfrue*."

Todd leaned back, stretched out his legs, and folded his hands behind his neck. "I saw a polar bear," he said proudly.

"No!" Katie said. "Not really."

"Yep. Really. Not up close, but it was a real polar bear. Lots of reindeer. Met some cool people. It was great."

Christy had insisted that he take her camera with him since he didn't have one. She asked, "And you did get a picture of you at the marker when the train stopped and let you off at the Arctic Circle, didn't you?"

"Took two pictures," he said. "Just in case one didn't turn out."

Christy smiled at him and said, "So you're glad you went, right?"

He nodded. Then, looking in Christy's eyes, he leaned closer and whispered so only she could hear, "Except I wish you had been with me."

The three reunited travelers spent the day playing like kids at
Tivoli Gardens in the glorious sunshine. They
ate ice cream that was served in cones with
whipped cream, a dollop of jam on top, and a
thin cookie tucked on the side. They knew they
had to try one when the sign said *Amerikan Cones*. They decided nothing was especially American about them.

By evening, even though it was still light, the air felt cool
and sweet. They rested on one of the many benches within
the garden, having gone on all the rides and then complained
that they were kiddie rides. The roller coaster was, in Katie's
words, "like going over speed bumps at Kelley High School."

"I think we're spoiled by all the amusement parks in California," Christy said. "Weren't you the one reading to me
about how this park was built more than one hundred and
fifty years ago?"

"Yeah, but I still had higher hopes," Katie said.

"It's really a beautiful park," Christy said. "Look at these
trees. Their trunks are almost black, and the leaves are minty
green. What kind of trees do you suppose they are?"

"Danish trees," Katie said. "Can we go see something
else?"

"Sure," Todd agreed. "What do you have marked there in

the book?" He broke off a triangle wedge from a Toblerone candy bar and handed it to Christy.

"I want a piece," Katie said.

"I thought you would." Todd handed Katie a piece of the honey-sweetened chocolate bar.

"I planned to eat a candy bar in each country we went to, but I blew it in Norway," Katie said. "I think I'll have to get double the bars here in Denmark. How did we end up not buying any chocolate there?"

"It's because I took you to all the bakeries, and we bought pastries instead," Christy said.

"Those haven't been too bad," Katie admitted.

"They've been fantastic!" Christy said. "I really can't wait to take both of you to my favorite little Konditorei in Basel." She turned to Todd. "Do you remember me telling you how I go there every Saturday morning? It's where I get my sanity back."

"I remember." Todd munched on the chocolate bar. "You order a coffee with cream and sit at the back corner table. Then Margie, or whatever her name is—"

"Marguerite," Christy corrected him.

"Marguerite brings you whatever they've just pulled out of the oven. Is that right?"

"Exactly." Christy felt warm inside as she realized how much Todd paid attention to her emails and how he did take notes on what was important to her. "I want to take you there. I want you to meet Marguerite and taste the delicacies she creates."

"We can do that." Todd stretched his legs out in front of him. He offered Christy and Katie another hunk of chocolate. "We'll plan our itinerary so that we get back to Basel on Sunday before you start classes, and we'll go to your bakery."

"Then the question is," Katie said, "what do we want to

see between here and Basel? I, for one, must see the Eiffel Tower."

Christy thought, *If you end up with the same feeling about the Eiffel Tower that you had about the fjords, Paris will be a really short stay.*

"Okay, we'll swing by Paris. I wouldn't mind seeing Notre Dame," Todd said.

"And the *Mona Lisa*," Christy added.

"Is she there?" Todd asked.

"Yes," Christy said. "We have to go to the Louvre. That's mandatory."

"How many more days do we have?" Todd asked.

It took the three of them a while before they could decide what day it was and how many more they had. The consensus was that this was, in fact, Thursday, and they had to be in Basel by a week from Monday. Or actually, they had to be back by Sunday so they could visit Christy's bakery.

"We have plenty of time," Todd said.

"You know what that means?" Christy asked. "Today our trip is half over. We've been traveling for eleven days, and we have ten more to go."

"Are you serious? We've only been traveling for eleven days?" Katie looked stunned. "It feels like a decade. Or at least a month. I hate it when I exaggerate so much." Shaking her head, she added, "You guys, we have to make a plan! This last week and a half is going to go by like that." She snapped her fingers for emphasis.

Todd and Christy looked at each other, and Christy burst out laughing. "That's what I've been trying to say for the past eleven days. We need a plan!"

"So I'm a slow learner. Be nice." Katie pulled out the tour book from her day pack, where she now permanently kept it. "I say we find a night train and get ourselves to Paris. No, cancel that. I wanted to try to talk you guys into going to Saint Petersburg first."

"In Russia?" Christy asked.

"I was reading about it," Katie said. "I think Moscow is too far to go. It takes something like three days by train from here. But Saint Petersburg isn't far from Helsinki, and Helsinki is only a day's train ride from here. Twenty-four hours. We could see those onion-dome churches, and they have a museum in Saint Petersburg that's supposed to be even better than the Louvre. It's the Heritage, or something like that."

"I think it's called the Hermitage," Todd said.

"Right." Katie flipped through a few tattered pages. "Here it is. The Hermitage contains 2.8 million exhibits. They built the museum out of the czar's former Winter Palace. It says, 'The staterooms in the Winter Palace, with their chandeliers and opulent marble and gold-leaf decoration, should not be missed.' See? 'Should not be missed.'" She pointed to the words in the tour book. "We should go to Saint Petersburg."

"What do you think, Todd?" Christy asked.

"Whatever you guys want is fine with me." With a grin he added, "I've been to Narvik and back. I'm happy."

Christy was glad all over that she had suggested he go to the Arctic Circle. It had been a good choice. She hoped they could come up with some more good choices now.

After an hour discussing options on the bench at Tivoli Gardens, Todd suggested they find a place to eat. He said he hadn't eaten much on his journey to the "end of the world." Today all he had eaten was an "Amerikan" ice cream and the Toblerone bar.

They went to a small restaurant off the main street at the recommendation of a distinguished gentleman Todd had stopped on the street once they were back in the main part of downtown Copenhagen. Christy ordered the special of the evening, which was listed on the menu as *"flaekesteg med rodka.''* The waitress spoke perfect English, and she told Christy it was roast pork with red cabbage and browned potatoes. Katie looked as if she was having a hard time not bursting out laughing.

As soon as the waitress left, Christy gave her a what's-so-funny look. Katie laughed and said, "I'm sorry. It's just that the way you said it, Christy, the last word sounded like 'road kill'! 'I would like to order the road kill for dinner, please.' " Katie kept laughing.

Christy realized how tired and hungry she was now that they were sitting in the quiet, dimly lit restaurant. Katie's laughter was fun while they were on the rides at Tivoli Gardens, but now it sounded loud and overdone to Christy. She knew Katie became punchy when she was tired and living on sugar. But the truth in Christy's heart was that she wanted to be alone with Todd. She wanted to hear all about his adventure to Narvik. She wanted to look into his eyes and listen to him without having to divide her attention between Todd and Katie.

Dinner was scrumptious, and they all mellowed after eating. A complimentary plate of various slices of cheese followed the meal. Todd ordered a coffee, and they went back to planning the next portion of their trip.

By the time the brightness in the sky had finally begun to soften into shades of tangerine and soft rosy pinks, the three of them had come up with a plan. Stockholm and Helsinki were off the list. Since they weren't headed for Helsinki, Saint Petersburg was also struck from the list.

They decided to travel to Paris with a one-day stop in Amsterdam so they could see a Dutch windmill. The train ride from Copenhagen to Amsterdam would take more than twelve hours.

Todd had been figuring out the train schedule with a book of Eurorail times. "It looks as if we can leave Copenhagen at

7:00 tomorrow morning and get to Hamburg around noon. We get on a different train at 1:00 and that takes us to Cologne, Germany. And that's as far as we can go, by my calculations. They don't list any night trains from Cologne to Amsterdam."

"What are you saying?" Katie asked. "Do you want to skip Amsterdam and go directly to Paris?"

"No, I'd like to go to Amsterdam. I'll keep checking. A night train is probably available, but it's just not listed here. If there isn't one, we could stay in Cologne tomorrow night and take a morning train to Amsterdam. I know some people we could stay with in Amsterdam. They were in Spain when I was there."

"Sounds good to me," Katie said. With a smile to Christy, she said, "Looks like we have a plan."

As they walked back to the youth hostel, Todd held Christy's hand, and she wondered how long it would be before she and Todd had a plan. He was so good at reviewing the tour book and figuring the train schedules. *Has he begun to review his school schedule to figure out when he'll finish? He's been trying to save money this past year. Was all that for college, or was he saving up for an engagement ring?*

Christy told herself she was jumping too far ahead. She knew from previous seasons of wondering and waiting in her life that if she ran ahead and tried to predict the future, she inevitably ended up robbing herself of the joy of the present.

This is where she wanted to be. Right here. Holding hands with Todd, strolling along the streets of Copenhagen under the peach-tinted trail of the midnight sun. They could discuss their future another time, but not tonight. Tonight was for dreaming, not discussing.

About halfway through their train ride to Hamburg the next morning, the train chugged into the belly of a huge ferry like the one Katie and Christy had seen at the harbor. Christy didn't know if they had been transported by a ferry on their way to Oslo because she had slept through most of that trip and wouldn't have noticed if the train was under the stars or under the sea.

She convinced Todd to exit the train with her and find a way to the top of the ferry. She wanted to wave to the tourists on the dock the way the school children in their yellow shirts had waved at Katie and Christy.

"I can take a hint," Katie said when Christy didn't include her in the invitation. "Don't worry. I'll stay here with the luggage. You two go and have a good time. Don't worry about me. I'm sure I'll be just fine."

"We'll find a candy bar for you," Todd said as they left.

"You're my hero!" Katie called out after him.

"What's it like being a hero?" Christy teased.

Todd grinned but didn't answer. She could see that the hot-water burn she had inflicted on his forehead hadn't improved much. Still red, it looked a little swollen.

"Does your face hurt?" she asked.

Todd gave her a funny look.

"I mean, your forehead. Does the burn bother you much?"

"No, I think it will be okay." Todd led her up some stairs until they reached the top deck. He immediately spotted a snack bar and stood in line for some food and for a candy bar for Katie. So many people were waiting it took nearly all of their fifty-minute ferry ride to buy the food.

At first Christy was disappointed they had spent their alone time standing in line. But when their train pulled into Hamburg a little late and they had to run to catch their next train to Cologne, Christy was glad she had something extra to munch on. The ride from Hamburg to Cologne took five hours. The three friends played chess and read the tour book to one another.

Katie was so caught up with reading every detail of every major city and giving Todd and Christy full reports, that Christy was beginning to think she actually had been to some of the cities. Katie said she had a philosophy. If they couldn't see Helsinki, Saint Petersburg, Moscow, and Berlin, they might as well know what they missed.

The descriptions Katie read of the Netherlands and France made Christy glad they had decided on those two places for their next destinations. The only problem was that Christy really wanted to see Luxembourg and Belgium, too, after hearing about them.

"I think after Paris we should go to a small city," Christy said. "Or at least a small country. We've been hitting the major cities, which is great, but we could see a lot outside the big cities. I think that way we would know more what people are really like in those countries."

"Sounds good to me," Todd said. "Where do you want to go after Paris?"

"Germany," Christy said.

"We're in Germany now," Katie said.

"I know, but we're zooming through. A Rhine River cruise is listed in the book that I marked. Did you see it, Katie? It sounds really wonderful."

"I saw that," Todd said. "Doesn't it start in Cologne?"

"No, you don't," Katie said. "Don't start changing plans on me. We're going to Amsterdam."

Christy couldn't believe how rigid Katie had become now that she had the power of the tour book at her fingertips. "What happened to the Katie Weldon who started this trip as a free-spirited woman on an adventure?"

Katie smirked. "She got information. Knowledge is power, you know."

"Knowledge can lead to arrogance and legalism," Todd

said. "Let's use the knowledge to make us a kinder bunch of grace-givers."

Christy remembered hearing Todd say those exact words at a Bible study he had taught years ago. He was referring then to the Bible and how some people can get so much information and knowledge about God that they turn into a bunch of rigid rule-makers. She knew he was talking about the tour book now with Katie, but the comparison was strong in her mind. At this point, all she could hope was that Katie would extend grace to her and agree to the Rhine River cruise.

"Oh, all right," Katie said. "I don't want to be a brat about this like I was about not going to the Arctic Circle. We have to stop in Cologne anyway, don't we? We can stay there tonight, take the river cruise in the morning, and be on our way to Amsterdam before the sun goes down. Then we'll spend one day there and go on to Paris because we're going to need at least a couple of days in Paris."

Even though Katie's plan sounded clear and easy, Christy had a feeling it wouldn't go as smoothly as all that. She was just glad that they would see more of Germany, the home of her ancestors. She hoped their boat tour would be a new highlight of the trip.

Once they arrived in Cologne, at Katie's insistence, they walked around the *Dom* before finding a place to stay. The Dom was a twin-towered cathedral close to the rail station. It dominated the area because it was so large. According to Katie, the cathedral was one of the largest Gothic structures in the world, with the foundation built in 1248.

"I'm so bummed we can't go inside," Katie said as they stared up at the massive, twin gray spires that pierced the evening sky. "They closed a half hour ago. I told you, didn't I, that this cathedral has relics of the wise men who brought their gifts to baby Jesus? The tour book didn't say what the relics were specifically. I wanted to see the display."

"We could come back tomorrow," Todd suggested.

"No, let's keep going. Youth hostel first, some food, and then in the morning we'll go see Christy's castles."

It didn't settle well with Christy that the reason they were spending an entire day floating down the Rhine River was because she wanted to see more castles. She would have felt better if Todd and Katie were as interested in this tour as she was.

The next day, an hour into the cruise, Christy could tell that Todd and Katie were being nice friends and acting as if this slow boat was fun. But she knew they were miserable, and that made it hard for her to enjoy the leisurely journey.

The first time they went past a castle high on the hillside, tucked behind ancient trees and overlooking the wide Rhine River, Christy could get Todd and Katie to look up and do a little imagining with her.

They answered with clever words when Christy said, "Who do you think lived there? A handsome prince, maybe? Do you think he ever had to fight any battles to defend the castle and his princess?"

By the third castle, no one, not even Christy, wanted to play twenty questions about the imaginary past of the castle. *I think I've seen too much. I feel numb. I mean, this is beautiful and romantic and wonderful, but all I want to do is find a patch of sunshine and curl up like a cat and sleep.*

The boat ride was restful, and more than any of them, Christy felt ready to rest. She knew she hadn't recovered from the exhaustion of her recent difficult school term. Traveling was exciting and fun, but it was anything but restful.

The clouds played hide-and-seek with the sun for the next few hours. While the weather never turned cold, Christy did end up pulling a pair of jeans out of her backpack, going to the rest room, and changing from her shorts.

The stretch from *Koblenz* to *Bingen* was spectacular. A hilltop castle gazed down on them every time they looked up. Christy had a feeling that this part of their trip would be something she would remember years later, as if it had been a dream.

But she was ready for the cruise to be over when they arrived in *Mainz* a little after one in the afternoon. Getting on a modern train and figuring out a way to sleep for the rest of the afternoon appealed to her, as if the gentle Rhine, with its fairy-tale guardian castles, had lulled her into a dreamland. She was eager to go there and allow her weary mind and body to rest deeply.

Todd, however, had different plans. "You guys, the Gutenberg Museum is here. Mind if we go there before heading to the train station?"

"What's at the Gutenberg Museum?" Katie asked.

"The first printed Bible. You've heard of Gutenberg, haven't you? He invented the modern printing press. And the first book he printed, of course, was the Bible. I really want to see it."

Off they went, with their bulky backpacks, to see the first printed Bible and a short movie on Gutenberg's life. Todd was really into the exhibit. Poor Christy couldn't help it; she dozed off when the lights went down for the movie.

They bought some cheese and bread at a corner market and walked to the train station, eating as they walked. Christy was happy to let Todd and Katie do all the discussing about which train to take and when. She couldn't care less where they ended up. The food hadn't helped make her headache go away, and now her throat hurt when she swallowed.

I wish I could go home to Escondido for one day and sleep in my old bed. My mom would bring me tea with honey for my throat. I would take a long bath before sleeping a full ten hours. Then I would wake up refreshed, clean, and energetic and instantly be transported back here. I wish I could do that. Then I'd be able to finish this jour-

ney and appreciate everything I'm seeing.

The train ride to Amsterdam was a blur to Christy. She carried her pack and changed trains when Todd told her to. When the conductor asked for passports and tickets, she automatically pulled her Eurorail pass from her travel pouch the way she had dozens of times before on this trip. The rest of the time, she snoozed.

When Christy finally began to come back around, she opened her eyes and peered out the window. The sun had set. The world they were rolling past was filled with shadows. Darkness covered the horizon.

"Where are we, you guys? Did we miss the stop for Amsterdam?"

She turned, expecting an answer from her travel companions. But they were gone.

Christy told herself not to panic. *Todd and Katie must have gone for something to eat and didn't want to wake me. We've done that before with each other; this isn't unusual.*

18 But something didn't feel right. They should have arrived in Amsterdam before dark. Christy vaguely remembered Todd waking her when they changed trains back in Cologne, around 5:00. He had said something about taking three hours to reach Amsterdam, that they would be there before dark, and he would call his friends when the train arrived to see about staying with them.

Christy looked up and down the long aisle for Todd and Katie. The train was slowing to a stop. All she could think to do was to grab her pack and be ready to exit if this was Amsterdam. She would figure out how to find Todd and Katie later. The worst thing would be to miss getting off at the right place the way Katie had almost done in Naples.

When Christy reached up for her pack on the overhead shelf, she noticed Todd and Katie's packs were still there. They wouldn't have left without their packs. They wouldn't have left without her. But where were they? And more important, what station was the train stopping at?

Christy tried to read the station's sign as they rolled in.

The sign said *Nancy*. Christy was stunned. *How did we end up in France?*

Just then Katie came bounding up and said, "Hey, Sleeping Beauty. You decided to wake and face the real world, huh?"

What Christy was experiencing at that moment felt like anything but the real world. "Katie, what are we doing in France?"

Todd was right behind Katie. Following him was a guy wearing a baseball cap and toting a backpack. "Christy, this is Seth. What was your last name?"

"Edwards," Seth said. He looked a little older than Todd and just as scruffy, evidence that he had been traveling for a while.

"Seth Edwards," Todd repeated. "This is Christy."

Then, to Christy's surprise, Todd added with a gentle smile, "Christy Miller, my girlfriend." Todd never had described her that way. If she hadn't still been confused and shocked about being in France instead of Holland, she might have taken Todd's words deeper into her heart.

"We met Seth in the dining car, and he has lots of great tips on what to see and do in Paris," Katie said.

"Would someone mind telling me what's happening?" Christy asked as the three of them sat down. "I thought we were going to Amsterdam."

"We changed plans," Katie said brightly. "We told you on the train from Mainz to Cologne, and you said that was fine; whatever we wanted."

"I don't remember," Christy said.

Seth smiled at her. He had nice eyes. They were deep blue and matched the dark blue denim shirt he wore over a stained white T-shirt. "It catches up with you, doesn't it?"

"What catches up?"

"Travel fatigue. All the new sights and sounds and food.

From what Todd and Katie told me, you guys have been going at it pretty hard and fast. I'm on a much slower pace, but it still hits me about every two weeks, and I have to stay somewhere for a few more days before I can go on."

"Seth has already been to Paris," Katie said. "He had way more information than our tour book. He's going back to meet up with some friends. He just spent the last two weeks in Venice. Can you imagine spending two weeks in one place?"

Right now that luxury sounded very nice to Christy. "Did these guys tell you that all we saw was the inside of the Venice train station for a few hours?"

"You have to go back," Seth said. "You can't come all this way and not see Venice, even if it's only for a day. However, fourteen days is better than one."

"Did you happen to notice a jewelry store called Santini?" Katie asked. "Wasn't that Marcos's last name? I have it written down somewhere. "

"Their name is Savini," Todd corrected her.

"And if you ever want a good place to stay on Capri," Katie told Seth, "go to the Villa Paradiso and tell them Carlos Savini sent you." She proceeded to tell Seth all about their free, deluxe hotel room in Capri.

Seth had a story about a Swiss family he had met on the train a few months earlier and how they had invited him to stay with them. After opening his pack and pulling out a small journal with several postcards sticking out, he asked if he could write their name in Christy's tour book.

"I'm serious," Seth said, pulling off the pen's cap with his teeth. "They would love to have you guys stay with them. They live in a chalet in this small Swiss alpine village called Adelboden." Seth flipped though his journal. "I'll write it all down here. You take the train from Bern to Thun to Spiez and then to Frutigen. You have to take a bus to Adelboden. The scenery is incredible."

"How long did you stay there?" Katie asked.

"Five days, I think. I slept in the hayloft, and during the day I helped out on their small farm. It was a kick. You guys would love it. I'm serious. Just tell them Seth Edwards sent you."

For the next two hours into Paris, they swapped travel stories with Seth. Christy felt a little more awake and coherent by the time they arrived, even though she was sure it was well after midnight.

Seth knew of a reasonable hotel near the train station. The four of them crashed for the night and met up the next morning at eight after taking showers.

"I need to get going," Seth said. "Sure was great meeting all of you. I hope the rest of your trip goes well."

"Yours too," Katie said. "Thanks for all the tips about what to see."

"I stuck a paper in your tour book with a list of those restaurants I was telling you about in Venice, in case you guys make it there."

"We will," Katie said. "If I have anything to say about it, we definitely will."

After saying good-bye to Seth, Todd suggested they eat something and head for the Eiffel Tower while it was still cool. He had heard someone on the train last night say that a heat wave was expected for the next few days in Paris, which was unusual so early in the summer. They could tour the air-conditioned Louvre during the hottest part of the day.

Christy hadn't slept as deeply as she needed to shake the fuzzy-headed feeling that had come over her. Their breakfast pastry and strong coffee didn't snap her out of her fog, either. She took pictures of the Eiffel Tower and agreed with Katie that it cost too much to tour the top. Todd coaxed them onto the *metro*, which was a modern subway system under the city, and directed them where to get off for Notre Dame.

As they approached the huge, light gray, west-facing front of the cathedral, Christy asked Katie if she could see the tour book. She wanted to find out how old this church was and how it compared to the cathedral in Cologne. They resembled each other some, but instead of twin spires in the front, Notre Dame had two identical towers that looked like open bell towers.

Katie handed her the book. When Christy opened it, three postcards fell out onto the pavement. The first card was of the Austrian Alps. Another one was of the Seine River in Paris. And the third was a picture of a gondola docked against a red-and-white-striped pole. The gondolier stood on the dock, complete with a wide-brimmed straw hat with a blue ribbon hanging down the back. He leaned casually against the pole and indicated with his hand that his gondola was available for the next rider.

These must be Seth's postcards. Christy turned over the one of the gondola from Venice. It was addressed to a Franklin Madison in Glenbrooke, Oregon. None of the postcards had a stamp on it. Christy tucked them into the back of the tour book and decided she would be nice and mail the postcards for Seth. They must have ended up in her book when he was sticking the list of restaurants in it.

Turning to the section on Paris, Christy skimmed the information on Notre Dame. "Can you believe this church was built almost a hundred years before the one we saw in Cologne? It says here that people have worshiped on this spot for nearly two thousand years."

She was struck with awe, the way she had been in Norway when they saw the simple, eight-hundred-year-old church and the sharp contrast it provided to Saint Peter's Basilica in Rome. "People want to meet God, don't they?" Christy said as they stood gazing up at Notre Dame. "Deep within the human heart is the desire to meet God. I never realized that as clearly as I have while we've been traveling."

"Look at that window," Katie said. "What does it say about the window?"

Christy read aloud, " 'The great rose window contains its original medieval glass. It was the largest such window of its time, and the design is so accomplished that it shows no sign of distortion after seven hundred years.' "

"Now, that's craftsmanship for you," Todd said. "Has anyone else noticed how art used to be used to demonstrate biblical truths? Man, have we come a long way from that being art's purpose!"

The three friends took more than two hours to tour the inside of the cathedral. It was dark and solemn. They climbed the winding stairs to the top, and Katie said, "Don't you feel as if you're caught inside a snail's shell when we go up these kinds of stairs?"

"It makes me dizzy," Christy said.

"I just think about what muscular legs those monks must have hid under their robes after climbing these stairs a couple of times a day to ring the bells," Todd answered.

At the top, they noticed how hot the day had become. The view of Paris looked hazy in the rising heat. From where they stood, Christy thought the Seine River looked appealing. Any kind of water at this point, either on her or in her, would feel refreshing.

It didn't take much for Todd to persuade them to descend the stairs and find something to eat before going on to the Louvre. To save money, they bought their food from a vendor's cart. Christy's hot dog–like sausage was too spicy for her, and she could only eat half of it. The Coke was as hot as the crate it was pulled from. She downed the hot, fizzy beverage but felt only thirstier.

At least inside the Louvre was cool. Christy felt spacey in the vast palace-turned-museum. She wished they had someone like Marcos to let them in a back door and lead them right to the rooms with the exhibits of greatest interest. As it was, they paid for their admission using their International Student ID cards to receive a discount. They entered through a modern, intricately designed glass pyramid, and from then on, Christy felt disoriented.

Katie was on a mission to find the *Mona Lisa*. Her determination to locate that famous little lady was much stronger than the interest she had expressed in finding the *Little Mermaid*. Once they entered the room where the small oil painting hung on the wall, Katie edged her way to the front of the crowd to have a close look. Christy and Todd stood at the fringes and peeked over people's shoulders.

"It's a lot smaller than I thought it would be," Todd said.

Christy smiled. "Funny how that goes, isn't it?"

Katie, still in her spunky mood, turned around at the front of the crowd of *Mona Lisa* viewers and shot a picture of Todd and Christy.

"That guard is going to take your camera away," Christy said as Katie came toward them.

"Why? It says not to take flash photographs of the *Mona Lisa*. It doesn't say anything about taking pictures of people looking at the *Mona Lisa*."

"Where to next?" Todd asked.

"Home," Christy said wearily.

"You want to go back to the hotel?" Todd asked.

"No, I think I want to go back to Escondido. I officially have hit overload. I don't think I can take in another wonder of the world. My brain can't hold it."

"How about if we get out of town," Todd suggested. "We could take a train or bus out to Versailles. It's only about a half hour away."

Christy didn't much care at this point. Sitting down for a half hour was what appealed to her the most. They briefly toured the Egyptian exhibit and several other rooms in the Louvre before Todd led the way back outside into the stifling afternoon heat.

After asking four people, Todd finally decided he knew where they should go to catch a bus to Versailles. They waited twenty minutes in the heat, rode forty minutes in air-conditioned comfort, and bought large bottles of water from a vendor immediately on arriving.

Standing back and surveying the massive, yellowish-cream-colored palace, Christy felt as if what she stared at couldn't be real. It was so perfectly balanced. Every window, column, and roof line seemed to be matched perfectly with the rest of the huge structure. Instead of being one long building with a flat front, the palace was constructed with stairstep-like indentations of buildings that led in tandem to the center.

Katie, who had been reading about this seventeenth-century home of the French monarchy, said, "Just look at that place. Can you image all those peasants starving to death and Marie Antoinette sitting somewhere inside that palace?"

Christy didn't know what Katie was getting at. Katie apparently read Christy's confused expression and said, "You remember, they came to her and said the starving citizens of France had no bread; so Marie Antoinette said, 'Let them eat cake.'"

For perhaps the first time on this trip, Christy wasn't intrigued by the history lesson. She liked the idea of cake, though. Or pastry. Or even a humble cookie. The half of a hot dog she had eaten for lunch wasn't doing her stomach any favors.

Blessedly, it felt cooler inside the gigantic palace. The water Christy had gulped also helped her to cool off. She found herself settling into a strange, robotic mode. Her feet moved her from room to room. Her eyes took in the sights. Each bedroom seemed more magnificent than the last. The ballroom made her think of something out of a Cinderella movie. She saw it all and took it in, but as she had told Todd earlier, she was on overload.

"Are you okay?" he asked on the bus ride back to Paris.

"I don't know," she said. "How can you take it all in? Doesn't everything you see make you feel something? And don't you reach the point where you don't have any feelings left to invest?"

Todd didn't answer right away. He seemed to be thinking about her questions. His answer came in the form of a few more questions for Christy. "Do you think that's why the work at the orphanage has been so draining this year? Do you think you take it all in and feel something deep every day about those kids? I wonder if that's what's been happening. Then you reach the point where you can't invest any more emotionally because you've spent so much of yourself."

"Todd," Christy said, leaning her weary head against his shoulder, "I think you have just figured out the answer to what has plagued me for months."

"I know you've been struggling with it because of your emails."

"The need is so great . . ." she said.

Todd turned his chin and gently kissed the top of her head. "But, Christy, the need is not the call. You are uniquely gifted by God. The key is finding out what it is you are uniquely gifted to do, and that's what you pour out of yourself. If you're operating within your gifts, you will feel energized, not emptied."

Christy pulled up her head and looked at Todd. "Are you saying I'm not gifted to work with children?" That possibility felt like a blow. For several years she had thought that was what she was supposed to do. It had started when Katie talked her into helping in the nursery class at church. Christy liked helping out. Ever since then, she had been making decisions about what to do with her life based on what she thought was a talent of working with children.

"I don't know exactly what God has gifted you to do or called you to do. That's something between Him and you. Ask Him. He'll tell you."

Christy leaned her head back on Todd's shoulder. Until this moment, she had thought her future was nicely structured. Her plans had been set long ago. She would earn a degree in early childhood education. Then she might be a preschool teacher, which was a plan she liked because she could do that no matter where she lived or if she was single or married or had children of her own.

"All I know," Todd said, leaning his chin against her head, "is that the future is wide open to you, Christina Juliet Miller. You are gifted by God, and He has called you to serve Him in a unique way. A verse in Romans says that the gifts and the calling of God are irrevocable. No one can ever take away from you who you are. You are free to dream as big a dream as you dare to dream."

If Christy thought her mind and emotions were on overload before, all circuits shut down now. Looking up into Todd's eyes, she knew he had just given her an important truth. With that truth came the freedom to become a person she had never dreamed of becoming before.

"Hold these tears for me," she whispered. Todd put his arm around her, and Christy leaned against his chest, letting the tears flow directly over his heart.

19 The next morning, Christy was hot when she woke in her room at the Paris hotel. She kicked off the sheet and lay in bed, wishing with all her heart that she could find a way to express to Todd how much she appreciated the gift of his words. Shortly after arriving in Basel and beginning her work at the orphanage, she had found herself fighting against a deep sorrow and weariness whenever she was around the children. What kept her there all those months was the knowledge that they needed her.

Deep inside, Christy had felt emptied. At first she thought something was wrong with her, because when she looked at the workers around her, they all seemed to get filled up and invigorated working with the children.

"What time is it?" Katie mumbled, kicking off her bed sheets, as well.

"It's only 7:00. We were going to try to sleep in today, but I can't. It's too hot."

"Let's wake up Todd and tell him we're ready for breakfast. Are you sure that window is open as far as it will go?"

"Yes. We didn't have much of a breeze last night. It's not that it's so hot; it's just that there's no air. If we had a fan it would be much better."

"I doubt they have any extra fans," Katie said. "This is a budget hotel, you know. Seth told us it was the best he knew of this close to town."

"That reminds me," Christy said. "I ended up with some of Seth's postcards. They need stamps so I was going to mail them for him today and write home to my family, too. Have you sent any postcards yet?"

"Are you kidding? When did we have time to buy postcards? Or souvenirs, for that matter. Do you realize the only thing I've bought so far is food? At least you were smart and bought that diary in Italy. I wish I had gotten one."

"We sure haven't done any shopping, have we?" Christy said.

"I wish now I had bought that sweater we saw in the shop window in Oslo. Do you remember? It was a blue-and-white hand-knit ski sweater. I think we figured out it cost about eighty-five dollars."

Christy could barely even think about a ski sweater in their present sweltering condition. "Do you have that much to spend on souvenirs? I'm impressed."

"Not really, but I could have bought it and then eaten bread and water the rest of the trip."

"I feel like all we've been eating lately has been bread and water," Christy said. "I don't even want pastry this morning, if you can believe that."

"No, I don't believe you for one second."

"I want some protein. Doesn't chicken sound good right now? Or a steak?"

"I'd settle for a Big Mac and French fries," Katie said.

"Oh, don't do that to me! Do you know how long it's been since I've had American French fries?" Christy sat up and reached for the clothes she had left hanging over the end of her bed. "Come on, let's get dressed and go find some French fries. We are in France, after all. If Todd wants to sleep, we'll let him sleep. I want to eat!"

"I'm with you."

Christy and Katie had just pulled on their shorts when a knock sounded on the door. "Just a minute," Christy called out. She shook out her last slightly clean T-shirt and pulled it over her head. "Are you decent?" she asked Katie.

"I'm never just decent. I'm always extra nice."

Christy gave her a pained expression and opened the door. Todd stood there, dressed and ready to go. He grinned when he saw Christy. "You guys couldn't sleep in, either, I take it."

"We've talked ourselves into a food frenzy, Todd." Katie quickly brushed her hair. "Join us, if you dare. But I warn you, it might not be a pretty sight. Our quest for French fries is not for the fainthearted."

"I think I'm up to the challenge. Although I've never heard of anyone actually buying French fries in France. When I was in Spain, the word was that the best French fries on the continent were in Brussels."

"How far away is that?" Katie asked.

"Three hours, I'd guess," Todd said. "It's between here and Amsterdam."

"Then, let's go," Katie said. "I'm ready to blow this town, aren't you? It's too hot. And what's left for us to see? We managed to fit in all the main sights yesterday."

"What about going to Spain?" Christy asked. "I mean, aren't we halfway there?"

"Not exactly," Todd said. "It's almost twelve hours from here to Barcelona and then seven hours from Barcelona to Madrid."

"I forgot that Paris was so far north," Christy said. "But don't you want to see your old friends?"

Todd thought a moment and then shrugged. "A lot of them have taken other posts around Europe or have gone back to the States. I can't think of anyone I was close to who's still there."

"So Brussels it is!" Katie announced, throwing clothes into her bag.

"I'll go pack." Todd headed back to his room.

Christy had noticed when she opened the door that his forehead was peeling slightly where her hot tea had burned him. At least it wasn't red anymore and looked as if it was healing.

"Do you think they have a place where we could do some laundry in Brussels?" Katie asked. "I'm on my last clean everything today."

"Me too," Christy said. "It's been a week since I washed my stuff in Oslo."

Katie stopped her frantic packing. "That means we have less than a week left."

Christy looked at the round clock on the wall. "It's 8:00. Exactly one week from right now I'll start summer term. And now I don't know if I even want to finish those classes."

"Why not?" Katie asked.

Christy tried to explain how Todd's words on the bus had given her freedom. She felt as if God had released her from the work at the orphanage and from the drive to earn a degree in early-childhood education.

Katie stared at Christy. Perspiration from their stuffy room glistened on Katie's forehead. "What are you going to do now?"

"I have no idea," Christy said with a smile.

"And that doesn't spook you just a little?"

"I think I was a lot more frightened when I was working so hard for a degree that didn't make me feel excited about the future."

"This is big-time, Christy. I mean, you were supposed to enter Rancho Corona in September with all the credits you were going to transfer from this program in Basel. You were on a fast track to graduate."

"I know."

"If you change majors now, aren't you a little freaked out about losing all those credits? It could take you a whole lot longer to finish."

"I know."

"Don't you get it?" Katie stood with both her hands on her hips. The perspiration was now streaming down her face. "That means even longer before you and Todd can get married."

Christy gave Katie a timid shrug. The same thought had crossed Christy's mind. But she was too euphoric about the thought that she could dream new, big, freer dreams to let that complication steal her sunshine.

"Let's head out of here," Katie said. "I don't want to get any more heated up in this room. I feel like I'm going to melt."

Once they walked out of the old building, the air movement allowed them to breathe again. It was warm, but nothing like it had been in their closed-off room. They walked to the nearby train station and bought rolls and cheese and funny-shaped cartons of yogurt to eat on the train.

The three hours to Brussels, Katie was quiet. Christy knew Katie wanted to talk more about Christy's life-changing decision to switch majors. But Katie seemed to be waiting until Todd wasn't around before she continued to give Christy the rest of her mind on the topic.

Katie got her chance about a half hour before they arrived in Brussels. Todd left them alone while he went to stretch his legs, and Katie jumped right in. "So do you think you would get married before you finish college?"

"Katie, I can't believe you're asking me that."

"I know you've thought about it. I'm just trying to get you

to answer your own question."

"I don't know, Katie. All I can do is take one step at a time, as God makes that step clear. Right now all I know for sure is that I have the freedom to change my major. I don't know what I'm going to change it to. I don't know if I'm going to stay in Basel for the summer session. And I really don't know what the next step is in my relationship with Todd."

"And that doesn't frighten you?"

Christy thought a moment before shaking her head. "No, it feels right. More right than anything has felt in a long time." She remembered how distinctly changed she had felt the night she and Todd had stood under the amber streetlight on the uneven cobblestone street in Capri. All doubts had flown from her heart. She knew then that she had passed through some invisible tunnel and was no longer a teenager. She was a woman. That same sense came on her now. Christy wondered if this was what a person was supposed to feel like after yielding every area of life to the Lord and waiting for Him to move.

She tried to explain it to Katie as an awareness of the Holy Spirit's presence comforting her. Katie said she thought she understood. Todd returned then and all talk of future plans ceased.

Christy didn't mind that she and Katie were done talking about that subject for the time being. However, Christy knew she needed to have an openhearted discussion with Todd. She had some decisions to make in the next few days, and she wanted Todd's input. More important, she wanted to hear what Todd's plans were for the future.

Their train arrived in Brussels, Belgium, at exactly noon. The first thing they did was search for a French fry cart. Todd said his friends from Spain had come back with stories of such carts on Belgium streets, just like Italy had gelato carts and New York had hot dog carts.

They didn't have to go far from the station before they spotted their first *frites* cart. As they stood and watched, large wedges of already fried potatoes were fried a second time until they were crackling hot. The vendor offered them several sauces to dip the frites in. One looked like mayonnaise. Christy passed on the sauce and tried her frites *au naturel*.

"Hot!" she said after taking the first bite.

Todd tried one of the darker-tinted sauces. "Not barbecue sauce. Not ketchup. I don't know. Shrimp cocktail, maybe."

"This is so bizarre," Katie said, trying the mayonnaise-looking dip. "I like it, so maybe I don't want to know what I'm dipping it in."

"In Switzerland the kids at the orphanage like their popcorn with sugar on it instead of salt and butter," Christy said. She realized that was the first time she had brought up anything about the orphanage this trip without feeling a tightening knot in her stomach. She was free. Really free.

Christy enjoyed her frites immensely. She surprised Todd and Katie by ordering a second helping when they were ready to walk away.

"We've had our French fries," Katie said. "What do you guys think? Do you want to stick around here awhile or jump on a train and head for Amsterdam?"

"We just got here," Christy said.

"I checked the train schedule," Todd said. "It's about three hours from here to Amsterdam. A lot of trains run during the day. We could stay here for the afternoon and then go on to Amsterdam for the night. If we decide to do that, I should call my friends to see if we can stay with them."

The next goal was to return to the train station, find a phone, check train schedules, and settle their plans for the day. A short time later Todd exited the phone booth with a piece of paper in his hand.

"They're expecting us at 6:30 tonight. Mike said he would

pick us up at the station and take us to The Rock for their 7:00 meeting. I'm going to help out with music tonight."

"Wait a second," Katie said. "What did I miss here? What is The Rock? What music are you talking about?"

Todd explained that a couple he worked with in Spain now ran a youth hostel in Amsterdam called The Rock. Every night they offered a worship service from seven to eight. Christy could tell Todd was excited about seeing his friends and probably even more excited to have a guitar in his hands again.

The heat wave wasn't as overwhelming in Brussels, but the afternoon sun was strong enough as they walked around with their heavy packs, killing time. Christy and Katie left their packs with Todd outside a small shop so they could go in and hunt for Belgian chocolate and some souvenirs. Christy bought three beautiful, delicate lace doilies that the clerk said were handmade. Katie said she wasn't exactly a doily kind of person, but the clerk talked her into buying four lace bookmarks.

"I thought they would be good gifts for people when I get home," Katie said. "Especially because they don't weigh anything." She strapped on her pack and groaned. "Is it my imagination or do dirty clothes weigh more?"

They found a park a few blocks away and stretched out in the shade.

"Oh, I was going to buy postcards," Christy said. "And stamps."

"I'll stay here with your packs if you and Katie want to go back into town," Todd said.

"You know, this seems crazy," Christy said. "We're all kind of tired and not energetic enough to see anything around here. We don't need to wait until the late afternoon train to Amsterdam. We could go now and spend our time buying postcards and stamps in Amsterdam as easily as here."

"I agree," Katie said. "Besides, I'm hungry for some more frites. Let's go."

They stopped at the same cart where they had bought the fries before and then ate them as they walked to the station. Their timing was perfect because the next train to Amsterdam was just pulling up. Once they were settled in their seats, Katie started to laugh.

"What?" Christy asked.

"Are we getting apathetic or what? We just spent two hours in an entire country. That was Belgium. Buh-bye, Belgium," Katie said, waving like a beauty queen as the train pulled out.

"It is pretty pathetic," Christy said, "when the only souvenirs we've bought this whole trip are from a country we only stopped in so we could eat their French fries."

All three of them laughed. The train pulled out of the station, and Todd challenged Christy to a game of chess. Katie announced she was going to find something to drink. "You guys want anything?"

"No, thanks." Christy pulled out a brush from her pack. While Todd set up the pieces, she worked on her hair. Most of the trip she had worn it in a loose braid. This morning, because of the heat, she had twisted it up on the back of her head, but it had been falling out slowly over the last few hours. Now she let down her hair and brushed out the tangles.

"I like your hair long," Todd said in one of his famous short statements.

Christy felt herself blush. Todd rarely made any comments about her appearance. Years ago he had said he liked her hair long after she had chopped it off. She had been growing it out since then, partly because she knew that's how Todd liked it, but mostly because she liked doing a lot of different things with it.

Todd made the first move on the chessboard. Christy playfully turned her back to Todd and then tilted her head all the way back. The ends of her straight hair almost reached to her waist.

"There," she said, her chin tipped toward the ceiling. "Is that long enough?"

She turned to Todd. He had a smile on his face. It was the same happy, contented smile she had seen when he kissed her in Norway on their way to see the *Kon-Tiki*.

She made her move on the chessboard, then twisted her hair and was about to fasten it with a clip, when Todd took his move and then said, "No, braid it. I want to see how you do it."

Christy divided her hair into three sections. "Like this," she said, quickly passing the sections between each other and making a braid in a few seconds.

"Wait, that was too fast. Do it again."

"Why? Do you want to learn how to braid or something?"

"Sure," Todd said as if her words were the only invitation he needed. Leaning forward and taking the strands from her, he said, "Okay, which side do you start with?"

"Either one. Doesn't matter." She sat patiently while Todd asked directions and slowly braided her hair. The first braid was too loose. On his second try, he pulled too hard, and Christy let out a yelp.

"This better?" Todd asked as he more gently tugged and twisted her hair.

"That's okay. It doesn't have to be really tight. Just tighter than the first time."

"There," Todd announced. "How's that?"

Christy took the braid from him and felt up and down with her fingers. "Not bad."

"Not bad?" Todd said. "I'd say it's better than not bad. I'd say it's pretty good."

"Okay," Christy said, turning and smiling at him. "It's pretty good."

Todd smiled back. "It's my move, right?"

"Very sneaky! You know it's my turn." Christy stared at the pieces on the chessboard for a long while. She wasn't thinking about chess, though. She was thinking about the way Todd had braided her hair and the way she knew he was staring at her now.

That had to be one of the most tender, romantic gestures you've ever made toward me, Todd Spencer. You're in love with me, aren't you?

She could tell he was leaning closer. Christy pretended to concentrate on the game board, but she couldn't because she could feel Todd's warm breath on her neck. All she had to do was turn her head slightly and she would feel what she wanted to—Todd's lips brushing her cheek.

"You're beautiful," he whispered after his lips touched her cheek. "In every way, Kilikina. You're beautiful." Then his lips meet hers in a warm, tender kiss.

20 Never before had Christy felt so overwhelmed emotionally, spiritually, and physically. The intensity startled her and caused her to pull away. With her heart pounding, she looked at Todd, who was now a foot away instead of an inch away. His expression was the most tender, gentle, wholehearted look of love she had ever seen.

"Todd," Christy said with a thin voice. "I . . . I . . ."

"I know." Todd rubbed the back of his neck with his hand. "I didn't mean to . . ."

"I know," Christy said.

"But I meant what I said."

Christy smiled. "Thank you."

Todd rose and moved to the seat across from Christy. He leaned forward and reached for her hand, holding loosely on to only her first three fingers. The words didn't seem to be coming to him.

Christy had words she wanted to give Todd. Her mind was clear, and her heart was full. "Todd," she said, leaning forward and speaking softly, "I thought about something while you were on your polar bear journey. I decided I like kissing you just a little too much."

Todd's surprised expression made her quickly add, "What

I mean is that we've never talked about standards or limits or guidelines or anything."

Todd nodded.

"Well, this may sound idealistic, but I thought about all this a lot, and I came up with some ideas."

"Go on."

Christy tried her best to explain to Todd her idea of saving her kisses and spending them sparingly. She told him about her imaginary piggy bank filling up with expressions of affection. "So you see, I wanted to spend one of my really big kisses on you just a minute ago, but I pulled back so I could save that one in my piggy bank. Then when . . ." Christy didn't want to say, "when we get married." Instead, she paused. Feeling her cheeks reddening, she finished the thought with, ". . . then it will be saved until the time is right, and I'll be able to freely spend everything."

Todd looked at Christy with what appeared to be deep admiration. He seemed to be moved by what she had said. But a minute passed before he finally spoke. "Thank you."

"For what?"

"For caring. For thinking through that part of our relationship. I'd thought about it a long time ago and decided I was only going to kiss you on special occasions. One of my guidelines was to keep our kisses short and in public so we would have nothing to hide."

Christy hadn't realized Todd had thought through this part of their relationship. But as she contemplated it, she saw that during the past five years his expressions of affection had fallen into those guidelines.

"Things are changing for us, and I'm glad they are." He gave her fingers a squeeze. "We're getting closer to each other. I think that means we're going to have a lot more decisions to make, separately and together. You've made a really wise decision ahead of me in this area. But your choice helps me, and I appreciate that. I'll be saving kisses in my bank, as well."

Christy glanced over Todd's head and saw Katie was returning.

Todd read her expression and said, "We can talk about this some more later."

Christy gave Todd a pesky little grin. In imitation of the teenager Todd used to be, with a chin-up nod, Christy pulled her hand from his and said, "Later."

Whether Todd caught the connection, Christy didn't know. Katie plopped down next to Christy, examined the chessboard, and said, "Who's winning?"

Christy glanced at Todd. He grinned back. In unison they said, "We both are."

"Whoa!" Katie said. "Did you two practice that while I was gone?"

What we almost practiced while you were gone was our kissing technique! If you hadn't gotten me thinking about setting my own limits, Katie, I think that's exactly what you would have found us doing.

"Christy was teaching me how to come out ahead," Todd said, his eyes fixed on the chessboard.

"Christy was?"

"Yep," Todd said. "And it's my turn, right?"

"Not exactly, pal," Christy teased. "It's my turn, remember?"

"This I have to see," Katie said.

All the way to Amsterdam they played a round of "group" chess in which Katie advised each of them on their moves. Once they arrived in Amsterdam, Christy grabbed her pack, and Seth's postcards spilled out on the floor. Katie accidentally stepped on one of the cards, and Christy picked them up, trying to brush off the dirt.

"I have to mail these before I lose them," she said, immediately realizing how crazy that sounded. These weren't even her cards. Yet someone on the other side of the globe in some place called Glenbrooke, Oregon, needed to receive those postcards from Seth. She wondered if she was taking this responsibility too seriously.

The three of them filed their way through the crowded train station, and Christy thought about how she took most of her responsibilities and commitments seriously. In some instances, such as in her relationship with Todd, that was a very good thing. But did she have to be so determined and responsible with everything—like postcards?

Their time to explore Amsterdam was shorter than they thought it would be. Todd's friend from Spain, Mike, showed up at 6:30 and drove them in his small car across town to the youth hostel he and his wife ran. At first Christy thought she might have met Mike and Megan during the short week she was in Spain more than a year ago. But they had come to Amsterdam and had been running the ministry at The Rock for almost two years now.

Christy liked Megan at once and asked Megan how she could help her get ready for the evening's event. Slim, energetic, blond Megan told Christy and Katie to relax. Every night they held a casual worship and praise service. She said sometimes half a dozen people came, sometimes it was just the two of them.

Mike handed Todd his guitar. Christy could hear him plucking out some of his old favorites, like one he wrote, "The Dust of His Feet." Katie and Christy settled themselves on a beat-up old couch toward the front of the small meeting room. Todd went on to play a song Doug had written, and Katie started to sing. Christy joined her, and a few people, hearing the music, shuffled into the meeting room.

Todd closed his eyes, and tilting his head toward the heavens, he sang out the lyrics, "Sing to the One who rides across the ancient heavens, His mighty voice thundering from the sky. For God is awesome in His sanctuary.' "

This is what Todd is gifted to do, Christy thought. *He told me God has uniquely gifted each of us. I believe that. And I believe Todd is gifted to lead people in worship. He has a shepherd's heart.*

The hour-long service turned into two hours. At first, only three students who were staying at the hostel entered. More began to come. Christy counted fifteen and then twenty. The worship time was awesome. About ten people stayed around to talk to Mike. Christy, Katie, and Todd had a discussion with a guy from Argentina. At nearly 11:00, Christy noticed that Mike was praying with two of the guys he had been talking with.

After everyone else left, Christy, Todd, and Katie gathered in the small kitchen with Mike and Megan. Megan had just found out that they hadn't eaten since their frites in Belgium that afternoon and was making grilled cheese sandwiches for them.

"And I'm even using white bread," Megan said with a smile. "This is my one comfort food around here. It's not exactly Velveeta and Wonder Bread like my mom used to make, but it's as close to Americana as you'll find in this part of the city."

"God really did something tonight," Mike said. "Did you see me praying with those two guys? They're from Scotland, and both of them said they wanted to give their lives to the Lord. It was incredible. God really used you, Todd."

"It wasn't me," Todd said. "It was God's timing."

"Yes, it was God's timing that you were here to play and lead worship on a night when those two guys happened to stay here. But I also think God used you, Todd, because you were available and open to Him."

Christy devoured two of Megan's sandwiches and thought about how she wanted her life to be like that—open and available to the Lord so He could use the gifts He had given her to further His kingdom.

Now, if only I could figure out exactly what those gifts are.

The next morning, in the same close kitchen, Christy and Todd sat eating bowls of oatmeal and talking with Megan and Mike. Katie was still asleep. As Christy listened, Mike asked Todd questions she had wanted to ask Todd for a long time.

"What are your plans for the future?" Mike asked.

"I'm working the rest of the summer at home to save some money. In September I'll start at Rancho Corona. I have about a year left. Maybe less."

"And then what?" Megan asked.

Todd was looking down into his oatmeal. He turned his head slightly and gave Christy a sideways glance. "Not sure yet," he said.

"Have you thought about going into missions work full time?" Mike asked. "You know, raise support and make the long-term commitment?"

"I've thought about it."

"What about coming back to Europe?"

"It's a possibility," Todd said.

"You probably have figured out what I'm getting at," Mike said. "We would love to have you here. We need help running The Rock. You are a perfect fit. Meg and I got excited last night talking about what could happen if you came on staff with us."

Todd quietly ate the last of his oatmeal without responding.

"Think about it," Mike said, pulling back. "Pray about it."

Todd nodded.

"So," Megan said, obviously trying to take the attention off Todd, "tell us about you, Christy. You said last night you're going to school in Basel. What are your plans after that?"

"Well, I'm not real sure. I've been doing some soul-searching on this trip, and I just realized a couple of days ago, as Todd and I were talking, that I'm headed in a direction I don't want to go."

"Do you mean with the orphanage and all that?" Megan asked. "You were saying last night that it really took a lot out of you to be with the kids."

Christy nodded. "I'm discovering that I don't have the gifts needed for a long-term commitment like that. I need to figure out where I'm gifted and see what I should be doing instead."

"Christy is exceptionally gifted," Todd said.

"Really?" Mike looked interested. "Do you sing, Christy?"

"No, not really."

"Do you like to teach?"

"Sort of. Little kids."

"What about counseling?" Megan asked.

Christy shook her head. She was beginning to realize that the quest to find out what she was gifted at might be a rather long journey. Nothing popped right out as her specialty. It made her feel insecure.

"Christy has a rare, pure, golden heart," Todd said. He looked at her with an open, caring expression. "She gives unconditionally and is a constant source of encouragement. She's gracious and patient and organized. She looks for the best in people and in every situation. She's willing to go the extra mile, even when it's inconvenient for her. She's flexible to change, generous, and wise beyond her years. God is going to use Christy's life in a powerful way."

When Todd finished, none of them spoke for a moment. Christy was stunned at his shower of praise.

Megan was the one who finally broke the silence. "Todd, why didn't you tell us? Christy's the one you were talking about before, isn't she?" Turning to Christy she said, "I should have figured it out. When Todd first came to Spain, we kept trying to fix him up with this woman on staff who was from Pennsylvania. Todd was nice to her. He was nice to everybody. But when he turned down all our dating tips, I asked him what the deal was. Do you remember that conversation, Todd?"

Christy glanced at Todd. He seemed to be trying to signal Megan that their conversation had been private.

Megan pulled back and said, "So he . . . I mean, you were . . ."

"I wasn't interested in Tina. That's what you're trying to say, isn't it?"

Megan grinned sheepishly at Christy. "We thought it was so cute. You know, we were Mike and Megan, and we figured Todd and Tina should be together. But Todd said he was interested in someone else, and he was waiting on God's timing. Now I guess we know who that someone was. It was you."

"It was," Todd said, giving Christy his full attention.

"Morning all," Katie said, making a grand entrance into the kitchen. "What did I miss?"

Only one of the most tender expressions of Todd's forever kind of friendship that he's given me since the day he first put this bracelet on my wrist. I'm his girlfriend, Katie! I really am. He loves me. He's loved me for a long time.

"Nothing," Christy said.

It wasn't that she didn't want Katie involved in this conversation, but the revelation had been perfect just the way it was. She didn't want anyone to repeat the details when it wouldn't have the same effect it already had had on her.

"I suppose you three are ready to see Amsterdam," Mike said, changing the subject for Christy. "Do you want to borrow a car, Todd?"

"No, we can use our train passes. You might want to give us a few tips. And if it's okay with Katie and Christy, I think we'll stay here tonight, too."

"Definitely," Katie said. "Only one small request. Do you have a washing machine, Megan?"

"Sure. It's small. Euro-size. You guys are welcome to use it. Or better yet, give me your clothes when you head out for the day, and I'll run them through for you."

"That would be great," Christy said. "Thank you."

Mike suggested several places to visit, including some art museums, the Hiding Place, where Corrie Ten Boom had lived, and the Anne Frank museum.

"Any preferences?" Todd asked.

"I'd love to see the Hiding Place," Christy said. "And at least one art museum. We sort of ran through the Louvre a little too fast. I'm feeling like we could use one more brush with culture before we go for our yodeling lessons in the Alps."

"Is that where you're going next?" Megan asked.

"Looks like it," Todd said. "But we're flexible."

Todd displayed his flexibility that day by doing whatever Christy wanted. Katie noticed it after they bought their admission for the Van Gogh museum. "I thought you said you weren't interested in any more art, either, Todd."

"Christy wanted to see this. I think it's a good idea."

In Christy's opinion, it was a good idea. Katie got more into the exhibit when she recognized some of Vincent Van Gogh's art and realized he was the tormented artist who cut off his ear.

For a long while, Christy stood in front of Van Gogh's famous painting of sunflowers. In some places, the paint was plopped onto the canvas so thick it stood up like freshly whipped cream stiffened into peaks. Only instead of white whipped cream, the colors were bright yellow. In other places, Christy could see the original canvas where no splotches of paint had landed. Such creative expression fascinated her.

When they went on to the Hiding Place, Katie complained again that she had voted for the Anne Frank museum, but Todd had decided on Christy's choice even though it was farther out of the city. To make matters worse, the Ten Boom clock shop, where the Hiding Place was located, was closed when they arrived so they weren't able to go on a tour.

The threesome returned to The Rock at 6:00, just in time for the homemade dinner Megan had promised them. Christy told Megan that was the best meat loaf, mashed potatoes, and green beans she had eaten since coming to Europe.

"Does it make you a little homesick?" Megan asked.

"A little."

"Are you going home with Todd and Katie, or are you going to stay and finish the course even though you're changing your major?" Megan asked.

"I haven't decided yet." As soon as Christy said it, Todd gave her a surprised look. "I need to decide pretty quickly. You know what? If I could borrow your phone tonight to make a collect call to my parents, that would really help me out."

"Oh, they're going to love that," Katie said. "If I called my parents collect from Holland, they would hang up on me."

"No, they wouldn't," Christy said.

"I'm not going to call them to find out," Katie said.

Christy phoned her parents after another incredible worship service. Even though it was late at night in Holland, it was still in the afternoon in California. Christy's mom answered and immediately asked Christy if she was all right.

"Yes, we're all fine. Everything is going great, Mom. But I'm going to change my major. I don't know what I'm going to change it to yet, but I know I can't do this kind of work with little kids for the rest of my life."

"Are you sure?" her mom asked.

"Yes, very sure. The question now is whether I should stay at school for the next term or come home. What do you think?"

Christy's mom paused before saying, "I think you have to decide that for yourself. Dad and I told you we would support your decisions from here on out. But they are your decisions, Christy."

21 The next morning, as Christy and Katie ate breakfast in Mike and Megan's kitchen, Christy said, "Sometimes I don't like being an adult."

"Really hard for you to make a decision about this next term at Basel, isn't it?" Katie said.

Christy nodded. "Last night I hardly slept. I kept thinking about what Todd and I decided when I was leaving England a year and a half ago and he was trying to figure out how much longer he should stay in Spain."

"Was that the conversation you two had at that little tea shop?" Katie asked.

"Yes, how did you remember?"

"You said it was the most romantic date you had with him—just the two of you, sipping tea and eating scones in London."

Christy smiled. "I think that's why I really wanted him to come to my Konditorei in Basel. I've sat at the back table so many times all by myself this past year. Every time I was there I would imagine what it would be like to have Todd seated across from me. Don't laugh, but sometimes I carried on imaginary conversations with him."

"And did he ever answer you?"

"Sometimes."

"Okay, now I'm scared." Katie reached across the table and gave Christy's arm a squeeze. "You and Todd need to talk about this. It's a big decision."

"That's what I was going to tell you. I kept remembering what Todd and I talked about that day at the tea shop. Todd had these verses from Psalm 15 that he quoted to me."

"Sounds typical. Todd would have a verse ready for any situation."

"It was about keeping your promises, even when it hurts."

Katie flipped her short red hair behind her ears and said, "Is that what you're going to do? Keep your commitment to the orphanage and the school, even though it hurts?"

Christy looked at her friend and quietly nodded. "Yes. I think that's what I'm supposed to do."

"And what are you supposed to do about Todd? Just keep him waiting?"

"I'll be back in September."

"I know," Katie said. "It's not that long. And I do think you're doing the noble integrity-thing by sticking with your commitment. I just thought that after this trip it would be hard to say good-bye because you guys have gotten so much closer."

Christy sighed. "You have no idea how hard it's going to be. But he and I seem to have said a lot of good-byes over the years. Still, I'd feel better about everything if we could define our relationship more clearly."

"You've always wanted that," Katie said.

"I guess I have."

"What woman doesn't?"

"What woman doesn't what?" Megan asked, entering the kitchen as Katie made her last comment.

"We were just talking about guys," Katie said with a smile at Christy. "So what's on the schedule today? I thought we were going to Switzerland, but I have a feeling Todd would like to stay here another night. That was a fantastic worship service last night."

Katie was right. When Mike and Todd returned from their breakfast with one of Mike's friends, Todd asked Christy and Katie if they would mind staying another night. The two of them had spent the morning helping Megan clean all the rooms and fix lunch. Christy didn't mind staying. She loved it there. Her morning chores had energized her. She quietly told that to Todd as they ate their vegetable stew and warm rolls for lunch.

"Would you like to work at a place like this more than at the orphanage?" Todd asked.

"Yes, definitely. It's hard to compare months at the orphanage with one morning here, but I understand what you meant about feeling energized instead of drained."

"Did Todd tell you about our breakfast?" Mike asked, breaking into their private conversation. "I introduced him to the group of men I partner with in this ministry. They asked if he wanted to come on staff here."

Christy hadn't expected to feel what she did at that moment. She wanted to grab on to Todd and say, "No, you don't! We're going to college together in the fall. You're not coming back to Europe in a few months, right when I'm ready to go home to California. You can't do this!"

"What did you tell them?" Katie asked, looking at Todd and then back at Christy.

"I told them the same thing I told Christy the other day. The need is not the call. I see the need here. I just don't sense the call from God. Not right now. I think my priority is to finish school. After that, I don't know."

Christy felt her heartbeat returning to a normal pace. She felt she would burst if she and Todd didn't have a chance soon to talk through what was going on in their lives and what they were deciding for the future.

"Well," Katie volunteered, "it looks as if I'm the only one who hasn't struggled with deciding what I'm going to do after this trip. Christy decided this morning that she's going to stay at the orphanage for the next term and finish her commitment there. I wanted her to come home, but she has this thing about keeping her promises, even when it hurts."

Christy looked over at Todd. She couldn't tell if he remembered that phrase or if his heart was yelling, "No, Christy, don't stay! Come home!"

Having these life decisions announced in front of others made Christy feel awkward and even more determined that she and Todd talk sometime soon.

Their alone time didn't occur that afternoon. Megan convinced Christy and Katie to go shopping with her, and Mike asked Todd to restring one of his guitars. The only good part of the afternoon was that both Christy and Katie were able to buy a few souvenirs and to find their way around Megan's local grocery store.

Thirty-two people came to the evening worship service, which was even better than the first two nights. Christy wondered how Todd was going to be able to pull away and leave in the morning. Maybe he would want to stay behind. Would he tell Christy and Katie to go on to Switzerland without him?

Christy considered the possibility of staying the rest of the week in Amsterdam. Her imagination then prompted her to ask, what if she stayed there longer than the rest of the week? What if she stayed permanently? What if she and Todd married and returned to Europe to work there or at a place like it? The possibilities of what she and Todd could do working together seemed endless. The more she thought about it, the more she second-guessed her decision to stay in Basel.

And why do I even need to finish college? I don't need a degree to sweep the floors of a youth hostel or to shop for carrots and chop them up for a stew. I'm already as equipped as I need to be to work at a place like this for the rest of my life. I love the atmosphere. I love using my hands to serve.

Christy hoped she could talk with Todd after the worship service that night. But so many people wanted to chat with him that she would have had to wait in line. Instead, she went to bed and stared at the ceiling, dreaming about what it would be like to be married to Todd and to live there.

Neither of us would have to finish college. We could start right now. We could even get married right now. The thought thrilled her. *No more of this waiting and wondering. We could both fly home on Monday. I'm sure we could pull off a wedding by the end of August, and then we could be back here in September instead of going to Rancho.*

Christy's dreams that night exhausted her. She woke with long, invisible lists wrapped around her like a mummy's bandages.

Dressing and heading for the kitchen before Katie awoke, Christy was pretty sure Todd would say he didn't want to leave that morning. When he announced his decision, she would say that she wanted to stay, too. If Katie wanted to go on, she could. She was strong and resourceful. Katie could travel around by herself for a few days and then find her way back to the Zürich airport.

Todd met Christy in the hallway. "Morning. I thought I'd be the early one today, but you're already up."

"Katie is still asleep. I thought I'd help with breakfast."

"You love it here, don't you?" Todd asked.

"Does it show that much?"

"You're using your gifts," he said.

"And so are you," Christy said. "If you're about to ask if I'd mind staying another day, I don't mind at all. I actually think we should stay here the rest of the week. As a matter of fact, I was thinking—"

He interrupted her with a motion to his backpack leaning against the wall behind him. "I'm packed and ready to go. I told Mike we would leave today. An early train rolls out of here at 7:20."

Christy felt as if the bottom had dropped out of her elaborate dream world. "Oh. You don't want to stay?"

"Not now. I don't have any peace about backing out of all my other plans and commitments. Actually, it was a God-thing that you were struggling with your decision about Basel and the orphanage. I realized I couldn't tell you that the need isn't the call unless I practiced that concept myself."

"Oh."

Todd reached his arm around her neck and drew her close in a warm hug. "You look bummed. We can take a later train. Why don't we get ourselves some breakfast? We can find a little bakery like the one you're always telling me about. I'd like to hear what's going on with you. You've been making some big decisions, too."

Christy nodded. She was ready to slip her arm around Todd's middle and have him hold her close, but Katie entered the hallway at that moment.

"What's up, guys?"

As soon as Todd mentioned the 7:20 train, Katie was ready to go. He didn't even tell her they could take a later one because he and Christy were thinking of going out to breakfast.

Disappointed, Christy left The Rock youth hostel with Todd and Katie fifteen minutes later. Mike and Megan drove them to the train station, still issuing invitations for them to return anytime. Todd told them again that he felt certain this was a matter of God's timing, and they all parted with warm hugs.

Christy knew she should take a nap as soon as they settled

on the train. She had learned on this trip that she didn't do well if she didn't get enough sleep. But her mind wouldn't slow down enough to consider sleeping. Last night her wild imagination had taken her so far in her relationship with Todd—married by August, returning to Amsterdam by September—that she had to force herself to stop and move way back.

Todd was being his easygoing self, which helped Christy to get a grip on reality. And Katie's challenging Christy to a long, well-fought game of chess helped to settle her down, too. She tried to convince herself that they were simply three friends on an adventure. She didn't need to discuss her future. She just needed the mercy that God had made new to her that morning.

By the time they arrived at the Frutigen train station twelve hours later, the sun was heading for its home in the west. A flock of fluffy, cream-colored clouds followed the sun like sheep trailing their faithful shepherd. Long shadows from the distant Alpine peaks fell across the barn-sized buildings that surrounded the humble train station.

Christy felt more peace. This was familiar. The German dialect the people beside her spoke sounded very much like the German spoken in Basel.

"I hope you really wanted to get off the beaten path," Katie said, "because this place is no metropolis."

"We take a bus from here. I called the Zimmermans last night, and they're expecting us. Seth was right. They're happy to have us stay with them."

"Of course they're happy," Katie said dryly. "We're their free farm labor."

The bus ride was longer than Christy had expected, but the scenery topped anything she had yet experienced on the trip. Her biggest regret was that the sky kept growing darker, making the looming Alps fade from view. The snow, however, acted as a light reflector. The first star of the night made a grand entrance, and Todd put his arm around her and pulled her close to the window so he could point it out.

They sat snuggled close together the rest of the journey. Christy felt she could think clearly again. They were just Todd and Christy. Forever friends. That's all they needed to be right now. Certainly by tomorrow morning, in a place like this, she and Todd could have a long talk and settle all the unfinished sentences of the past few weeks.

Mr. Zimmerman met them at the bus stop. Christy wanted to laugh gleefully when she saw the look on Katie's face. Mr. Zimmerman looked like the grandfather on a *Heidi* video Christy and Katie had watched together several times. He had a huge white beard and wore a dark green felt hat with a jaunty red feather stuck in the side. With broken English, he graciously invited them to be his guests and come to his home.

"I can't believe this," Katie muttered as they followed the "grandfather" down the cobblestone street. Katie couldn't hold her amazement in any longer when they saw where Mr. Zimmerman had led them. His mode of transportation was a horse-drawn wagon. With lots of laughter, Katie, Christy, and Todd climbed up and rode on their own private hayride to the Zimmermans' home.

In the dark Christy couldn't tell how quaint the chalet was. But from what she could see by light of the handheld lantern, they were walking into a fairy-tale music box.

Mrs. Zimmerman, a round woman with a thick braid wrapped around the top of her head, greeted them warmly and insisted they eat some soup. Everything inside the house was meticulously clean and brightly decorated. Christy was certain that the ornate wooden cabinet in the corner was an antique.

When they finished the scrumptious soup, Katie and

Christy were led upstairs to a tidy, small bedroom with two child-sized beds. Todd was ushered out to the barn to sleep in the straw with several wool blankets.

As soon as the door closed, Christy and Katie grabbed each other's arms and spun around in a giddy twirl. "If this weren't so cool, I'd think it was freaky," Katie said.

"Why?"

"It's like we left reality and entered the fairy-tale zone! I'm Heidi! Tomorrow morning, Peter the goat herder will come to these windows and call out for me to join him in the high country."

Christy giggled. "Look at these beds! I think they once belonged to Hansel and Gretel."

"And they were bought at Snow White's garage sale after two of the dwarfs moved out. We're going to have to sleep curled up in little balls."

Christy curled up under the thick down comforter and slept blissfully through the night. Katie, however, complained the next morning that she hadn't slept at all and her back hurt.

"Oh, come on. You're just trying to make excuses to get out of chores this morning," Christy said. She was already up and dressed and ready to milk the cows.

When she found Todd and Mr. Zimmerman, they were in the barn. Christy stood back and watched Todd try to milk a cow. Her muffled laughter prompted Mr. Zimmerman to motion for her to come closer. Christy didn't want to get anywhere near Todd's line of fire. Sprays of milk were flying everywhere.

"Come on, Christy. Help me out here, will you?" Todd said, getting up from the milking stool. "Watch my girlfriend," he said proudly. "She was born on a farm."

Christy hadn't milked a cow in years. Maybe in almost a decade. Even when she was a child on their dairy farm in

Wisconsin, the milking was all done by machines. But she did know how to milk a cow. Her father patiently had taught her what he called "the dying art" when she was five.

With shaky confidence, Christy positioned herself on the stool and leaned her shoulder and head against the side of the brown Jersey cow. "Come on, girl," she said calmly. "It's okay. Stay calm."

The first squirt went right in the metal bucket and made a lovely, familiar sound that caused Christy to smile. She continued to milk with impressive success until her hands were sore and the bucket was more than half full.

"You never cease to amaze me, Kilikina," Todd said.

"Me too," Katie said, stepping in from where she had been watching in the shadow by the door. "And milking a cow is such a useful talent these days for young women of marital age."

Christy stepped back and invited Katie to give it a try.

"No, thanks. Bungee jumping I would try. Eating raw squid I would try. This, I will not try."

Before the morning was over, Katie did try several new adventures, including churning butter and feeding the chickens. She took a liking to one of the plow horses, and Christy found Katie hand-feeding it a fistful of oats.

"Do you want to go up the ski lift with us?" Christy asked.

"Who is 'us'?"

"Todd and me. Mrs. Zimmerman packed a picnic lunch for the three of us to take to the high meadow. You might see Peter the goat herder up there."

"Sure, I'll go. Unless you were hoping that you and Todd could have the time alone."

Christy was, but she didn't want Katie to know that. "Come on. It will be fun for all of us."

As they slid onto the rickety wooden benches of the chair lift and rose above the charming village of Adelboden, Christy waved at Todd. He was in the seat in front of her. Katie was in the seat in front of him. Christy could hear Katie call out as the lift pulled them to dramatic heights, "We're finally on an adventure!"

Christy smiled. *So this is what you meant when you said you wanted an adventure. Good. I'm glad you got what you wanted, Katie. It's Friday. My final chances to talk with Todd are melting away by the second. One final weekend is all we have. You got your adventure, Katie. Now that my heart has finally settled down, will I get what I hoped for—a plan for the future?*

At the top of the ski lift, Todd took the large, wooden lunch basket from Christy and offered her a hand. They had to walk quickly to keep up with Katie.

"She thinks she's Heidi," Christy explained to Todd as they watched Katie spin around in a field of wild flowers.

Katie burst out singing, " 'The hills are alive!' "

"Wrong country," Todd called to her. "We did that one already, remember? The fountains and the abbey?"

Christy drew in a deep breath of the cool Alpine air. Over her head hung a pure blue sky, pulled taut and held aloft by jagged, snow-covered peaks. At her feet was spread an endless carpet of green meadow sprinkled with wild flowers like colorful confetti. The beauty left her speechless.

Katie, undaunted by Todd's comment, kept dancing around and singing. Christy thought how funny it was that she had been the one who had wanted to get out into the country. Now that they were there, Katie acted as if this were her adventure.

This isn't an adventure. This is a calming rest. An adventure would be dancing at San Marcos Square in Venice or horseback riding along the beach in Spain.

Todd put down the picnic basket in the middle of the wild flowers and stretched out next to it. He leaned on his elbow and gave Christy a contented smile.

I guess my friends are happy to spend our last few days together here in the Alps. How odd that, looking back, I wish we could have done the trip differently. I wish we were going camping with Tonio. I'd be a completely different camper now. I'd go fishing with Todd and bathe in the stream every day. I'm just now ready for my vacation.

"This has to be one of the most incredible, spectacular, amazingly beautiful corners of God's green earth," Todd said. He leaned back and gazed at the sky. "It's just a breath away from heaven."

"It is amazing, isn't it?" Christy sat down next to him and reached into the picnic basket. "Are you hungry? This bread looks homemade."

Katie flitted over to them and said, "Okay, I'm a happy woman. I've danced in an Alpine meadow. Now all I need is a ride in a gondola, and my life will be complete."

"Yeah," Todd agreed. "We passed that one up, didn't we?"

"I can't believe we made it all the way to the train station and then left," Katie said. "What were we thinking? We were in such a rush to get somewhere. I don't even remember where."

Christy remembered. It was Salzburg. And their decision had been a group choice, but she felt responsible since she was the one who had pushed them to go and see and do so much at the beginning of the trip.

Katie bent over and plucked a wild flower. "Did you ever hear that Norwegian legend about the wild flowers?"

"No. Where did you hear it? In Oslo?" Christy asked.

"No, it's an old tradition my grandmother taught me when I was around eight or nine. I did it at her house when I was staying there once on Midsummer's Eve."

"That's tonight," Todd said. "Mr. Zimmerman was talking

to me about it in the barn this morning. I didn't understand what he was saying, but then I figured it out when he said today is the longest day of sunlight in the year. That's Midsummer's Eve, right?"

"Yes!" Katie's excitement colored her cheeks rosy. "This is perfect! Chris, do this with me. You're supposed to pick seven wild flowers and sleep with them under your pillow."

"Seven of the same kind or seven different ones?" Christy asked.

"I don't think it matters," Katie said, quickly moving on with the rest of the legend. "If you sleep with seven wild flowers under your pillow on Midsummer's Eve, you'll dream of the one you'll marry."

"I want to try," Todd said with a teasing grin. "How many? Seven?"

"You can't play," Katie said. "This is a girls-only game."

"Katie," Christy said, "are you sure this isn't some kind of medieval incantation? I don't believe in doing any of that."

"I don't, either," Katie said. "It's just a little folklore. You don't say anything magical or throw in any bat wings. It's just a bit of tradition from my heritage. Like making a wish when you blow out candles on a birthday cake."

Christy took off with Katie to find seven wild flowers while Todd watched. When they were far enough away that he couldn't hear them, Christy asked, "How are you doing with the whole boyfriend-jealousy thing?"

Katie stopped and gave her a pained expression. "Why do you ask?"

"I'm wondering. I think it must be uncomfortable for you sometimes around us, even though you don't act like it."

"I'm doing better than I was at the beginning of the trip. I guess if Antonio or Marcos had acted at all interested in me, it wouldn't have hurt so much whenever I saw you and Todd falling in love right before my eyes."

Christy smiled. She couldn't help it. And her cheeks blushed.

"You guys are so perfect for each other," Katie said with a sigh. She bent over and plucked her first yellow wild flower. "I'm happy for you, really. Deep down, I'm thrilled. If the two of you ever broke up for good, I think a part of me would shrivel up and die. You give me hope that some God-lover guy is out there who will think I'm the sun and moon and stars and one day will look at me the way Todd looks at you."

Christy plucked a tiny white flower. "There is, Katie. I know he's out there."

"Oh, he'll probably be an 'out there' kind of guy, all right," Katie said with a laugh. "He would have to be to put up with me."

"He'll probably be shy and kind of quiet," Christy guessed. "You know how they say opposites attract. What about the baseball player at Rancho? What was his name? Number 14, wasn't it? Is he shy?"

"I don't know. Matt wasn't shy or quiet when I met him, but then, they had just won their final game. He has such a look of honesty and simpleheartedness about him. He seemed like an uncomplicated person, and I like that.

"You know," Katie said a moment later, after they each had picked three more flowers. "What I really want is to trust God more in this area of my life, and I'm learning about how to do that a little bit better. Weren't you the one who told me that God gives His best to those who leave the choice with Him?"

"I don't know. I might have said that. It sounds more like something Todd would say."

"I want to trust God more," Katie said decisively.

"That's funny because I've been saying the same thing on this trip. I keep thinking I know what's best or what the future holds, but really, I don't have a clue. Only God does."

Katie looked up with her bouquet of tiny flowers in her hand and gave Christy a grin. "Guess it doesn't matter what stage we're at in life, does it? With a boyfriend or without a boyfriend."

Christy quickly added, "With a major in college or without one."

Katie nodded. "We have to, as they say, 'let go and let God.' I'm just glad we've had each other on this journey, Christy. This journey through life, I mean, not just this journey through Europe. I'd be a mental case by now if I didn't have you and Todd and the rest of our friends as my circle of sanity."

"I like that," Christy said. "Circle of sanity. You guys are that for me, too."

"Okay, we better stop this before I burst out crying. My sobs and loud wailing would start an avalanche!"

Christy laughed and held out one of her seven wild flowers to Katie. "Here, you take one of mine, and I'll take one of yours."

They swapped, and Katie said, "This means we have to be each other's maid of honor, right?"

"Definitely. We're creating our own version of this folklore."

They laughed and linked arms as they headed back to where Todd lay stretched out on the picnic blanket. Then, carefully pressing their flowers in a cloth napkin, they secured the napkin inside the picnic basket.

"Did you ever wish on these when you were a kid?" Todd plucked a dandelion with a full, fuzzy white head. "We used to pick them in the schoolyard, make a wish, and then blow off all the dandelion fuzz. I think my friends and I single-handedly kept our schoolyard seeded with dandelions."

Christy reached over and picked one of the dandelions

near her. She closed her eyes and heard herself say, "I wish we could still go to Venice."

When she opened her eyes, Todd was sitting up and looking at her with a wild, blue-eyed gaze. "Are you serious? You'd be up for that?"

"Yes, I really would. I want one more adventure before Monday."

"That means we probably won't make it to your bakery for morning pastries."

"That's okay."

Todd looked at Katie and then back at Christy. "We can do it, you know. We catch the bus back to Frutigen, and then we pick up the train out of Basel that stops at Spiez. We change trains in Milan, and we're in Venice before midnight."

Katie laughed and broke off a piece of bread. "You're scary, Todd! What did you do, memorize the whole train schedule in the hayloft last night?"

"No, I looked up how far it would be from here to Venice this morning because I had the same feeling Christy must be having. I could go for one more adventure."

"Wait a minute," Katie said. "What would be wrong with staying here another night and then tomorrow going to Christy's school in Basel and hanging out there on Sunday?"

"Are you turning down an adventure?" Christy asked. "You sound like me when we started this trip, and now I'm sounding like you."

"I like it here," Katie said.

"You'll like it in Venice, too." Todd plucked a dandelion. "I wish Katie would change her mind about Venice." Then he blew the fuzzy part right in her face.

"Okay, okay! If you're going to torture me like that, we can go." Her face brightened. "Oh yeah, and we can see Marcos again. I'm with you."

Their ride down the mountain on the rickety wooden ski

lift felt charged with electricity that shot between the three of them. They called out back and forth and pointed to the magnificent scenery as they rolled toward Adelboden with their faces to the world below them. A quick explanation to the Zimmermans, an even faster packing job, and they were out the door, climbing up into the back of the "grandfather's" horse-drawn wagon.

Christy felt more charged up than she ever had before. Then she remembered. "Wait! Our wild flowers!" She jumped off the back of the wagon and ran into the house, trying to explain to Mrs. Zimmerman that she had left her flowers in a cloth napkin at the bottom of the basket.

Mrs. Zimmerman chuckled and gave her the whole napkin, flowers and all, before shooing her out the door. The wagon rambled down the narrow road to the bus stop. From their uphill view of the village's main street, Todd spotted the bus as it came winding around the corner.

"That's our bus," Todd told Mr. Zimmerman. Todd had been consulting the train schedule and now announced to all of them, "If we don't catch that bus, we won't make our connection at Spiez."

"Can this buggy go any faster?" Katie asked Mr. Zimmerman.

His reply was in German, or perhaps it was French. Whatever he said the horses understood, and they took off. Christy and Katie tumbled into each other and held on, laughing all the way.

"Hold the bus!" Todd yelled when they were still a few yards off.

The bus let out a billow of smoke, and the door closed.

"Wait!" Todd yelled.

Mr. Zimmerman seemed to enjoy the chase more than any of them. He kept the horses headed straight for the bus. As it pulled out, he put his thumb and finger in his mouth and gave a sharp whistle. The bus driver didn't seem to hear it, but the horses did. They were confused and reared back.

Two men came out of the shops along the main road. One wore a long white butcher's apron. A woman in a local *Dirndl* dress exited a shop at the end of the street with two little boys wearing leather *Lederhosen*. When everyone saw Mr. Zimmerman chasing the bus and whistling, they all joined in, waving their hands, yelling, and running after the bus, as well.

Christy couldn't stop laughing. She felt as if their fairy-tale land had turned into Busy Town, and they were now cartoon characters on a mad romp. All they needed was Sergeant Murphy and his trusty whistle.

Someone in a blue Mercedes pulled around their wagon and took off after the bus, honking until the bus pulled over just outside of town.

"Thank you, thank you," Katie said, reaching out from the wagon like a parade princess, shaking the hands of all the helpful townsfolk. She hopped down, swung her pack over her shoulder, and kept shaking hands. "Thank you. We couldn't have done it without you. You guys were awesome, really."

The jovial crowd gleamed with appreciation. Mr. Zimmerman waved and laughed as Todd, Christy, and Katie ran to the bus. The bus driver was the only one who didn't find the antics of these three backpacking students humorous. As a result, Todd led them to the back of the bus so they could finish laughing and could retell every detail without the driver's critical eye staring at them in the rearview mirror.

Not until they were safely on board the train headed for Milan did Christy begin to relax. The scenery was breathtaking, and she felt as if she were still on top of the world. She didn't want this time with her two best friends to end, ever.

◆

All their connections were smooth until they hit Milan. The train station was packed on this Friday night. Todd directed them to a ticket booth where they had to wait in a long line to make reservations and upgrade their tickets to first class. Todd kept checking his watch.

"Are we going to make the next train?" Christy asked.

"We have five minutes. Unless the train has been delayed, I don't think we'll make it."

"What if we run to the train? We could stand in second class," Christy said.

"Sure," Katie agreed. "We've done it before."

With another mad dash, they found the train to Venice, but the conductor wouldn't let them on. Reservations only. The train was packed. Everyone seemed to want to travel to Venice for the weekend.

They went back to the ticket booth and stood in an even longer line than before.

"How about if Christy and I find some food and bring it back to you?" Katie asked.

"I could sure use something to eat," Todd said. "Thanks."

"Sure. We'll be right back. Just don't leave this area, and we'll be fine."

Christy stayed close to Katie. Their backpacks kept bumping into the mob of travelers. This was the busiest she had seen any of the train stations so far. She wondered if it was because school was out in the States as well as in Europe and throngs of students were just starting out on their adventures. Christy knew they had avoided some of that crowd by leaving on their trip so early in June.

"There's a pizzeria," Katie said. "Let's buy some extra in case we're stuck here all night."

After waiting in another long line, Christy and Katie bought a whole pizza and three sodas. The fragrant garlic and spices tortured Christy as she carried the pizza with both hands back to the ticket booth. Todd still hadn't reached the front of the line.

Fifteen minutes later he joined them on a bench with the news that he had miraculously secured three seats in first class. The seats apparently were the only ones available for the next twenty-four hours.

"The only thing is," Todd said after he handed them their tickets, "the train leaves at 6:00 in the morning."

"Should we look for a youth hostel here in Milan?" Christy asked.

"I have a feeling it might be full already," Katie said. "The tour book said the hostels in the major Italian cities fill up quickly, and you should check in early."

Todd looked at his watch. "I'd say let's find a hotel, but I'm getting low on money. Which reminds me, I need for you both to pay me back for these first-class tickets. I'd like to say I could cover them for you but—"

"We planned to pay for them," Christy said. "And the pizza is on us."

They found a corner of the station away from the mobs and settled their money. Then they ate their cooled pizza and drank their warm soda.

"Where did all these people come from?" Todd asked.

"It looks as if summer travel in Europe has officially begun," Christy said. She didn't like feeling sweaty, smelly, and sticky. Whatever they did tomorrow morning when they arrived in Venice, she hoped it included a shower.

The three of them took turns walking around the huge station. Katie bought some chocolate and a key chain souvenir. Several other American students stopped to talk to them. The travelers compared stories and gave one another advice and names of places to stay. Sometime around 2:00 in the morning, Todd ate the last slice of cold pizza. The scent of garlic in their small corner of the station overwhelmed Christy.

She turned down Todd's offer for another round of chess and tried to find a way to curl up against her backpack to sleep. Their spontaneous adventure to Venice was quickly losing its glamour.

Christy closed her eyes and leaned her head against her backpack. That's when she remembered the wild flowers. "Katie, where did we put that napkin with the wild flowers?"

"Oh yeah! The night is half gone, and we haven't been sleeping with our wild flowers. I think you put the napkin in your day pack."

Rummaging around, Christy found the cloth napkin and opened it carefully. The brightly colored wild flowers were not only pressed, but they also had gotten crumpled and squished with some of the stems broken off. "Do you think it will still work?" she asked Katie. "Will we dream of our future spouses even if our flowers are mangled?"

"Hey, if we can manage to have any kind of pleasant dream in a place like this, I think we're doing okay." Katie carefully extracted her seven flowers and folded them up in a wrinkled bandana scarf.

Christy found a piece of Italian newspaper and made a crooked sort of envelope in which to place her flowers. She slid the envelope into the zippered pouch on the front of her pack and tried to settle in so that her head rested against the pouch. She wiggled to get comfortable and opened her eyes. Todd was watching her with a smile. She smiled back.

"I want a full report on who you meet in your dreams tonight," he said.

You know it will be you, Todd. It's always you. Only you.

But all she said was "Okay."

Christy didn't know how long she dozed. She didn't know whom she dreamed of or if she dreamed at all. Her sleep ended abruptly when she heard Katie scream.

"Get away from me, you creep!" Katie cried.

Through bleary eyes, Christy saw a large bald man bending over Katie, trying to talk to her. He reeked of alcohol.

As soon as Todd woke and said, "Be on your way, buddy," the man ambled off, talking to himself.

"So much for the wild flower theory!" Katie said, sitting up and adjusting her sweat shirt.

"Are you okay?" Christy asked.

"That was a living nightmare," Katie said. "There I was, dreaming of my mystery man, and then I felt someone touching my hair. I thought I was about to see the face of my true love, but when I opened my eyes, I saw *him!*"

Christy couldn't help but laugh. "Oh, Katie."

Katie pouted.

Todd chuckled. "The moral of the folklore lesson could be that some mysteries are best left in God's keeping."

"No kidding!" Katie said. "What about you, Christy? Who did you dream of? Or can we all guess?"

Christy could feel Todd looking at her, but she suddenly felt too shy to look back. She especially didn't want to say that she hadn't dreamed at all. "Some mysteries are best left in God's keeping," she answered quietly.

The rest of the uncomfortable night on the floor of the Milan train station and the three-hour, early-morning train ride into Venice gave Christy plenty of time to think. The panic she had felt in Amsterdam had subsided. Now she knew how crazy it had been to even think of getting married in two months and going back to work at The Rock with Todd. The decision to finish her commitment at the orphanage and complete her course work was a good choice. She felt peace about following through on what she had begun.

What remained to be settled was her relationship with Todd. It bothered her a little that he hadn't kissed her since she had talked with him on the train ride into Amsterdam about saving her kisses. She hadn't meant for him to pull back completely. While they had still been close these last few days, they weren't snuggly the way she wanted to be. Christy wasn't sure how she felt about that. Couldn't they be a little more affectionate? Or was this Todd's way of honoring her request to save their kisses?

Christy knew it would all settle itself once she and Todd had a chance to be alone and have a long talk. *But when is that going to happen? Our time together is slipping away. It's already Saturday morning. I don't mind staying in Basel another two months, but I don't think I can wait that long to have a heart-to-heart talk with Todd.*

CHRISTY AND TODD
THE COLLEGE YEARS

When the train pulled into Venice at nine that morning, the
place seemed like a different station from the
quiet, nearly empty one they had stayed in
two weeks earlier. It was alive with noise and
throngs of travelers. Todd, Christy, and Katie
found their way to the water taxi and climbed aboard with
dozens of other students.

As the boat sped across the water, Christy shielded her
eyes from the sun and tried to memorize the sight before her.
Across the gleaming water was one of the more than one
hundred islands that made up the ancient city of Venice. A
tall spire stretched toward the sky. Dozens of tall, very old
buildings stood close together. They reminded Christy of
plump old ladies dressed in their Sunday best, sitting snugly
beside one another on a church pew. Some wore hats. Some
seemed to be holding large handbags on their laps. All the
faces of the matronly buildings were adorned with smug
grins, as if the women were listening to a sermon being proclaimed to them from the heavens, but all the while, they
held in their hearts mischievous secrets of their past.

"What a place!" Christy declared as they stepped out of
the water taxi. "I mean, I've seen pictures, and I've seen Venice in movies, but this place is larger than life."

"Something is in the air, isn't it?" Todd said.

Christy sniffed but didn't catch any whiffs of garlic.

"No," Todd said to her, "I mean, a sort of spirit is in the air. This city has seen it all."

"Yes," Christy agreed. "I was just thinking how the buildings all looked like smug old ladies sitting next to each other."

Todd grinned at her. "What should we do first? Eat or find a place to stay?"

Christy knew Todd would prefer finding some food. She would prefer a shower. Katie made the choice for them when she said, "Let's call Marcos."

"We know where his father's jewelry shop is, right?" Todd said. "Let's go there and ask for him. He's more likely to be at the shop than at home. We can't assume that we can stay with him."

"Can we stow these packs someplace?" Katie asked. "I'm sick of carrying this thing everywhere we go."

"We can find the youth hostel," Christy suggested.

A girl who had been standing nearby turned to them and with a British accent said, "They won't let you check into the youth hostel until three o'clock. It's very crowded. We found a hotel that's much closer. Would you like the address?"

"Yes, thanks," Todd said.

The hotel turned out to be a good choice except that it was more expensive than the hostel. Todd admitted he was almost out of money; the plane ride from Narvik to Copenhagen had taken a huge chunk out of his budget. Katie said she figured she had about seventy-five dollars left, and Christy had a little more than that.

"We can pool our money," Christy said. "Together we have enough to eat and pay for the hotel. What more do we want? We'll have to ride second class back to Basel, but that's no big deal. I think we'll be fine." Her optimism as well as her suggestion that they all take showers before they headed out again helped tremendously. They were starving by the time they left their hotel, but at least they were clean and didn't have to carry the heavy packs.

"Let's find a quaint, authentic place to eat," Katie suggested. "None of these tourist traps. Then we can go to Savini Jewelers and see the rest of San Marcos Square."

Following their noses, the three famished friends tromped down narrow alleys and over ornate bridges with absolutely no idea where they were going.

"I haven't seen a single restaurant," Christy said. "Don't you think we should consult the tour book?"

Katie pulled out the book, and three postcards fluttered to the pavement.

"I can't believe I haven't mailed those cards yet," Christy said, bending to pick them up.

"Isn't that a post office over there?" Todd asked, motioning toward the building two doors down from where they stood. "At least, that looks like a post office. That is a mailbox out front, isn't it?"

While Todd and Katie consulted the tour book for a good restaurant, Christy ventured into the small building. She found a short man sitting behind a desk, reading a newspaper. He wore wire-rimmed glasses that rested precariously on the end of his pointy nose. Christy handed him the postcards but didn't understand what he said to her. Trying to speak slowly in English, she handed him some change for the stamps. He licked the stamps for her and looked at her over the top of his glasses. Then he motioned with his free hand that she needed more money. Christy reached into her pocket and pulled out two more coins. The peculiar man shook his head as if it wasn't enough and then waved his hand and spoke a string of Italian words. She thought he was indicating that the amount was close enough, and she could go.

Christy walked back into the bright daylight shaking her head.

"Was it a post office?" Katie asked.

"I have no idea, but the odd little man in there put stamps on the cards and took my money, even though I don't think it was enough. If Seth's postcards ever reach Oregon, it will be a little miracle."

"Those weren't your postcards?" Katie asked.

"No, can you believe it? Remember the guy we talked to on the train to Paris? He dropped them. I've been meaning to mail them for the last week."

Todd stretched his arm around her shoulder and drew her close. "My little Good Samaritan," he teased.

Christy liked feeling him close to her, especially when he smelled fresh, like soap and shampoo. She slipped her arm around his middle and rested her head against his shoulder.

"Come on, you two snuggle bugs," Katie said. "We have to find some food. I don't care anymore if it's a tourist trap. Let's find our way to San Marcos Square."

Following the map and crossing several bridges, they were almost to San Marcos Square when Christy caught the scent of garlic in the air. "Oh, just smell that."

Katie sniffed and began to follow the scent. It led them down a narrow alley to a tiny place that looked like a pizzeria. The door was open, but no one was inside.

"Should we go in?" Christy asked.

"Hello?" Katie boldly entered. "Ciao. Do you sell any chow here?"

A short, round woman wearing a white apron over her dress greeted them. "Americanos!" she said. "Come in. You are hungry, yes?"

"Yes!" all three of them answered in unison.

"You like to make your own pizza?" the woman asked. "I am, how do you say . . . breaking now."

"You're taking a break?" Todd said. "Sure. We'd love to make our own pizza." He walked behind the counter and went to wash his hands in a small sink. Christy and Katie followed him.

"You tell us what to do, and we'll do it," Todd said. "By the way, I'm Todd. This is Katie and Christy. We're from California."

"I am Cassandra. We lived in New York for a little while. What kind of pizza do you like?"

"Any kind," Todd answered for them. "Did you hurt your foot?" He motioned to where her right leg was resting on a stool.

"Yes. I did this morning."

"Have you put ice on it?"

"No."

"Here." Todd made himself at home, looking through the small refrigerator in the back while Katie and Christy grinned self-consciously. He returned with a towel wrapped around a hunk of cold mozzarella cheese. "It's not ice-cold, but this should help."

"You are an angel," Cassandra said dramatically. "Come here. Let me kiss you."

Todd bent over to apply the chilled mozzarella to the ankle, and Cassandra kissed him with a big smack on both cheeks. Christy thought she saw him blushing.

"Where do you keep the pizza dough?" Todd asked, reaching for an apron he saw under the counter.

For the next two hours Christy thought she had never laughed so much in her life. While Cassandra sat with her foot up, Todd, Katie, and Christy learned the fine art of tossing pizza dough into the air and then covering it with Cassandra's special tomato sauce. Two young girls entered the pizzeria while Todd was sliding their masterpiece pizza into the oven with a wide paddle.

Cassandra said something to the girls in Italian. They giggled, took a seat, and watched Todd as the perspiration glistened on his forehead.

"I told them you would make their pizza," Cassandra said.

"One Todd Special coming right up."

This time Katie tried her hand at tossing the dough into the air. Christy was certain it would come down over her head like in a cartoon, but Katie actually was better at the task than Todd had been. At Cassandra's insistence, Christy gave it a try, but on the first toss, her fist went right through the middle. She ended up wearing the pizza crust like a huge, sagging bracelet around her wrist.

"You spread it out too thin," Cassandra said. "Try it again."

Christy's second attempt was a twirling, flying success and gained her a round of applause.

Todd served the first slice of his pizza to Cassandra with a towel over his arm, like a classy waiter. Cassandra praised him and offered him a job.

"Hmm," Todd said, playfully rubbing his chin as if seriously contemplating her offer.

"Remember," Christy said, "the need is not the call."

Todd laughed and wrapped his arm around Christy's shoulders. He turned to Cassandra and said, "Sorry, but my girlfriend says no."

"Ahh!" Cassandra said excitedly. "Your girlfriend, is she? Why didn't you tell me?" The woman worked to get to her feet, all the while saying, "Stand there. Wait."

Once she was up, she patted her apron, and a cloud of fine white flour rose up to encircle them. "I must give to you a blessing."

As Todd stood there with his arm around Christy's shoulder, she slipped her arm around his middle. Cassandra raised her hands and pressed her fingers on each of their closed lips. She spoke a melodic-sounding string of Italian words. Then she pulled her hands back to her lips, where she kissed her fingers and then pressed her fingers to their cheeks.

With a wistful look, Cassandra said, "I do not know how to say it in English. It is not the same. I wish for you all God's goodness."

"Thank you," Christy said in barely a whisper. "Grazie, Cassandra. Molte grazie."

"Molte grazie," Todd repeated, squeezing Christy's shoulder and pulling her close.

"Do you happen to have any blessings for those of us who are still available?" Katie asked.

Cassandra didn't seem to understand Katie's question.

"She wants a blessing, too," Todd explained.

"You come back here when you have a man, and I will bless you both."

Christy thought those words would break Katie's heart, but to Christy's surprise, her friend didn't make a joke or let out a forlorn moan. Katie stood tall and said, "I'll do that someday, Cassandra. You wait. I'll be back. And whoever he is, he'll be worth every word of your blessing."

Christy had never felt more proud of her friend.

It took Todd, Christy, and Katie several hours before they could pull themselves away from Cassandra's pizzeria. The next stop was Savini Jewelers.

From outside, the shop didn't look like much. But once they stepped inside, they realized they were in an exclusive and expensive jewelry store. A glittering, golden chandelier hung from an ornate, domed ceiling. Marble statues stood guard in each corner. Cushioned sofas covered in gold brocade enabled buyers to sit back in comfort as they browsed the lowered glass cases.

A large man in a black suit immediately stepped up to Todd, Christy, and Katie. He looked like a bouncer.

"Hi. How's it going? We'd like to speak with Marcos Savini, if he's here," Todd said.

"Mr. Savini is not in," the bouncer said.

"Okay, but we were wondering about his son," Katie explained. "Is Marcos here?"

"Mr. Carlos Savini is not here, and Mr. Marcos Savini is not here," the hulking man said.

"Could we leave a message for him?" Katie asked.

The bouncer pulled a business card from his pocket and opened the door for them to leave.

"Thanks." Katie took the card. As soon as they were all outside she said, "Boy, was that the opposite of Cassandra's or what? I take it they don't like poor American college students around here. I guess we're not welcome here the way we were at Antonio's."

"Should we try calling and leaving a message?" Christy asked.

"No," Katie said. "He's probably out of town anyway."

"Let's go exploring," Todd suggested. "I want to check out San Marcos Square."

The sight that impressed Christy most in the square was the pigeons. They were everywhere. People held out hands full of food that could be purchased at vendor carts, and the birds would come and sit on their hands to eat. One little boy was frozen with a mixture of terror and delight as two birds sat on his head and four more perched on his arms. A man spoke to him in German and stepped back to take the boy's picture. Christy pulled out her camera and snapped a few shots of the square. She had taken only three rolls of film the whole trip. Most of the time she had been so busy absorbing and observing that she hadn't thought to use her camera.

That afternoon she made up for it by finishing the roll of film in the camera and taking another entire roll. She took pictures of the unique church at the end of San Marcos

Square and then shots of the square from the top of the church. She took several shots of the Rialto Bridge as the gondolas passed under it.

Katie didn't bring up the topic of a gondola ride, and Christy didn't, either, because she had read in the tour book that the gondolas could be very expensive. It was doubtful if they had enough money left to rent one. She wondered if Katie had figured that out, as well.

Or are the gondolas another Lille Havfrue, *an illusive mermaid we traversed the globe to find? Now that we're here, is Katie feeling it's no big deal? Why do so many things in life turn out like that? Like the fjords and the castles.*

By sunset, all three of them were exhausted. The all-nighter at the Milan train station and walking around all afternoon had caught up with them. Christy wasn't even hungry. All she wanted to do was sleep.

The next morning Katie was the first one up, and she woke Christy. "Come on, sunshine," she teased. "Venice awaits you."

"What time is it?" Christy asked.

"Almost nine. This is a new record for you, isn't it? Todd and I have been up for hours. We went for coffee, and I brought you back a pastry. Wait until you taste this one. I think this is the winner of the trip so far." Katie held out a flaky pastry shaped like a cone and filled with chocolate.

"I can see why you liked this one," Christy said, indulging in a big bite while she was still in bed. "Thanks for bringing it back for me. Sorry to keep you guys waiting."

"No problem. I've decided that today none of us is going to apologize to anyone for anything. This is our last day; it's going to be perfect."

Christy thought the delicious pastry was a pretty perfect way to start the day. She felt like a new person after so much sleep.

After she took a quick shower, Todd arranged for them to take a boat to the island of Murano to watch the glassblowers. Christy loved being out on the water and feeling the wind in her hair. She was standing by the rail snapping pictures when Todd came up behind her. He put both his hands on the rail so that Christy stood securely within the circle he had created.

"I don't want you to go," Christy said softly.

"I'm not going anywhere." Todd pressed his cheek against the side of her head.

"Yes, you are. Tomorrow at this time you'll be on a plane back to California, and I'll be in class. No, actually, my first class will be over, and I'll be at my little Konditorei, drowning my sorrows in whatever Marguerite baked."

"Our plane doesn't leave Zürich until two tomorrow afternoon," Todd said.

"Okay, so I'll be at the Konditorei, and you'll be at the airport. We'll still be apart, Todd. I don't want tomorrow to come." She turned and buried her head in his shoulder. She wanted Todd to tell her he would leap into the sky, lasso the sun, and with his bare hands hold it back from circling the globe so that this day would never end. Or if he wouldn't attempt that, she wanted him to at least kiss her.

But Todd did neither.

The aching she felt inside only grew as they toured the island of Murano. They watched a skilled craftsman demonstrate the ancient art of blowing glass through a long, hollow pipe and then quickly shaping the fiery hot liquid into vases. On the boat ride back, Todd talked with a retired track coach and his wife from Ohio, while Christy stood alone at the rail, watching the lacy ripples the boat produced in the water.

"We need to make some decisions," Todd said once the three of them had disembarked and found a shady spot to stand.

"I think we should try calling Marcos again," Katie said.

"I don't know if we'll have time to see him," Todd pointed out. "We need to check out of the hotel by 1:00, which is in twenty minutes. I've checked the schedule, and we have a couple of times when we can catch the train. No matter which train we decide on, it takes ten hours to reach Basel."

"That long?" Katie said. "I thought we were closer. I also think we need to walk while we talk so we can get to the hotel in time to check out. If they decide to charge us an extra night, I don't know if we could pay for it."

Todd started to walk and asked Christy, "Do you think it's okay if we stay at the dorms tonight in Basel?"

"Sure. Then would you take the train to Zürich in the morning?"

"Yes. It's only an hour from Basel to Zürich."

"I know." Christy wondered if that would allow them time for a short visit to her Konditorei. If they could fit that into the schedule, somehow she felt saying good-bye wouldn't be as hard.

"We could take the 2:00 train and be in Basel by midnight. Three other trains leave after that one. The last one would be the 8:30 train. That one would take us into Basel at 6:30 Monday morning, which is cutting it close for Christy's class."

"That's okay." Christy wanted to be with Todd as long as she could, and she didn't mind going to class directly from the train. If she could cut that class, she would. That way she could go to Zürich with Todd and Katie and see them off for their 2:00 flight. But the summer term was so short. If she missed even one class, her grade could be dropped as much as half a grade. Since her grades last term weren't the best, she knew she needed to do all she could to keep her scores high. Otherwise the partial scholarship she had been awarded for Rancho Corona in the fall could be affected. "We could take that last train. That would give us a few more hours here in Venice."

Katie, who was agreeing with everything that day, said she thought that was a great idea. Todd suggested they retrieve their packs, go to the train station to see about making reservations, and then, with whatever money they had left, they could fill up on pizza.

After standing in line at the train station for more than two hours, they found out all first-class seats for the 8:30 train were booked. They would have to go in second class, which could mean standing for ten hours. Or at least for the first three hours to Milan.

They bought some pizza at the train station. Christy was down to her last bit of money. With only three more hours left in Venice, none of them knew what to do.

Christy's feet and her heart felt heavier and heavier. Todd was quiet. The thought of their trip ending was too depressing to even talk about how to spend their final hours together.

Katie was the one who kept them going with her bright, optimistic attitude. She suggested they find their last taste of Italian gelato, and she said she knew just the place. They followed Katie onto a water taxi and disembarked at San Marcos Square. Christy thought Katie would suggest they call Marcos. But she didn't.

Instead, Katie marched them right up to one of the gondola stands, pulled out the last of her money, and said to the gondolier in the straw hat, "My friends here need to go for a ride. How much do you want?"

"Katie, that's all the money you have left," Christy protested.

24 "You don't have to pay for this."

"Yes, I do. You two don't have any money left, so this is my treat. Now, don't spoil it for me. Just take off your backpacks; I'll watch them for you. And get in the man's boat."

The gondolier took Katie's money while Christy, still protesting, was ushered by Todd into the gondola's cushioned hull.

Then the gondolier asked Katie, "You are paying for your friends? And this is all the money you have left?"

"We're going home tomorrow," Katie explained. "I just thought they couldn't come all this way and not go for a ride in a gondola."

"And neither can you!" the gondolier said. "Come. No charge. My honor. You must have your gondola ride, too."

"Do you guys mind?" Katie asked.

"Of course not," Christy said, snuggling up close to Todd. It would have been wonderfully romantic for the two of them to be alone for one final hour, but how could she say no after Katie had been so generous?

"Come aboard," Todd said.

With a burst of glee, Katie climbed into the gondola and

reached for each backpack as it was handed down to her. She joked around by resting one of the packs beside her on the seat and putting her arm around it. "Oh, Milton, you are so strong! I always did go for the strong, silent types."

Christy smiled at Todd. He put his arm around her and drew her close.

"We have many beautiful palaces here along the *Canal-azzo*," the gondolier said, pushing off from the dock and pointing the gondola down the Grand Canal. "The canal is two miles long, and the water is only nine feet deep. Less, in some places. It is not recommended for swimming."

Christy could see why. A disagreeable odor rose from the water, and trash floated on top. She kept her attention directed upward, toward the magnificent mansions that lined the canal, each more splendid than the last. Katie carried on a lively conversation with the gondolier while Christy and Todd sat close. Todd turned out to be as strong and silent as Katie's backpack partner. Christy wondered again when she and Todd would have their heart-to-heart conversation. On the train? So much had happened in her heart these past few weeks. She didn't know how much she needed to tell Todd and how much he had figured out.

I don't need you to promise to hold back the sun, Todd. I just need you to promise to always hold me this close.

Their ride ended near the train station, and they clambered out with smiles and waves for their gondolier. Todd took Christy's hand in his, and they ambled into the very familiar train station. Todd suggested they walk to the platform a little early so they could try to find seats in second class. He held Christy's hand the whole time they stood waiting in the crowd for the train. She wondered if he was feeling the same sadness she felt.

The train pulled in, but unlike some of the other trains they had boarded on the trip, the conductor wanted to see each person's ticket before boarding. When they finally reached the front of the line, Christy, Todd, and Katie pulled out their Eurorail passes.

"No!" the conductor yelled. He thrust Todd's train pass back at him.

"No!" he said again after looking at Katie's pass and jabbing it into her hands.

"Si!" he said to Christy, handing the pass to her nicely and pushing on her back to hurry her onto the train.

"Wait!" Christy cried out, pulling away from the crush of people. "What's wrong with their passes?" She maneuvered her way out of the crowd and moved around to where Katie and Todd stood, talking to another uniformed conductor.

"What do you mean expired?" Katie said.

"The date is stamped here," the man said. "June 5 to June 25. That was yesterday."

Christy quickly looked at her pass, which she had bought separately from Katie's and Todd's. Hers was stamped June 6 to June 26.

"We had them issued a day too early," Todd said. "We flew out of L.A. on the fifth, but we didn't arrive until the sixth." He turned to the conductor. "Can they be extended for one day? We didn't even use them the first few days."

"No. You can buy a separate ticket. This pass is no longer valid."

"We don't have any money," Katie said solemnly.

"I cannot help you," the man said. "Every day I hear the same stories. You should next time plan your trip better."

He turned to help another frantic student, who was speaking to him in French. The train now was loaded, and the grumpy conductor was giving a final boarding call.

"What do we do?" Christy asked.

"You better get on that train," Katie said. "We'll figure

something out. This is our problem, not yours. You can't miss class in the morning, Christy."

Christy turned to Todd, her eyes wide with panic. He seemed to be frantically searching her face, reading every detail as if trying to memorize it. Tears began to well up in his eyes as he said, "Go, Kilikina, go."

The train began to move. Christy turned, and the conductor reached out and grabbed her arm as she leaped onto the lowest step. "Ticket," he said gruffly.

With trembling hands, Christy handed him her Eurorail pass, and he motioned for her to enter the packed second-class compartment. As Christy moved down the aisle toward the back of the train, she saw Todd out the window, walking quickly alongside the train, scanning the compartments for her. She pushed her way through the first compartment and into the second. Spotting an open window at the end, she ran with her heavy pack bumping against the seats. The train was picking up speed, and Todd was running to the platform's end, waving at her.

Out of breath, Christy reached the open window. Todd was less than twenty feet away, with very little platform left. As tears streamed down her face, she planted one of her very special, saved-up kisses on the palm of her hand and threw it to Todd out the open window.

He reached into the air, closing his fist around her invisible kiss. Then, with a sharp movement, he pounded his fist against his chest, right over his heart, as if he were placing her kiss in that deep place where she already knew he held all her tears.

The train entered a tunnel, and suddenly everything went dark.

Christy spent the longest ten hours of her life on that train out of Venice. For the first hour she stood by the open window. The warm breeze dried her tears. A wild confetti of thoughts sprinkled themselves into her mind. She remembered standing on the boat's deck on the way to Capri and feeling the warm air behind her. The Lord had felt so close that she could feel His breath. Tonight, He came near again.

The verse Todd had found in 2 Timothy from Paul's time in the Mamertine Prison came back to her: *"But the Lord stood at my side and gave me strength."* Christy found strength in knowing that if she was going to stand on this train all the way to Basel, at least the Lord was standing with her.

She thought of the Alpine meadow and the wild flowers she had picked, pressed, and slept on. Those wild flowers still held dreams that she had not yet extracted. She decided she would frame those wild flowers, now buried in their Italian newspaper envelope.

Closing her eyes, Christy remembered the tingling sensation from when she bathed in the stream at the campground. She could almost taste Tonio's strong coffee and see the sheer lace curtains at his mama's house as they fluttered in the breeze the morning Marcos arrived in the taxi. She thought of the brilliant midnight sun pouring through the window of their room in Oslo, and how handsome and adorable Todd had looked right after he had shaved his scruffy face.

She touched her lips and thought of how they had tingled after his kiss in Oslo when he went off to the ends of the Earth without her. Christy missed him with every part of her being. She felt as if now she was the one going to the ends of the Earth without him. Only instead of being apart two days, they wouldn't see each other for two long months.

Christy managed to sleep after Milan, when a seat opened up and she could lean her head against the window. She missed Todd's navy blue sweat shirt. It had made the best pillow. She missed Katie's laugh and the faint scent of chocolate that had followed her through every country.

When the train finally pulled into the Basel train station,

Christy experienced an odd sensation. This was "her" train station; the one she was most familiar with. Yet being alone made her feel as if the station was foreign and cold. She walked with weary steps uphill to her dorm room. The only thing that came close to bringing a smile to her lips was the wonderful aroma she smelled as she passed the Konditorei. Marguerite was placing a basket of bread in the window. She waved when she saw Christy and motioned for her to come in.

"I'll be back," Christy promised. "Later."

Later. Now, that's a laugh, isn't it? All those years Todd told me "later," and here we are, going our separate ways again. Will it always be "later" for us?

She made it to class in plenty of time, even after stopping at her room to shower and change. The seven other tour books were still sitting on her desk, untouched for the last three weeks. Christy laughed to herself when she realized she now probably owed a library fine on all of them.

As soon as class was out, Christy headed for the Konditorei. She had borrowed her roommate's bike to get to class faster, and now she rode the bike's brakes all the way downhill, bumping on every cobblestone she hit. The front tire wobbled on the old contraption, and Christy laughed aloud at herself when she barely managed to come to a stop in front of the Konditorei.

Securing the bike, and with a smile still on her face, Christy entered. The cheery bell over the door lifted her spirits, and she walked up to Marguerite, who stood behind the counter with a big grin on her face.

"*Guten Morgen*, Marguerite. *Wie geit's?*"

"*Gut, gut. Danke. Gut.*"

Christy thought Marguerite acted a little odd. After ordering her pastry, Christy turned toward her usual seat in the back of the café.

Someone was sitting there this morning. Blocking the person's face was a huge bouquet of white carnations.

Christy stopped breathing.

Todd moved the bouquet away from his face. With his easygoing grin brightening the place like a Norwegian sunrise, he said, "Hey, how's it going?"

Christy ran to the table and threw her arms around him. "What are you doing here?"

"Having coffee with you. Here, these are for you." He motioned to the carnations that now lay across the table.

"Did you miss your plane?"

Todd leaned back and took a sip of coffee from his mug, ignoring her question. "You're right. Marguerite makes the best pastry in the world."

"You did, didn't you? You missed your plane. Todd, what are you going to do? What about Katie?"

"Our plane doesn't go out until 2:00." Todd smiled. "I'm going to have coffee with you, and then go back to Zürich and fly home."

"What happened? How did you guys get out of Venice?"

Todd slipped his arm around the back of the seat Christy had fallen into and playfully tugged on the ends of her hair. He acted as if sitting there chatting was the most natural thing in the world for them.

"Tell me everything," Christy said.

"Well, after your train left, we tried to call Marcos. He answered the phone, which was a God-thing because he had just gotten back from a trip to Vienna and was about to leave for a trip to Zürich."

"So you rode the train with him, and he paid your way?"

Todd shook his head. "We drove to Zürich last night in his Ferrari. Katie and Marcos are in Zürich right now. He let me borrow his car so I could come have breakfast with you."

"You drove his car here?" Christy hadn't noticed any fancy

cars parked out front, but then she had arrived on a rather wobbly set of wheels and hadn't been paying much attention to anything outside her immediate path.

"I parked at the train station. Seemed safer than parking in the *verboten* zones along here."

"I can't believe this," Christy said, smiling at Marguerite as she delivered Christy's coffee, cream, and pastry to the table.

"Believe it," Todd said. "And are you ready to believe something else?"

"What?"

"Marcos became a Christian."

"You're kidding! That's awesome! When?"

"About a week ago. He said he started to read Romans because we told him that was the letter written just for Italians. God's Word is powerful. Marcos read it, he believed, he repented. You should see him; he's totally on fire and telling everyone on all his business trips about his new relationship with Jesus."

Christy shook her head. "God is so incredible."

"Yes, He is."

"And it's so incredible to see you. Todd, I hate to say this, but I don't know if I can stand saying good-bye to you again. I mean, this is exactly what I wanted—to sit with you here and talk with you from my heart, but it's only for a moment, and then you have to go again."

"I know," Todd said. "I feel the same way. But I needed to see you one more time."

Todd hesitated and Christy froze. *This is it!* a torturing voice of doubt chanted in her head. *This is when he breaks up with you for good. He's probably going to leave you and go serve the Lord on some remote island, alone, for the rest of his life.*

No, Christy told herself decisively. *No more fear. No more doubting. Take each mercy that comes every morning. Whatever hap-*

pens is in God's care. He's the Master Designer of our lives. He's in control.

Todd looked at his hands and then back at Christy. "I thought we might have had a few more times to talk on the trip than we did. Alone, I mean."

Christy nodded. "I know. I thought the same thing."

"I wanted to tell you a couple of things."

Christy nodded, waiting.

Todd swallowed and looked at her intently. "You have become a part of me. Not a day goes by that I don't think of you and pray for you. When we've been on the opposite ends of the Earth, I feel you right here." He patted his chest. "I hold you, Kilikina. I hold you close in my heart. I always have. I always will."

Christy felt the tears rush to her eyes.

"But," Todd said and then seemed to draw in a deep breath as if gathering the courage to finish his sentence.

No! Christy screamed inwardly. *Don't say anything else!*

"But I honestly believe I need to tell you something I've never told you before. And I feel certain this is the best time to tell you."

Todd, don't do this! Don't break my heart. Not here. Not now.

"It's not because I think you don't already know this, because I think you do." Beads of perspiration glistened on Todd's forehead. "I want to . . . No, I need to tell you this because I think you need to hear it. You need to know . . ."

Tears were now streaming down Christy's face as she braced herself for the worst.

Todd reached up and brushed away her tears with a tender hand. "You need to know, Kilikina, that I love you."

Christy couldn't breathe. She couldn't blink. She couldn't feel her heart beating.

A shy grin inched up Todd's face. "Do you need me to say it again?" He leaned closer and whispered, "I love you."

A breath of relieved joy burst from Christy's lungs, followed by a ripple of laughter.

"You seem so surprised," Todd said.

"Oh, Todd, I wasn't expecting you to say that!"

"You don't have to respond," Todd said. "Not right away. Think about what that means. We have a couple of months to pray through what the future might hold for us."

Christy nodded and blinked back the rest of her tears. She felt her lower lip quivering. "These are going to be the longest two months of my life."

"It's only a short time, really," Todd said. "Sixty-seven days, to be exact."

"You counted?"

Todd nodded. "And you know what we'll do for those sixty-seven days, Kilikina? We'll pretend we're at the ends of the Earth, where the sun never goes down. Instead of sixty-seven days, it will be one long day. And then we'll be together again."

"One extremely long Narvik day," Christy said.

"That's right."

"Then you know what I will say sixty-seven times during that extremely long Narvik day?" Christy asked.

Todd reached over and brushed back her hair with his hand. "What?"

"Sixty-seven times I will say, 'I can't wait until tomorrow.' "

Todd grinned and pulled her close. Right before his lips kissed her earlobe, he whispered, "Until tomorrow."

NEW

Possibilities for Disciples

and

Independents

NEW
Possibilities for Disciples
and
Independents

With a History of the Independents—
Church of Christ Number Two

A. T. DeGroot

The Bethany Press • St. Louis, Missouri

To

LEWIS H. McADOW

Pastor, Scholar, Friend

The Commission on Cooperative Policy and Practice of the International Convention came into being to help all of us face the problem of division in our brotherhood. One of its purposes is to understand the causes of this division and to interpret these causes to our brotherhood. It is hoped that out of an appreciation of our history there will come a better understanding and good will.

This commission is interested in encouraging books, monographs, and pamphlets that will promote better understanding and good will. It is in this context that the commission requested Dr. De Groot to rewrite *Church of Christ Number Two*. It comes to you now under the title *New Possibilities for Disciples and Independents*.

Members of Commission on
Cooperative Policy and Practice

Spencer P. Austin	Lester B. Rickman
George G. Beazley	Hugh M. Riley
A. T. DeGroot	Jo M. Riley
Velva Dreese	Harlie L. Smith
Willis R. Jones	Mark Rutherford
Albert M. Pennybacker	Gaines M. Cook
Morris H. Pullin	Gertrude Dimke

George Earle Owen, General Chairman

Introduction

THE growth and consolidation of Independent churches into the equivalent of another denomination is still in process but for all sociological intents and purposes is *fait accompli*. A number of our Christian Churches (Disciples of Christ) and Independent churches, to say nothing of the large group of "unrelated" churches, know little or nothing of the forces and factors that have brought the Independents to such a stage they can be denominated as Church of Christ Number Two.

So little has been written in this field by a church historian, with one or two exceptions, that it is very desirable we have such a history and interpretation. This need led the Commission on Cooperative Policy and Practice to encourage Alfred T. DeGroot to revise his earlier book, *Church of Christ Number Two*. This volume speaks to this need. It is written as history with a valid bias, to set the record straight about some controversial issues. It is also written in the spirit and context of *unity with liberty* which brought the Christian Church (Disciples of Christ) into being. It is written in a readable style so that the average layman can understand who the Cooperatives are and who the Independents are, and why they constitute separated brethren among the Christian Churches.

7

Christian unity, as we have always insisted, is our business. But how do we bring it about? What the author has done has been to show two basic approaches to Christian unity: *the exclusive approach,* "Come join us," the unity by pattern approach of the Independents; and *the inclusive approach,* "Let us join together," the unity approach of fellowship, cooperation and possible union of the Christian Churches (Disciples of Christ) with other like-minded bodies. There is a big difference between unity by some blueprint and unity by concensus.

Dr. DeGroot is well qualified to write in this field. His doctor's thesis was a study of the Restoration Movement and an examination of the Independent-Restoration formula for Christian unity—restore the pattern of the New Testament Church. Dr. DeGroot by a documented study of the application of this principle concludes: *"The principle of restoring a fixed pattern of a primitive Christian Church is divisive and not unitive."*

Until he turned them over to the Disciples of Christ Historical Society, through the generosity of the Christian Board of Publication, Dr. DeGroot had the most complete file of Independent journals and publications to be found anywhere. In collaboration with Winfred E. Garrison he has written a comprehensive history, *The Disciples of Christ: A History.* In addition he has made a study of the whole Restoration Movement from New Testament times until now, in *The Restoration Principle.* Both of these histories are recommended as auxiliary reading along with this book for understanding the division in the brotherhood of the Christian Church (Disciples of Christ).

George Earle Owen

Preface

IT IS NOT an unusual thing for a church to have its first histories written by persons who stand outside of its organized life. New religious movements usually are so concerned about their peculiar messages or purposes that they give little attention to an evaluation of these matters in the light of history.

The first narratives about the Christian Churches (Disciples of Christ) were written by "outsiders." In 1807 Richard McNemar wrote *The Kentucky Revival; or a Short History of the Late Extraordinary Outpouring of the Spirit of God in the Western States of America. . . .* (Cincinnati: J. W. Browne), and in the same year he brought out *Observations on Church Government, by the Presbytery of Springfield. To Which is Added the Last Will and Testament of That Reverend Body; With a Preface and Notes by the Editor. . . .* (Cincinnati: J. W. Browne). In 1811 Robert Marshall and John Thompson wrote *A Brief Historical Account of Sundry Things in the Doctrines and State of the Christian, or as it is commonly Called, Newlight Church. . . .* (Cincinnati: J. Carpenter & Co.).

1955, the year of the publication of its first *Yearbook*, may be termed the birthday of "Church of Christ Number Two." It will have to employ some designation like

9

this if it is to have a suitable descriptive name by which to be recognized. There is adequate precedent for this type of name. The Plymouth Brethren now have eight separate denominations, each demanding its own particularisms for fellowship. The United States Census and other annual handbooks of religion list them in just that manner—Plymouth Brethren Number I, etc., to Number VIII.

The writer will endeavor to be objective in all reports of historical incidents, and fair in the selection of the material presented. He cannot, however, dissociate himself from that cooperative wing of the common Restoration Movement from which his own body (Christian Churches, Disciples of Christ) descends nor from the principles which he believes it embodies—and from which he sees both Church of Christ Number One (the anti-instrumental music body) and Church of Christ Number Two (the "Independents") as *groups which have abandoned the historic purpose of Unity with Liberty.*

It should be noted that after all except the final chapter of this book was written, the Independents did produce a history from within their own ranks. It is a book of high quality entitled *Christians Only,* by James DeForest Murch.[1] We shall deal with its theme in our final chapter.

---

[1]Cincinnati: Standard Publishing, 1962.

Contents

11

-1-

The American Restoration Movement of the Nineteenth Century

ONLY THE PURPOSES and principles of the restoration movement of the nineteenth century will be discussed in this chapter.[1]

The Christian Churches (Disciples of Christ, the Churches of Christ Number One, and the Churches of Christ Number Two) originally were one movement, stemming from the evangelical revivalism of Barton W. Stone which was combined with the English puritanism and Lockean rationalism of Alexander Campbell. It was an easy thing for individualistic frontiersmen of the early 1800's to assume that they could leap over all of Protestant Reformation and medieval and ancient church history to start afresh in building a church movement which would reflect only the New Testament commands. In this manner they would be a "peculiar people," reproducing the exact polity and practices of the apostolic church. It is not surprising that this commendable effort

---

[1]The detailed history of the three families or church brotherhoods into which the original movement has fallen may be found in these large books:

For the Christian Churches (Disciples of Christ): W. E. Garrison and A. T. DeGroot, *The Disciples of Christ: a History.* The Bethany Press, St. Louis, Mo., 1948; revised, 1958.

For the Churches of Christ (anti-instrumental music): Earl Irvin West, *The Search for the Ancient Order.* Vol. I, 1849-1865, Gospel Advocate Co., Nashville, Tenn., 1949. Vol. II, 1866-1906, Religious Book Service, Indianapolis, Indiana, 1950.

For Church of Christ Number Two: James DeForest Murch, *Christians Only, a History of the Restoration Movement.* Standard Publishing, Cincinnati, Ohio, 1962.

actually was molded as much by popular eighteenth-century philosophy as it was by the biblical record. We shall see how this showed itself in creating ideas of the full capability of the individual as a person and small groups of individuals as churches to discover the whole realm of truth and to act as "independent" bodies without any real need for the joint thought of others in the long search for truth, or any need of common action with others in making ideals operate and be effective. Much as we may respect and applaud A. Campbell and Walter Scott in the rejection of the Calvinistic doctrine of the depravity and inability of man, we may yet recognize that this very act in behalf of liberty was a part of the American Jeffersonian idealism which, across the years, had to be reduced to constitutional, limited freedoms.

To put our situation in religious language, any rediscovery of the "ancient order of things" and the "primitive gospel" would have to win the approval of not just a few folk who would have their own peculiar way or go off to form a schismatic group; instead, this rediscovery must be made in terms of things that would commend themselves to the whole group, the *consensus fidelium*, the whole body of the faithful.[2] The tragedy of the larger American restoration movement of the nineteenth century is that it has been victimized by parties that were impatient to build upon partial truths, or peculiar vagaries, rather than to create a fellowship bounded only by those things in which all could agree.

The one new note in the restoration program, which was to give it a timeless relevance and quality, was its rediscovery of the importance of *unity* in the message of the New Testament. Even after the seeming defeat of

---

[2]Robert W. Burns writes: "It seems to me that one of the elements of Mr. Campbell's contribution was the idea that those who were competent to deal with the subject were to be listened to. It was really an adaptation of the conciliar theory of the Church. A council of scholars were the ones to whom appeal was to be taken."

the movement by the tragedy of a threefold division, it is possible that the holding of this ideal will call the divergent elements back into a common identity. The Campbell program was loosed in a day when concern for church unity was absent in most circles. Long preaching of this ideal as a basic New Testament demand eventually won its way in the larger Christendom. Even the tragedy of failure by the restoration forces to find an infallible program for unity does not invalidate the goal; it is only the means toward that goal which obviously were not embodied by all of the restoration advocates. We shall be suggesting throughout this study that the neglected element here is failure to keep ever in eye and mind the need for *consensus fidelium* as the boundary mark for fellowship. Only when consensus can be reached does the church have a true standard of its nature, in faith or in organization.

When the Campbells and their associates proclaimed their program for a restoration of New Testament doctrines and practices, it sounded to their contemporaries on the frontier like something entirely fresh and unparalleled. Isaac Errett in the 1860's was discerning enough to write that Disciples of Christ were but one of a series of restoration movements. In 1960 the writer of this book published a fairly large treatment of the subject, entitled *The Restoration Principle,* which identifies many scores of such church groups or denominations.

The genius and resulting good fortune of the Campbell program was that it added one new element and purpose lacking in the others. This was the overarching goal of unity. Other reformation and restoration actions normally were designed to uncover some neglected idea or practice of historic Christianity. Henry VIII wanted to restore to England a national, nonpapal administration of the English church patterned on the type of church tradition before the Norman Conquest. Some movements were set up to revive the (presumed) Christian ideal of celibacy, as with the Shakers, who thereby soon died out as an organization. Others were devoted to the recapture of ancient ways of dress, such as without any adornment. Still others had will-of-the-wisp hopes for male supremacy as would be gained by commanding, with the Apostle Paul, the silence of women in church affairs.

Different from these narrow aims, the Campbell program sought the unity of the church by making essential to its life and structure only those things on which all Christians could agree. As Thomas Campbell wrote in his founding document, the *Declaration and Address,* 1809, ". . . every effort toward a permanent Scriptural unity among the Churches, *upon the solid basis of universally acknowledged and self-evident truths,* must have the happiest tendency to enlighten and conciliate. . . ." (italics added). Reiterating his unity principle, he added,

Indeed, if no such Divine and adequate basis of union can be fairly exhibited as will meet the approbation of every upright and intelligent Christian, nor such mode of procedure adopted in favor of the weak as will not oppress their consciences, then the accomplishment of this grand object upon principle must be forever impossible.

The only book ever written about the *Declaration,* Frederick Doyle Kershner's *Christian Union Overture,* 1923, says, "So sure is Mr. Campbell, in the main, of the substantial infallibility of his platform for unity [i.e., unity won by consensus of faith] that he discusses only incidentally the possibility of its being erroneous."[3]

What we shall be seeing in this book is that Churches of Christ Numbers One and Two are those groups which have retreated to the status of many prior restoration

[3] p. 67.

movements whose object was to be "right" in their own eyes (as a small, homogeneous group), excluding the search for correctness of judgment by the *whole* body. This is why both Churches of Christ refuse to participate in present-day studies and conferences and in interchurch service projects which together constitute "the great new fact of our age," the movement toward church unity. Both of these churches say, in effect, to other Christians and churches, "We are completely right, and you are wrong; you must join us to find unity." The difference between this program for unity and that of the Roman Catholic church is solely a matter of what agency is making the statement and what bill of particulars it is demanding. The *means* to unity are the same.

In our final chapter we shall endeavor to show how this difficulty can be resolved. Meanwhile, it is necessary to review the history by which the problem has been created.

-2-

Early Problems of Unity
Within the Unity Movement

THE RESTORATION MOVEMENT in America was never a completely united brotherhood which only subsequently lost its pristine oneness. To speak of "restoring the restoration" is to allure with fiction but with little more. The unity of the founding fathers was in their quest, not in the specific programs under which they found their several groupings. There was much agreement on what the various leaders and their followers were against; there was much less consent to what, together, they were advocating.

With nothing less than than a testy spirit Alexander Campbell took dead aim on Walter Scott in 1838 and wrote, "I am thankful that I never put the title 'Christianity Restored' nor 'Gospel Restored' to any thing I ever wrote." Yet they remained one in fellowship within the search for the divine intention for their lives.

The first congregation formed by Thomas and Alexander Campbell was the Brush Run church, established in 1811. It began as an open membership body, with a human creed. It soon became a closed membership church and eliminated the creed, causing the loss of a few members.

The most careful study of the baptismal question among Disciples of Christ that has been made in the

18

twentieth century is that of Joseph Belcastro. At the conclusion of his extensive book he says,

The Disciples must know that they have never been united in their understanding of New Testament baptism. In their beginning there were at least five baptismal positions with at least four attitudes toward the unimmersed and church membership. In the course of history there have appeared at least three types of closed membership churches with about eight types of open membership churches. There is a greater theological difference between some of the closed membership churches than between some open and closed membership churches. Some of the differences contain highly controversial-explosive elements. Yet every position has been advocated by sincere and honest followers of Jesus Christ, believing that the New Testament, either in word or spirit, supported them. Loyal men have been on all sides. It is not loyalty to the New Testament, but the contradictory understanding as to what the New Testament taught that has plagued the brotherhood with many controversies.[4]

The union of the forces of Barton W. Stone and of Alexander Campbell in 1832 was much less than complete, because of real differences of belief. Colby D. Hall's book entitled *The New Light Christians* says:

There were several other "spats" back and forth between the two leaders, of much the same flavor, but as Stone expressed it, they "agreed to disagree." As will be observed later, throughout the process of unifying, Campbell was more neutral rather than enthusiastic.[5]

James DeForest Murch estimates that the lack of unity between the Campbell and Stone forces was far more serious than other historians have noted. Concerning the union conference in 1832 he says,

When the news of the happenings at Lexington and beyond came to his ears, Campbell was stunned. While he earnestly

[4]From a manuscript *The Disciples of Christ and Baptism* (Nashville: The Historical Society of the Disciples of Christ), pp. 197-198.
[5]Fort Worth: Colby D. Hall, 1959, p. 110.

desired Christian union, he was not ready for such precipitate action.

. . . Indeed, differences in opinion on central doctrines needed to be resolved. . . . Among these central issues were the Trinity, the atonement, the name of the church, church government, revivalism and the work of the Holy Spirit in conversion, and Christian baptism.[6]

As early as 1831 A. Campbell felt the need for a general cooperation of churches to do those works which a single congregation could not successfully accomplish. In that year he began a series of articles in his *Millennial Harbinger* on "The Cooperation of Churches." A Mr. "A. B. G." promptly replied, "There never was, and there never can be, any occasion for such a combination of 'the churches' to build up the Redeemer's kingdom."[7]

Mr. Campbell returned to the same subject with another series of articles in the same paper in 1842. They were under the general title of "Church Organization" and continued into 1848. During this discussion there arose the opposing opinions which were to create the antisociety party within the movement which became Churches of Christ (Number One), and which issued its first *Yearbook* as a separate people in 1906.

The opposition to Mr. Campbell and his associates included some misrepresentation. It was said that the "cooperatives" wanted to create a new entity, apart from the New Testament, which was a "general church" with "general church officers" and general obligations. This was never true. On the other hand, it was the case that the Campbell program saw that there was a duty for Christians in separate congregations to become involved in the whole growth-by-study and effective witness-by-work which they could do only by voluntary cooperation

---

[6]*Christians Only* (Cincinnati: The Standard Publishing Co., 1962) pp. 113-114.
[7]*Millennial Harbinger*, 1832, p. 201.

in *and beyond* their local churches. Specifically at issue was the task of undertaking missions, "unto the uttermost parts of the world."

With this, however, was a further task, the finding and speaking of the agreed mind of the whole church for sounding its message and pronouncing its judgment in the world. The church is a living church only as it comes to grips with the world for the purpose of cleansing the life of persons and society. It does this with its word of faith. But no one man controls this faith. The whole church is worthy of its name only as it works earnestly at the difficult, spiritually demanding task of bending the mind of all its people to the mind of their Lord. It is this hard-won and slowly reached "consensus of faith" with respect to the issues of life which is the goal of church cooperation. Cooperation in general work always must wait upon a spiritual factor, which is a common faith.

Members of the families within the restoration movement in America should not be surprised that they have had deep problems of unity. They are still a young people in the total life of the church universal. They may be a long time coming to the unity of spirit which is prerequisite to any unity in work.

In 1849 the majority of the ministers and members of "Christian Churches" and "Churches of Christ," as they were called almost interchangeably, agreed to form an agency to represent them in tasks too large for local congregations. It was the American Christian Missionary Society. Other service organizations were added later.

Unfortunately, this development became involved with new issues, especially instrumental music. This aid to worship had wrought havoc in other churches earlier and now was going to do the same with Christian Churches that were wrestling with the physical problem of hauling their first church organs over the Alleghenies.

With the growth of local churches full-time pastors were needed. It is not surprising that isolated frontier congregations that had not been able to afford either church organs or full-time ministers looked upon the county-seat and city churches that adopted these measures as "different" and, consequently, "heretical." The New Testament was searched and, while it yielded no specific instructions against musical instruments, at least it was silent on the theme and this silence was claimed as divine disapproval. Thus there came about the greatest single evidence of disunity in the restoration program.

There were other instances of different theology and practice, however. Open or closed communion is one example. Consider two *dicta* of Alexander Campbell, one in 1829 and the other in 1850. An inquirer had asked Mr. Campbell whether the unimmersed should be given even occasional access to the Lord's table. The Bethany editor replied,

I know of no scriptural authority for such a discrimination. It is arbitrary and unreasonable. If I can admit an unimmersed person once a month for a year to all social ordinances, I can for life or good behavior. When I say, *I can do so,* I mean that all precepts, precedents, and scriptural reasons, authorize such a course.[8]

But in 1850 it was the same man who wrote,

This kissing of the cheek, this extending of the right hand of Christian fellowship, this complimentary compellation of our "orthodox fellow-Christians of different communions," while not a crumb of consecrated bread, nor one drop of consecrated wine, will be extended to us any more than to Turks, Jews, or Infidels, is the quintessence of sublimated hypocrisy; the very spirit of guile and dissimulation from which every pure, and generous, and sensitive heart recoils in mortification and disgust.[9]

---

[8]*Christian Baptist* VI, 68.
[9]*Millennial Harbinger,* 1850, p. 312.

It is one of the strangest experiences of doctrinal meta-morphosis that any communion should undergo such a change from closed to open communion and do so with-out significant controversy. It is possible that here we have a key to the problem of unity and division in the church. The existing practice of open fellowship at the communion table rests upon the injunction of the Apostle Paul to "let a man examine himself, and so partake." It was the intention of Thomas Campbell, as he wrote the *Declaration and Address* in 1809, to extend this principle widely in all church life. His definition of church mem-bership is,

The Church of Christ upon earth is essentially, intention-ally, and constitutionally one; consisting of all those in every place that profess *their* faith in Christ. . . .[10]

Alexander Campbell elaborated this principle in his "Lunenburg Letter" of September, 1837, saying,

But who is a Christian? I answer, Every one that believes in his heart that Jesus of Nazareth is the Messiah, the Son of God; repents of his sins, and obeys him in all things according to *his* measure of knowledge of his will.[11]

Until restoration advocates "catch up" with their founding fathers by providing fellowship with large lib-erty for honest convictions arising from study of the New Testament, they will continue to proliferate Churches of Christ Numbers One, Two, etc.

---

[10]Proposition 1
[11]*Millennial Harbinger*, 1837, p. 411.

-3-

Origins of Church of Christ Number Two

In 1955 THERE WAS PUBLISHED *A Directory of the Ministry of the Undenominational Fellowship of Christian Churches and Churches of Christ*. The same title was used on similar books in 1957, 1958, 1960, and 1963.

In the congregational tradition of Christianity, the unity of the church is recognized as effective through:

(1) The free movement of ministers and members among all of the local churches.

(2) The cooperation of the local congregations through voluntary societies which are noncombative even if sometimes competitive for support—and which are constantly in consultation to respond to the will of the many churches (the consensus of the group).

(3) A continuous fellowship, as in conventions, to proclaim the "like precious faith" and to be effective in producing, checking, and ordering those agencies recognized as arms of the body.

Alexander Campbell stated the necessity of these principles, through some consultative and directing body, as early as 1842, in the *Millennial Harbinger*. He said,

I cannot conceive of a kingdom without a constitution, an organization, a joint and common interest, and a constant co-operation in reference to its self-preservation and comfortable existence. If Christ have a kingdom on this earth, it must be a community organized, united in common interests, in harmonious concert, and conservative of its own integrity and prosperity. . . .

It allows not persons to send themselves or to ordain themselves to office; but every where intimates the necessity of choice, selection, mission, and ordination. . . .

. . . I lay it down as a maxim not to be questioned, that where there is Christian communion of any sort, special or common, there must be an amenability of the participants to some common tribunal, and a mutual responsibility to watch over, and nourish, and comfort one another. . . .[1]

It will be seen that 1955 was the fateful year of overt schism, for the second time, in the ranks of the American restoration movement. The separation of Church of Christ Number Two was in repudiation of the basic principles enunciated in the statement by Mr. Campbell, given above. We must now trace the steps by which this schism was generated.

A long process of discussion of issues took place before Church of Christ Number One (the anti-instrumental music group) consolidated itself fully into a separate camp by the publication of its first *List of Preachers* in 1906. The removal of the antiorgan faction still left within the parent movement many believers in the "independent principle" of church relations; that is, those who felt that there was no inherent obligation, no constitutive element or practice, by which local congregations become fully the Church by growth into a unity or consensus of faith and by common acts of service. It was this remaining body of convinced Independents, who conceived of the church as finding its highest reality within local congregations which bear no dependence

---

[1] *Millennial Harbinger*, 1842, pp. 59, 62, 63.

upon one another, who were going to grow into Church of Christ Number Two.

The exact point of origin of a body of sentiment which later becomes an organization is not easy to designate. Stephen J. Corey in *Fifty Years of Attack and Controversy* (published 1953) suggests 1903 as the dividing line, but the issue was older than that. The issue, or resident feeling, was without organized leadership and without a journalistic voice, until Russell Errett changed the policy of the *Christian Standard,* about the year 1901. That paper had been one of the bulwarks of cooperation among the restoration forces for a generation after its origin in 1866.

Federation of churches in common ideals and work was the overt issue in this controversy. In order to be able to work as a distinct fellowship in consultation and cooperation with other existing religious communions of Christendom, Disciples recognized the utility, indeed, the need, of an intercongregational structure among their Christian Churches. This meant that the church in its wholeness was greater than one local congregation, and even greater than the sum of its parts. When, through federative activities with Christians of other communions, the Christian Churches (Disciples of Christ) began to affirm that they were really only a part of a much larger Christendom, the Independent sentiment in the brotherhood found an issue congenial to its basic belief. This belief was: All but "our own" are defective Christians—so defective as not to be deserving of fellowship in "loyal" local churches and not deserving of participation in enterprises common to all churches.

This is the real issue today. We shall note in the closing two chapters that an occasional voice (Orval Crowder, Fred Thompson, James DeForest Murch) cries out for some effective fellowship on the part of Church of Christ

Number Two with other Christians, in ministerial associations, councils of churches, and joint community projects of churches. As a whole, however, Church of Christ Number Two refuses to have this type of cooperation and stands quite apart from all of the rest of the Christian world—more so than the Roman Catholic church in current times. This is an assertion by a fraction of less than one tenth of one percent of the world's Christians that all the others have no real consequence in the providence and plan of God except that they are a part of the mission field waiting to be evangelized with the true gospel. Cooperative Christian Churches (Disciples of Christ) believe that such an attitude is a tragic denial of God's work in the unfolding life of his church.

This does not mean that Disciples of Christ believe that all that has happened in the career of the church was for good. The powers of evil have been real and infernally able in misdirecting the church time after time. But the use of the Bible has been the salvation of the church just as frequently. Wise and devoted Christians have called it back closer to ways of truth on many occasions. A major problem of Disciples has been their lack of historical orientation with regard to the nature of their own movement. The proper function of the restoration program ought to be an effort to join forces with all other earnest Christians in a rediscovery of God's intention for his church. The genius and true intent of the founding fathers of Disciples of Christ was stated by one of their British leaders, Lancelot Oliver, who wrote in the *Bible Advocate*, May 6, 1910,

We have never held that a return to New Testament Christianity *and acceptance of what we think constitutes it* are necessarily one and the same thing; and at needed moments the fact has been recalled that we must ever be ready to diminish or enlarge, as further truth breaks forth from God's word.

Disciples of Christ believe this statement; the Independents (Church of Christ Number Two) deny it. The issue is simple and clear.

It is only by intimate conference and joint study with other Christians that the purpose of Proposition Two of the *Declaration and Address*, by Thomas Campbell, 1809, can be fulfilled. It stated,

> . . . although the church of Christ upon earth must necessarily exist in particular and distinct societies . . . there ought to be no schisms. They [are] . . . to be perfectly joined together *in the same mind, and in the same judgment.*

Acceptance of the principle of recognizing the essential Christianity of earnest followers of our Lord in other churches, and seeking joint study and work with them in pursuit of a true program of restoring New Testament Christianity, is the only way of coming to a *consensus fidelium,* the mind of the faithful. There can be no consensus of faith achieved by a denomination which draws its skirts of self-righteousness around it and refuses to participate in the slow processes by which truth is perceived and even more slowly embodied in the daily work and worship of the church.

-4-

Development of Church of Christ Number Two:

(1) COOPERATION AS AN ISSUE

THE *Christian Standard* WAS STILL A VOICE of cooperation among Christian Churches under Russell Errett's early management, in 1901. Archibald McLean wrote in J. H. Garrison's *Reformation of the Nineteenth Century* (1901):

> One man to whom the [Foreign Christian Missionary] society owes as much as to any other is one who has never had a prominent place in any of our conventions. He has been a steadfast and generous friend of the society since its organization. . . . Russell Errett has been in a position where he could help; he has quietly and persistently and joyfully done what he could to send the gospel to those who are sitting in darkness and in the shadow of death.[1]

When E. B. Sanford, secretary of the National Federation of Churches and Christian Workers encouraged federation of churches as a practice before the National Convention of Disciples of Christ in 1902, at Omaha, Nebraska, and J. H. Garrison, editor of *The Christian-Evangelist,* encouraged it, J. A. Lord, editor of the *Christian Standard,* began the unrelenting campaign of that paper against such recognition of and cooperation with other Christian bodies. Church of Christ Number Two

---

[1] St. Louis: Christian Publishing Co., p. 442.

29

truly may be identified as the child or creation of this work by the *Christian Standard.*

Fellowship with "the denominations" has continued to be a major issue in the division which was effected somewhat formally in 1955. In 1907 the Norfolk, Virginia, convention of Disciples gave practically unanimous approval to joining the Federal Council of the Churches of Christ in America (organized 1908). In combatting this fraternal attitude and life, the *Christian Standard* battled those groups and actions which favored such cooperation. The Campbell Institute, organized in 1896, consisted of college- and seminary-trained Disciples ministers, most of whom favored cooperation. Since it also studied the new biblical criticism with zeal, the *Standard* attacked this organization steadily.

When John D. Rockefeller made a financial gift to the Foreign Christian Missionary Society through his Standard Oil Company, the *Christian Standard* seized the opportunity to attack the society. This soon developed into a bitter personal attack upon A. McLean, secretary of the F. C. M. S. Mr. McLean's reply was in three parts.

(1) J. A. Lord, editor of the *Standard,* had been a private agent for an oil company and endeavored to sell stock in its undertakings. He solicited sales from his Christian friends. He even stated that his company was a subsidiary of the Standard Oil Company, in order to make his point more conclusive.

(2) The *Christian Standard* had been continuously receiving Standard Oil "tainted money." It ran paid Standard Oil advertisements in the paper.

(3) The *Standard* editor, Mr. Lord, wrote strong editorials against taking "tainted money" and demanded that the Foreign Christian Missionary Society return the entire amount to Mr. Rockefeller. Yet Russell Errett,

owner of the *Standard*, apparently wrote editorials for one of his papers in which he took the other side of the issue. (The reference was to a statement, "Several Things," *Christian Weekly*, September 16, 1905, p. 10, published by the Standard Publishing Company.)

Attacks upon the Foreign Christian Missionary Society were accompanied by the setting up of a new, separate missionary enterprise, sponsored by the *Standard*. Using a "Hors de Rome" (out of catholicism) movement as its device, it solicited support for A. E. Seddon to develop a church in Paris, France, in 1909. Much money was poured into this venture, but no church grew out of it and it was abandoned during World War I.

When Disciples missionary leaders decided to abandon their Monterey, Mexico, station in favor of the Methodists, who were already strong there, and concentrate Disciples work in Central Mexico, the *Christian Standard* agreed to support an independent mission station in Monterey under the direction of E. T. Westrup.[2]

The movement toward cooperation in all general work of the churches came to a new stage of unity by the creation of the United Christian Missionary Society, voted in 1919 and legally effected in 1920. The object of this organization was to give unity of planning and direction in the work of the many agencies that entered the Society, to avoid overlapping and unnecessary competition, and thus to render a better stewardship of the funds given to Christian causes. This plan was attacked by the *Christian Standard*, which called a "Restoration Congress" rally in Cincinnati in 1919 immediately prior to the national convention of the churches.

In this Congress attacks were made against persons who were leading in the unification, and charges were laid against the merging societies. This rehearsal in the

---

[2]See *Christian Standard*, June 14, 1919.

31

Congress was promptly carried to the larger national convention. Dr. Corey's detailed account shows that in the presence of this larger assembly the organized opposition to cooperation and coordination of the general work of the churches was seen for what it was—i.e., it was the work of a magazine and a publishing company dedicated to destroying the missionary and benevolent movement which it could no longer control. The *Standard* had lost the respect and loyalty of the new generation of ministers and other church leaders whose study and learning had been pronounced dangerous and heretical by the magazine. W. R. Warren wrote about the charges that were hurled in the convention, and said,

Some of the most violent were aimed at F. M. Rains, a hero of Christ's service who was known to be on his deathbed at that moment, twenty years before his time because of his abundant labors. With quiet self-control the officers allowed the storm to break its fury upon its own violence. Even the opposition paid high tribute to the forbearance and fairness with which they were heard. Most of those present recognized the plain marks of strength and courage, integrity and unselfishness in all of the official group. The vote was overwhelmingly in favor of organizing the United Christian Missionary Society as proposed, and later for all other recommendations of the boards.[3]

Cooperation of churches seeking to achieve a common mind and faith, accompanied by its natural outcome, cooperation in work and service, thus is seen to be the basic issue leading to the withdrawal of persons and churches into Church of Christ Number Two. Decision to join the Federal Council of Churches in 1908 was the first clear test of the thought of Disciples about their place in the larger kingdom of Christ. It was termed by the opposition as an act of "recognizing the denominations." When J. A.

---

[3]Warren, *Life and Labors of Archibald McLean* (St. Louis: Bethany Press, 1923), p. 273.

Lord used this phrase in questioning W. E. Garrison at Omaha in 1902 the latter said that such cooperation recognized that the denominations exist, and that there are Christians in them, but not that they represented an ideal or final form of organization for the whole church. This is the principle that has led Disciples of Christ to *work from within* the existing larger Christian community to reform it to New Testament principles. The Independent position, on the other hand, is to stand apart from the existing Christian world and to show by its life and deeds so superior a type of character that all others will join them in unconditional surrender. The difference between the two bodies is clear.

-5-

Development of Church of Christ Number Two:

(2) OPEN MEMBERSHIP AS AN ISSUE

THE STORY OF HOW OPEN MEMBERSHIP has been a problem to the thought and practice of Disciples of Christ has been written in detail by Joseph Belcastro in *The Relationship of Baptism to Church Membership*.

The earliest churches of the American restoration movement were open membership congregations. Some of the churches that "came out" of Methodism under James O'Kelly in North Carolina in 1792 retained optional forms of baptism.

Barton W. Stone wrote about baptism in the *Christian Messenger*, October, 1827:

It was unanimously agreed that every brother and sister should act according to their faith; that we should not judge one another for being baptized in this mode [immersion]. The far greater number of the church submitted to be baptized by immersion, and now there is not one in five hundred among us who has not been immersed. From the commencement we have avoided controversy on this subject; and, directed the people to the New Testament for information on this matter.

In August, 1831, he added:

We have seen many unimmersed possess the spirit of the kingdom; and we have seen many immersed destitute of it. To receive the latter, and to reject the former, we cannot view divine.

Alexander Campbell rejected closed membership. He believed that redemptive grace was not bound by im-

34

mersion. To him, baptism was a sign, a pledge, and an assurance that God had forgiven his sins by the Holy Spirit through the atoning blood of Jesus Christ.[1] He did not agree with some of his followers who maintained that only the immersed were Christians.[2] Baptismal regeneration was never a part of his thinking.[3]

Briefly, while he was serving the Brush Run church, Campbell wrote a few items that reflected a closed membership position—but these, later, were specifically disavowed.

In 1827 Alexander Campbell affirmed his church membership fellowship with the unimmersed. He added that while he could do this, it did not mean that a church should abolish the use of immersion. In the July issue of the *Christian Baptist* for that year he wrote:

Some of them receive unnaturalized persons into his realm on the ground of forbearance. On this subject I write with great caution, for I know this question of forbearance has in it some perplexities of no easy solution and is at least of as difficult solution as that concerning the amalgamation of the Jews and Gentiles in the Christian church, decided by the apostles and elders in the city of Jerusalem. . . . Now, although I could feel myself at perfect liberty, in full accordance with the requirements of the Great King, to receive into the most cordial fellowship everyone which I have reason to recognize as a disciple of Jesus Christ, with all of his weaknesses, as I would call them; yet I could not, and dare not, say to all the members of the Christian congregation, that they must do so too; and I could not approve the adoption of a rule to receive such persons, which in its direct tendency, aims at the abolition of one of the fundamental laws of the empire.

The major early incident clearly showing Alexander Campbell's acceptance of open membership was the

---

[1]See *Campbell-Rice Debate*, 1843, pp. 458, 459, 519.
[2]See *Millennial Harbinger*, September, 1837.
[3]*Ibid.*, November, 1837, and December, 1837; also *Campbell-Rice Debate*.

Christian-Reformer union of 1832. L. L. Pinkerton, who was baptized by Mr. Campbell in 1831, wrote:

Nothing was said [about baptism] at the time the two bodies united, and so immersion was not made an indispensable prerequisite to membership in the new organization.[4]

The importance of this event and its terms is seen in the fact that Isaac Errett, when defending W. T. Moore's right to use open membership in Great Britain, argued that it was justified upon the basis of A. Campbell's attitude and practice in the Christian-Reformer merger of 1832.[5]

The final and mature thought of Alexander Campbell on the subject is seen in his book entitled *Christian Baptism*, published in 1851. Here he rejected baptism as a requisite of church membership. He said,

The baptisms of the New Testament were all for the remission of sins, and for no other specific purpose. . . .

Some have such a puerile and inadequate conception of Christian baptism, as to regard it as mere ceremonial introduction into the church—a way of making a profession of the Christian religion—no way of affecting the spiritual relations of the subject. This view of it ought to have been expressed by such a precept as the following: "Repent and be baptized, everyone of you, for the admission into the church." But no such precept, in form, in substance, or in sense, is found in God's own book.[6]

This was a position more radical than that of Barton W. Stone, who thought some mode of baptism was essential to membership in the church.[7] The full implications of Campbell's final baptismal position, says Belcastro, never were "fully grasped by the brotherhood." Instead, it was swamped by the forensic success of other Disciples in the second generation (the time of their

---

[4]*Christian Standard*, June 28, 1873.
[5]*Christian Standard*, October 7, 1885.
[6]pp. 253, 256.
[7]See *Millennial Harbinger*, September, 1849.

greatest growth) over advocates of infant sprinkling, in debates held in a literalistic and proof-text age.

The characteristic position of Disciples of Christ on baptism was thus fashioned not by A. Campbell and B. W. Stone but by leaders in the middle period of the life of the Christian Churches. Isaac Errett was the editor of the *Christian Standard* from its founding in 1866 (the first issue announced the death of Alexander Campbell) until 1888. To him, salvation was by faith, but the unimmersed were "Christians in error" who could not be received into "our" churches (Missouri Christian Lectures, 1888), even though they could be fellowshiped on an informal basis (*Christian Standard*, July 5, 1873). Christian union, he said, must wait upon all Christendom practicing immersion exclusively (Missouri Christian Lectures, 1888).

Isaac Errett's position became general among Disciples, but some "strict constructionists" went to greater extremes. Campbell had felt obliged to dissociate himself from Walter Scott on baptism, because the latter used a formula which said, "For the remission of your sins and the gift of the Holy Spirit, I immerse you into the name of the Father, and of the Son, and of the Holy Spirit."[8] Moses E. Lard was even more explicit in his exclusions. He wrote, "I mean to say distinctly and emphatically that Martin Luther, if not immersed, was not a Christian—this is what I mean to say. . . . It is not that I love Luther less, but that I love truth more, which impels me to think him not a Christian. . . . I recognize no human being a Christian who is not immersed."[9] John Thomas required Baptists to be re-immersed, as did Nathan Smith.[10]

---

[8]See *Evangelist*, 1830, p. 60.
[9]*Lard's Quarterly*, September, 1863, pp. 44, 47, 49.
[10]*Gospel Advocate*, March 14, 1867.

In summary, says Belcastro, there were four Disciples' attitudes toward unimmersed believers:

Dr. John Thomas and Moses E. Lard denied the unimmersed fellowship, because they did not consider them as Christians. Isaac Errett considered them as Christians, but denied them church membership unless they were immersed as a fulfillment of the formal requirements of the New Testament. Barton W. Stone acknowledged them as Christians and invited them into church membership hoping that the truth of immersion, through love and forbearance, would eventually be accepted. Alexander Campbell accepted them as Christians and as church members without any mode of baptism, but presented immersion as the New Testament mode as a pledge and formal assurance that sins are forgiven.[11]

Open membership as a practice (not only as a theory) began with W. T. Moore, an American aide (missionary) to churches in England, 1878-1896. He practiced immersion only, but received the unimmersed into full fellowship. Oddly enough, when he was called into question about this behavior by American supporters, it was Isaac Errett (who did not himself favor the practice) who defended him. The latter said,

Brother Moore is not preaching or practicing anything out of harmony with the faith and practice of the Disciples generally. He is faithfully preaching the gospel just as it is preached in our pulpits all over this land, without compromise and without perversion.[12]

J. A. Lord argued in 1885 in his Missouri Christian Lectureship in favor of open membership, saying that freedom in Christ places one above forms or rituals. However, when Mr. Lord became the editor of the *Christian Standard* in 1889 he changed his ground and became as dogmatic in opposing open membership as he had been earlier in defending it. J. W. McGarvey, contrib-

---

[11]Belcastro, *op. cit.*, p. 58.
[12]J. S. Lamar, *Memoirs of Isaac Errett*, II, 235.

38

uting editor of the same paper from 1892 to 1911 set the pattern for most Disciples in opposing open membership.

H. R. Cooley introduced open membership in America at the Cedar Avenue Church, Cleveland, Ohio, in 1895. In 1906 the Monroe Street Church, Chicago, adopted W. T. Moore's "London Plan." W. B. Craig introduced open membership at Central Christian Church, Denver, Colorado, about 1909.[13] However, the practice was so uncommon that at the Centennial convention, 1909, Samuel H. Church, a grandson of Walter Scott, created something of a sensation by delivering an address favoring individual liberty in the matter of baptismal forms.

In 1914 the Northern California convention felt impelled to do something about the growing threat, and became the first state body to exclude a church for its membership practices. Graham Frank, secretary of the General Convention, and a guest on the program, said that the refusal of seats to representatives of the Berkeley church "was implicitly impossible in the General Convention," the preamble of whose constitution affirms "the independence and autonomy of the local churches."

The Hyde Park Church, Chicago, adopted open membership in 1919. It became apparent by this time that this practice was held in favor by a significant minority of the churches. The next question was, Should the Christian Churches (of the American restoration movement) have doctrinal and baptismal standards and practices which would be creedal and required for fellowship? One alternative was to maintain fellowship within the quest for "New Testament Christianity" by allowing liberty and autonomy for local churches in the pursuit of this quest. A dissenting faction, however, was in favor of separation, demanding uniform practices.

---

[13]W. E. Garrison, *An American Religious Movement*, p. 138.

-6-

The Decision to Separate

THE *Christian Standard* TOOK THE INITIATIVE and responsibility for making open membership an issue requiring division of the Christian Churches. It did so upon the charge that open membership was being promoted in the church colleges and on the mission fields. Long-time leaders in both fields denied the charge.

In 1918 the *Standard* editorialized that "The Time Has Come for Action." It announced and promoted a preconvention congress to gather prior to the International Convention of Disciples of Christ (which was then its name) at St. Louis in that year. The influenza epidemic cancelled both meetings. The same paper then sponsored a preconvention rally at Cincinnati in 1919. At that meeting a resolution was adopted which said that since certain men were advocating and practicing open membership, this Congress expressed the conviction that such persons and churches had apostatized from the restoration movement, and should be so regarded by the agencies that served the brotherhood.[1]

The *Standard* forces were surprised that the churches as a whole were not radically fearful of open membership. Accusations of disloyalty against long-respected leaders caused much resentment and the 1919 conven-

---

[1]*Christian Standard,* October 25, 1919.

tion, contrary to the expectations of the *Standard*, refused to call them apostates.

The *Christian Standard* called another Congress prior to the convention at St. Louis in 1920. In that convention, L. N. D. Wells, highly respected middle-of-the-road leader, argued that open membership in China did not have the same meaning as it did in this country. He added that the brotherhood was arguing about a "membership roll" problem, of which the New Testament tells us nothing, since it is the Lord who adds to the church (Acts 2:47).

After continued but fairly moderate agitation from 1920 to 1925, the *Standard* initiated a series of nine regional rallies in the latter year to combat open membership. It also created a new paper, the *Spotlight*, with Robert E. Elmore as editor, "to expose and counteract evils." The name of the paper soon was changed to the *Touchstone*. It featured such headlines as "The Betrayal of Our People," "A Campaign of Deception," and "The Failure of the United Christian Missionary Society." The latter, it said, "must be destroyed to preserve purity, liberty, and unity in the churches of Christ."[2] This was a clear promise by the Standard Publishing Company, publisher of the *Christian Standard*, that it proposed to rule or ruin the American restoration movement.

The time of the convention at Memphis, Tennessee, 1926, was nothing less than the "year of decision" for unity among the Christian churches. This writer was in Memphis for his first experience of attending an International Convention of Disciples of Christ. He heard Leslie Wolfe make the claim of "quoting" a report from an American inquiry committee that had been sent to the Orient to investigate church practices. John Golden, a respected pastor, arose and shouted, "Finish that sen-

---

[2]*Touchstone*, October, 1926.

tence" (of quotation). When all of the sentence was read, it was apparent that Mr. Wolfe had endeavored to deceive the audience of several thousand people about the intent and content of the inquiry report.

Other equally strong charges were hurled by opponents of the attitudes held by the majority of the convention people. Leaders of the assembly endeavored to give suitable and fair attention to the protests, but refused to be dominated by the minority.

One reason for this attitude was the inconsistency of the conservative forces. In the questioning at Memphis, W. D. Cunningham, a missionary supported by the *Christian Standard*, acknowledged that he was an officer of an open membership church in Tokyo, Japan.[3]

Repulsed in its plan to control the International Convention at Memphis in 1926, the *Christian Standard* led in calling a competing assembly, the North American Christian Convention, the first session of which was held at Indianapolis in 1927. This annual gathering became the means of encouraging the formation of agencies to compete with those organizations that were doing the general work of the churches and reporting to them through the International Convention. Thus new colleges, missionary societies and missionary families, benevolent homes, hospitals, and other service organizations were established. The object was to create a whole new fabric of agencies which would serve the "loyal" churches —those loyal to the *Christian Standard* and its interpretation of New Testament Christianity.

The new grouping did not have a rapid growth. One cause of delay was the influence of Edwin Errett. He became editor of the *Standard* in 1936 and remained in this post until his death in 1944. He attended the Interna-

---

[3] Other instances of open membership being practiced by Independents on the mission field will be cited in a later chapter.

tional Convention and took part in some of the world-wide assemblies of the ecumenical movement that were to lead to the formation of the World Council of Churches in 1948. In these gatherings he became aware of the honesty of representatives of scores of denominations who were investing so much time, money, and talent in the search for unity. He toned down the bitterness of some of his associates in the North American Christian Convention by his moderation. Attacks upon his own honesty may have contributed to his comparatively early death.

The illness and loss of control by Edwin Errett permitted the radical independents to mount their pressure for separation, and in 1943 the *Christian Standard* issued "A Call for Enlistment." It proposed to replace the "unfaithful leadership" of The United Christian Missionary Society, the International Convention, and the Christian Board of Publication, with "new and consecrated" leadership. The major advocates of this "Call" were W. R. Walker, R. C. Foster, P. H. Welshimer, Burris Butler, Peyton Canary, Lester Ford, S. S. Lappin, Fred Smith, T. K. Smith, and Orval Morgan.

The Christian-Evangelist for December 15, 1943, promptly rendered its judgment that "This Is Divisive." Stephen J. Corey called it "a blueprint of separation for the brotherhood of the Disciples of Christ."[4] That these were correct statements is shown in the fact that in the July 29, 1950, issue of the *Christian Standard* that paper took the responsibility for announcing the reality of a separation of its followers from Disciples of Christ.

The clarity of the separation has been made more explicit in recent years. The *Dallas Christian College Contender* for March, 1956, said,

---

[4]*Fifty Years of Attack and Controversy*, p. 185.

It is either independent OR Disciples since there is no connection, it cannot be both. It is just a simple fact that the independent work is connected in no way with this apostate organization.

Harold W. Scott wrote in the *Christian Standard* of January 18, 1958, ". . . there are now separate conventions, separate publishing houses, separate yearbooks, and separate youth camps." He added, "We are in duty bound to take action when folk depart from the faith," but concluded, "We want freedom; let us give freedom."

-7-

Results of the Separation

"A SCORE OF LITTLE SECTS"

ONE RESULT OF THE SEPARATION of Church of Christ Number Two is its loss or abandonment of the original aim and end-method of the American restoration movement. Barton W. Stone epitomized the over-all objective of the Christian Churches when he pleaded, "Let the unity of Christians be our polar star!"[1] The method by which this grand objective of unity was to be reached was by creating congregations controlled in their thought and life by the New Testament.

Such a method requires an operating principle. This principle involves a common, brotherhoodwide search of the New Testament for agreement on what it says a church should be and do. The search must be continuous and include the representatives of all points of view, seeking a consensus of the faithful. The whole movement represents "one body" so long as majority opinion is allowed to be normative, even while permitting liberty of thought and of action—so long as these do not separate themselves into "other bodies."

Continued fellowship in search of agreement is the only way of achieving a *consensus fidelium*. Destruction of fellowship by a minority which accuses the historic

---

[1]This slogan is carved in the stone pillar at the entrance of the Disciples of Christ Historical Society building, Nashville, Tennessee.

main body of apostasy can lead only to schism and continued fragmentation. We have quoted in Chapter 3 the keen insight of Lancelot Oliver about what a return to New Testament Christianity involves.

Church of Christ Number Two has abandoned the only path that can take a body of people to a consensus of faith. Instead of coming into conference in a genuine search for truth, it stands apart, hurling anathemas at those with whom it refuses to consult.

In 1906 Church of Christ Number One set up three standards of orthodoxy as grounds of fellowship. These were—

> Anti instrumental music
> Anti societies
> Anti pastors

In 1955 Church of Christ Number Two set up two marks of separation. They were—

> Anti open membership
> Anti consensus of faith

There were very often others added to these, including—

> Anti evolution
> Anti social gospel
> Anti modernism

Instead of engaging in a search for community of thought, or consensus of faith, the body now coalescing as Church of Christ Number Two assumes that *it has agreement,* already reached, on all major items of faith and practice. It is the object of this chapter to show that this assumption is a fiction, and that disunity already is a problem to the new church body.

The *Christian Standard* saw the threat of fragmentation and stated it editorially, October 13, 1951:

Within the "Independent" group are the seeds of from one to a score of little sects, all the more sectarian because of its insistence that it alone is right.

46

How censorship and tests of orthodoxy work in the ruling factions of Church of Christ Number Two are shown by E. E. Scates. He wrote,

It should be recognized that many of the folk who support "Direct Support" missions are making tests of fellowship out of many non-essentials and do not have within their forces as much of the inherent urge to unite and work together as do the "Co-ops." In my journeyings and correspondence I encounter much "splinter party" type of thinking. The Horizons magazine had to re-write our ad last year before accepting it although we feel we were using New Testament language. The Brazilian Christian Mission and the Christian Missionary Fellowship are not treated equally with pure "direct support" types of missions because of their use of some forms of organization. Bible colleges are sometimes organized by one local church and sometimes by representative Boards and there is some contention as to the rightness of each policy. All these signs indicate further division and we will follow the pathway of divisiveness followed by the Churches of Christ non-instrumental, unless we have a greater passion for unity and fellowship than often exhibited. I still have the strong conviction that one's love of Jesus Christ and loyalty to His teachings is the only basis of Christian fellowship and unity. If love is the most important New Testament Doctrine I cannot conceive of happiness where harsh and vituperative words sometimes replace love and fellowship.[2]

Since Church of Christ Number Two was so largely the creation of the *Christian Standard*, it is not surprising that the publishers of other journals envied and sometimes challenged *Standard* domination. One competitor is *Horizons*. It ran in its January 1, 1955, issue an article charging "*Christian Standard* Quits." This had reference to the move, said Harrold McFarland, editor of *Horizons*, "without fanfare or previous preparatory announcement," by which the *Standard* dropped its page or column about Independent missions. Through *Horizons* Mr. McFarland

---

[2]*Intermountain Christian*, January 27, 1955.

promised "we will do our best to replace the great void left by the *Standard* abandoning the independent, direct support, missionary cause."

R. M. Bell, President of Johnson Bible College, showed how division among the Independents arises. He wrote in *Blue and White*, May, 1950, concerning a meeting of the Independents, and said:

. . . Everyone with whom I talked seemed to be having a good time. One man was pointed out to me who seemed to be an exception. He moved about the convention hall like an evil spirit seeking whom he might destroy. Of course I could be mistaken about him as he usually is about others. He may have been suffering from joy. He was described to me by one of his friends as a man "who lives on his hates." He appeared to be looking for someone to hate.

For a probable identification of the person thus described with the editor of the *Restoration Herald*, one needs only refer to that journal, the issue of July, 1950.

The result of these attitudes is narrated by Mr. Jessup in the *Gospel Broadcaster*, May 1950:

. . . many churches are torn by strife. Ecclesiasticism and modernism are not the main curses among our people. Those who deny Christ and His Word are not of us and there isn't any basis for unity. Our main problem is sectarianism, among free churches of Christ. Evangelists and elders have assumed authority and legislated where God has not spoken. . . . It is time for us to . . . begin marking the trouble makers who are disturbing the peace and harmony of local congregations.

The disappearance of any effective unity among the Independents is shown in the reports which describe the only public evidences of cooperation among these workers, which are the rallies and conventions. The conference at Minnesota Bible College, reported in the *Restoration Herald*, April, 1950, was presided over, in large part, by S. S. Lappin. His position and actions were described in this fashion:

This, then, is the apology of the appeaser, the program of the palliator, the confession of the "conservative" compromiser, the sale of the Lord for 30 pieces of silver.

To this spokesman of the cult, support of the UCMS is purely an affair of "expediency"; it is not a question of motive, but of "method"; not a matter of faith, but "a matter of opinion," . . . .

The same issue of this journal described the third Direct Support Missions Conference, Indianapolis, as a "tiny side show," put on in March with the knowledge that the "second National Missionary Convention" was to gather in the same city in April. The defense of this action was stated as follows:

The committee (Chase et al) was in fear of offending the NACC ("North American convention" meeting Ap. 26-30, H. Poll local chairman) by putting on a better program than they offered. They seem content to be a tiny side show since they're not admitted into the main tent.

This discontent with the North American Christian Convention, largest rally of the Independents, is of long standing. Because, prior to the first such convention, in 1927, P. H. Welshimer insisted that it should be constructive and not used for internal quarrels, the *Restoration Herald* said the Independents were "double crossed" (April, 1946). A review of twenty years of the NACC by Mr. Elmore (*Restoration Herald,* May, 1949) concludes that it is "giving succor to the enemies of Christ" and "hindering the work of those who are really fighting the good fight of The Faith. . . ."

What is meant by these strong statements is made clear later. Tibbs Maxey wrote about the Christian Missionary Fellowship (*Restoration Herald,* January, 1952) that it "insists on fellowshiping those of liberal Protestantism who are historically connected with the Restoration

49

Movement . . . ," meaning the larger Disciples body. This is intolerable, says Mr. Maxey, and he dismisses the CMF by saying, "Its existence is a criticism of independent missions."

In the *Restoration Herald,* May, 1955, there began a series of discussions, not yet ended, about "dangerous missions trends." This paper is particularly unhappy about the conduct of certain Independent Korean missions, which are defended by *Horizons.* The *Restoration Herald* is also a stern critic of the North American Christian Convention, upon which Mr. McFarland leans for much of the support of his publishing enterprises. Some persons claim that the Convention and *Horizons* aspire to dictate policies to the Independent movement. Concluding a review of events, the *Restoration Herald* said, in the March, 1956, issue: "There you have it in all of its naked infamy. And that is handed down from the would-be Headquarters of 'Direct-Support' Missions."

A missionary, writing in the October, 1955, issue of the *Restoration Herald,* says of the "Chapels for Korea" Fund, "I am angry with no one but myself, for ever allowing myself to become a part of something worse than the United Christian Missionary Society."

Robert E. Elmore, a stern Independent, writes in the Fall, 1955, issue of the *Seminary Review* (Cincinnati Bible Seminary):

The independent brethren are now confronted with the problem of their own conventions. Some of these conventions have departed from the simplicity and purity of their original character and purpose. A little Campbell Institute has been operating behind the scenes, watering down the faith and collaborating with the Disciples hierarchy. Self-appointed and self-perpetuating clerical cliques have taken over control, subtly corrupting the ministry at large insofar as their influence reaches.

Divisions in Church of Christ Number Two have continued to increase. A letter by Burrus Butler, then editor of the *Christian Standard* and dated January 3, 1952, said that "for various reasons of policy" it refused to make any reference to the following colleges:

> College of the Scriptures
> Intermountain Bible College
> Louisville Bible College
> Midwest School of Evangelism
> Roanoke College

Thus it is apparent that it is not a single and united Church of Christ Number Two which stands over against the historic main stream of the American restoration movement seen in the Christian Churches (Disciples of Christ).

An editorial in the October, 1957, *Church and Home Christian Leader* is entitled "A Protest! We Bolt over Grahamism," an action which was seconded the next month by the *Restoration Herald*. The *Herald*[3] took a peculiar satisfaction in reporting that the North American Christian Convention would release no registration figures, but its [the *Herald's*] representative estimated that "at none of the sessions were there present as many as one thousand people." However, the North American meetings have subsequently grown much larger.

A stringent cartoon against the use of the North American Christian Convention was published by *The Church Speaks*, September, 1958. The *Restoration Herald* and its constituency were differentiated from the larger Independent body in the June, 1960, issue. In it James DeForest Murch had perhaps a novel experience in being condemned as a "liberal." The paper said:

---

[3]June, 1957, p. 15.

Our readers are referred to the February, March and May (1959) issues of the *Restoration Herald* for the story of Mr. Murch's official affiliation with and service for an organization of some 40 denominations, sects and cults which calls itself the National Association of Evangelicals, among which are the Pentecostal Holiness church, the Mennonite church, the Reformed Presbyterians, the Church by the Side of the Road, and Holiness Methodist Church, Six-Principle Baptists, the Foursquare Gospel church, and so on. His fellowship and salaried service for this denominational hodgepodge has continued since 1945. He is now an employee of the denominational organ, *Christianity Today*.

The last-named paper is described in the *Restoration Herald* as follows, quoting Bob Jones:

Christianity Today was founded to "sell" compromise with liberalism, and with great pretensions to scholarship seeks to break down the lines of demarcation between those who believe the Bible is God's word and those who question or deny it. The Bible demands separation. . . .

It is not difficult to identify who is being referred to in the editorial quoted below from *The Seminary News* (Phoenix, Arizona), September, 1958, when we recall that the editor of the *Restoration Herald* long has attacked the Arizona seminary. A part of the editorial reads,

A frustrated old man, weakened by personal habits, frustration, and loneliness, has made himself pathetically ludicrous by a series of articles attacking THE SOUTHWEST CHRISTIAN SEMINARY and other loyal agencies and individuals among us.

A few have wondered why we have chosen to remain somewhat indifferent to such false and ridiculous tirades. There have been three reasons why we have ignored, in large measure, the Philippics of the barbarous Bard.

In the first place, most of what was written is too absurd to merit reply. The absurdity reached an all time high when the author attempted to justify his own ministry, strewn with altercations, split churches, and disgrace. His own failures are known, and no amount of "glossing" covers up the fact that he has failed repeatedly, and his failures are partly the cause of his absurdity.

More than "meets the eye" is involved in a special, dark-type, front-page editorial by President W. F. Lown in *Manhattan Bible College News*, October, 1957, under the title "Love the Brotherhood." One paragraph says,

How sad it is that Christian people who professedly have as their ministry the bringing of men to Christ, will sometimes coldly try to exclude their fellow Christians from the body of Christ! What logic prompts this thoughtless deed?

This is a mild and mediating statement from a school which endeavors more than any other institution to maintain ties with both Cooperative and Independent churches.

Conclusive evidence of division within Church of Christ Number Two is seen in the appearance, in the winter of 1961, of the "Red" *Tokyo Christian*. The original *Tokyo Christian*, now in its 61st year, was the organ promoting the mission work of the W. D. Cunninghams, who were among the earliest Independents. Their daughter, Eloise, became an Episcopalian. Since the properties accumulated by the Cunninghams for mission work were owned by the missionaries (as is now true of much Independent mission property), the daughter probably reasoned that they should become her possessions. With the help of Dr. Wm. S. Boice of Phoenix, Arizona, she began another *Tokyo Christian* imprinted with a red banner across its front page. It is sufficient, here, to let Harold Sims, editor of the older *Tokyo Christian*, tell the substance of the story, in the Winter, 1962, issue of that paper.

There is much talk of the successful plan of work followed by the Cunninghams and our failure to follow it. From all we can learn, the plan followed through the years was simple—Mr. Cunningham was the dictator, and all who didn't accept that fact were dismissed. The old-time readers of the Tokyo Christian will remember a long, sad line of missionaries who came for one term or part of one and then quit. The wicket was also busy with incoming and outgoing Japanese pastors. The Mission had only 1 essential officer—"director." His authority was maintained by the classic method of paying salaries to all preachers and Mission workers—even $5.00 monthly to all Sunday School teachers.

The account concludes:

It really saddens us to see the churches at home and in Japan involved in this controversy over Mission policy, but perhaps it is inevitable in these changing times. The irony of history is that in the name of the first independent mission among our people the old organizational and paternalistic notions of missionary work should make one of their last stands; and that being led by the Episcopal daughter of the founders and some opportunist businessmen.

Schism of Church of Christ Number Two into a variety of nonfellowship groups is threatened by such actions as that of editor Harrold McFarland, who made the major article in the January 5, 1963, issue of *Horizons* one entitled "I Do Not Recommend Support of the Christian Missionary Fellowship." Christian Missionary Fellowship is one of the two principal missionary agencies of Church of Christ Number Two. Denial of its right to exist will not lose it many supporters, but more likely will be a cause of further subdivision into Church of Christ Number Three and other bodies.

-8-

Problems in Education

IT IS POSSIBLE THAT PERSONAL AMBITION to be a "college president" has been a real factor in the rise of Independency. Grover Lee Hardison was one, but returned to the pastorate in the Carson Street Christian Church, San Antonio, Texas. He runs this advertisement about his congregation in the newspaper:

A cooperative brotherhood Christian Church in the direct support of 600 Independents (local church sent) missionaries, 60 Bible Colleges, and many other benevolent and charitable causes and institutions of the Christian Churches and Churches of Christ.[1]

The effort here to mislead Disciples newcomers to the city into thinking his is a "cooperative brotherhood" congregation may be passed over just now in noting the claimed "60 Bible Colleges." Independent papers are almost unanimous now in claiming only 37.

Even this number is too many, say some Independent leaders. Russell E. Boatman, President of Minnesota Bible College, wrote in the *Minnesota Bible College News*, February, 1960, an article entitled "College Poor! Poor Colleges?" He said:

---

[1]*San Antonio Express and News,* Jaunary 21, 1961.

As a people we have more colleges per capita, and per number of congregations, than any other religious body. The fact is we are college poor. Scarcely a college among us is not struggling with deficit budgets. . . . we are in jeopardy of becoming "poor colleges." . . . their presidents must be raised above the role of perennial beggars. . . .

William R. Nash, President of Dallas Christian College, wrote in the August, 1962, issue of the *Dallas Christian College Contender:*

Financial crises are commonplace among our Bible Colleges also. Were it not for the dedicated interest of one particular individual, Dallas Christian College would be "out of business" now. Because of this man's concern our doors are still open. BUT, the problem is how long will they remain that way. And, this man must be repaid $10,000 on December 1, 1962.

Another phase of the problem was presented in a letter of Bruce Parmenter, of Tuscola, Illinois, and published by the *Christian Standard,* December 9, 1961. He said:

One of the actual sites now being proposed as the location of a new Bible college will reach into an area which is already supporting three [to five] other Bible colleges!

The present understanding of what is a college, by the Independent leaders, is those educational institutions purporting to offer "four years of studies basically designed for those who possess high school certificates, or their equivalent."[2] The roster given in the latest Independent *Yearbook,* 1960, is:

	Founding date
Alberta Bible College—Calgary, Alberta, Canada	1932
Atlanta Christian College—East Point, Georgia	1928
Boise Bible College—Boise, Idaho	1945
Central Christian College of the Bible—Moberly, Missouri	1957
Central Washington School of the Bible—Selah, Washington	1948

---

[2]Letter of Vernon Newland, February 25, 1961.

Churches of Christ School of Evangelists—Portland, Oregon	1952
Cincinnati Bible Seminary—Cincinnati, Ohio	1924
College of the Scriptures—Louisville, Kentucky	1945
Dakota Bible College—Huron, South Dakota	1942
Dallas Christian College—Dallas, Texas	1950
Eastern Christian College—Bel Air, Maryland	1946
Great Lakes Bible College—Lansing, Michigan	1949
Grundy Bible Institute—Grundy, Virginia	1956
Gulf States Christian College—Baton Rouge, Louisiana	1953
Intermountain Bible College—Grand Junction, Colorado	1946
Johnson Bible College—Kimberlin Heights, Tennessee	1893
Kentucky Christian College—Grayson, Kentucky	1919
Lexington Christian Bible College—Lexington, Kentucky	1954
Lincoln Bible College—Lincoln, Illinois	1944
Louisville Bible College—Louisville, Kentucky	1948
Manhattan Bible College—Manhattan, Kansas	1927
Maritime Christian College—Charlottetown, PEI, Canada	1960
Memphis Christian College—Memphis, Tennessee	1959
Midwest Christian College—Oklahoma City, Oklahoma	1946
Midwestern School of Evangelism—Ottumwa, Iowa	1946
Milligan College—Milligan College, Tennessee	1881
Minnesota Bible College—Minneapolis, Minnesota	1913
Nebraska Christian College—Norfolk, Nebraska	1945
Northwest Christian College—Eugene, Oregon	1895
Ozark Christian College—Joplin, Missouri	1942
Pacific Bible College—Long Beach, California	1928
Platte Valley Bible College—Scottsbluff, Nebraska	1951
Puget Sound College of the Bible—Seattle, Washington	1950
Roanoke Bible College—Elizabeth City, North Carolina	1948
St. Louis Christian College—Florissant, Missouri	1956
San Jose Bible College—San Jose, California	1939
Southern Christian College—San Antonio, Texas	1947
Southwest Christian Seminary—Phoenix, Arizona	1947
Winston-Salem Bible College—Winston-Salem, North Carolina	1950

Mr. Newland's letter indicates that two of these, Gulf States, and Lexington, "discontinued operation even before Directory publication," and Maritime college, "while projected, did not actually open." However, Toronto Christian Seminary was subsequently opened in Canada.

It is unrealistic to include Northwest Christian College in this list. It sends many if not most of its graduate students into accredited, cooperative institutions. In the

57

1960-1961 Review of the Independent Colleges (*Christian Standard*, August 27, 1960) and the 1961-1962 College Report (*C.S.*, August 18, 1962), Northwest Christian College did not report.

A few of the Independent colleges have made significant progress educationally and financially in the past few years. Others have had to struggle against lack of support and show little if any improvement within the past decade. *Boise Bible College News*, October, 1954, said:

Because of the number of members on the faculty, and because each one has other responsibilities besides his teaching in the school, none has time enough to teach a full schedule of classes. For that reason two years' classes are taught each year. This year the second and fourth year classes are being taught. We realize that this arrangement is not ideal. There are some first year students taking a fourth year class.

Regimentation and thought control in these colleges is charged by Robert E. Elmore, in the *Restoration Herald*, April, 1952. He relates rumors "that in some 'independent' schools, operating for the professed purpose of training Gospel preachers, the professors are under orders and the pupils are muzzled and there is a rigid ban on discussing the thing called the U.C.M.S. . . ."

Writing of "that segment of the Disciple fellowship known as 'Independents,'" Hoyt S. Canary gives a summary of their educational results in the *Seminary News*, December, 1952. He says:

This brotherhood that I love has basked in the mud of mediocrity. Even if the charge angers, the charge is still true. New Testament preachers do not have a national audience; our professors are not writing books; our schools are not producing scholars; our impression on the life of the world is pathetic.

Just what is a college is a question not agreed upon by all who are in association with one, but some factors should be recognizable. Normally, there should be a president who gives his whole time to this work—or, if that is asking too much, there should be at least one teacher around whom the program centers. Yet, some Independent institutions do not have this much staff. The following is a quotation from the August, 1954, issue of the official journal of one of the listed colleges:

Since the close of school Mr. (X) has resigned as president of the school. Mr. (X) came to the school three years ago to fill the vacancy in the teaching staff occasioned by the departure of Mr. (Y). He has driven bus for the (Z) Bus Company, mainly on their school runs, for the major portion of his support since coming to (Z). He has made two trips among the churches in behalf of the school during the summers. He has taught Evangelistic Singing, Acts and Hermeneutics, Logic, Homiletics II, Apologetics, I Corinthians–Galatians.

. . . (his) departure has left quite a gap in the teaching staff of this institution.

Any observer is obliged to honor the devotion and generosity with which the teachers in some of the Independent colleges have given their time to the teaching work. What happens to the quality of the educational program under staffs made up of marginal-time teachers is another matter. A statement of the Financial Policy of Boise Bible College, published in the April, 1955, *BBC News* is as follows:

Whatever amount comes into the school in the way of gifts is divided among the teachers as "salary." It is divided on a percentage basis. Each man teacher receives twenty per cent (20%) and each woman teacher receives ten per cent (10%). If the amount of the gifts in a single week exceeds one hundred dollars ($100), just that amount is divided, and the remainder is kept in the treasury till the following week. The maximum that any teacher receives in a given week would then be $20 for a man teacher and $10 for a woman. The only exceptions to this in the past year have been a special gift at Christmas time and a special gift at the close of the school when each received more than the regular maximum. Another factor in this division of the money is that there is never any such thing as a "back salary." If the money comes in, it is divided; if it doesn't, it isn't. Last year we went as high as three weeks on one occasion without receiving anything. On another occasion we received a full check for as many as four consecutive weeks. By operating in this way the school can never go in debt and have to borrow money to pay back salaries or come under obligation to anyone else. This is not intended as a criticism of any other school or policy, but it is a statement of how we operate and why.

The natural result of this is that each member of the faculty must provide for his basic needs in some other way. Brothers Beckman and Knowles are co-ministers of the church at 18th and Eastman in Boise, and each receives a weekly salary of $40 plus parsonage. Brother Richards ministers at the church in Meridian and receives a salary of $50 plus parsonage. Brother Thomas teaches in the public school and receives a somewhat higher salary but must pay his own rent.

Park H. Netting, minister at Owosso, Michigan, in his parish paper comments that "the average Church of Christ (Independent) minister has far less education than many of his religious neighbors." Mr. Netting believes that this situation is the result of the educational program of the Independent Bible college. He points out that there are 38 such Bible Colleges in the United States and Canada. Their enrollment is 2,638. "This averages out to 69 students per school. Actually, this figure is misleading, as 64% of those enrolled are in the seven largest schools. . . . The total graduate enrollment was only 135."

The fact that Church of Christ Number Two is not to be thought of as one body is seen in the public declaration of basic differences among its colleges. In the first catalog of the Churches of Christ School of Evangelists,

1953-54, the reason for starting this college was explained as follows:

> The crisis has been aggravated by the existence and toleration of deficiencies of the gravest character, ranging from obscuring Bible Ideals and methods to rationalism, in schools allegedly committed to the program of the church of Christ.

The reference here is to other Independent colleges.

Robert Elmore, a leading Independent, has no confidence in large numbers of his "loyal" brethren. He wrote in the February, 1950, issue of the *Restoration Herald:*

> In calling attention to the schools as the chief cause of trouble, our friend has in mind particularly the schools which fly the "loyal" flag . . . .
> It is the half baked, self seeking aspirants and appeasers from some of the independent schools who are doing most of the damage now being wrought among churches of Christ.
> We doubt if the earth was ever before so overrun with such a plague of grasshopper preachers as is the case today. . . . We are thinking now of the "independent" or "loyal" preachers, who specialize as "the pastor" of this or that church of Christ. We have seen church after church reduced to the same state as the once great church to which our correspondent refers has fallen.

Further charges of internal problems and shortcoming are made by some of the workers. Luke D. Elliott says in the *Dallas Christian College Contender,* April, 1953, with regard to the missions so largely staffed by Independent college graduates, that there is "Non-cooperation among the missionaries themselves. This has been due many times to: jealousy distrust, greed, and fear."

In support of this he says, "The difficulty of getting out a cooperative missionary publication that would save all the missionaries money and duplications is one evidence. . . ."

61

More directly and doctrinally, he complains of "making tests of fellowship out of non-essentials in regard to methods of procedure."

In addition to these clear demonstrations that unity and cooperation are absent among Independent colleges, it may be added that they have their share of personality weaknesses and disloyalties. Minnesota Bible College published a sheaf of mimeographed "evidence" in 1942 telling of the troubles it had with Luke Elliott, who has since started and left other Independent operations. The material charges that Elliott had the Dakota Bible College started by accusing Minnesota Bible College of disloyalty. It says that Mr. Nystrom reported that Elliott was forced to resign from the MBC faculty because of "radicalism, fanaticism, and dogmatism." It further relates a specific charge of falsehood against Elliott, who in another place is quoted as saying "God cannot save a sinner without his being immersed. . . ."

The desire of an occasional Independent college to get away from the confining narrowmindedness of its fellowship is made plain in this report. It states:

Mr. Elliott preaches glibly the doctrine of unity among God's people and practices division, while denominational ministers preach union and accomplish what they preach. His frequent attacks against denominational churches and preachers has brought us nothing but silent contempt and isolation. He never loses an opportunity to warn and admonish the students against the danger of having anything to do with the denominational churches and preachers. What self-righteous bigotry and hypocrisy!

Independent Disciple colleges speak with mixed voices on the strategic subject of accreditation. Hosts of young people attend unaccredited colleges, then desire to complete their preparation elsewhere, only to find that their "credits" are of no value.

Southwest Christian Seminary, Phoenix, Arizona, published an editorial in the *Seminary News,* October, 1950, entitled "Our Goal," which included this statement: "a standardized undergraduate college where men and women may come for preliminary training in many secular professions as well as for the ministry." It added, "Leaders in the Seminary see no incompatibility between scholarship and a passion for souls."

Puget Sound College of the Bible, Seattle, Washington, said in the *Pacific Christian Chronicle,* March, 1953, that "our charter forbids the college ever to become an affiliate of any organization or institution." However, it added that PSCB is approved by the Washington State Board of Education for training in religion, by the Veterans Administration for training in theology, by three Independent schools (Cincinnati Bible Seminary, Minnesota Bible College, and Lincoln Bible Institute) for undergraduate work.

Lester Ford, president of Midwest Christian College, encourages conference and co-operation between the independent colleges, saying "these Bible Colleges must work together" or become provincial and isolated (M. C. C. *Bulletin,* January, 1952).

Minnesota Bible College has made it known for some years that it seeks to be accredited. In the M. B. C. *News,* June, 1954, it announced that its music certificate had been accredited by the Minneapolis College of Music. In the November, 1955, issue of the same paper an article announced with satisfaction, "We Passed." It referred to being admitted as a college into the Accrediting Association of Bible Institutes and Bible Colleges.

Lincoln Bible Institute announced its membership in this accrediting society in the *Restorer* of November, 1954.

Apart from these minority voices, most of the listed colleges keep discreetly quiet about the subject of accreditation.

In December, 1955, the Ford Foundation made financial grants to all of the accredited private colleges in the United States. The cooperative colleges of the Disciples of Christ received $2,600,000 as their share of the grants, because these colleges are recognized as worthy and as colleges which provide standard, acceptable educational work.

The independent colleges of Church of Christ Number Two did not receive any support from the Ford fund.

A student of Lincoln Bible Institute wanted to enter the military chaplaincy, but was denied admission because his B.D. degree from L. B. I. was not from an accredited school. President Hargrove of L. B. I. wrote to the Christian Churches (Disciples of Christ) chaplaincy director saying L. B. I. was accredited (i.e., by the Association of Bible Institutes and Bible Colleges). The Director wrote to the Association, which replied that L. B. I.'s Bachelor of Divinity degrees should not be considered as accredited, for while it recognized its undergraduate institutions as standard, it did not so claim for its "graduate" work.

A milestone of real significance for education among Independent colleges was marked in 1960 when Milligan College was accredited by the Southern Association of Colleges, and thus became the first truly accredited Independent college. Lincoln Bible College seems to have fair prospect of reaching the same standard.

To any person acquainted with the history of the American restoration movement it comes as nothing less than a shock to find a portion of this family, the Independents, pulling away into a separate fellowship which demands of its leaders and their institutions that they shall commit themselves in writing to theological creeds and theological speculation. Some Independent schools have taken membership in the Accrediting Association of Bible Institutes and Bible Colleges, which consists mostly of extreme Fundamentalist colleges which are parts of denominations with long and involved theological creeds. Perhaps this is one point of origin for the prevailing tendency of the independent colleges to write speculative creeds into this charters and their payroll systems.

Items in Article X of Midwestern School of Evangelism are said "not to be taken as a church creed or discipline. . . . They are merely statements which disqualify men from places of authority in this institution. . . ." The required beliefs include:

 . . . . The use of such names as . . . "The Christian Church" . . are not befitting the body of Christ; hence are sectarian.
 . . . denominations . . . deceive more souls into condemnation than any other form of sin.
 . . . a Christian must leave alone . . . movies (even the so-called "good ones"), dancing, cards, lodges . . . tobacco in any form.

Under Article XVIII it is further provided that "arts and sciences cannot at any time exceed twenty per cent of the curriculum hours."

It is further provided in Article VII that "said Corporation shall never be endowed."

A frequently used form of doctrinal requirement is Article III of the Constitution of Great Lakes Bible College, which reads, in part:

 . . . every trustee and teacher or other worker in any capacity must be a member of the church of Christ (undenominational) and *must believe, without reservation,* in the full and final inspiration of the bible to the extent that it is to him the infallible Word of God, and therefore the all sufficient rule of faith and life; in the deity and supreme authority of Christ; obedience to the Gospel; the edification of the church; and the restoration of its unity on the New Testament basis.

Occasionally other topics are introduced into the required doctrinal statements, as at Nebraska Christian College:

. . .

8. A strict weekly observance of the Communion.

9. That the terms of Salvation and Church membership are one and the same.[3]

10. That God will answer prayer, when approached in the name of the Lord Jesus.

Dakota Bible College states that it believes and teaches:

1. That the Bible is the revealed Word of the Living God.

2. The Deity and Lordship of Jesus Christ.

3. That we are saved by the blood of Christ.

4. The personal bodily resurrection of Christ.

5. That Christ is coming again in person.

6. That Christ's plans for His Church are sufficient, without any human additions, subtractions, or substitutions.

7. That the Bible plan of salvation involves faith in Christ, repentance of sin, confession of Christ, and a burial in Christian baptism in the name of Christ for the remission of sins, and a consecrated regenerated life after conversion.

Such a creed, of course, would not qualify a person even for baptism in the usual Protestant or any Catholic denomination, since it lacks baptism in the name of the three Persons in the Godhead, and otherwise is so vague in terminology as to mean little in relation to the historic subjects with which it deals.

---

[3]This is exactly contrary to what Alexander Campbell said in the Campbell-Rice debate, 1843, p. 785. Campbell said, "...we do not...make conditions of ultimate salvation out of the conditions of church membership."

All colleges have problems, but the Independent institutions have some that are peculiar to themselves. With so many of their colleges existing, some graduates do not find work. The *Restoration Herald,* December, 1957, reported "the fact that in Phoenix were residing at that moment half a dozen or more student preachers who had completed their work at the [Southwest Christian] Seminary, and were then employed in some secular business and preaching for no church in Arizona."

In view of the "orthodoxy" and Bible-centeredness of Independent schools, it is surprising to find Lincoln Bible Institute reporting in the July 30, 1958, issue of the *Restorer* that its freshmen know less of Bible content than students in "denominational" colleges.

The November, 1957, issue of the *Restoration Herald* reported that Southwest Christian Seminary was the personal property of the president and his brother. Many examples of misleading news from the seminary were claimed in that edition of the paper.

-9-

Missionary Promotion

APART FROM DOCTRINE, the principal appeal of Independent missions to its supporters is the claim that "every penny goes to the field." Unpaid "forwarding agents" in the United States represent the foreign missionary individuals, families, or teams, to acknowledge receipt of contributions and to forward them in lump sums periodically. The only expense involved is a little postage and some stationery. This gives the appearance of a system which avoids the "overhead" or promotional costs of having a staff of scores of people on salary in Indianapolis to conduct the home base work of The United Christian Missionary Society.

But the picture, examined more closely, does not turn out to be a contrast in black and white, even of heavy costs for overhead compared with light costs. Indeed, it is likely that the actual promotional costs in money that never gets to the missionary field is at least three or four times the percent that is freely acknowledged as overhead by the cooperative missionary system.

"Did you know that forty per cent of our time is spent writing and corresponding," writes Robert M. Small, editor of *Small News* (issue of June, 1951) and one of the staff of Kiamichi Mountain Missions. If missionary money is for missionary work and time, this is an acknowledged

40 per cent overhead, without counting travel and related items. Selected at random is one of Mr. Small's monthly statements of expenditures. It reads:

"God of Creation" (film) _____$ 20.94
Oklahoma City trip _____ 15.00*
Gasoline—bulk _____ 38.65
Mimeograph paper _____ 23.00*
Amp. payment, repairs _____ 21.00
Bank charges _____ 1.94*
Postage _____ 22.00*
Salary _____ 200.00
Dallas trip _____ 34.00*
Native M. Fund _____ 10.00
Gifts designated _____ 16.00
Bus repairs _____ 103.80
Office help _____ 11.00*

$527.33

If only the items which have had an asterisk added to them (total $115.94) are counted as promotion, here is an addition of more than 20% to be counted in with the "over forty per cent" of time spent in correspondence, or a cost of 65% for overhead in this mountain mission project by the Small family.

"Do you know that the expenses of an evangelist while making his 'tour' to raise funds for his support equals that of six to nine months on the field?" Thus writes Burl Shoemake in a printed folder (recent but undated) concerning his work in the Bahama Islands.

Just exactly what the cost of missionary promotional tours really is, seldom is revealed. Owen Still reported in *Hawaiian Challenge* (November, 1953) the cost of a three-month tour in the United States. His figures show:

Money sent to Hawaii _____ $1588.11
Money paid on bldg. loan _____ 1538.48

                                                 3126.59
Money for expenses _____   929.62

This means that 23% of the total offerings were spent for tour expense. This was a great deal better for the mission than Mr. Still was able to do earlier in the same year. He reported in the May, 1953, issue of the same paper on three months of a promotional tour as follows:

For the Mission _____ $1312.56
For expenses _____ 606.31

This is a cost of over 31% overhead.

When a new missionary sets out, lacking oversight from experienced workers, he may or may not find a field ready to accept his services. An example of this problem is seen in the case of the C. W. Callaway family, who left the United States in 1946, with two children. They were in England until early 1948 under missionary support while studying. They then went to Burma, only to be refused residence visas (all this is avoided by arrangements in advance through the oversight in cooperative missions). After five months they moved to China, and began studying another language, but communist control was unfavorable and in less than a year they moved to Hong Kong, for a brief stay, followed by another move to Siam. By this time there were six in the family. Following two years of language study and other work in Siam they announced their plans to return to the United States in 1953, nearly seven years after leaving, the most of which was spent in study and travel.[4]

Disruption of independent missionary work, with resulting travel expenses, because of lack of oversight and

---

[4]See *Tribes and Trails in Thailand*, April, 1952.

planning through legal channels, is increasing as world conditions become more unsettled. The *Assam Messenger*, December, 1952, carried this notice:

On Sunday night November 23rd, Mrs. Mabel Nichols flew from New York by way of London to Calcutta where she was to arrive November 27th. Her return to Assam at this time was made necessary because her husband Edgar Nichols has been denied permission to remain in Assam after November 30th . . . .

Even though "every penny goes to the foreign field" through independent missions it may be spent for various purposes. The December, 1953, issue of *Nagoya Christian News* carried an appeal for $789.00 per year for tuition in the United States Air Force school for children of the Howard Davis family at work in Japan.

The African Christian Mission was begun when the Guy Humphries family left the United States in 1948, and organized their first church in 1949. Various emergencies developed in the staff, and in the Fall, 1952, issue of the *African*, notice was given that "due to recent developments . . . it has become imperative that Brother Humphries return to the States briefly. He plans to arrive by air sometime during this month and return in March. . . ." The notice further indicated that a daughter would fly the round trip with her father, and that other members of the family "may have opportunity to come home briefly later." These brief visits via round trip plane flights to Africa are immense elements in the overhead and promotional costs of independent missions.

Even an occasional Independent magazine editor becomes alarmed at the prodigality of some Independent missionaries in connection with their travel. Tibbs Maxey wrote in the October, 1955, issue of the *Restoration Herald:* "It costs real money to fly a family home, two thousand dollars of widow's mites. Who put up the money? Why not send them boat tickets?"

Perhaps the most unhappy experience that can come to young missionaries is to volunteer, take long training, travel to the field, then find that a clash of temperaments makes the work impossible, only to be stranded, physically and financially—plus being presented with a bill by the missions operator for part of the expense of getting out to the field. This is what happened to Mr. and Mrs. Robert Williams, as related in the First Quarter, 1953, issue of the *African*. After five months' service, the mission decreed:

To protect the churches and the Lord's money, the trustees of the African Christian Mission have already required the following, to which the Williamses agreed orally before the Trustees previous to leaving for the field: "The Mission will expect any missionary who leaves the field before the end of five years, EXCEPT ON DOCTOR'S ORDERS, to pay his own transportation home. Furthermore, any missionary who leaves the field in less than two years of service, EXCEPT ON DOCTOR'S ORDERS, will be expected to pay a share of his transportation to the field in addition to his own transportation back home. This share will be arbitrarily set at $25.00 for each month required to fulfill the two years."

It is a very common thing to read notices like this headline: "Ray Carlson Family on Furlough From Philippine Islands; Will Make Home in Kentucky for One Year" (*Christian Standard*, November 11, 1950). The article which followed added, "During his one-year stay in the States, Mr. Carlson will endeavor to secure funds. . . ." One year of promotional travel represents a large per cent of the missionary income.

The Woodrow Phillips family, of six, issued a notice in 1953 that "we are planning to begin visiting among the churches in the middle of December . . . to return to our

Jamaica work before Fall of 1954," a tour of almost one full year.

However, some promotional campaigns last longer than this. One missionary family reported in the *India Christian,* May, 1953, "It has been nearly a year and a half now since we returned to the States for furlough," indicating that medical checkups and slowness in raising money were the causes of such a long stay.

The Bills family, of Christian Radio Mission, Japan, announced in *Wave Lengths,* March, 1955, a tour of at least eight months to raise money in the United States.

Even greater expense is involved when a whole mission group falls into disagreement and, without any overhead missionary society control, simply disintegrates. The *Christian Standard* for January 17, 1959, published a notice entitled "Missionaries and Committee Resign." It stated:

Effective October 25, 1958, Joe and Maxine Seggelke, Bert and Marge Ellis, and Flora Maye Guernsey, missionaries on the field of Korea, resigned from Christian Radio Mission. . . . Mr. and Mrs. Seggelke and Mr. and Mrs. Ellis plan to continue to work in Korea, whereas Miss Guernsey's plans are indefinite.

Going out as missionaries without health or other requirements leads occasionally to special problems. A letter from the Mediterranean Christian Mission, dated February 27, 1953, appeals for "between $2500.00 and $3000.00" promptly to bring a sick worker and family home and send out another family of volunteers in their places.

Health emergencies inevitably arise which involve Independent missionaries and put them to great expense because, contrary to the cooperative missions program, few doctors are included in the Independent work (only one doctor had gone out independently, in more than fifty years prior to 1956). A "special news letter" from the Nagoya Christian Mission, dated January 8, 1954, relates that the five members of the Howard Davis family must return to the United States promptly because Mr. Davis was ill and no other provision had been made for such needs. Some thousands of dollars of emergency missionary overhead expense was involved.

Missionary travel is expensive, under any system of support, and Independent missions does not escape this problem simply by implying that every penny goes to the foreign field. A postcard sent by the South African Church of Christ Mission, dated November 7, 1953, gave sailing dates and added:

We have tickets purchased, $1900.00.
Balance on hand to cover all needs is $800.00.
We need $1000.00 for freight costs.
We need $500.00 for duty and freight in Africa.
Mrs. Nicholson and one son need living link—this is $1500.
We need to borrow $3500.00 for down payment on house.

When Luke D. Elliott closed his work in Jamaica a special appeal for travel funds was made, in the *Christian Standard*, January 28, 1950:

We will also need funds to return to the States, for travel and for shipping our personal goods. We will need some funds to get started again, and to get a little rest, if possible. We would greatly appreciate it if in addition to the regular support of this work you could send a love offering to help our present small and entirely inadequate repatriation fund.

Promotional tours necessarily are always being operated or the next one is being planned under the Independent system. The *Jamaica Christian*, August–September, 1953, gave this report:

Mr. and Mrs. Donald Fream concluded their six-months' tour in September, and are returning to Jamaica October 1st

74

by Pan-American Clipper from Miami, Florida. They covered 25,000 miles through 14 states . . . .

The Freams have also been able to purchase a new Plymouth, which they badly needed, to take back to Jamaica.

Promotional touring as a basic and continuing method of meeting missions costs results in large numbers of missionaries and a large per cent of the Independent force always being in the United States for "furloughs" that are really promotional trips. *Report,* the journal of Cincinnati Bible Seminary, in July, 1950, listed eleven alumni of that school alone who were then on or arranging promotional tours. The *Christian Standard,* December 9, 1950, listed twenty-five so engaged as of that date. The list also showed one hundred and twenty-five on the field—but a number of these were working in industry abroad and were not full-time missionaries. At least one was included of whom another Independent missionary says he is deceiving the American supporters because for years he has made his living by operating a popular school which opens each year with a grand ball (dance). The unreliable nature of what is "missionary" is apparent.

An editorial in *Among Ourselves,* April, 1951, says:

In many cases, furloughs would be unnecessary if it was not vital to remind the supporting brethren at home that we are still in this world. . . . Too much of our strength and effort is used in teaching the churches at home to give to missions that might better be used on the field.

Just what is to be called "missions" is a matter of entirely private interpretation in the Independent system. *Horizons* magazine announced in its May, 1953, issue that that journal is a missionary venture and appealed for $1500.00 per month as an organ in the missionary field. This, of course, is 100% "overhead."

The greatest hue and cry raised by Independent missions advocates, until recently, has been concerning the cost for "secretaries' visits" to foreign fields under cooperative missions as a part of its supervisory oversight. With the growth of Independent work, apparently it has seemed wise to encourage an occasional visit abroad by American pastors or observers. Previously, such visits by cooperative administrators were called "junkets"—wasting the Lord's money. Less of this kind of argument appears now. The *Jamaica Christian,* February–March, 1953, told of a six-day visit, by plane, to the Jamaica work by V. G. Gilbert, a professor at Atlanta Christian College. Mr. Gilbert paid for his trip personally, but the object of the journey was to be able to aid in Independent missionary promotion, so the funds could otherwise have been used for work on the field rather than for visitation or promotion. A much more extensive and expensive trip was made by W. L. Jessup, president of San Jose Bible College, early in 1952. The *Christian Standard,* January 5, 1952, announced that the "independent missionaries located in Japan have chosen William L. Jessup" to visit the work, adding "when Brother Jessup returns he will report to us in this country the things that he has seen and heard. . . ." The editorial then appealed for contributions to meet the costs of this visitation, somewhere around two thousand dollars, all "overhead" expense.

Notwithstanding a rising resentment among Independent workers at self-appointed leaders who find "reasons" for supervisory visits to the field, John T. Chase put out a feeler with regard to another proposed trip to the Orient for the gathering of information. The *Restoration Herald* criticizes such costly overhead expenditures this way (May, 1955):

He has returned to Korea four times, spending this amount of time each trip: six months, three months, three months, and two weeks. The last trip was to go out and set-things-in-order. Who can comprehend Oriental thinking in two weeks?

The formerly denied or ignored costs of Independent missions, along with a large growth in the number of persons setting out to go abroad on their own volition and then expecting the churches to feel a duty to underwrite their unsupervised programs, has in time led to mounting misgivings. The *Pacific Christian Chronicle,* December, 1952, said, "there are now 308 'direct support' missionaries of churches of Christ . . ." but "less than 500 churches professing New Testament origin have financial fellowship with these 300 New Testament workers." Tibbs Maxey wrote an article entitled "Overreaching Ourselves in Missions" in the *Restoration Herald,* January, 1951, saying, "One of these ministers claimed that his church was swamped with appeals for money and requests from those who wanted to occupy his pulpit."

When it is remembered that all this Independent program grew out of attitudes sponsored by the *Christian Standard,* it seems a bit strange to hear this uncertain sound issuing from the editorial page of that journal, May 30, 1953:

This is what we mean—why is it that so many of the reports, and so much of the promotional material of missionaries is taken up with asking for funds rather than with informing the Christian public of work done and victories achieved? One missionary needs a new tire for his jeep; another needs a new jeep. One needs travel funds to get to the field; another needs travel funds to get home. One has made a down payment on a property and wants the brethren to come through with the rest of the purchase price—we could go on and on. While every need is real and ought to be met, the cumulative effect is to give an entirely false impression of what is involved in the great work of world evangelism. There is a pettiness in such mendicancy that leads people to look upon missions itself as something petty.

What is involved, of course, is utterly unsupervised and irresponsible initiative and promotion of the missionary impulse. "Independency" and "irresponsibility" in the complicated work of international missions are equivalent terms.

The result of some years of experience in costly promotion is that some papers are denying support to certain of the operations which they deem to be unworthy and too expensive. Tibbs Maxey writes as follows in the May, 1955, issue of the *Restoration Herald:*

That brings up the fascinating Chapels for Korea Fund. The Christian Standard refuses to raise funds for particular missions. Every rule has one exception. It helped John Chase raise $50,000 for the Fund.

❋ ❋ ❋ ❋ ❋

NOT ONE CENT HAS BEEN SPENT FOR A CHURCH BUILDING IN KOREA UP THROUGH JANUARY 1, 1955, BY THE CHAPELS FOR KOREA FUND.

The Fund never had the total desired, but rather $32,000. Of this $10,000 was invested in two houses in Japan and $2,000 was spent for land in Korea on which was to be built the seminary. The ground proved to be too tied up in red-tape, so it lies now unused.

The strength of the Independent missions system is its intimate relationships between supporters and workers, and the family solidarity and concern that it encourages. *News from Kanpur,* April, 1954, tells its readers that the young Harter family, in India, had found a new forwarding agent in the United States to replace the mother of La Von Harter who had been doing the receiving and publicity work for five years. Givers to this cause across even these few years developed a personal knowledge about the three generations of missionary workers which made for ties of love and concern that should be long lasting.

The Harter financial report for January and February, 1954, was probably typical of many missions. It reads:

Salaries, Harters	$400.00
Indian publication	176.94
Indian evangelism	84.50
Indian children	347.72
Travel to India	620.60
Supplies	550.69
Promotion (postage, etc.)	599.70
Operation (US postage, etc.)	131.19
Bank charges	7.50
	$2,918.84

Disregarding the heavy travel cost, and using only the last three items in the list as overhead, this shows $738.39 for promotion and $1,578.24 for work on the field, or more than 25% for overhead.

The difficulties in Korea have not subsided. The August, 1962, issue of *For Christ in Korea* says:

In KCM [Korean Christian Mission] we found several men who were in positions of influence and responsibility, but who seemed to regard lightly what we call Christian Principles. Because of their position we trusted these men at first. We trusted until we saw we should not; we cooperated until we saw that our purposes pointed up different directions.

. . . .

In the last three weeks (June, 1962) I have been asked to "bite" on bait which would have bankrupted this Mission before Christmas, and another bait which would have put me in jail. These were deals being promoted by preachers!

. . . .

these men who are seeking a man to give them foreign support, have a cloud of encouragement on the eastern horizon. This "cloud" includes a plan for another mission in Seoul now under consideration! If this plan is carried out, it will present an opposition to the principles we have been establishing in Korea. . . .

The kind of business chicanery and deceit referred to in this report is made possible by the Independent practice of having many of its mission agencies and their properties owned and operated in the form of private business enterprises. So conducted, "missionary work" can descend to barter and trade. Some Independent mission projects are supervised by boards of responsible trustees and thus avoid such disrepute.

In a column entitled "The Voice of Dissent," written by Art Harrington, *Horizons* magazine, August 4, 1962, carried these judgments:

A modern missionary uses up half the support he would get traipsing around the country looking for more support. I say, let's put an end to this and put the responsibility on the individual congregation. . . . Let the missionaries use that "traipsing" money to the glory of God by publishing better materials for the missionary education of our churches and the furtherance of their missionary effort. Let them use furloughs working with the church which supports them and in preparation. We would run them to death and then send them back with a nervous breakdown.

The *Assam Messenger* of December, 1962, reveals how large a proportion of the missionaries' time and expense must be spent for promotion. Mr. Fairbrother indicated that he and his family would be in the United States some fifteen months for fun-raising purposes. He added:

Certain expenses have had to be met in clothing after five years. . . . All eight of us had our immediate needs. When we return to India, some of our children will have to have enough clothing for boarding school. . . . If purchase of supplies is made too close to the time of our arrival in India, there will be extra duty to pay.

It is seldom that any guidance is given in print to prospective independent missionaries, but a very sane and helpful two-page statement on this theme was written by Mark G. Maxey, of the Kyushu Christian Mission. He recommended seven years of college training in two or more widely separated colleges; be married if at all pos-

80

sible; obtain physical health approval from doctors; take a year of language study in the United States; serve as a full-time pastor at least two years; and, be sure to have no race prejudice. Other practical advice was added.

A long editorial in *Horizons*, December, 1952, discussed missions support. It also urged that experienced pastors rather than untested recruits go into the work, and quoted an appeal to "reduce the overhead of travel expense." It cited one mission that accepts but never solicits funds, its operators preferring to provide self-support, if necessary, by taking employment on the field. The editorial concluded by saying:

In a recent survey it was discovered that most missionaries now on the field went there as "faith" missionaries without guaranteed livinglink support, and remain there in the work with inadequate livinglink support, and meagre funds for the work itself.

The matter of going out on "faith" is sometimes conceived in the most complete terms, wherein the candidate is sure that God gives orders or direct approvals on most of the details of the work. Max Randall is sure that God told him not only to buy an airplane and use it in the South African mission, but adds (*Among Ourselves*, November, 1951): "Truly the Lord was leading us. . . . He led me to buy the Stinson [plane], I am sure. . . . He led us in buying the Frigidaire, deep freeze, and washing machine. . . ."

While the "faith" element is common in Independent missions support, not all agencies hold to this principle. As reported in the *Christian Standard*, October 13, 1951, the Cunningham mission in Japan then had a reserve fund of over $26,000, and received bequests in the forms of annuities for which the fund stood as security in this type of endowment.

The appeal of a particularistic message, accusing all other Christians of being sectarians, gets results of a kind, but also suffers the danger of losing leaders to other particularisms which may be able to make a case for themselves as the true church, with the Independents then being viewed as the sect. This attitude, so contrary to the position of the founding fathers and of the *Declaration and Address,* is the background of an announcement in *Horizons,* May, 1953: "Paul Marteeny, Homer, Alaska, is preaching for the Community Church (interdenominational) since the former pastor split off part of the group to start a Baptist church. Marteeny no longer has fellowship with the Church of Christ in Homer."

Further dissatisfaction with "modern" Independents, who are seen as being inferior to their leaders of less than a generation ago, is voiced by Lester Ford, a man with a nostalgic memory, in the *Midwest Christian College Bulletin,* November, 1953. His editorial on "What's the Matter with our Evangelism?" says:

Among Christian Churches (independent) it is increasingly difficult to hold great revival and evangelistic meetings. Instead of the great crowds, intense enthusiasm and the large ingathering of souls characteristic of such efforts among our people a generation ago, we have to be satisfied with the anemic, discouraging, half-hearted attempts at evangelism that are so common among us today.

Independent operation without informed oversight sometimes results in the most serious mistakes. Mrs. William O. Rees reported in *Christian Mission to the Chinese,* May, 1954, that "through misinformation by an official, Bill has lost his right to Canadian citizenship."

What to do about irresponsible persons who undertake missions and only later are found in their unfortunate colors is a problem heightened in unsupervised Independent work. The *Christian Standard,* August 21, 1954, carried an editorial entitled "Investigate First" which said:

Just because an itinerant who comes to your door claims to be a missionary is not sufficient reason for opening the pulpit of the church and the purse of the people to him. Investigate first. It may save headaches and heartaches. . . . There is nothing quite so harmful, not only to the local chrch, but to the cause of missions itself, as for a congregation to discover that it has been "taken in" by a glib-talking rascal.

Are we making so bold as to admit that there are unworthy characters who appropriate themselves the sacred name missionary? Yes, of course there are. The more valuable the coin the more frequently it is counterfeited. And in this country, with its postal service, its telegraph and telephone systems, it is inexcusable that a single congregation should be victimized.

Two weeks later the same paper published with approval a telegram from John T. Chase which read, in part:

However, I regret to state that due to certain facts, the exact knowledge of which has only recently come to me, I feel compelled to withdraw all personal endorsement of Mr. and Mrs. Hill as far as work in Korea and among the Korean people is concerned. . . . It is with deepest regret that I withdraw my endorsement. I believe that Mr. and Mrs. Hill should not return to work in the Korean Christian Mission, nor among the Korean people.

In the January 15, 1955, issue of *Horizons* the editor began a discussion of who could properly be called a responsible Independent missionary. In brief, it concluded that each missionary should, among other things, be endorsed by at least one local church. It added, "the truth is that not many of those on the field . . . have this kind of relationship to a local church." For this reason *Horizons* felt obliged to withdraw the privilege of news releases through its columns to certain missionaries of which it did not approve. This action drew an extended blast from the pen of Tibbs Maxey in the July–August, 1955, *Restoration Herald*. He further accused Mr. McFarland of suppressing the facts essential to judging a certain missionary in question. However, the December 10, 1955, *Horizons* charged that there were still missionaries going to the field without the endorsement of any local congregation, and then expecting their news notices to be published by papers in the United States so that the missionaries could thus solicit support funds.

Much of the factual data given above was published in 1956 in a booklet of 50 pages entitled *Church of Christ Number* Two. Since that year few reports of expenditures are printed in the mission papers. Occasionally one is found, and it is apparent that promotion overhead remains a large proportion of total money raised for this type of work. *Harter Throbs*, journal of the Ralph Harter missionary team in India, gave this report in its issue of January 14, 1960.

Disbursed, Oct., Nov., & Dec., '59

Salary for Three months	$ 300.00
Bus, train, taxi, baggage	175.34
Housing on Tour	7.25
Postage	9.00
Telephone	7.05
Publicity	64.97
Spent/India	
Bookstore	38.73
To Kulpahar for Andriyas	80.00
Travel to India—Deposit	508.50
Hindi Typewriter Repair	6.50
Postage	5.25
	1,202.59

It will be noted that only a little over $100 of this total was actually spent in India; the remainder was for furlough and other promotional costs.

With the Troyers, journal of the Troyer family in Lecce, Italy, in the issue of August, 1957, gave a report of some eleven months spent in the United States in an effort to raise funds for the Italian mission. They traveled 37,000 miles, spoke 155 times, and published the following aims and receipts—

Aims		Receipts
$ 500.00	per month for support	$ 231.50
1,500.00	travel fund back to Italy	1,100.00
4,000.00	for a printing press	50.00
100.00	per month living link support	5.00

Apparently all other funds received, but unreported, were required to pay the cost of raising the money.

A further financial problem, of a most serious nature, is basic to independent missionary operations. Some gifts sent to "direct support" agencies are not tax deductible, although all established and cooperative religious activities are granted this privilege and encouragement by the United States government. The nation's decision on this was reported in the *Christian Standard,* February 13, 1960.

It is no fault of the devout independent mission workers themselves that the very nature of their "organization," with little responsible oversight, permits dishonest individuals to deceive the churches in America by false claims and thus to raise funds for work that does not exist. *Horizons* magazine in the April 18, 1959, issue was obliged to warn unsuspecting churches against another such free-lance promoter who was imposing upon the churches.

-10-

Statistics of Church of Christ Number Two

A YEARBOOK ENTITLED *Directory of the Ministry of the Undenominational Fellowship of Christian Churches and Churches of Christ* was issued in 1955, with subsequent editions in 1957, 1958, 1960, and 1963. It is not surprising that the Directory makes no effort to learn what is the membership or constituency of the churches served by the Independent ministers. There are reasons which are adequate to the sponsors which recommend that no count be made. This has been the long-time practice of Church of Christ Number One, the antiorgan group. In 1954 it used in its major magazines the round figure of 1,000,000 members as its constituency. However, when *Life* magazine was making up its special issue on Christianity in 1955 they reported 1,500,000 members. In 1962 this church was reporting claims of over 2,200,000.

Actually, there is no substantial ground on which any of these membership figures can be supported. This writer is the owner of the only set of the published yearbooks of Church of Christ Number One in existence. He has repeatedly offered to make the set available to various colleges or other centers of these churches, either the original copies or a microfilm edition of them. None of the libraries has shown any interest in an effort to study these records, which are the only data from which a statistical report could be projected. The same attitude prevails in Church of Christ Number Two.

With the help of a number of student associates this writer has made certain studies in the 1955 *Directory* and its successors. Part of the information may be tabulated as follows:

STATISTICAL STUDIES IN THE INDEPENDENT YEARBOOKS
Summarized as of 1960

	1955	1957	1958	1960
Total number of names listed	3,712	4,094	4,536	4,527
Students (preaching and non-preaching)	856	711	877	269[1]
Missionaries (home and foreign)	311	322	339[2]	329[3]
Engaged in Education	203		273[4]	293[5]
Retired ministers	46	62	53	62
Rel. Educ. Directors and Associates		111	252	169
Mission Stations	66	84	85	79[6]
Churches represented	2,301	2,789	3,504[7]	3,570

[1]The editor states that there is no carry over of students from previous books (p. 2), therefore 269 students returned forms in order to be counted. The editor then lists 3,589 students in Independent colleges in a summary on p. 104.

[2]Not counting Recruits. The 1957 count, without recruits, is 299 (p. 92).

[3]Does not include Recruits.

[4]On p. 106 of the 1958 Independent Yearbook the editor claims 373 such persons. A careful count of the actual names in this yearbook giving education as their occupation shows 273.

[5]This figure represents a careful count of those listed who are engaged in education in one way or another, drawn from the 1960 yearbook. On p. 104 of that same book the editor gave a summary in which he stated there are 431 total (part and full-time) such people.

[6]This is only foreign mission stations. It is impossible to gather an accurate count of home mission stations.

[7]All three of these figures, for 1955, 1957, 1958, represent the Independent yearbook claims. The figure of 3,504 for 1958 includes over 400 churches for which no report was sent to Mr. Newland, but he continues to include them. This is why our subsequent listing of churches, summarized by states, and drawn very carefully from the names of the ministers and the churches they are serving, will show 2,806 churches (in the U. S. A.).

	Indep. Yearbook	Total[8] Churches	With member figures	Resident	Non-resident	Total
Alabama	5	0	0	0	0	0
Alaska	4	1	1	60	0	60
Arizona	30	0	0	0	0	0
Arkansas	31	20	9	1,014	85	1,099
California, N. California, S	186	54	20	8,208	681	8,889
Colorado	38	21	11	821	237	1,058
Delaware	1	1	1	345	0	345
Florida	59	19	5	914	156	1,070
Georgia	74	40	8	894	365	1,259
Hawaii	4	3	3	400	0	400
Idaho	15	9	9	4,679	688	5,347
Illinois	379	275	96	25,015	5,092	30,107
Indiana	413	329	329	69,251	18,489	87,740
Iowa	102	55	22	5,157	746	5,903
Kansas	142	109	108	21,267	2,348	23,615
Kentucky	305	212	211	33,500	3,183	36,683
Louisiana	13	0	0	0	0	0
Maryland	15	11	9	1,582	289	1,871
Massachusetts	1	0	0	0	0	0
Michigan	74	44	12	1,967	352	2,319
Minnesota	51	36	3	1,027	59	1,086
Mississippi	16	10	3	405	56	461
Missouri	272	192	181	23,173	7,169	30,342
Montana	13	8	8	984	139	1,123
Nebraska	59	40	28	3,763	1,282	5,045
New Jersey	4	2	1	127	5	132
New Mexico	24	11	4	854	173	1,037
New York	24	8	5	313	121	434
N. Carolina	97	53	40	4,765	95	4,860
N. Dakota	2	0	0	0	0	0
Ohio	323	179	97	39,979	6,721	46,700
Oklahoma	103	62	62	14,030	2,651	16,681
Oregon	139	108	92	21,523	3,289	24,812
Pennsylvania	99	86	75	17,838	2,843	20,681
S. Carolina	10	4	1	65	0	65
S. Dakota	21	10	1	87	0	87
Tennessee	85	68	23	6,223	1,022	7,245
Texas	93	41	22	3,008	260	3,268
Utah	1	0	0	0	0	0
Vermont	1	1	1	66	77	143
Virginia	104	34	11	3,322	377	3,699
Washington	42	15	11	2,600	492	3,092
West Virginia	56	34	15	2,690	532	3,222
Wisconsin	27	17	2	230	14	244
Wyoming	12	2	0	0	0	0
	3,569	2,224	1,540	322,166	59,888	382,234

[8]For legend see opposite page.

Copies of these figures were sent to all cooperative state secretaries and their comments were invited. Only a few state officers had made their own statistical studies. The Pennsylvania office was fully informed and reported that of the 75 churches in both books, and with membership figures, 18 congregations with a total of 6,069 members were quite thoroughly cooperative, and the other 57 churches continue to participate in some phases of cooperative work. Although one set of state figures is not enough on which to generalize, this particular report shows over one fourth of the known membership in churches claimed as independent to be actually cooperative. This would make our estimate of something over 600,000 independent members a very generous one.

The subject of statistics for a church group which makes no effort to study itself seriously as a growing body leaves us without dependable data. *Horizons* magazine for December 3, 1960, claims "605 missionaries"— but an examination of the report indicates that within this figure were all editors of magazines for the Independent churches, pastors of new churches who were receiving aid, and other general workers.

Additional Notes on Statistics

Concerning the 1958 yearbook

It will be noted that a large percentage of the churches listed in the Independent yearbook are also listed in the cooperative yearbook. In 1957 of the 2,789 churches in the Independent yearbook, 1,567 were in the Cooperative

---

[8]i.e., total in cooperative yearbook of those in Independent Yearbook. Average church size (1,533 into 382,234) is 249 members, for Independent churches. Total estimate for Independent churches (3,569 × 246) is 888,930. But one half of the members in the 1,533 churches (or even of the 2,218 churches) which are listed in both yearbooks should be counted as Cooperative members. So, ½ of the 1,533 church's members (382,234) is 191,117; deduct these from 888,930 and you arrive at a total Independent membership of 697,813. However if we deduct one half of the members of the whole 2,218 that are in both yearbooks, we get (2,218 × 249 divided by 2) 276,141 members, which, deducted from 888,930, gives a more accurate estimate of 612,789 as the actual membership strength of the Independents.

yearbook, or 56.1%. For 1958 we worked only one fourth of the figures, i.e., states Oklahoma through Wyoming, alphabetically. These states show 678 churches in the Independent yearbook, but 463 of these are in the Cooperative yearbook, or 68.3%. As a very generous minimum figure, we may say that at least 50% of the churches in the entire Independent yearbook are in the Cooperative yearbook.

The 452 churches reporting membership figures in 1958 constitute 16.1% of the total of 2,806 churches listed in the Independent yearbook. These 16.1% have a total membership of 151,795. This is an average of 366 members per church. No statistician, Mr. Newland included, claims this high an average figure. However, by using this generous figure for all 2,806 we get an estimated grand total of 942,816 Independent members in the U. S. A.

However, since well over 50% of the churches in the Independent yearbook are also in the Cooperative yearbook, we may properly claim one half of the members of these one half of the churches, or one fourth of the total shown above, as Disciples rather than as Independents. Deducting one fourth leaves an estimated 707,112. It should be remembered that this figure represents a most generous high estimate. My own estimate is that a true figure would be near to, perhaps below, 600,000.

Concerning the 1960 yearbook

First, it should be noted (as many state secretaries did *not* see when we sent our tabulations to them) that this is a faithful count of Independent *claims*. Several secretaries wrote back briefly, saying simply, You are wrong; your figures are inaccurate. Our list is just a record of claims.

In Pennsylvania the Independents include in their list 18 churches that are reported as fully cooperative by the State Society. These 18 churches have 6,069 of the 20,681 members claimed as Independent. In Ohio 18 churches with 13,761 members were also reported by the State Society as fully cooperative.

One state secretary says: "So many of our churches are not independent, they are just unrelated. They are small, ineffective, and have no program beyond their local interest."

Concerning the 305 (or 302) churches claimed as Independent in Kentucky, the state secretary writes: "Only 165 of these congregations are antagonistically independent toward the cooperative work. These 165 congregations represent 19,000 members. There are 137 congregations that remain in splendid isolation from any involvement beyond the local community. . . . These congregations represent approximately 15,000 members."

As the Independents consolidate into a separate, self-promoting body, a new program is beginning to emerge in any study using the two yearbooks. Maurice Lyerla reports that in Colorado "the Independents have independent churches in many of the communities where we have cooperating churches." If only one "Christian" church is listed in any such town, it makes accurate distinctions impossible in our type of statistics. However, since this kind of situation is not widely general, our estimates remain a valid study method.

-11-

Relationships of Church of Christ Number Two

CHAPTER 7 IN THIS BOOK noted that Church of Christ Number Two is not a single, united body. Its majority faction, however, is fairly well identified through the larger Bible colleges, the *Christian Standard,* and the North American Christian Convention.

A major ground on which these churches have separated themselves from the original American restoration movement is that of its pristine purpose. The opening chapters of this book have shown that the program formulated by the Campbells, Scott, and Stone conceived of it as a movement among Christians. Other churches were truly churches, with greater or lesser degrees of correctness in their perception of the many marks or standards which constitute their Christian nature. "Our" restoration was designed to bring all such churches around to the use of only such practices and such public declarations of faith as all could agree were prescribed in the New Testament. This movement was *within* the church, and was designed for its purification and more exact definition. As such, it moved in fellowship with all churches, and recognized their members as Christians—even if it did not, in many instances, feel that these Christians were eligible to be members of our own congregations until they met our own understanding of the ordinance of initiation and membership, that is, baptism. A good example of the basically fraternal spirit of the movement was Alexander Campbell's promotion and participation in the work of the Evangelical Alliance, a worldwide program for church unity that began in 1846.

The Independents, however, have repudiated this ground, and the vast majority of them have dissociated themselves from other churches and Christians, not only saying that they are not churches and Christians, but also acting out this belief by refusing to participate with them in joint worship, in ministerial associations and other interchurch agencies. They also refuse to work in the great conference movement of the twentieth century known as the ecumenical movement which has as its goal the greater unity of the church. Instead, the Independents say only, "Come and join us—this is our program for Christian unity."

The assumption of Thomas Campbell's *Declaration and Address*, 1809, was expressed in the historic slogan of Disciples, "We are not the only Christians, but Christians only." As the Independents have been led more and more apart from all fellowship with their parent movement by individual leaders, these spokesmen have found that they can keep their constituency together only by claiming for themselves alone all virtue which makes for real Christianity and denying that Christianity can exist outside of the particular definitions held by the Independents. The editor of the *Voice of Evangelism* published this dialogue in the issue of December 16, 1950:

Question: "Is it all right to go into the homes of denominational people and pray for them?"

Answer: . . . we would need to be careful what we prayed for. . . . If we prayed too directly, they might get the idea that we are asking God's covenant-blessings upon them as if they were actually His very own.

Question: "Are denominational people to be classed as unbelievers?"

Answer: The word "unbelievers" in II Cor. 6:14-18 surely includes denominational people.

When *Horizons* began a youth program page, its editor, Ralph McLean, stated the typical independent attitude toward other church bodies. He said: "Even Christian Endeavor, the pioneer church youth movement, whose principles are similar to those of the Restoration movement is being shunned by our 'loyal' brethren because of its denominational associations."

The editor of the *Alberta Bible College Evangel* answered a number of questions in the April, 1957 issue. One was, Do you belong to a ministerial association? He replied:

No, I do not. This question is asked me usually by people who want to make me admit that I do not believe sufficiently in the New Testament doctrine to stand aloof from leaders of denominations. I have not attended a ministerial meeting in seven years.

The *Dakota Evangel* for September, 1959, confirmed this position. It said:

4. They do not enter into interdenominational programs; not because of any prejudice or dislike toward those in the denominations, but because of a conviction that to do so would mean compromising scriptural doctrines.

The *Dallas Christian College Contender* was of the same opinion, as given in the January, 1959, issue. It said, ". . . association with the sects and extrabiblical organizations of men contributes little and hinders much."

With this being the position in the United States, it is natural that it should be the same on the mission fields. Mark G. Maxey wrote in the *Christian Standard* on "Christians in Japan" as follows: "fellowship between

Kyodan-related Churches of Christ and other [Independent] Churches of Christ is nonexistent."[1]

Not all papers of the Independent movement will reduce to public print the logic of their refusal to have fellowship in any way with members of other communions —but at least one does. In the December 9, 1956, issue of *The Church Speaks,* its editor said:

"WE" are the ONLY Christians, or there is nothing to Christianity that is definite. God has told us what to do in order to become Christians, and if we have done that, then we are Christians, and if we have not done that, no matter how religious a person may be, he or she is not a Christian. . . . We can say, "WE are not the *only* Christians" and straightway begin to call Baptists, Christians; Presbyterians, Christians; Disciples, Christians; Lutherans, Christians; and so on down the line until we will be calling good sincere Unitarians, Christians; and the sincere Communists, Christians; and the good sincere Masons, Christians; and rabid, false Jehovah's Witnesses will be met by Christian; and if the Devil happens to come to us smiling, we will meet him with "Hail, Christian," too.

Upon the basis of this type of righteousness it is not surprising that occasional ministers and churches of the Independent group will employ practices which make public their real faith. Requiring Southern Baptists to be reimmersed in order to become "Christians" was reported as the practice of Stanley Letcher, Jr., minister of the Cleveland, Oklahoma, Christian Church.[2]

Failure of the Independent work to be effective in the larger realm of Christendom and of the world is deplored by Orval C. Crowder, president of Atlanta Christian College, in the *Christian Standard,* June 5, 1954. He says:

From another point of view, it is a tragic failure on our part that we are almost completely unknown, unknowing,

---

[1]February 22, 1958.
[2]*Christlike News & Digest,* June, 1956, p. 7.

and uncaring with relation to the World Council and the themes of its assemblies. Jesus said, "go into all the world . . . preach," but we are failing to make our voices heard, even within the boundaries of Protestantism! Paul summons us to wake out of our sleep, but most of us have no intelligent awareness of today's challenge to our faith. Jesus said we were to be the salt of the earth, but we isolate ourselves just where the savor of our presence is most needed.

We are not even facing the Christian issue of life among ourselves. We have no effective medium for serious discussion, no effective plan for mutual study, and no effective voice for the expression of our united convictions before the world. What is worse, we show few signs of any real desire or purpose to improve the situation. Unless we accept this task, our only future will be that of the wicked and slothful servant when his Lord returns.

Our impotence cannot be charged to the fact that we are few in number. The Quakers also are a little people, and a peculiar people, but they have made their influence felt to the far corners of the earth. They have done so with a minimum of ecclesiastical machinery and with a lesser degree of clericalism than exists among us today. What they have done, we could do, and more!

It will be noted that while this quotation, and the rest of the article, provides much diagnosis and description, it offers no plan, no program or prescription for becoming effective. This is the unfortunate situation of the Independent missions movement; completely apart from and indeed thoroughly critical of perhaps 99.75% of Christian work and workers in the world and in history, it lives with the hope that competitive effort without plan through conference or democratic agreement will bring in the kingdom, which, by its definition, will exclude these 99.75%. Such a movement is quite devoid of the statesmanship needed in worldwide missions.

With the passage of time some Independent missionary families or groups are becoming discontented with the complete aloofness of Church of Christ Number Two to

96

the rest of the Christian world. The Christian Missionary Fellowship published a long article in the October, 1954, issue of *Missionary Fellowship* asserting that it would now stand "in friendliness toward the denominational world." In brief, it proclaimed "a desire for fellowship in the discharge of the Great Commission."

The one distinctly irenic voice with influence in Church of Christ Number Two is that of Fred P. Thompson, Jr., minister, in Chicago, Illinois. In reporting the 1962 North American Christian Convention, for which over 7,000 persons were registered, the *Christian Standard*, August 11, 1962, gave this account.

If the brotherhood in convention assembled was inclined to congratulate itself on Wednesday night, however, it was brought sharply back to less complimentary self-evaluation in the Thursday morning address, "The Unity We Seek," by Fred P. Thompson, Jr., of Chicago. In the more spectacular part of his address, quoted in daily papers, Mr. Thompson left the impression that we are not very consistent and have accomplished very little toward the goal of oneness in Christ. The suggestions he gave for greater accomplishment in the future made his address one of the most talked-about features in the convention.

-12-

The Future of Church of Christ Number Two

PROPHECY IS AN UNSURE PRACTICE for human beings. However, history must have a few lessons to teach or it would not be studied. The problem examined in this book is, How can a religious democracy function serviceably? Shall self-appointed (even though sincere) leaders start colleges, missionary agencies (and personally own the property), orphans homes, and other general work, then lay the burden of their support upon persons and churches who were not consulted about the beginning of the work?

The answer is not a clear-cut case of Yes or No. Democratic or congregational churches have as a principal merit that in them private initiative can devise good ideas and release as much devoted energy as is true of the republican (Presbyterian) or monarchial (Roman) types of churches. *New ideas and new agencies must have a chance to rise and flourish on their merits.* When the fresh sap of a vibrant life turns to woody stalk, pressures will be set up that require new buds and branches. Any church organization must have the means of welcoming new life. But the new life must be within the brotherhood, or schism mars the face of the church.

Let's face the truth. If a cooperative college, for example, fails to serve its state or area with an earnest effort to provide sufficient numbers and quality of church leaders, good church folk will be ready to support an independent program of education which features the numbers and which hopes that the quality may in time be better. It is the duty of democratic brotherhood leaders to be aware of this fact and to be at work concerning it. When recruitment lags, independent initiative will rush into the vacuum.

However, the issue still remains one of how to maintain the unity of the church in all its work.

No system of church government is perfect in human hands. Democratic methods are more true to the spirit of the New Testament than any other. *Democracy has duties.* We must exhaust every democratic effort to live in mutual helpfulness before concluding that God simply cannot get along without making another fragment of the already shattered cross.

Any Christian worker has liberty to invest his life in meeting what he thinks is an unmet need. But he has no right to call others bad names because their judgment leads them to focus on a dozen mission fields instead of fifty, at this stage of total church development. And, in any democracy, the ultimate goal must be to convince the brotherhood by work and by spirit that it should see its way clear to embrace the duties of meeting the proven need. The final objective of every independent agency should be group approval. In the life of Disciples of Christ, this means the sanction of the International Convention.

It is this writer's opinion that the main body of the restoration movement of the nineteenth century, generally known as Disciples of Christ, has about as fair and as effective a method for free churches to pursue the historic goals of their spiritual ancestors as a democratic society will ever witness. Let us grant errors of judgment and expression on the part of individual leaders; yet there always remains for the correction of mistakes as fair a method as any free association can construct. This is the International Convention constitution, written in the main by Z. T. Sweeney, then of Columbus, Indiana. When the only alternative to the Sweeney program is the demonstrated subdivisions and disharmonies of Church of Christ Number One, there is little promise of anything better in the impending subdivisions of Church of Christ Number Two.

A democratic brotherhood thinks slowly and moves cautiously, but it is more apt to find the truth about polity and faith than are oligarchies and monarchies in religion.[1] The long story of our adoption of loose co-operations, district and state and then national societies, the relating of these to each other in behalf of the welfare of the total cause, shows that the Christian Churches (Disciples of Christ) have pondered seriously and experimented hopefully in a search for biblically authorized ways of common life and work. Their career clearly shows a trend of movement among originally independent churches toward awareness of their common responsibility.

There is a distinct theological connotation, even an affirmation, of the nature of the church, in the adoption of certain terms by the major working agencies of the Christian Churches (Disciples of Christ). These include The *United* Christian Missionary Society, and *Unified*

---

[1]A very careful study of this idea, as it appears in the thought of Alexander Campbell, is presented in *Apostle of Freedom*, by D. Ray Lindley (St. Louis: Bethany Press, 1957). A paragraph in Chapter IV, p. 171, says: "Campbell thus appeared to seek for the congregation of believers the status of what McDougall calls the 'deliberative group.' Just as McDougall affirms that in a deliberative group it is possible for the group thought to result in a decision and an action 'higher than that which its best minds, independently could have achieved,' Campbell said that he had often been led, not only to reconsider, but to abandon some of his former conclusions, 'on suggestions and objections made by those whose education and capacity might be regarded as of a very humble rank.' Such group action, he said, sought not simply the communication of knowledge, nor the execution of a program but 'the proper development and direction of the human powers.' " An earlier student noted this crucial idea thus: "Campbell falls back on a principle which is uniquely his own, his unswerving faith in the correct judgments of the enlightened common mind. In a word, the majority of those who love the Lord must always decide such questions, and the minority, as in all social compacts, must quietly bow to its will." Jesse Kellems, *Alexander Campbell and the Disciples* (New York: R. R. Smith, 1930), p. 392.

Promotion. The lordship of Christ in the work of the church implies a responsibility to elicit a *wholeness of response* from all persons and churches in their living witness to faith. There is equally a demand for some device for ascertaining the *mind* that exists in the total church, and the education of that mind into continued and new expressions. This is what the International Convention does. There is a basic theology which produces a principle and an agency of cooperation in religion—a strong belief about God-given freedom within fellowship, because *positive declaration of fellowship is basic to the biblical understanding of the church.*

The older, uncritical or unthought assumption in International Convention fellowship was that the agencies in it were there on the dog-eat-dog basis of each one for himself, promotionally, regardless of the fortunes of the others. Across the years, a new understanding of the meaning of fellowship has arisen. There were days, not long ago, when a large home mission agency would not grant the use of its list of supporters for circulating the materials of other agencies. This is no longer the case. All agencies now in the International Convention (with one exception—and that one has been largely "independent" from its beginning) understand that they aid each other; that an attack upon one is an attack on the others. This does not mean that attack cannot be permitted or never would be justified, but it does mean that such attack is to be an open thing within the whole group, and is not to be a covert or single attack apart from the wisdom of the whole community. The several agencies see themselves as parts of a larger whole, with inescapable mutual responsibilities.

This means the end of the era when some agencies took membership as "reporting" agencies within the International Convention with the expectation of reporting—only; they did not mean to subject themselves to the group thinking and group disciplines. Any such agency clearly was only *using* the International Convention as a means of reaching a large constituency for its own support with no sense of having a responsibility for the welfare of the whole brotherhood and all its agencies. When this became clear, the Brazil Christian mission withdrew, in 1961, rather than to be associated with agencies that it did not want to help. There is one agency still within the Convention which from its beginning has refused to be anything other than a free-wheeling society, making its own requests for money but having no significant participation in the larger task of mutual aid.

The choices before the American restoration movement are fairly clear. We are discussing the question as to whether these churches need to have any visible organization apart from an utterly independent local congregation. They could choose (1) episcopacy in church government with its priestly assumption parallel to the divine right of kings. They could choose (2) an oligarchial church superintendency derived from Reformation state churches. They could choose (3) a representative congregationalism which expresses awareness of the wholeness of the church being made up of local congregations in responsible, democratic cooperation, much after the pattern of our great American political government. Or they could choose (4) complete anarchy as the theory of any relationships beyond the local independent congregation.

History shows that thus far the Independent fellowship has chosen Type No. 4 above. But the honest student can understand why this present choice has been made. One reason is that conservatives do no want to be in fellowship with liberals. One speaker at the Stillwater Consultation (1961) said, "I am an ultraconservative biblicist." He added, "We must have a uniform attitude toward the Bible for unity." This is a sure recipe for endless schisms, but not a way to unity. The editorial in

Christianity Today, November 24, 1961, also demanded doctrinal uniformity, but its view of the Bible would have shut out the Independent speaker at Stillwater. Apart from this theological reason for present-day separation there is a more practical one, which affects such jobs as ministers, and missionaries, and professors in Bible colleges, and presidents thereof. The most difficult problem is, Can we have a united brotherhood in which there are whole local churches honestly committed to a united interchurch promotion of missions and other general work, as in Unified Promotion, but also whole local churches equally committed to supporting the faith-sent missionary who may or may not make any reports of his work? And, even more problematical, Can we expect to succeed with some cases of local churches in which a "United Society" group exists and lives in genuine peace with an "Independent Missions" group?

It is possible to have such a united brotherhood. It can be done, however, only by understanding clearly in what unity consists. It is not to be determined by missionary methods. It must be a unity determined by a common commitment to the lordship of Christ as only Savior. Under such a commitment there is room for a variety of methods in Christian work. It is important, however, that something positive be done about *declaring* unity within a "like precious faith." We may sketch a possible step toward a greater unity.

The proposal made here is not really new, but simply the application of what many European Christians have found to be joyfully helpful in growing together. There several national, international, and interdenominational groups have (in Germany, for example) a *Kirchentag* (church day). It is much more than a day; it is a couple of weeks with varied programs for study, inspiration, and witness. The heart, the powerhouse of it is its witness in behalf of unity. In Germany the vastly predominant church is the *Evangelische Kirche in Deutschland* (Evangelical Church in Germany), called the E. K. I. D. Even its founders and present-day administrators cannot agree on whether it is one church, or a federation of churches, or just what it is. They are fully agreed, however, that it has become a precious fellowship for all of them, and a real experience of growth toward unity, particularly at the point of the Kirchentag and its public witness of a felt unity.

What could be happier for all spiritual descendents of the historic American and international restoration movement than to participate in a day of public witness to their common faith? Leaders in all portions of the larger family certainly have the ability to make this possible. All that is needed is the will. In this day when group life and group power is more and more a reality, we have an increasing duty to pay heed to our Lord's prayer, which is his command, for the fullest possible unity of his people. As only one step toward this end, we could plan to have the national conventions of our existing major groups meet occasionally in the same or nearby cities at the same time. For the present let us acknowledge that in theology, which is human thought, we have not arrived at agreement.[2] Let us agree that for an undetermined period we shall disagree about methods of work. But on a Sunday common to the coordinate conventions would

---

[2]"We could nullify our message for the unity of the whole church by setting the seal of official sanction upon some set of theological formulations which would be supposed to 'tell the world where we stand' doctrinally. Beyond the affirmation of loyalty to Christ and the acceptance of his lordship as the bond of unity among Christians, nobody can tell the world where we stand, because we do not all stand on the same theological ground. There is almost as much theological diversification among Disciples as there is in the whole body of American Protestantism. This diversification has tended to increase as more and more Disciples have emerged from the state of theological naïveté which characterized our leaders in earlier days, and it will probably increase still more in the future. This gives Disciples an unprecedented opportunity to demonstrate to the world by a concrete example that it is possible for a wide variety of doctrinal views to coexist peacefully and fraternally within one fellowship of Christians. Our central thesis is that this kind of unity with freedom and diversity can be projected on a larger scale which will include all Christians, and that no other kind of unity is either possible or desirable. Meanwhile, as to where we stand, let us stand on a platform as broad as that upon which we think a united church ought to stand." W. E. Garrison, *Heritage and Destiny* (St. Louis: Bethany Press, 1961), p. 153.

come the "church day," for which some good term should
be chosen. It might be—

> United Church Day
> Primitive Church Day
> New Testament Church Day
> Restoration Rally Day

The central magnet which for a few years might be our
only common act (for unity is a thing that must grow)
should be a whole participation in the observance of the
Feast of Remembrance, with Christ our Lord as the inviting host. Already our people have the greatest annual
Protestant Eucharistic Congress, in the Lord's Supper at
our various conventions. Christ is the source and the
cause of our unity; who not say so, unitedly? If we will
do only this for a few seasons, other kinds of unity will
come as unstructured gifts. Churches of Christ brethren,
as individuals if not as church units, will be happy to
share in that part of our life as Christians about which,
historically, we have never been divided, that is, that it
is the privilege of the church to spread the Lord's table,
and the duty of the individual Christian to examine himself, and so partake. If we examine ourselves honestly in
this day of increasing power in mass witnessing and mass
movements, how can we do any less than to exhibit our
given unity? Methods in missions and schools of thought
in theology must wait for the mind of the persons to
render judgment upon them, but judgment will be upon
us if we fail to witness to the unity that our Lord has
given to us. Together we should reverently praise the one
Name that is above every name. His blessing and his
design for unity will in time be his gift to his people.

-13-

The Future of the American Restoration Movement

IN THIS BOOK WE HAVE REFERRED FREQUENTLY to "the American restoration movement." There have been scores of restoration programs in the history of the church, as we showed in a former volume entitled *The Restoration Principle* (1960). The problem we must consider in this final chapter of evaluation is whether the particular plea generated by the Campbells, Stone, and Scott in America in the early nineteenth century will, like so many other efforts in what historians are now calling "primitivism," break into a score of little sects, each fixed upon some interesting hobby or particularism. W. Carl Ketcherside, an extremely capable editor among Churches of Christ Number One, wrote: "The restoration movement today is splintered into more than two dozen antagonistic parties."[1] He adds:

This is not all. Other divisions must follow in the future. Every time a truth is discovered, every time honest investigation forces a change of mind, there will be another division. This philosophy bars the door to further scriptural research, makes real unbiased study a crime, and places a premium on mediocrity. It throws a dam across the channel of thought, freezes the acquisition of knowledge, and constitutes an unwritten creed. It makes blind conformity a blessing and enthrones orthodoxy as the ideal.[1]

---

[1]*Mission Messenger*, February, 1962.

It is possible for a group, excited by a rediscovery in the Bible (such as the practice of foot-washing, or the use of one common cup in the Lord's Supper, to cite only two examples) to become almost hypnotized by what it suddenly sees as a long-lost value in worship or in fellowship. In the wider judgment of total Christendom, however, these particular practices in antiquity may have little relevance for Christian life in today's world. We are confronted with these problems: (1) What should be restored, and (2) Who shall decide on what should be restored. These two become one problem, actually, since an answer to 2 will also give the answer to 1.

James DeForest Murch's history, *Christians Only*, written to defend Church of Christ Number Two, approaches our problem in Chapter 23, "The Restoration Plea in an Ecumenical Era: an Evaluation." He notes on page 343 that the American restoration movement by "a conservative estimate of the total membership would approach five million." How can so large a congregational type of church body have unity and move effectively within the vibrant activities of worldwide Christendom today as it seeks ecumenicity (oneness)? Dr. Murch gives a proposed solution on pages 369, 370:

As Thomas Campbell put it, "the church of Christ upon earth is essentially, intentionally and constitutionally one; consisting of all those in every place that profess faith in Christ and obedience to Him in all things according to the Scriptures. . . ." The task is to liberate the captive church of the New Testament and restore its functions as they were in apostolic times.

Purposely or otherwise, Dr. Murch has misquoted the one sentence from Thomas Campbell's *Declaration and Address* that is best known among restoration movement students. He has done so by leaving out one word, and this word carries the genius and intent of Campbell's proposal for church unity. The correct quotation is—

The church of Christ upon earth is essentially, intentionally and constitutionally one; consisting of all those in every place that profess THEIR faith in Christ and obedience to him in all things according to the Scriptures, and that manifest the same by their tempers and conduct.

We have capitalized THEIR, the word left out by the Independent historian. This is the very heart of Thomas Campbell's proposal. It is the sure and intentional guide to the freedom of Bible study and of theological speculation which must be embraced in any scheme of union which holds promise of working effectively in Christendom's vast world of study and learning.

The Christian Churches (Disciples of Christ) constitute the historic, main stream of the American restoration movement because they follow the search for the pure gold of Christian truths that are refined from the total ore of the Bible and Christian tradition. In terms of creed, this pure gold is the faith first enunciated by the apostle Peter, "Thou art the Christ, the Son of the living God." There are many other interesting creeds, some of them revered for their age, but they are less than the solid truth of the New Testament creed. But a place must be found in a united church for, say, an Episcopal church, whose people bring with them THEIR faith in those things stated so speculatively in the Nicene Creed, A.D. 325. This does not mean, of course, that the whole church must agree with that part of the church which wants to make its own use of the so-called Nicene Creed (we say "so-called" since the creed of Nicea is not in use by any church today).

In like manner, a united church must spread its reach of fellowship to encompass the deep concern of Christians which became (mistakenly, and unfortunately, in our opinion) the eventual practice of infant baptism. Dr. Murch's wise studies, taking advantage of earlier work by Stephen J. England, note that biblical theology today is retreating from infant baptism because it is historically and theologically indefensible. A united church could quite well encompass in its full fellowship the practice of parent-and-child dedication—again demonstrating how honest and earnest Christian parents can bring THEIR faith into a common fold. Other examples could be added.

If there is to be any significant future for the American restoration movement, it will be created by the use of the *liberty* that is inherent in Thomas Campbell's reference to diversity of faith within a truly ecumenical, universal church. There will be no "coming great church" except as agencies like the World Council of Churches—and the restoration movement—seek unity upon the agreed principle of wide liberty. This freedom can be bounded only by the universal creed, Jesus is the Christ and our Savior. Individual Christians and many of the historic groupings of Christians must be allowed to contribute to the enlarged fellowship THEIR faith in what this creed helps them to be and do, in worship and work, today.

If we may draw an illustration from the field of esthetics, it will be noted that the essence of beauty is unity through diversity. Complete uniformity in color or even in shading or line is destructive to great art. Richness through depth and surface in tension, and other forms of variation, are the soul of wide appeal.

The greatest art is worship of the divine. In it we come, for example, to the Lord's Supper with humility and dedication. In this we are related to God and to one another. But, someone asks, shall we drink from one common cup; another asks, shall we meet for this purpose on the first day of the week or on the seventh day? The answer is, within the bounds of the universal creed, rich liberty must be allowed, and full fellowship must encompass these liberties. Leaders in the search for Christian unity have as a primary obligation the leading of the fragmented church to be adventuresome so as to objectify helpful historic varieties of worship aids and methods. In the case of Church of Christ Number Two, thus far it has sought unity by binding many specifics of thought and practice which are really peculiarities rather than universals.

Not only did Dr. Murch leave out "THEIR"; he left unquoted the vital conclusion of the prescription which sees Christianity proven by "temper and conduct." It is probably true that, within the total American restoration movement, efforts toward harmony and inclusiveness have considered almost solely theologies and liturgies to the exclusion of Christianity proven by character and conduct.

Dr. Murch says:

> Liberal Disciple ecumenists have rejected congregational polity. They brand the freedom of the local church as the culminating "Protestant heresy" or "the sin of Protestantism." They say that it derives chiefly "from Protestant biblicism, and from an utterly unimaginative form of biblicism."[2]

No documentation is given for the quoted words, and perhaps the intention is to employ them as impressions gathered by the author rather than as specific utterances or writings. A more serious misdirection of historic Disciples thought occurs on page 372. Here Dr. Murch quotes a portion of Frederick D. Kershner's *How to Promote Christian Unity* and proceeds to discuss the quotation as though it favors pure congregationalism in the

---

[2]*Op. cit.*, p. 353.

110

form of absolute independency as now practiced by Church of Christ Number Two. This is an unfortunate misrepresentation. The writer of this present book was for years the private secretary of Dr. Kershner and later a member of the theological faculty of which he was the Dean. Fortunately, no element of personal memory needs to be employed here, for Dr. Kershner put himself on record clearly in a book entitled *The Religion of Christ.*[3] He said:

> The polity of the Apostolic Church, in the New Testament days, so far as it can be determined, was therefore unquestionably Congregational. That there was any specific injunction laid upon the Church of future ages to continue this polity, may be questioned. That the creed and the ordinances, as fixed and fundamental factors in the constitution of Christianity, cannot be changed, except by the great Head of the Church Himself, seems clear; but the same is not equally true of any distinctive polity. That form of government which will best subserve the spiritual interests of the whole Church would seem to be the form required by Scriptural authority. . . .

We have related in an earlier chapter that it was Kershner who got Z. T. Sweeney to write the constitution of the International Convention of Christian Churches (Disciples of Christ), under which cooperative Disciples operate today. Under this structure all affairs affecting local churches alone are left to those churches alone. Intercongregational services, relationships with other Christian bodies, and the inevitable problems of Christian thought arising within a living church are brought to the Convention for slow, patient, and reverent consideration in an effort to enable the church as a whole to "make up its mind," to reach a *consensus fidelium* (consensus or agreement of the faithful) on these vital matters.

---

[3]Cincinnati: Standard Publishing Co., 1917, pp. 137-138.

We began this book by saying that from the start and throughout its treatment this problem of how consensus of faith can be achieved within the needed freedoms of congregationalism would be a major concern. Dr. Murch observed the need at this point when he wrote:

The testimony and challenge of this company of "Christians only" committed to the "restoration of the New Testament church in doctrine and life" by an appeal to "the Bible alone as a rule of faith and practice" *deserves the consideration of the whole Christian world* in this new day.[4]

The italic print has been given to the key words. Co-operative Disciples of Christ are committed to entering into "consideration" with "the whole Christian world." Church of Christ Number Two thus far in its career is opposed to such conference activity, calling it "recognizing the denominations." Dr. Murch is not only one of the most capable editors in American religious journalism, as proven by a long and honored career, but he is urging his companions in Church of Christ Number Two to abandon their isolation and move into the pulsing streams of life throughout a rich and varied Christendom. The future of the entire American restoration movement will depend upon a favorable response to this urging, which thus far has been rejected by Churches of Christ Numbers One and Two. The Christian Churches (Disciples of Christ) have felt immensely enriched by their fellowship in the larger stream of universal Christendom.

---

[4]*Op. cit.*, p. 374.